Here are fifteen fascinating stories of imagination which have never before appeared in paperback:

JOHN BRUNNER's story of a city hovering on the edge of time

R. A. LAFFERTY's wry narrative about a valley that was only a few yards wide—until you tried to enter it

JORGE LUIS BORGES' powerful evocation of the life of an immortal man

KATHERINE MAC LEAN's surprising tale of a strange being living in the mind of a little boy

RAY RUSSELL's story of a man with a talent so powerful it could destroy him

Plus ten more tales of strangely altered realities . . . unpredictable and engrossing. You'll love all of them.

TERRY CARR was born in Grant's Pass, Oregon in 1937, but moved with his family to San Francisco before he was five. After studying at City College of San Francisco and University of California, he moved to New York and began writing professionally; his short stories and articles have appeared in *Fantasy & Science Fiction, Esquire, The Realist, If Magazine, The Saint Mystery Magazine* and others. His previous anthologies include SCIENCE FICTION FOR PEOPLE WHO HATE SCIENCE FICTION, published by Doubleday, and the WORLD'S BEST SCIENCE FICTION annual series coedited with Donald A. Wollheim for Ace Books. He and his wife Carol live in Brooklyn Heights with two cats, Gilgamesh and George.

NEW WORLDS OF FANTASY

~~~~~~

Edited by

TERRY CARR

ACE BOOKS, INC.
1120 Avenue of the Americas
New York, N.Y. 10036

CONTENTS

INTRODUCTION

THIS IS NOT a collection of ghoulies and ghosties and things that go bump in the night. There isn't a conventional monster within these pages, though there are any number of unconventional ones . . . and if they move around at night, they usually do it silently.

There are no heroic swordsmen here to chop up scheming sorcerers, either. We do have a young prince on a magic quest, a couple of honest witches and a good number of authentic sorcerers, but none of them are quite what you'd expect . . . nor quite what they expect themselves, for that matter.

What this book does contain is imagination, originality and fresh writing. Here you'll find creatures from worlds stranger than unreality, peculiar ideas that will nibble away at your mind long after you've finished the book, haunted relics of the past in human form, and a few apparently standard fantasy themes suddenly turned on their heads.

These stories were all written in the last few years—with the exception of Jorge Luis Borges' story, which was published in Spanish perhaps 25 years ago but only made available to English-speaking readers comparatively recently. I include the latter not only because it will be another "find" for those who love good fantasy, but also because it is as modern in conception and execution as any story here. (In

9

fact, perhaps even more modern: Borges was and is an amazing man.)

The theme of this book, if a collection of superior contemporary fantasy *needs* a theme, is almost journalistic: the borders of man's imagination, and his means for communicating what he is now thinking, are constantly moving outward as he explores fresh territory, and it is these *New Worlds of Fantasy* which are presented here. They are fascinating worlds, dreams and nightmares and notions and insights which show our own world with the outer layer peeled back.

That's the delightful thing about really good fantasy stories: they're enjoyable in themselves, and they can also set you to thinking . . . about things you may never have considered before, or if you did you've probably long since forgotten about it. And in a world saturated with entertainment media designed to provide diversion by turning off the mind, it's a delight to run across stories which will turn you *on*.

Here are fifteen such stories. May you enjoy them as much as I did.

—TERRY CARR

In this story of a bewildering syndrome which causes time to run backward, Roger Zelazny once again demonstrates the difference between an imaginative gimmick, which captures your curiosity, and an imaginative *idea*, which involves you on the emotional level. And he shows that he's a master of both.

DIVINE MADNESS
Roger Zelazny

"... *I IS THIS* ?*hearers wounded-wonder like stand them makes and stars wandering the conjures sorrow of phrase Whose* ..."

He blew smoke through the cigarette and it grew longer.

He glanced at the clock and realized that its hands were moving backwards.

The clock told him that it was 10:33, going on 10:32 in the P.M.

Then came the thing like despair, for he knew there was not a thing he could do about it. He was trapped, moving in reverse through the sequence of actions past. Somehow, he had missed the warning.

Usually, there was a prism-effect, a flash of pink static, a drowsiness, then a moment of heightened perception ...

He turned the pages, from left to right, his eyes retracing their path back along the lines.

11

Helpless, there behind his eyes, he watched his body perform.

The cigarette had reached its full length. He clicked on the lighter, which sucked away its glowing point, and then he shook the cigarette back into the pack.

He yawned in reverse: first an exhalation, then an inhalation.

It wasn't real—the doctor had told him. It was grief and epilepsy, meeting to form an unusual syndrome.

He'd already had the seizure. The Dilantin wasn't helping. This was a post-traumatic locomotor hallucination, elicited by anxiety, precipitated by the attack.

But he did not believe it, could not believe it—not after twenty minutes had gone by, in the other direction—not after he had placed the book upon the reading stand, stood, walked backward across the room to his closet, hung up his robe, redressed himself in the same shirt and slacks he had worn all day, backed over to the bar and regurgitated a Martini, sip by cooling sip, until the glass was filled to the brim and not a drop spilled.

There was an impending taste of olive, and then everything was changed again.

The second-hand was sweeping around his wristwatch in the proper direction.

The time was 10:07.

He felt free to move as he wished.

He redrank his Martini.

Now, if he would be true to the pattern, he would change into his robe and try to read. Instead, he mixed another drink.

Now the sequence would not occur.

Now the things would not happen as he thought they had happened, and un-happened.

Now everything was different.

All of which went to prove it had been an hallucination.

Even the notion that it had taken twenty-six minutes each way was an attempted rationalization.

Nothing had happened.

. . . Shouldn't be drinking, he decided. It might bring on a seizure.

He laughed.

Crazy, though, the whole thing. . . .

Remembering, he drank.

In the morning he skipped breakfast, as usual, noted that

12

it would soon stop being morning, took two aspirins, a luke-warm shower, a cup of coffee, and a walk.

The park, the fountain, the children with their boats, the grass, the pond, he hated them; and the morning, and the sunlight, and the blue moats around the towering clouds.

Hating, he sat there. And remembering.

If he was on the verge of a crackup, he decided, then the thing he wanted most was to plunge ahead into it, not to totter halfway out, halfway in.

He remembered why.

But it was clear, so clear, the morning, and everything crisp and distinct and burning with the green fires of spring, there in the sign of the Ram, April.

He watched the winds pile up the remains of winter against the far gray fence, and he saw them push the boats across the pond, to come to rest in shallow mud the children tracked.

The fountain jetted its cold umbrella above the green-tinged copper dolphins. The sun ignited it whenever he moved his head. The wind rumpled it.

Clustered on the concrete, birds pecked at part of a candy bar stuck to a red wrapper.

Kites swayed on their tails, nosed downward, rose again, as youngsters tugged at invisible strings. Telephone lines were tangled with wooden frames and torn paper, like broken G clefs and smeared glissandos.

He hated the telephone lines, the kites, the children, the birds.

Most of all, though, he hated himself.

How does a man undo that which has been done? He doesn't. There is no way under the sun. He may suffer, remember, repent, curse, or forget. Nothing else. The past, in this sense, is inevitable.

A woman walked past. He did not look up in time to see her face, but the dusky blonde fall of her hair to her collar and the swell of her sure, sheer-netted legs below the black hem of her coat and above the matching click of her heels heigh-ho, stopped his breath behind his stomach and snared his eyes in the wizard-weft of her walking and her posture and some more, like a rhyme to the last of his thoughts.

He half-rose from the bench when the pink static struck his eyeballs, and the fountain became a volcano spouting rainbows.

The world was frozen and served up to him under glass.
. . . The woman passed back before him and he looked down too soon to see her face.

13

The hell was beginning once more, he realized, as the backward-flying birds passed before him.

He gave himself to it. Let it keep him until he broke, until he was all used up and there was nothing left.

He waited, there on the bench, watching the slithey toves be brillig, as the fountain sucked its waters back within itself, drawing them up in a great arc above the unmoving dolphins, and the boats raced backward across the pond, and the fence divested itself of stray scraps of paper, as the birds replaced the candy bar within the red wrapper, bit by crunchy bit.

His thoughts only were inviolate; his body belonged to the retreating tide.

Eventually, he rose and strolled backwards out of the park.

On the street a boy backed past him, unwhistling snatches of a popular song.

He backed up the stairs to his apartment, his hangover growing worse again, undrank his coffee, unshowered, unswallowed his aspirins, and got into bed, feeling awful.

Let this be it, he decided.

A faintly-remembered nightmare ran in reverse through his mind, giving it an undeserved happy ending.

It was dark when he awakened.

He was very drunk.

He backed over to the bar and began spitting out his drinks, one by one into the same glass he had used the night before, and pouring them from the glass back into the bottles again. Separating the gin and vermouth was no trick at all. The proper liquids leaped into the air as he held the uncorked bottles above the bar.

And he grew less and less drunk as this went on.

Then he stood before an early Martini and it was 10:07 in the P.M. There, within the hallucination, he wondered about another hallucination. Would time loop-the-loop, forward and then backward again, through his previous seizure?

No.

It was as though it had not happened, had never been.

He continued on back through the evening, undoing things.

He raised the telephone, said "goodbye," untold Murray that he would not be coming to work again tomorrow, listened a moment, recradled the phone and looked at it as it rang.

The sun came up in the west and people were backing their cars to work.

14

He read the weather report and the headlines, folded the evening paper and placed it out in the hall.

It was the longest seizure he had ever had, but he did not really care. He settled himself down within it and watched as the day unwound itself back to morning.

His hangover returned as the day grew smaller, and it was terrible when he got into bed again.

When he awakened the previous evening the drunkenness was high upon him. Two of the bottles he refilled, recorked, resealed. He knew he would take them to the liquor store soon and get his money back.

As he sat there that day, his mouth uncursing and undrinking and his eyes unreading, he knew that new cars were being shipped back to Detroit and disassembled, that corpses were awakening into their death-throes, and that priests the world over were saying black mass, unknowing.

He wanted to chuckle, but he could not tell his mouth to do it.

He unsmoked two and a half packs of cigarettes.

Then came another hangover and he went to bed. Later, the sun set in the east.

Time's winged chariot fled before him as he opened the door and said "goodbye" to his comforters and they told him not to grieve overmuch.

And he wept without tears as he realized what was to come.

Despite his madness, he hurt.

... Hurt, as the days rolled backward.

... Backward, inexorably.

... Inexorably, until he knew the time was near at hand.

He gnashed the teeth of his mind.

Great was his grief and his hate and his love.

He was wearing his black suit and undrinking drink after drink, while somewhere the men were scraping the clay back onto the shovels which would be used to undig the grave.

He backed his car to the funeral parlor, parked it, and climbed into the limousine.

They backed all the way to the graveyard.

He stood among his friends and listened to the preacher.

".dust to dust; ashes to Ashes," the man said, which is pretty much the same whichever way you say it.

The casket was taken back to the hearse and returned to the funeral parlor.

He sat through the service and went home and unshaved and unbrushed his teeth and went to bed.

He awakened and dressed again in black and returned to the parlor.

The flowers were all back in place.

Solemn-faced friends unsigned the Sympathy Book and unshook his hand. Then they went inside to sit awhile and stare at the closed casket. Then they left, until he was alone with the funeral director.

Then he was alone with himself.

The tears ran up his cheeks.

His suit and shirt were crisp and unwrinkled again.

He backed home, undressed, uncombed his hair. The day collapsed around him into morning, and he returned to bed to unsleep another night.

The previous evening, when he awakened, he realized where he was headed.

Twice, he exerted all of his will power in an attempt to interrupt the sequence of events. He failed.

He wanted to die. If he had killed himself that day, he would not be headed back toward it now.

There were tears within his mind as he realized the past which lay less than twenty-four hours before him.

The past stalked him that day as he unnegotiated the purchase of the casket, the vault, the accessories.

Then he headed home into the biggest hangover of all and slept until he was awakened to undrink drink after drink and then return to the morgue and come back in time to hang up the telephone on that call, that call which had come to break . . .

. . . The silence of his anger with its ringing.

She was dead.

She was lying somewhere in the fragments of her car on Interstate 90 now.

As he paced, unsmoking, he knew she was lying there bleeding.

. . . Then dying, after that crash at 80 miles an hour.

. . . Then alive?

Then re-formed, along with the car, and alive again, arisen? Even now backing home at a terrible speed, to re-slam the door on their final argument? To unscream at him and to be unscreamed at?

He cried out within his mind. He wrung the hands of his spirit.

It couldn't stop at this point. No. Not now.

All his grief and his love and his self-hate had brought him back this far, this near to the moment. . . .

It *couldn't* end now.

After a time, he moved to the living room, his legs pacing, his lips cursing. himself waiting.

The door slammed open.

She stared in at him, her mascara smeared, tears upon her cheeks.

"!hell to go Then," he said.

"!going I'm," she said.

She stepped back inside, closed the door.

She hung her coat hurriedly in the hall closet.

".it about feel you way the that's It," he said, shrugging.

"!yourself but anybody about care don't You," she said.

"!child a like behaving You're," he said.

"!sorry you're say least at could You"

Her eyes flashed like emeralds through the pink static, and she was lovely and alive again. In his mind he was dancing.

The change came.

"You could at least say you're sorry!"

"I am," he said, taking her hand in a grip that she could not break. "How much, you'll never know."

"Come here," and she did.

John Brunner has established a solid and growing
following as a writer of thoughtful extrapolative science
fiction, of colorful space-adventure, of the most tech-
nically precise hard-science fiction, of satirically barbed
or poetically evocative stories. In this dreamlike tale
of a doomed city wavering on the edge of chaos, he
shows that his versatility extends to the field of high
fantasy as well.

BREAK THE DOOR OF HELL
John Brunner

*I will break the door of hell and smash the bolts; I will
bring up the dead to eat food with the living, and the
living shall be outnumbered by the host of them.*
—THE EPIC OF GILGAMESH

In those days, the forces were none of them chained.
They raged unchecked through every corner and quarter
of the cosmos. Here ruled Laprivan of the Yellow Eyes,
capricious, whimsical, and when he stared things melted in
frightful agony. There a bright being shed radiance, but
the radiance was all-consuming, and that which was

18

solid and dull was flashed into fire. At another place, creatures in number one million fought desperately with one another for the possession of a single grain of dust; the fury of their contesting laid waste whole solar systems.

—IMPRINT OF CHAOS

Time had come to Ryovora.

The traveler in black—who had many names, but one nature—contemplated the fact from the brow of the hill where he had imprisoned Laprivan of the Yellow Eyes, more eons ago than he cared to count. Leaning on his staff made of light, curdled with a number of interesting forces, he repressed a shiver. Single though his nature might be, unique though that certainly was, he was not immune to apprehension; his endowments did not include omniscience.

Time had come to that great city: Time, in which could exist order and logic and rational thought. And so it was removed from his domain forever, gone from the borderland of chaos which exists timeless in eternity.

The task for which his single nature fitted him was the bringing forth of order out of that chaos; accordingly, he should have felt the satisfaction of achievement, or even a mildly vain pleasure. He did not, and for this there were two most cogent reasons and a third which he preferred not to consider.

The first, and most piquing, was that a duty lay on him: that at a certain season following the conjunction of four significant planets hereabout, he must oversee that portion of the All which was his charge. And he had grown accustomed to terminating his round of inspection at Ryovora, known far and wide as the place where people had their heads screwed on right. There if anywhere he could look on his work and be pleased.

Lapses and backsliding had occasionally minded him to alter this habit; still, he had never done so, and to discover that Ryovora was—elsewhere—annoyed him.

The second reason was not annoying. It was alarming, and absolutely unprecedented, and dismaying, and many other distressing epithets.

"In sum," the traveler in black announced to the air, "it's unheard of!"

Another city had arisen in the borderland of chaos, and it was stamped all over with the betraying mark of Time. How was it possible? Carried in some eddy whose flow ran counter to the universal trend, so that from reason and logic it receded to the random laws of chance? Presumably. Yet the means whereby such an eddy might be created seemed inconceivable; some great enchantment would be required, and in the grip of Time enchantment was impossible.

"Fantastic!" said the traveler in black, speaking aloud again to distract his mind from the third and least palatable reason for regretting the loss of Ryovora. It was known to him that when he had accomplished his task all things would have but one nature; then they would be subsumed into the Original All, and time would have a stop. Beyond which point . . .

He glanced around him at the hillside. It was sparsely overgrown with gray-leaved bushes, and dust-devils rose among the rocks to sift their substance, fine as ashes, over the footprints he had left on the path. That was the doing of Laprivan, to whom memories of yesterday were hurtful, and who accordingly used what small power remained to him to wipe away the traces of the past.

The staff tapped, once, twice, and again. At the third tap the elemental heaved in his underground prison and cracks appeared in the road. From these a voice boomed, monstrous, making the welkin echo.

"Leave me be!"

"What do you know of the city which stands yonder?" said the traveler in black.

"Nothing," said Laprivan sullenly.

"Nothing? You say so to spare yourself the pain of memory, Laprivan! Shall I send you where Ryovora has gone, into the domain of Time?"

The whole hill shuddered, and an avalanche of gray rock rattled on its further side. The sourceless voice moaned. "What should I know of the city yonder? No man has come from it and passed this way."

"Bad," said the traveler thoughtfully. "Very bad."

After that he was silent for a long while, until at last the elemental pleaded, "Leave me be! Leave me to wipe clean the slate of the past!"

"As you wish, so be it," said the traveler absently, and tapped with his staff again. The cracks in the ground closed; the dust-devils resumed their whirling.

Ignoring all this, the traveler gazed over the green and orderly meadows in the valley. The city lay in noon-tide sunlight like a worn-out toy cast aside by a giant's child. The heedless ruin of Time was everywhere about it, tooth-marks of the greatest leveler on brick and stone and metal.

20

It had been fair and rich, that was plain; its gates were of oak and bronze—but the bronze was corroded green; its towers were of silver and orichalcum—but their bright sheen was overlaid with a dull mist like the foul breath of a swamp; its streets were broad and paved with marble—but the flags lifted to the roots of wild plants, and here and there one found holes filled by the rain and noxious with algae and insect-larvae.

Out of Time and into chaos. Almost beyond belief.

At length he stirred himself. There was nothing else for it—so he reasoned—but to set off on his journey of obligation, and come at last not to familiar, welcome Ryovora, but to this enigma wished on him by fate and boding no good whatever.

Relief carried him far and fast. To learn that Acromel stood where it had, the place where honey itself was bitter; to know that they yet fished Lake Taxhling when the stars came out, and that the river Metamorphia fed it with strange unspawned creatures, greedy and unwholesome—this was reassuring, an earnest of balance continued in the cosmos.

And at these places and many many more he did what on this journey was required of him.

A lonely hut stood on the shelf-edge of a mountain pasture in the land called Eyneran; here where he paused to ask a crust of bread and a sup of ewe's milk from the flock high and distant as clouds on the steep meadow, a woman with a frightened face opened the ill-carpentered door to him, and met his request with a silent shake of the head.

She was wrinkled and worn out beyond her years; yet the hut was sound, a savory smell filled the air, and the clean floor and many copper pots the traveler could see assorted badly with the woman's ragged gown and bare feet. He waited. Shortly a cry—man-deep, yet edged with a child's petulance—rang out.

"Mother, come here! The pot's boiling over! What's keeping you, you lazy slut?"

"Mintra!" whispered the woman, and a patter of feet announced the passage of a girl, some twelve years old, across the floor to tend the pot.

Another cry, still louder: "Mother, come and give me some of it! Mintra can't lift the pot, you stupid old bag of bones!"

"We can't give you food," the woman said to the traveler. "It's for my son."

The traveler nodded, but waited still. Then at last with
21

great heaving and panting came the son into view: gross-bulging in his apparel of velvet worked with gilt wire and stained with slobberings of food, so tall he nearly scraped the roof with his pate, yet so fat he breathed hard for the simple effort of standing upright. His fist, big as a ham, cracked his mother behind the ear.

"Why don't you die, you lazy old cow, and get it over with?" he bellowed.

"It'd be a merciful relief," the woman whimpered. "And die I would of my own free will, but that I stand alone between you and your sister! With me gone you'd take her like a harlot, sister or no!"

"And wouldn't she be a tasty bit for my bed?" chortled the son with an evil grin, his tongue coming out thick as an ox's to stroke his lips lasciviously.

"As you wish," said the traveler, "so be it." And he knocked his staff on the threshold and took his leave.

That night the plague stole silent from the mountain mist, and took the mother as the son had wished; then the girl Mintra fled on light feet down the hill-trails and the fever-giddy glutton went calling her among the heedless sheep till his gross weight dislodged a rock and sent him like an animal to feed the crows.

In the rich city Gryte a thief spoke to curse the brief-ness of the summer night, which had cut short his plan to break the wall of a merchant's counting-house.

"Oh that dawn never came!" he cried. "Oh that I had lasting darkness whereby to ply my trade!"

"As you wish," said the traveler, "so be it." And darkness came: two thick gray cataracts that shut the light away.

Likewise in Medham was another rogue, striving to seduce a lady who feared her charms were passing with the years so that he might win to a coffer of gold secreted in her chamber. "I love you!" declared the smooth-tongued de-ceiver. "I'd love you had you no more than rags and a shack!"

"As you wish, so be it," said the traveler, and the bailiffs came down the street to advise the lady that her house and treasure were forfeit on another's debt, so that the liar turned and ran, not staying to hear the city officers who followed hard on the bailiffs' heels to report the honoring of the debt a day past due.

So too in Wocrahin a swaggering bully came down the street on market day, cuffing aside children with the back of his hand and housewives with the flat of his sword. "Oh that my way were not cluttered with such riffraff!" he exclaimed, his shoulder butting into the traveler's chest.

"As you wish, so be it," said the traveler, and when the bully turned the corner the street he walked was empty under a leaden sky—and the buildings either side, and the taverns, and the shops. Nor did he again in all eternity have to push aside the riffraff he had cursed; he was alone.

This, however, was not the sum total of the traveler's doings as he passed from place to place within his realm. In Kanish-Kulya they had built a wall to keep Kanishmen and Kulyamen apart, and from either side, set into the masonry, grinned down the skulls of those dead in a war for which the reason had long been forgotten. In this strange and dreadful place Fegrim was pent under a volcano; shadowed by its cone the traveler halted and spoke long and seriously with that elemental, and when he was done the country for a mile on every side was dusted with cinders, little and bright as fireflies.

At Gander's Well, branched Yorbeth brooded in the guise of a tall tree whose main root tapped a wonderful subterranean spring and whose branches, fed with miraculous sap, sprouted leaves and fruit of which the like had not been seen under any sun before. The traveler spent an hour in the shade of that tree, and for the questions he asked was constrained to carry away a red twig and later catch a cat and perform a ceremony with these two objects—a price he paid with heavy heart, for he had been told nothing of any great use in his inquiries.

Also he consulted with Farchgrind, and in Leppersley he cast the bones of a girl's foot to read the runes they formed, and after great labor he incarcerated Wolpec in a candle over whose flame he smoked a piece of glass which thereupon showed three truths: one ineluctable, one debatable and one incomprehensible. That was in Teq, when the end of his journey was near.

So finally he came to Barbizond, where there was always a rainbow in the sky because of the bright being Sardhin, chained inside a thundercloud with fetters of lightning. Three courses remained to him: he might free Sardhin and let him speak, and from here to the horizon nothing would be left save himself, the elemental and that which was of its nature bright, as jewels, or fire, or the shining edge of a keen-bladed knife; or he might do as once he had done in similar circumstances—address himself to an enchanter and make use of powers that trespassed too far toward naked

23

chaos to be within his own scope—or finally he might go forward in ignorance to the strange city and confront the challenge of fate without the armor of foreknowledge.

Some little while remained to him before he needed to take his final decision. Coming to Barbizond, therefore, he made his way down a fine broad avenue where plane and lime trees alternated in the direction of a steel-blue temple. There stood the altar of Hnua-Threl, who was also Sardhin when he chose to be; the people invoked him with daily single combats on the temple floor. They were not a gentle folk, these inhabitants of Barbizond, but they were stately, and they died—in tournaments, or by the assassin's knife, or by their own hand—with dignity.

Such a death had lately occurred, that was plain, for approaching the city gate came a funeral procession: on a high-wheeled cart drawn by apes in brazen harness, the corpse wrapped in sheets of lead, gold and woven leaves; a band of gongmen beating a slow measure to accompany musicians whistling like birds on pipes no larger than a finger; eight female slaves naked to the ceaseless warm rain; and last a straggle of mourners, conducting themselves with appropriate solemnity.

He who passed penultimately of the mourners was a fat and jolly person on each of whose shoulders perched a boy-child sheltered by the enormous brim of his leather hat. The traveler stared long at him before stepping out from the protection of the nearest tree and addressing him courteously.

"Your pardon, sir, but are you not Eadwil?"

"I am," the fat one answered, not loath to halt and let the funeral wend its way to the graveyard without his assistance. "Should I know you, sir?"

"Perhaps not," said the traveler in black. "Though I know you. I'd not have expected to see you here; you were formerly one of the chief merchant enchanters of Ryovora."

"A long time ago, sir," Eadwil answered with a deprecating smile. The two children on his shoulders giggled and one of them tried to reach for the traveler's staff, almost lost his balance, and righted himself with the aid of a pat from Eadwil's broad soft hand.

"May I ask what brought about your change of residence?" the traveler murmured.

"My change of employment," Eadwil shrugged, again nearly dislodging the more venturesome boy. "You spoke of me as a merchant enchanter—but when the decision was taken, many years ago, to let rational thought rule Ryo-

24

vora and put an end to conjurations there, certain consequences followed. For myself I have no regrets; there was a geas upon me which made my feet grow red-hot when I walked, and now nothing worse attends a long tramp like today's except an occasional blister. And these my grandsons, too—hey, you little nuisances?—they'd not be here today if I'd submitted to the other main restriction which purchased my powers." He rubbed the boys' backs affectionately, and they responded by pulling his ears.

This was quite true, as the traveler knew well; Eadwil had postponed the growing of his first beard till unusually late in life by making the trade on which his command of magic had been based.

"So there came an end to my conjuring of fine silks and spices, of rare wines and exotic perfumes!" Eadwil pursed his lips. "And there were, one must confess, certain persons in Ryovora who felt the lack of those luxuries and accused us ex-enchanters of—ha-hm!—betraying them. Barbizond is a fair city in its way, though the local customs are not to my taste; still, no one plagues me for magical doings and I've lived to be a grandfather to my own surprise. . . . You have late news of Ryovora, sir? For it comes to my mind that I've heard nothing from my old home in quite a while."

The traveler shook his head and gave a wry smile. "It's a fair span since I last set foot there. Indeed, I was hoping you might be able to give me certain information which I lack, rather than vice versa."

Eadwil looked politely downcast at being of no help; then one of the boys grew impatient and started to fidget.

"Home?" said his grandfather, and laughed indulgently. "Very well—old Harpentile is in no state to notice that we failed to attend his burying. Good day to you, sir," he added to the traveler. "It's been pleasant to renew our acquaintance, and I greatly hope you find someone who can aid you in these inquiries where I failed you."

"As you wish, so be it," said the traveler under his breath, and a great weight seemed to recede from his heart.

That accomplished, there was no more to do than to wait till the course of fate worked itself out. The traveler took a seat at a curbside tavern; with his elbows on a green tabletop he watched the passersby and wondered in what guise his helper would come. The avenue grew crowded as the day wasted. Men in gay jerkins with armor clanking at their saddle-bows came by, challengers in some tourney for the hand of an `heiress; pedlars and wonder-workers with a few small tricks, for which they had paid excessively to judge by their reddened eyes, pocked cheeks, limping gait or even womanly shrill voices—no wonder, the traveler reflected. Eadwil felt he had had the better bargain.

Women, too, passed: high-wimpled dames attended by maids and dandling curious unnamable pets, harlots in diaphanous cloaks through which it was not quite possible to tell if they were diseased, good wives with panniers of stinking salted fish and honest bread and sealed jars of pollywogs for use in the commonplace home enchantments of this city.

And children also: some naked not necessarily from poverty but because skin was the best raincoat under Barbizond's light continual shower, others in fantastical costumes to match the whim of one or other parent—helmets of huge eggshells, bodices of leaves glued like scales, coats like tents and breeches like plant stems with the knees made to resemble knots in springtime. With spinning paper windmills, toy lances, tops, hoops and skipping-ropes they darted among the adults and left a trail of joyful disorder.

There was no joy in the heart of the traveler in black—only a dulled apprehension.

The places at the tables before the tavern filled with customers, till only one was left—the second chair at this table where the traveler waited. Then, to the instant, appeared a curious bewildered figure from the direction of the city gate: a pale-faced, wild-haired man in a russet cape, clinging to a pitiful bag of belongings as though to a baulk of timber in an ocean of insanity. Time had etched his brow with suffering, and the traveler knew him the moment he clapped eyes on him.

Abreast of the tavern the stranger stopped. Enviously his eyes scanned the delicacies placed before the customers: fragrant jars of wine, mounds of mashed fruit stuck with silver spoons, crisp sheets of moonbark that only this city's enchanters knew how to bring across the freezing gulf of space without spoiling. Huddling his bag under his arm, he felt in his scrip for money, and produced one solitary copper coin.

Hesitant, he approached the traveler in black. "Sir, by your leave, will this purchase anything at your tavern here?" he muttered, and offered the coin on a trembling palm.

The traveler took it and turned it over, and was at pains to conceal the shock he felt on seeing what name the reverse of the coin bore.

26

Ys!

A city in Time so great and famous that rumors of it had crossed the tenuous border of chaos, running ahead of those who bore its news until the stories were magnified beyond believing, until there were prophecies caused by the recirculation of those rumors through one corner of eternity and back to Time—ahead of reality.

"No?" said the stranger sadly, seeing how long the black-clad one spent staring at his only money.

"Why—!" the latter exclaimed, and rubbed the coin with his fingertips, very lightly. "I should say so, friend! Is it not good gold, that passes anywhere?"

"Gold?" The stranger snatched it back, almost dropping his shabby bag in his agitation, and scrutinized it incredulously. Through the coppery tarnish gleamed the dull warm yellow of precious metal.

Without more ado he slumped into the vacant chair at this table, and the waggle-hipped serving girl came to his side. "Food and drink!" he commanded, letting the miraculous coin ring on the table. "I starve and I'm clemmed with thirst—be quick!"

Eyes twinkling, the traveler regarded his new acquaintance. "And how are you called, sir?" he demanded.

"Jacques of Ys is my name," the other sighed. "Though truth to tell I'm not overmuch inclined to add my origin to my name any longer."

"Why so?"

"Would you wish to be shamed with a city full of fools?"

"Considering the matter with due reflection," said the traveler, "I think—no."

"Well, then!" Jacques of Ys ran his long bony fingers through his already untidy hair; the water had been trying to sleek it down, but half an ocean would probably have been unequal to the task. He was a gaunt man, neither old nor young, with burning gray eyes and a bush of tawny beard.

"And in what way are the people of Ys foolish?" probed the traveler.

"Once they were a great people," Jacques grunted. "And that's where the trouble started. Once we had a fleet—and not on any inland lake, either, but an Oceanus itself, mother of storms and gulls. Also we had an army to guard our trade routes, skillful money-changers, wise counselors . . . Ah, Ys was among the finest cities of the world!"

"I believe I've heard so," the traveler agreed.

"Then your news is stale, sir!" Jacques thumped on the

table. "Listen! There came changes—in the times, in the weather, in the currents of the sea. To be expected, *I* say, for did not Heraclitus teach us *panta rhei,* all things flow? But soft living and much ease had stolen the brains out of the people's heads! Faced with the silting-up of our great harbors, did they go to it and build dredgers? They did not! Faced with a landslide that closed our chief silk-road, did they go scouting to locate another way? They did not! Faced with long winters that killed our autumn wheat in the ground, did they sow barley or the hardy northern oat? They did not!"

"Then—what did they do?" the traveler inquired.

"Fell first to moaning and wringing their hands, and lamenting their sad fate; then, when this proved unfruitful and incapable of filling the granaries, turned to a crowning imbecility and invoked the impossible aid of magic. I see you scowl, sir, and well you may, for all the world knows magic is a vain and ridiculous snare laid by evil demons in the path of mankind."

This was a stubborn and pigheaded fellow, clearly; with his hand closed around a coin that veritable magic—and no petty domestic hearth-spell, either—had turned from copper to gold, he could still make such an assertion. He would not care for this domain in which he now found himself. Still, there was no help for that.

"And to what purpose did their researches in—ah—*magic* tend?" the traveler asked.

"To bring back the great days of the past, if you please," said Jacques with majestic scorn, and on the last word crammed his mouth full from the dish the serving girl placed before him.

While he assuaged his hunger, the traveler contemplated this news. Yes, such an event as Jacques had described would account for the paradox of Ys reversing the cosmic trend and exchanging Time for eternity and its attendant confusions. But there must have been a great and terrible hope in the minds of very many people for the change to be brought about; there must have been public foolishness on a scale unparalleled in the All. Thinking on this, the traveler felt his face grow grim.

He got to his feet, grasping his staff, and Jacques glanced up with his cheeks bulging. Having swallowed frantically, he spoke. "Sire, did I intrude on your meditations? Your pardon if—"

"No, Jacques. You merely recalled me to some unfinished business. You are right in your description of the people of

Ys. They are fools indeed. So do not—if you will take my advice—go back there."

"Where else shall I go, then?" Jacques countered, and for a second despair looked out from behind his eyes. "I set off thinking no place could be worse than my home had become—yet on this brief journey I've seen wonders and marvels that make me question my own good sense. I met a creature on the road that was neither man nor beast, but a blending; I saw a shining sprite washing feet like alabaster in a cloud rimmed with rainbows; and once when I bent to drink from a stream I saw pictures in the water which—no, I dare not say what I thought I saw."

"That would be the brook called Geirion," said the traveler, and gave a crooked smile. "Don't worry—things seen there can never become real. The folk round about go to the brook to rid themselves of baseless fears."

Jacques glanced over his shoulder at the motley crowd and shivered with dismay. "Nonetheless, sir, I'm not minded to remain in this—peculiar city!"

"It would be better for you to adapt to the local customs than to go home," the traveler warned. "A certain rather terrible doom is likely to overtake Ys, if things are as you say."

"Doom!" cried Jacques, and an unholy joy lit his face. "I told them so—over and again I told them! Would I could witness it, for the satisfaction of seeing them learn how right I was!"

The traveler sighed, but there was no help for it now; his single nature bound him to unique courses of action. He said sourly, "As you wish, so be it. Go hence toward the city men call Acromel, where honey itself is bitter, but do not enter it; go rather around it toward the setting sun, and you will reach a gray hill fledged with gray bushes where there are always dust-devils. Look behind you and see how they wipe out your footprints a moment after you have passed. From the brow of that hill you can see Ys. Wait there."

"Now just a moment," said Jacques, rising. "From my boyhood up I've wandered around and about Ys, and I know of no such hill as you describe!"

The traveler shrugged and made to turn away. Jacques caught at him.

"Wait! What's your name, that you say such strange things and send me on such an improbable errand?"

"You may call me Mazda, or anything you like," the

black-clad man said, and shook off the claw-like grip with a moue of distaste.

"Hah! That's rich!" Jacques put his hands on his hips and laughed. "But still . . . For the sake of wanting to see how Ys goes to its fate, I'll follow your instructions. And my thanks!"

He parodied a bow, flourishing a hat that was not on his head.

"You may not thank me more than this once," said the traveler in black sadly, and went his way.

Lord Vengis sat in the Hall of State in Ys, and gazed at the nobility assembled in his presence. Once this had been a building to marvel at: mirrors higher than a man lined its walls, set between pilasters of marble, gilt and onyx, and the arching roof was painted with scenes in eleven bright colors, showing the birth of Saint Clotilda, the martyrdom of Saint Gaufroy—that one was mostly in red—and the ascension of Saint Eulogos to heaven on the back of a leaping dolphin; the floor, moreover, had been carpeted with ermine and bear-pelts.

The pelts had gone. Some of them, to be exact, had returned—but in unusual fashion: they had been cut into paunches and bosoms with the aid of gilt girdles. Worse yet, some of the underlying slabs of marble had been prized up to expose crude stone flags—a rumor having got around as to the effectiveness of marble for sacrificial altars—and on an irregularity of this kind, in an ill-lit corner, Lord Vengis had twisted his ankle on the way into the hall.

That was the trouble with Ys now. The harbors that once swallowed the twice-daily ocean tides were blocked with stinking mud; grass grew on the stone moles as it did in the wheel-ruts of the fine old roads leading away from the city—though none of the personages present had seen this fact with his or her own eyes, all having declined to leave Ys since things took their turn for the worse. In the gardens of the great houses a plant like, but not identical with, mistletoe had spread over the handsome trees, letting fall a sticky fruit on those who walked beneath; in the deep sweet-water wells servants claimed to have heard ominous voices, so that now they refused to let the buckets down for fear of drawing up those who spoke: last week's market had reduced to two old men squabbling over a cracked earthen pot and a comb of dirty wild honey.

Lord Vengis glowered at the company, and they fell silent by degrees. Their attendants moved, silent as shadows, to the double doors of entrance, closed them, barred them against all intrusion—for this was no discussion which the common people were permitted to overhear.

With the clanging down of the final bar, one leaped to his feet at the end of the front rank of gilded chairs, uttering a groaning cry and cramming his fingers into his mouth. All eyes turned.

"Fool, Bardolus!" Lord Vengis rapped. "What scares you?"

"In that mirror!" Bardolus gibbered, trying to point and finding his shaking arm disobedient to his will. "I saw in the mirror—!"

"What? What?" chorused a dozen fearful voices.

Bardolus was a small man whose manner was never better than diffident; he was accounted clever, but in a sly fashion that had won him few friends and none who would trust him. He said now, mopping sweat from his face, "I don't know. I saw something in the mirror that wasn't also in this hall."

Time hesitated in its course, until Lord Vengis gave a harsh laugh and slapped the arm of his chair.

"You'll have to become accustomed to manifestations like that, Bardolus!" he gibed. "So long as the things are in the mirror, what's to worry you? It's when they emerge into the everyday world that you must look out. Why, only the other day, when I was in my thaumaturgic cabinet testing a certain formula I—but enough of that." He coughed, and behind his polite covering had glanced to see if his words had had the desired effect. They had, even though the episode to which he referred was an invention. True, he'd spent much time in his cabinet; true, he'd rehearsed many formulae; nothing had so far come of his efforts, not even a harmless shadow in a mirror.

Still, that would change. One could tell by the feel of the air. There were forces in it that no man could put a name to, and sometimes scalps prickled as they do before a thunderstorm.

"We are here for a reason you know," he said after an impressive pause. "We are agreed on the only course open to us. We admit that modern Ys stands on the shoulders of very great men and women; unkind fate has burdened us with such difficulties as they never encountered, and we eat stale bread and rancid meat where they ate pies running with gravy and soft delicious fruits from the ends of the earth. We drink plain water, none too clean, where they enjoyed wine and mead and beer like brown crystal.

"We have agreed that for all their—admitted—greatness,

31

they are responsible, not us! We did not ask to be born at a time when our trees die, our crops wither, our harbor is blocked. In every way they are responsible: for siting Ys where it stands, for breeding children to inherit such a miserable legacy!"

"Ay!" came a rumble of assent from all around the hall.

"Some faint-hearts, some ignorant fools, have argued with us," Vengis went on, warming to a speech he hadn't intended to deliver at length. "These, of course, were base-born, lacking the insight which nobility gives. Jacques the scrivener, for example, would have had us turn to with hoes and shovels and clear the harbor with our bare hands!"

This time, it was a chuckle that circled the hall. "What's become of him, by the way?" someone asked audibly.

"Does it matter?" Vengis countered, drawing his beetling brows together. "We know we are doing the right thing. We have decided that we must employ something other than crude—ah—agricultural implements to cope with so massive a disaster. We shall, in short, restore all our fortunes, and the splendor of our city, *and* root out once and for all the disaffection among the common rabble spread by such as Jacques, by using the mightiest means available to us. Magically, by decree of the will, by harnessing supernatural forces, we shall again make Ys the envy of the world!"

A roar of approval and a barrage of clapping went up. Unnoticed in the shadows, one listener alone did not clap, and he stood leaning on his staff, shaking his head very slowly from side to side.

"Let us have news, then—encouraging news of our progress!" Vengis cried. "I call first on Dame Seulte, around whose home last time I rode by I could not help noticing an aura pregnant with remarkable phenomena."

Silence. At length a portly woman near the back of the hall rose with some difficulty and spoke.

"Dame Seulte, as you know, is my close neighbor, and as she is not here I think perhaps I ought to mention that yesterday she was in high spirits and confident of success. She had obtained a free-will gift of a child to offer to—well, to a creature best not named directly—and was leading the pretty thing home on a leash of green leather. Such a sweet sight!"

"Dame Rosa!" said a man from nearer the front, turning in his chair. "A free-will gift—are you sure?"

And his companion, a pale girl of no more than eighteen in a dress of brown velvet, said doubtfully, "My maid said something about a fire at Dame Seulte's house this morning. . . ."

Vengis slapped the arm of his chair again, making a noise as sharp as a gavel's. He said sternly, "No defeatist talk, *if* you please, Lady Vivette!"

"But are you *sure* it was a free-will gift?" persisted the last man who had spoken.

Dame Rosa said stiffly, "Dame Seulte promised to raise the child as her own, and the parents were poor and hungry; they parted willingly with it."

"Then there was a fire at her home this morning," said the man, and shrugged. "My copy of the book she conjured from has a leaf that hers lacks, and on it the authorities are cited by dozens—deception is of no avail with that ceremony."

There was a stunned pause. Dame Seulte, after all had only been trying to manifest a comparatively straightforward elemental.

"I have better news," said a sweet, enticing voice from the opposite side of the assembly. They turned gratefully; this was Lady Meleagra, whose eyes like sapphires, lips like rose-petals and skin like snow had broken hearts for ten of her twenty-one years. As Eadwil had once done in Ryovora, she had accepted a basic proviso for her wished-for powers; she, though, had not suffered in consequence, but she had imposed a most regrettable condition upon those who craved to share the pleasures of her chamber at night. It was an efficacious precaution, but the number of suitors calling on her had signally reduced since she imposed the rule.

"I have sensed a change here in Ys," she mused aloud. "A great wonder has overtaken this city. So far I do not know its precise nature, but the fact is indisputable. See!"

She stretched out one graceful arm, swathed in white lace so fine her skin tinted it pink, and in the central aisle dividing the company a thing appeared. It was dark; it writhed, and it had no distinguishable feature except two glowing eyes alight with hatred. It lasted half a minute before it slowly faded, and at its going the air was full of a dank steamy odor against which those lucky enough to have brought them buried their noses in bouquets of flowers.

By degrees a clamor arose, as on all sides the nobles strove to show that they had been equally successful. "Look!" cried Messer Hautnoix, and between his hands he strung a chain of gleaming bubbles from nowhere, and again and yet a third time before the glamor faded. And: "See!"

cried Dame Faussein, shaking a drum made of a gourd capped either end with tattooed skin from a drowned sailor; this made the hall pitch-black for as long as it sounded, and all present had the eerie sense that they were adrift in an infinite void. And: "Watch!" bellowed rough old Messer d'Icque, spreading a scarlet cloth at the full stretch of both arms; on the cloth, a mouth opened and uttered five sonorous words that no one present understood.

Smiles greeted these achievements, and loud approbation gave place to a babble of inquiry as to means—"Five nights drunk under a gallows!" boasted Messer Hautnoix; "A day and a night and a day kissing the mouth of the man who bequeathed his skin!" bragged Dame Faussein; "Doing things to a goat I can't discuss with ladies present," Messer D'Icque muttered behind his hand.

"But that creature came to me when I did no more than call on him," Meleagra said, and at these disturbing words those closest to her chair drew as far back as they could from her without appearing rude.

Vengis on his high chair joined neither in the praising nor in the questioning; his heavy-jowled face remained set as stone. Had he not submitted himself to worse indignities? Had he not made pledges which in retrospect made him quail inwardly? And nothing had yet come from all his struggles—not even a pretty tricksiness like Messer Hautnoix's shining bubbles!

He thumped on his chair-side again, and cut through the chatter with a furious roar. "Enough! Enough! Are you children early out of school, that you disgrace our meeting with mere gossip? How far do these cantrips advance us to our goal? That's the question!"

A little embarrassed at their own enthusiasm, the company subsided into a period of asking each other with their eyes if any was bold enough to claim success in the central problem. At first they avoided looking at Meleagra; then, no other offer being forthcoming, they took that plunge and were rewarded with a sigh and a shake of the head.

"As I thought," Vengis crowed in scorn. "You're overwhelmed with bright spectacle and have forgotten the urgent need confronting us. Next time you go to conjure, ask yourself first this: if I succeed, what comes by way of benefit? Can I eat it? Can I put it on my back, or mend my roof with it? In fine, how will it serve not only me, but the community and nobility of Ys?"

He glared at the now fidgety assembly. "It's not going to be easy, I know that well. I've had no success to speak of, myself. But at least I haven't been diverted down illusory byways!"

The one standing unnoticed in shadow shook his head once more. Here truly was a company of fools, and chief of them their chief Vengis: a man of consuming arrogance and vanity, blind to his faults and proud beyond description. In which case . . .

He gave a gentle cough, and heads whisked around to see from whom the noise issued. Vengis half rose from his seat in astonishment.

"What are you doing here?" he thundered. "Who let you in without my leave?"

The traveler in black walked without a sound along the aisle dividing the company until he was face to face with Vengis, and there was that in his eyes which stifled further speech prior to the answering of the double question.

At last he said, "As to what I am doing here, I have been listening and considering what you've said. As to the leave that was granted me, I go where my presence is required, whether you wish it or no."

The ranked nobles of the city held their breath. This was the speech of one holding an authority they dared not challenge.

"What—what do you want of us?" whispered Vengis when he had regained some of his composure.

"Say rather what you want of me," the traveler countered with a sardonic cock of his head. "From the confusion of your meeting here I've been unable to make it out. Put it in words for me. That is, if you are sure you know what you are after . . . ?"

There was a gently insulting turn to that last phrase. Vengis bridled.

"Of course we know!" he blustered. "Have you not seen the miserable pass to which our fair city is reduced?"

"I have," acknowledged the one in black. "And as nearly as I can discern, you hold your ancestors to blame."

"We do so!" Vengis snapped. "And we seek to make them rectify their fault. We seek to call them back, that they may behold the ruin they have bequeathed to us, and compel them to save us."

"Compulsion is no part of my task," said the one in black. "I know only choice. And you say you have chosen; what then restrains you from action?"

"What do you think?" That was Bardolus, half-frantic with the tension of the moment. "We want the power to bring it about, and so far all we've managed to achieve is

35

some minor manifestations and a few personal calamities like the one which now overtakes Dame Seulte!"

"Is this the desire of you all?" said the traveler with very great sadness, casting his burning gaze to the furthest corners of the company.

"Ay!" came the chorus of replies.

"As you wish," said the traveler softly, "so be it."

Where he went, none of them saw. He passed from among them swiftly as thought, silently as shadows, and they had no more stomach for their consultations once he had departed. Yet they felt a lightness, a sense of promise, as they called to the servants to unbar the doors and made their several ways toward their homes.

The streets by which they passed seemed more crowded than of late, and not a few of them had the impression that they recognized among the throng a familiar face, a known gait, or a garment of distinctive cut. However, such ideas were of a piece with the general mood, and served only to heighten the taut anticipation they had brought away from the hall.

"What think you of Dame Seulte's fate?" said the Lady Vivette to her companion—who was also her brother, but they had judged that an advantage in making their earlier experiments. She spoke as their carriage creaked and jolted over the courtyard of their ancestral home, a short ride only from the Hall of State; behind, the hinges of the gates complained of rust and lack of oil when the retainers forced them too.

"I think she was unwise," her brother said. His name was Ormond to the world, but recently he had adopted another during a midnight ritual, and Vivette knew what it was and held some power over him in consequence.

"Do you believe that we have been gifted by this—this personage?" Vivette insisted.

"We can but try," shrugged Ormond. And added, "Shall we now, or wait till after dinner?"

"Now," Vivette said positively. "I have a feeling . . ."

So, duly, they made their preparations: putting on fantastical garments which contained surprising lacunae, and over these items of no further use to their original owners, such as a necklace of children's eyes contained in glass for Vivette and a mask made from a horse's head for Ormond. Arrayed, they repaired to a room in the high tower of the mansion, where by custom the heads of their family had been laid in state for a day and a night before burial since untold generations.

There, in a pentacle bounded by four braziers and a pot of boiling wax over a lamp, they indulged in some not unpleasurable pastimes, taking care to recite continually turn and turn about a series of impressive cantrips. The room darkened as they went on, and great excitement almost interrupted their concentration, but they stuck to it and . . .

"Look!" whispered Vivette, and pointed to the catafalque removed to the corner of the room. Under the black velvet draperies a form was lying—that of a man armed and armored.

"Why! Just so, in the picture downstairs, did Honorius our great-grandfather lie when he was waiting burial!" Ormond snapped, and leaped to his feet to pull back the velvet.

Impassive, a steel visor confronted them. Vivette pushed it open, and in the dark interior of the helmet eyes opened and a rush of fetid breath began. Stiffly, with effort, the occupant of the armor arose from the catafalque.

"Come, let me kiss you both," said a rusty voice, and the arms resistlessly encircled them, though they struggled to get away. "What, have you no feeling for your own kin?"

There was a hollow hideous chuckle, and strong as the steel enclosing them the arms forced them close; the horse-mask went thudding to the floor, and spittle-wet lips clamped on one mouth, then the other.

Both fainted. When they recovered, the figure in armor was gone, but where it had taken shape on the catafalque lay a manuscript book in bindings of leather and brass, open to the page recording the death of Honorius from a contagious fever against which no medicine was of use, in the three-and-thirtieth year of his age.

Dame Rosa, in her palanquin borne between two white female donkeys, passed the corner on which stood the house formerly owned by Dame Seulte, and drew aside the curtains to peer curiously upward. Sure enough, from the window of the room in which her friend had been accustomed to conduct her experiments, a licking tongue of greasy black smoke had smeared the walls.

She clucked with her tongue. Poor Seulte! Had she but waited another day she might have had the full fruit of her efforts. That at least was Dame Rosa's belief; she trusted the promise the one in black had made, and looked forward with impatience to the earliest moment she could closet herself with her books and apparatus and rehearse with improvements the most promising of her formulae.

Her family had in the past numbered among the most lascivious of Ys, and excessive indulgence by the womenfolk in the pleasures of the bed had often threatened to over-populate the resources of their not inconsiderable estates. Accordingly there was a cellar where excess children had been discreetly disposed of, not by any crude and direct means but by consigning their nourishment to the fates. She entered this cellar by a bronze door, which she locked with a heavy key, and passed between rows of wooden stalls in each of which a set of rat-gnawed bones lay on foul straw, gyves about one ankle.

She had chosen this place after much thought; surely, she reasoned, the point of departure to eternity of so many spirits must have a peculiar potency!

Her method of working involved feathers, four liquids of which the least noxious was fresh blood, and long silent concentration while seated on a stool of unique design with no other covering for her ample frame than her age-sparse hair would afford. Briskly she carried out the introductory rites; then she sat down and closed her eyes, shivering from excitement and not from cold.

She had, the books stated, to keep her eyes shut until she had completed the recital of a cantrip that lasted eight whole pages in minuscule script. There were two pages to go when she heard the first rustlings and clicketings behind her. There was one page to go when the first touch came on her fleshy thigh. Desperately wanting to know what marvels her work had brought about, she raced through the last page, and on the concluding word came the first *bite*.

Thirty starving children, mad with hunger and their teeth keen as any rat's left gnaw-marks on her bones too.

Bardolus trembled as he piled the curious ingredients high on the charcoal-filled brazier before his mirror. He had chosen the mirror spell out of those known to him because he had, after all, come closest to success with it before—even if he had been taken aback to see a manifestation in the unconstrained mirror of the Hall of State.

He wished he could find the courage to abandon the entire project, but fear and conceit combined to drive him on. He was beside himself with jealousy to think that a slip of a girl like Meleagra—not to mention that coarse peasant type d'Icque, or stupid complacent Dame Faussein!

—had mastered simple powers while he still cried out in terror at the consequences of his own thaumaturgy.

He struck a light and ignited the pile. Saturated with the fat of a sow that had devoured her own farrow, it blazed up and gave off a choking smoke that veiled the mirror till it was all consumed.

Then the air cleared, and in the mirror was a face he knew: that of his own mother.

"My son Bardolus," she said with fawning sweetness. "Look behind you. There is an oaken cupboard which you have known since you were a child. Press the last knob in the carved design, and a drawer will open. In the drawer is that which gave me power over your father. Take it as my gift."

The image faded. A little puzzled, Bardolus hesitated before doing as directed. He remembered his father only dimly; he had been a strange man, alternating between hysterical gaiety and depression so deep he would sit by the hour contemplating a knife or a dish of poison, plucking up the courage to take his own life.

Yet—*power*.

He pressed the knob and the drawer slid open, revealing a packet made of a strange yellow paper and sealed with green wax. He broke the seal convulsively, and a fine powder drifted up from it, seeming to seek his nostrils of its own accord. He tried to dodge, but it was useless; he inhaled it all, and the packet lay empty on his palm.

Another few seconds, and vast elation filled him. Why, he could do anything! He was ten feet tall, stronger than an ox, more potent than the heroes of legend and so handsome no wench could withstand him if he courted her!

He threw down the packet and raced toward the street.

From the mirror drifted mists, that coalesced into the shape of his mother, and ultimately grew strong enough to take up the empty packet in gnarled old fingers and regard it out of bleary eyes.

"You deserve no better fate than the one who got you on my body against my will," she whispered. "One hour, Bardolus—one hour of delirium! And afterwards despair. For it will be no use hunting for more of the drug, Bardolus! I never compounded more than one dose at a time, and it was by postponing for a day the next mixing that I held power over your father. There is no one to mix it for you, Bardolus! No one at all!"

But these were not all the calamities that overtook Ys,

the once-fair city. For those whom the black-clad traveler had challenged truly did not know what they were after, and for fear of letting slip a unique opportunity had demanded as much as they could conceive. Lost in this plethora of plenty—somewhere—was precisely and exactly what was needful; that much the traveler was bound to grant. But as he had warned, he had nothing to do with compulsion. Choice was what he understood.

And those who made a wrong choice did so because of what they were.

His friends had generally liked Messer Hautnoix, who was engagingly like a child with his delight in such baubles as the pretty colored bubbles he had displayed to the nobles of the city; it was characteristic of him that, compelled to spend five nights under a gallows for the privilege, he spent the entire time drunk to avoid excessive contemplation of his situation.

Yet when he repaired to his chosen ground of the execution dock and chuckled while he cut the throat of a white cock and a black hen, the one who came to him proved to be the first bearer of his line's name, professionally the municipal hangman, who had so loved his work that more than once he bought the silence of witnesses that would have saved victims from the rope; this being discovered they had set him swinging on his own gallows at the last.

Much time having passed since he had performed his welcome task, he seized his chance with both hands, and sunset found Messer Hautnoix dangling from a noose while his forebear walked back to the city gate, rubbing his bloated hands to think of what was promised.

Dame Faussein, who had paid a drowned man so generously for the loan of his skin, made further use of her curious little drum when she came home, thinking that the tried and tested means must be superior to any not yet proved workable. It was regrettable—and she certainly regretted it—that this time the darkness to which its beating carried her was the musty interior of her ancestral vaults, where the warmth of her living body, so long as it lasted, gave strange comfort to an aunt and two uncles whose relationship even now was more complex than the ordinary ties of kinship; her eyes continued to perceive darkness when the three together had lifted off the enclosing marble lid of their mausoleum and gone to see how Ys now stood.

Messer d'Icque was indeed of peasant stock—that was no secret in Ys. His inclinations were toward country matters, and it has never been any secret anywhere that events transpire in lonely country districts at which the sophisticated of the cities invariably wonder or grow nauseated. The whole of his city residence had been stunk out for weeks by a dung-pile he had made in the central courtyard, because it was said to be in the warmth of rotting manure that homunculi came to artificial life. This heap of foulness he passed by today, however; his mind was set on the proper employment of his stock of what the French call *animelles,* a springtime by-product of farms where sheep and cattle are bred. His plan was not, moreover, to cook and serve them as a seasonal delicacy.

To him came a progenitor who had felt the frustration of an aging wife, racked with child-bearing, and had turned to the daughter of his bailiff; it being Spring. The bailiff had returned early from the task of which the *animelles* were typically a by-product, and had made use of the implement in hand to avenge the slight to his family honor. For twenty-one generations the sufferer had sought the chance to inflict on another the operation performed on himself, and he did so without asking permission upon Messer d'Icque as the subject convenient to him. After that he set forth to multiply his valued possessions from all possible male sources.

No word of this had been brought to the beauteous Meleagra when she came home. She had never cared for Messer d'Icque, thinking him rough and ill-bred, and the news that he had been involuntarily qualified to share her overnight company would have interested her not at all.

In a boudoir hung with lace draperies, containing a round golden bed and a mirror abstracted from the Hall of State as being the largest in Ys—which she had mounted cunningly on the ceiling—she caused her maids first to draw all the curtains at the many high windows, then to light candles which gave off a fragrant, intoxicating aroma. She suffered them to remove her clothing, to prepare her a bath in which she dissolved a handful of polychrome salts, and to sing in harmony while they sponged her from head to toe. Sweetmeats were brought on a white platter and a silver filigree dish, and twenty-four new gowns were displayed before her on the body of a dumb girl who matched the dimensions of her figure.

All the while this was going on, she was musing over a crucial decision: should she, or should she not, act upon the promise the black-clad one had made?

That he had the power to which he laid claim, she never

doubted. Two years before anyone else in Ys saw what needed to be done, she had closed the bargain about her virginity
which she had scrupulously kept—at first purely from determination, but latterly partly from honest fear.

And what she had purchased with this bargain had enabled her to recognize the single nature of their unaccount-
able visitor.

A single nature! It implied that the possessor of it could
neither lie nor deceive, surely . . . ? In which case she
might employ her talents and be safe as she ever was. Her
whole life since the age of eleven had been on the edge of
a precipice, and there were creatures at the bottom of the
chasm she had eluded only by extreme foresight and planning.

She had naturally said nothing of what she had learned
to anyone else. It had been an uncharacteristic yielding to
vanity which made her call Ub-Shebbab to the Hall of
State—the purpose had been to discountenance Vengis because he was a boastful donkey. The mark had been struck.
Yet Ub-Shebbab was the meekest and mildest of the beings
she had called up.

Why share her hard-bought knowledge with fools and
bunglers? Let disaster overtake them in due time. Meanwhile, she herself . . .

In the end, it was curiosity as much as anything that
decided her. She dismissed her maids and put on a gown
that had not been displayed during her bath, worked all
over in gold wire with a single sentence in a forgotten
language; then she opened a brass chest and took out gifts
she had exacted from various suitors in the days before information about her inflexible rule was noised abroad.

There was a twig from Yorbeth, bearing a leaf trans-
parent as glass and a brown, blotched fruit which tinkled
like a bell; there was a vial of rain water caught at the
foot of the rainbow overarching Barbizond, that had a trifle
of Sardhin's essence in it; there was a block of pumice from
the volcano where Fegrim slumbered; there was a jar of
gray dust from the hill where Laprivan was shut away;
there was a hair from the head of Farchgrind, an inch of
candle that had revealed the secret thoughts of Wolpec but
had been allowed to burn one instant longer than was
safe, and a drawing of two birds and a crocodile made by
a possessed child.

Also there was a book.

Following with care the instructions it contained, she
danced around her boudoir keening, went twice backward

across the floor with a knife between her teeth, and at last cut her forearm and let three drops of her blood fall on the carpet. When she looked again the stains had vanished.

Nothing else happened in the room. She had expected that; humming, she changed her gown for something more conventional and went down to the dining-hall where supper was to be served.

Already as she approached it she could hear the clatter of dishes, the murmur of conversation. That boded a great company. She hurried the last few steps and threw open the door.

Every place at her great table—and there were thirty-six—was taken; the servants had pressed into use benches from the kitchen, too, and the sideboards and the serving-tables were alike packed with a hungry horde. For all the scullions and maids could do, the food, brought on trolleys because there was more of it than a man could lift, disappeared within instants of being set down. The bread had gone, the meat, the wine; now it was boiled turnips and hedge-greens, broth of bones and barley, and beer too new to serve by ordinary.

Yet that was not all. Behind, between, among those who ate were others looting. The fine brocade drapes had been torn down to clothe naked bodies, leather-backed chairs stripped to afford protection to sore feet, tapestries turned to cloaks and ponchos. One wild-eyed woman, lacking anything else, had smeared herself with gravy to break up the maggot pallidity of her skin.

Meleagra stood in the doorway for a long heartbeat of time before the chief steward caught sight of her and came running to beg for help.

"Mistress, what shall we do? They are in every room—five hundred of them at the last count! And all, all have the right to what you have, for they say they are your ancestors and this is their home!"

"That is so," whispered Meleagra. Her eyes, drawn by a magnet, went to him who had taken her seat at the head of the table, and a silence overcame the entire company.

The one at whom she gazed was a cross-eyed, ill-favored fellow in a dirty doublet, unshaven and with black around his nails. He gave her a smile that showed gapped yellow teeth, and spoke in a soft voice with a peasant's accent.

"We are in your debt, Meleagra, that you set your table for us and bid us back to enjoy what was ours and shall be again! You have worked most potent magic, child; the family is proud of you."

43

"Who—who are you?" she choked out.

"Damien, who built the house and founded the family's fortune in the earliest days of Ys. And at my side Cosimo, my first-born here—though I had byblows aplenty in another town! And Syriax his wife and their children Ruslan, Roland and Igraine, and their children Mark, Valetta, Corin, Ludovic, Matthaus, Letty, Seamus; theirs, Orlando, Hugo, Dianne, twins Nathaniel and Enoch—"

"Stop! Stop!" Meleagra put her hands to her temples; the room seemed to be spinning, and from every side gross faces leered at her, or thin drawn faces gazed in stony regard, or dull faces moped, or . . .

"There is no more food!" the steward shouted. "We have killed all the poultry, the pantry is bare, the wine-casks are drained, the last carp is gone from the pond, the beer-barrels are exhausted and even the *well* is dry!"

"You've done this to me, for that I gave you breath and life and this new opportunity?" Meleagra whispered to her remotest ancestor Damien.

"What do we care for you?" said Damien with contempt. "We are here and alive, your ancestors; how then can you be of importance? Here we are alive, who died before you saw light—how then can you be mistress in this house? You are a thing not thought of, less than dust for dust can be seen to dance in sunbeams. You are the flame of a candle guttering out. So—*poof!*"

He blew at the candle closest to him upon the great table, and with the death of its flame there was no such person as Meleagra—never had been—never could be.

Long hours Lord Vengis had paced in the high room above the Hall of State, pondering the day's events and screwing himself to the point where he would again begin his rituals. The day wasted; shadows lengthened; evening cold began to permeate the building and he called for fire.

He was afraid.

He had seen in the eyes of the traveler in black a warning which his pride forbade him to heed; he was ashamed because he was afraid, yet shame could not break fear's grip. He wished to do as doubtless many others were doing—what if he alone remained untalented in sorcery when blockheads like Bardolus or half-grown wenches like Vivette boasted powers unnameable?

Nonetheless, he dithered and delayed, and had not yet cast the first runes nor recited the first line of any formula

44

when the sergeant of the guard came stiffly to report a disturbance in the town.

"Disturbance?" rapped Vengis. "Man, be precise! What do you mean?"

"Why, sir"—and the sergeant rubbed his chin dolefully—"some hours agone there were complaints of desecration in the graveyard by the cathedral, the curate saying that a vault was open and the bones removed, but seeing as how we've had call for similar extraordinary materials that your lordship required I decided best not to say anything. Now, though, it's serious, and the side wall of the building here is cracked where they entombed alive a woman named Igraine—you've seen the plaque—accused of commerce with a familiar spirit in the guise of a cat. . . ."

From the street outside came a howl as of maddened beasts, and the sergeant flinched visibly. But he continued in his best official manner.

"Then, your lordship, at dusk reports came of strangers in the city and we called out the patrols for fear of infiltration by some jealous invader. Myself, I've stopped twenty-one persons and all spoke with the accent of the city and gave names that fit our habits, but it seems I've seen all those names on gravestones before now—some, indeed, earlier today when I answered the complaint at the cathedral. And what brings me in to you, begging your pardon, is the curious business of the man and two wives."

"What?" whispered Vengis, sweat pearling his face.

"Well, sir . . . There was this man, whom I'd challenged, walking with a girl of fifteen-odd, and comes up from nowhere a woman aged as he was—forty, maybe—and says she is his wife and what's this hussy doing with her husband? So the little girl says they were married legally and then there follows screaming of insults and hair-pulling and at the last we must clap 'em in the jail. Which is—uh—difficult. For every cell, they tell me, is full, and that's more than I can understand; this morning the records say there were one hundred and one places vacant for new prisoners."

Vengis's voice had failed him. He could not speak, but chewed his nails and stared with burning eyes at the sergeant.

"What shall I do, your lordship?" the man finally asked.

"I—I . . ." Vengis spun around and strode to the window overlooking the main square. He thrust the casement open and leaned out. By the last dim light of the dying day he could see a myriad people gathering. Some were colorful and substantial, but these were few; most were gray as the

45

stones they trod, and they trailed curious wispy streamers behind them, like cobwebs. But all alike had the same air of bewilderment, as though they were lost in the mazes of time and eternity, and could not find the way back to the present moment.

Vengis began to babble incoherently.

There came a thundering knock at the door of the room where they were, and a cavernous groaning voice said, "Open! Open in the name of the Lord of Ys!"

Shrugging, the sergeant made to obey, but Vengis came after him, clawing madly at his arm. "Don't! Don't let them in!" he wailed.

"But, your lordship," said the sergeant firmly, "it *is* in your name that they demand entry, so it must be a matter of importance. Indeed, with your permission, I'm expecting further reports from my patrols."

Vengis searched the room with feverish eyes. In the far corner he spied a cupboard large as a man; he dashed to it, and slammed the door behind him.

The sergeant, astonished, went nonetheless to answer the knock, and fell back in dismay before the apparition which confronted him. Gaunt, tall, with a second mouth gaping redly in his throat, was the figure of legendary Lord Gazemon, who had laid the first stone of the city with his own two hands.

Now those hands held a broadsword; now he advanced with slow terrible steps upon the closet in which Vengis thought to secrete himself, and battered down the planks to the door to hail that miserable successor of his into the wan torchlight.

"You know me?" croaked the city's founder.

Gulping, moaning, Vengis contrived a nod, and the huge spectre shook him as a terrier shakes a rat. "Oh, to what a miserable stature have shrunk these weaklings of today!" he bellowed. The sergeant, cowering in the opposite corner, could not tell by which mouth Gazemon spoke—his natural one, or the second which had let out his life.

Again the door rattled to an imperious knock, and he scuttled to answer before Gazemon could address him. With trembling hands he admitted those who stood without: Lorin, who had slain Gazemon by treachery and usurped his throne; Angus, who had taken the throne back into the rightful line of descent; then Caed, then Dame Degrance who passed for a man and ruled like one until the physicians at her deathbed unmasked her sex, then Walter of Meux, then Auberon, then Lams and the first Vengis who was a

46

stout and brave leader for the one short year he survived, and others and others to the latest who had sat the chair below before this current weakling.

With axes, maces, swords, with pens and scrolls and money-changer's scales according to the sort of power by which they had made Ys great, they gathered around the hapless victim of their contempt.

"We have been abroad in the city since we were called from rest," rumbled Gazemon, his grip still fast on Vengis' shoulder. "We have seen the stagnant puddles in the streets, the shutters dangling from one hinge on the cracked walls of the fine houses, the dirty beggars and the starving children in this which we all gave our lives to make into a city that the world should envy! You have given our golden towers to tarnish, our iron doors to rust; you have given our splendid harbor to the mud and our fat grain-fields to the weeds; you have squandered our treasury on baubles when we bought it with blood. How say you all, you who listen here? Is it not time that we held an accounting?"

"Ay, time," they said as one, and hearing the menace in the voices Vengis rolled his eyes upward in their sockets and let go his hold on life.

"Oh, there you are!"

Perched on a rock at the top of the gray hill, Jacques turned and forwent his gazing at sunset-gilded Ys in favor of a scowl at the traveler in black who had come to join him. There were no footprints to show by which path he had arrived; still, where Laprivan wiped away the past that was no wonder.

"You've been long enough, in all conscience," he complained further. "It's cold here, and for all you promised I should witness the doom of Ys I see nothing but what I've always seen when I looked on the place. Though before you say anything I concede you were correct in describing this hill. I must have missed it somehow when I wandered around in my youth."

"No, that's not the case," the traveler sighed. Now the course of events was grinding to its inexorable conclusion, he felt downcast, despite there never having been an alternative. Also he did not like Jacques, regarding him as too self-righteously opinionated.

"So what's the form this doom will take?" Jacques pressed him.

"It is already in train," the traveler said. He raised his staff and pointed across the twilight gray of the valley.

47

"Do you not see, there by the gate, a certain number of persons making in this direction?"

"Why—yes, I believe I do." Jacques peered hard. "But I cannot make out who they are at this great distance."

"I know who they are."

"Then tell me!"

"They are those of the people of Ys who have remembered you—Jacques the scrivener. And who are now bent on finding you and regulating an account with you. There is a great balancing going on, and you are an uncanceled factor."

"What?" Turned sidewise in the gloaming, Jacques' face was ghastly pale. "Why me? What do they want with me?"

"I will explain if you wish," the traveler agreed wearily, and shifted his grip on his staff to afford a more comfortable angle of support. "You must understand first that the would-be enchanters of Ys have succeeded beyond their wildest dreams, and have called back—as they desired—those who made the city and visited their present plight on them. And they have found, as was inevitable, that their ancestors were ordinary human beings, with human faults and failings, and not infrequently with remarkable outstanding faults, because this is the way with persons who are remarkable and outstanding in other areas of their lives."

"But—but I counseled against this foolishness!" cried Jacques.

"No," corrected the one in black. "You said: you are pig-headed fools and I am absolutely, unalterably right while everyone else is wrong. And when they would not listen to such dogmatic bragging—as who would?—you washed your hands of them, and even wished them a dreadful doom."

"Did I wish them any worse than they deserved?" Jacques was trying to keep up his front of bravado, but he had to link his fingers to stop his hands from shaking.

"Discuss the matter with those who are coming to find you," suggested the traveler sardonically. "Their belief is opposite to yours; they hold that by making people disgusted with the views you subscribed to, you prevented rational thought from regaining its mastery of Ys. Where you should have reasoned, you flung insults; where you should have argued calmly and with purpose, you castigated honest men with doubts as purblind idiots. This is what they say, and I have no business disagreeing with them. I leave it to you to convince them of the truth—

48

but it seems likely to be a tough task, in view of what they carry."

Jacques looked again at the column of people winding out from the city, and now saw what the traveler referred to. At the head of the line was a blacksmith with a hammer on his shoulder; behind him, a ditcher came with a mattock, then a gardener with a sickle and two coopers with heavy barrel-staves. And those behind still bore each their handiest weapon, down to a red-handed goodwife wielding the stick from her butter churn.

"But—but!" Jacques leaped to his feet, glancing wildly around for a way of escape. "You must stop them! You told me to come here, and I think you knew this would happen if I did!"

"It happened because you wished to witness the doom of Ys," said the traveler. "You did not stop to ask if that doom was one you must share to witness it."

Slightly louder, for Jacques had begun to stumble downhill into the gathering night, he added, "Running away won't help for long, my friend. Those are incredibly determined people yonder; though you hid in the pit of Fegrim's volcano, they would track you down."

"Is there nothing I can do?" moaned Jacques. "How can I stop them from coming after me? Tell me! Tell me!"

"As you wish, so be it," said the traveler, and cheered up somewhat, for that put a very satisfactory end to this momentary aberration in the smooth course of the cosmos. It had happened, which was bad, but now it would cease, which was good.

He tapped three times on a nearby rock, and under his breath he said, "Laprivan! Laprivan of the Yellow Eyes!"

Jacques screamed.

Below, in the valley, the column of determinedly advancing men and women bound to wreak their vengeance on Jacques hesitated, halted, and broke in disorder that grew to panic. For out of the side of his hill Laprivan was peering, and what was behind his eyes belonged to the age when chaos was the All.

Some small power remained to him so long as he survived, and he put it to this single and unique purpose: to wipe clean the slate of yesterday.

So he looked down on Ys, and saw there what was to him an abomination: the shadows of the past given substance. He reached out one of his arms, and erased—and erased—and erased. . . .

Honorius, sowing his contagious fever on the streets, was not.

Thirty sated children, smeared with blood on faces and fingers, were not.

Bardolus' mother, chortling over the fate of her son, was not.

Knotting a noose from every rope in a cord-seller's shop, the first of the line of the Hautnoix was not.

Brandishing his bloody trophies, the adulterous d'Icque was not.

Three who had come forth from a vault were not.

Stripped of its food, its draperies, its gold and silver and precious artworks, the house of Meleagra was silent.

And those who had come to regulate accounts with the decadent lordling Vengis took their leave.

Also many who had come forth from graves and sepulchres, from hollow walls and wayside ditches, from dungeons and the beds of rivers and the bottoms of wells—were not.

"So!" said the traveler in black, when he had restored Laprivan to his captivity. "You have a reprieve, Jacques—are you glad of that?"

The tawny-bearded man beside him moaned an affirmative.

"And will you learn a lesson from it?"

"I'll try—as heaven is my witness, I will try!"

"Fairly said," the traveler declared. "Go then after those who are hiding in the valley. Approach them as a friend, not showing that you know why they set forth with cudgels and bludgeons. Say to them that the rule of chaos in Ys is ended, and so is Ys; they must return home for the last time and pack their belongings before they and all the people scatter to the ends of the Earth."

"But—is this Earth?" Jacques whimpered. "On the way to Barbizond—and now here—I've seen . . ."

"Don't worry. You'll have no more of that. It belongs to yesterday, and with other traces of yesterday Laprivan has wiped it out." The traveler allowed himself a smile. "And do not lament excessively for Ys. For cities, as for men, there comes a Time . . . Besides, there is a prophecy: a prince shall seek a name for his new capital, and he'll be told of Ys, and out of envy for its greatness he will say, 'I name my city Parys, *equal to* Ys.'"

"I have little faith in prophecies as a rule," said Jacques, staring. "But in this extraordinary place . . . Well, no matter.

Sir, I take my leave of you—and I thank you. You have held up an honest mirror to me, and I cannot resent that."

"Go now," the traveler said. "Be quick."

He waited long on the brow of the hill while the last daylight dwindled away and the stars wheeled gradually to the angle marking midnight. It became more and more difficult to see Ys: the towers melted into mist, the walls and gates were shadow-dark among shadows. For a while torches glimmered; then even they failed to be seen any longer, and when dawn came there was neither the city, nor the traveler in black, for anyone to behold.

Jorge Luis Borges is an Argentine fantasist whose strange, individualistic stories have gained a steadily increasing reputation first in Europe (where Andre Maurois unhesitatingly called him "a great writer") and now in the U.S. (where Borges is so In that he recently had three stories in one issue of *The New Yorker*). Yet most pure-fantasy readers, sadly, aren't familiar with his work. The following narrative is distinguished not only for its descriptions of strange beings and the insane City of the Immortals, but for its echoing-mirror glimpse of what a really immortal man's mind might be like.

THE IMMORTAL
Jorge Luis Borges

Salomon saith, *There is no new thing upon the earth.* So that as Plato had an imagination, *that all knowledge was but remembrance;* so Salomon giveth his sentence, *that all novelty is but oblivion.*

Francis Bacon: *Essays,* LVIII

In London, in the first part of June 1929, the antique dealer Joseph Cartaphilus of Smyrna offered the Princess of

Lucinge the six volumes in small quarto (1715-1720) of Pope's *Iliad*. The Princess acquired them; on receiving the books, she exchanged a few words with the dealer. He was, she tells us, a wasted and earthen man, with gray eyes and gray beard, of singularly vague features. He could express himself with fluency and ignorance in several languages; in very few minutes, he went from French to English and from English to an enigmatic conjunction of Salonika Spanish and Macao Portuguese. In October, the Princess heard from a passenger of the *Zeus* that Cartaphilus had died at sea while returning to Smyrna, and that he had been buried on the island of Ios. In the last volume of the *Iliad* she found this manuscript.

The original is written in English and abounds in Latinisms. The version we offer is literal.

I

As far as I can recall, my labors began in a garden in Thebes Hekatompylos, when Diocletian was emperor. I had served (without glory) in the recent Egyptian wars, I was tribune of a legion quartered in Berenice, facing the Red Sea: fever and magic consumed many men who had magnanimously coveted the steel. The Mauretanians were vanquished; the land previously occupied by the rebel cities was eternally dedicated to the Plutonic gods; Alexandria, once subdued, vainly implored Caesar's mercy; within a year of the legions reported victory, but I scarcely managed a glimpse of Mars' countenance. This privation pained me and perhaps caused me precipitously to undertake the discovery, through fearful and diffuse deserts, of the secret City of the Immortals.

My labors began, I have related, in a garden in Thebes. All that night I was unable to sleep, for something was struggling within my heart. I arose shortly before dawn; my slaves were sleeping, the moon was of the same color as the infinite sand. An exhausted and bloody horseman came from the east. A few steps from me, he tumbled from his mount. In a faint, insatiable voice he asked me in Latin the name of the river bathing the city's walls. I answered that it was the Egypt, fed by the rains. "Another is the river I seek," he replied sadly, "the secret river which cleanses men of death." Dark blood surged from his breast. He told me that his homeland was a mountain on the other side of the Ganges and that on this mountain it was said that if

53

one traveled to the west, where the world ends, he would reach the river whose waters grant immortality. He added that on its far bank the City of the Immortals rises, rich in bastions and amphitheaters and temples. Before dawn he died, but I had determined to discover the city and its river. Interrogated by the executioner, some Mauretanian prisoners confirmed the traveler's tale; someone recalled the Elysian plain, at the end of the earth, where men's lives are perdurable; someone else, the peaks where the Pactolus rises, whose inhabitants live for a century. In Rome, I conversed with philosophers who felt that to extend man's life is to extend his agony and multiply his deaths. I do not know if I ever believed in the City of the Immortals: I think that then the task of finding it was sufficient. Flavius, proconsul of Getulia, gave me two hundred soldiers for the undertaking. I also recruited mercenaries, who said they knew the roads and were the first to desert.

Later events have deformed inextricably the memory of the first days of our journey. We departed from Arsinoe and entered the burning desert. We crossed the land of the troglodytes, who devour serpents and are ignorant of verbal commerce; that of the garamants, who keep their women in common and feed on lions; that of the augyls, who worship only Tartarus. We exhausted other deserts where the sand is black, where the traveler must usurp the hours of night, for the fervor of day is intolerable. From afar, I glimpsed the mountain which gave its name to the Ocean: on its sides grows the spurge plant, which counteracts poisons; on its peak live the satyrs, a nation of fell and savage men, given to lewdness. That these barbarous regions, where the earth is mother of monsters, could shelter in their interior a famous city seemed inconceivable to all of us. We continued our march, for it would have been dishonor to turn back. A few foolhardy men slept with their faces exposed to the moon; they burned with fever; in the corrupted water of the cisterns others drank madness and death. Then the desertions began; very shortly thereafter, mutinies. To repress them, I did not hesitate to exercise severity. I proceeded justly, but a centurion warned me that the seditious (eager to avenge the crucifixion of one of their number) were plotting my death. I fled from the camp with the few soldiers loyal to me. I lost them in the desert, amid the sandstorms and the vast night. I was lacerated by a Cretan arrow. I wandered several days without finding water, or one enormous day multiplied by the sun, my thirst or my fear of thirst. I left the route to the judgment of my horse.

In the dawn, the distance bristled up into pyramid⟨s⟩
towers. Intolerably, I dreamt of an exiguous and n⟨ear⟩
labyrinth: in the center was a water jar; my hands almost
touched it, my eyes could see it, but so intricate and per-
plexed were the curves that I knew I would die before
reaching it.

II

When finally I became untangled from this nightmare, I
found myself lying with my hands tied, in an oblong stone
niche no larger than a common grave, shallowly excavated
into the sharp slope of a mountain. Its sides were damp,
polished by time rather than by human effort. I felt a
painful throbbing in my chest, I felt that I was burning
with thirst. I looked out and shouted feebly. At the foot of
the mountain, an impure stream spread noiselessly, clogged
with débris and sand; on the opposite bank (beneath the
last sun or beneath the first) shone the evident City of the
Immortals. I saw walls, arches, façades and fora: the base
was a stone plateau. A hundred or so irregular niches, ana-
logous to mine, furrowed the mountain and the valley. In
the sand there were shallow pits; from these miserable holes
(and from the niches) naked, gray-skinned, scraggly bearded
men emerged. I thought I recognized them: they belonged
to the bestial breed of the troglodytes, who infest the shores
of the Arabian Gulf and the caverns of Ethiopia; I was
not amazed that they could not speak and that they
devoured serpents.

The urgency of my thirst made me reckless. I calculated that I was some thirty feet from the sand; I threw
myself headlong down the slope, my eyes closed, my hands
behind my back. I sank my bloody face into the dark
water. I drank just as animals water themselves. Before losing myself again in sleep and delirium, I repeated, inexpli-
cably, some words in Greek: "the rich Trojans from Zelea
who drink the black water of the Aisepos."

I do not know how many days and nights turned above
me. Aching, unable to regain the shelter of the caverns,
naked on the unknown sand, I let the moon and the sun
gamble with my unfortunate destiny. The troglodytes, in-
fantile in their barbarity, did not aid me to survive or to
die. In vain I begged them to put me to death. One day,
I broke my bindings on an edge of flint. Another day, I
got up and managed to beg or steal—I, Marcus Flaminius

Rufus, military tribune of one of Rome's legions—my first detested portion of serpent flesh.

My covetousness to see the Immortals, to touch the superhuman city, almost kept me from sleep. As if they penetrated my purpose, neither did the troglodytes sleep: at first I inferred that they were watching me; later, that they had become contaminated by my uneasiness, much as dogs may do. To leave the barbarous village, I chose the most public of hours, the coming of evening, when almost all the men emerge from their crevices and pits and look at the setting sun, without seeing it. I prayed out loud, less as a supplication to divine favor than as an intimidation of the tribe with articulate words. I crossed the stream clogged by the dunes and headed toward the City. Confusedly, two or three men followed me. They were (like the others of that breed) of slight stature; they did not inspire fear but rather repulsion. I had to skirt several irregular ravines which seemed to me like quarries; obfuscated by the City's grandeur, I had thought it nearby. Toward midnight, I set foot upon the black shadow of its walls, bristling out in idolatrous forms on the yellow sand. I was halted by a kind of sacred horror. Novelty and the desert are so abhorred by man that I was glad one of the troglodytes had followed me to the last. I closed my eyes and awaited (without sleeping) the light of day.

I have said that the City was founded on a stone plateau. This plateau, comparable to a high cliff, was no less arduous than the walls. In vain I fatigued myself: the black base did not disclose the slightest irregularity, the invariable walls seemed not to admit a single door. The force of the sun obliged me to seek refuge in a cave; in the rear was a pit, in the pit a stairway which sank down abysmally into the darkness below. I went down; through a chaos of sordid galleries I reached a vast circular chamber, scarcely visible. There were nine doors in this cellar; eight led to a labyrinth that treacherously returned to the same chamber; the ninth (through another labyrinth) led to a second circular chamber equal to the first. I do not know the total number of these chambers; my misfortune and anxiety multiplied them. The silence was hostile and almost perfect; there was no sound in this deep stone network save that of a subterranean wind, whose cause I did not discover; noiselessly, tiny streams of rusty water disappeared between the crevices. Horribly, I became habituated to this doubtful world; I found it incredible that there could be anything but cellars with nine doors and long branched-out cellars; I do not know how long I must have walked beneath the ground; I know that I once confused, in the same nostalgia, the atrocious village of the barbarians and my native city, amid the clusters.

In the depths of a corridor, an unforeseen wall halted me; a remote light fell from above. I raised my confused eyes: in the vertiginous, extreme heights I saw a circle of sky so blue that it seemed purple. Some metal rungs scaled the wall. I was limp with fatigue, but I climbed up, stopping only at times to sob clumsily with joy. I began to glimpse capitals and astragals, triangular pediments and vaults, confused pageants of granite and marble. Thus I was afforded this ascension from the blind region of dark interwoven labyrinths into the resplendent City.

I emerged into a kind of little square or, rather, a kind of courtyard. It was surrounded by a single building of irregular form and variable height; to this heterogeneous building belonged the different cupolas and columns. Rather than by any other trait of this incredible monument, I was held by the extreme age of its fabrication. I felt that it was older than mankind, than the earth. This manifest antiquity (though in some way terrible to the eyes) seemed to me in keeping with the work of immortal builders. At first cautiously, later indifferently, at last desperately, I wandered up the stairs and along the pavements of the inextricable palace. (Afterwards I learned that the width and height of the steps were not constant, a fact which made me understand the singular fatigue they produced.) "This palace is a fabrication of the gods," I thought at the beginning. I explored the uninhabited interiors and corrected myself: "The gods who built it have died." I noted its peculiarities and said: "The gods who built it were mad." I said it, I know, with an incomprehensible reprobation which was almost remorse, with more intellectual horror than palpable fear. To the impression of enormous antiquity others were added: that of the interminable, that of the atrocious, that of the complexly senseless. I had crossed a labyrinth, but the nitid City of the Immortals filled me with fright and repugnance. A labyrinth is a structure compounded to confuse men; its architecture, rich in symmetries, is subordinated to that end. In the palace I imperfectly explored, the architecture lacked any such finality. It abounded in dead-end corridors, high unattainable windows, portentous doors which led to a cell or pit, incredible inverted stairways whose steps and balustrades hung downwards. Other stairways, clinging airily to the side of a monumental wall, would die without leading anywhere, after making two or three turns in the lofty darkness of the cupolas. I do not know if all the examples I have enumerated are literal; I know that for many years they infested my nightmares; I am no longer able to know if such and such a detail is a transcription of reality or of the forms which unhinged my nights. "This City" (I thought) "is so horrible that its mere existence and perdurance, though in the midst of a secret desert, contaminates the past and the future and in some way even jeopardizes the stars. As long as it lasts, no one in the world can be strong or happy." I do not want to describe it; a chaos of heterogeneous words, the body of a tiger or a bull in which teeth, organs and heads monstrously pullulate in mutual conjunction and hatred can (perhaps) be approximate images.

I do not remember the stages of my return, amid the dusty and damp hypogea. I only know I was not abandoned by the fear that, when I left the last labyrinth, I would again be surrounded by the nefarious City of the Immortals. I can remember nothing else. This oblivion, now insuperable, was perhaps voluntary; perhaps the circumstances of my escape were so unpleasant that, on some day no less forgotten as well, I swore to forget them.

III

Those who have read the account of my labors with attention will recall that a man from the tribe followed me as a dog might up to the irregular shadow of the walls. When I came out of the last cellar, I found him at the mouth of the cave. He was stretched out on the sand, where he was tracing clumsily and erasing a string of signs that, like the letters in our dreams, seem on the verge of being understood and then dissolve. At first, I thought it was some kind of primitive writing; then I saw it was absurd to imagine that men who have not attained to the spoken word could attain to writing. Besides, none of the forms was equal to another, which excluded or lessened the possibility that they were symbolic. The man would trace them, look at them and correct them. Suddenly, as if he were annoyed by this game, he erased them with his palm and forearm. He looked at me, seemed not to recognize me. However, so great was the relief which engulfed me (or so great and fearful was my loneliness) that I supposed this rudimentary troglodyte looking up at me from the floor of the cave had been waiting for me. The sun heated the plain; when we began the return to the village, beneath the first stars, the sand burned under our feet. The troglodyte went ahead; that night I conceived the plan of teaching him to recognize and perhaps to repeat a few words. The dog and the horse (I reflected) are capable of the former; many birds, like the Caesars' nightingales, of the latter. No matter how crude a man's mind may be, it will always be superior to that of irrational creatures.

The humility of wretchedness of the troglodyte brought to my memory the image of Argos, the moribund old dog in the *Odyssey*, and so I gave him the name Argos and tried to teach it to him. I failed over and again. Conciliation, rigor and obstinancy were completely in vain. Motionless, with lifeless eyes, he seemed not to perceive the sounds I tried to press upon him. A few steps from me, he seemed to be very distant. Lying on the sand like a small ruinous lava sphinx, he let the heavens turn above him from the twilight of dawn till that of evening. I judged it impossible that he not be aware of my purpose. I recalled that among the Ethiopians it is well known that monkeys deliberately do not speak so they will not be obliged to work, and I attributed Argos' silence to suspicion or fear. From that imagination I went on to others, even more extravagant. I thought that our perceptions were the same, but that he combined them in another way and made other objects of them; I thought that perhaps there were no objects for him, only a vertiginous and continuous play of extremely brief impressions. I thought of a world without memory, without time; I considered the possibility of a language without nouns, a language of impersonal verbs or indeclinable epithets. Thus the days went on dying and with them the years, but something akin to happiness happened one morning. It rained, with powerful deliberation.

Desert nights can be cold, but that night had been fire. I dreamt that a river in Thessaly (to whose waters I had returned a goldfish) came to rescue me; over the red sand and black rock I heard it approach; the coolness of the air and the busy murmur of the rain awoke me. I ran naked to meet it. Night was fading; beneath the yellow clouds, the tribe, no less joyful than I, offered themselves to the vivid downpour in a kind of ecstasy. They seemed like Corybantes possessed by the divinity. Argos, his eyes turned toward the sky, groaned; torrents ran down his face, not only of water but (I later learned) of tears. Argos, I cried, Argos.

Then, with gentle admiration, as if he were discovering something lost and forgotten a long time ago, Argos stammered these words: "Argos, Ulysses' dog." And then, also without looking at me: "This dog lying in the manure."

We accept reality easily, perhaps because we intuit that nothing is real. I asked him what he knew of the *Odyssey*. The exercise of Greek was painful for him; I had to repeat the question.

"Very little," he said. "Less than the poorest rhapsodist. It must be a thousand and one hundred years since I invented it."

IV

Everything was elucidated for me that day. The troglodytes were the Immortals; the rivulet of sandy water, the River sought by the horseman. As for the city whose renown had spread as far as the Ganges, it was some nine centuries since the Immortals had razed it. With the relics of its ruins they erected, in the same place, the mad city I had traversed: a kind of parody or inversion and also temple of the irrational gods who govern the world and of whom we know nothing, save that they do not resemble man. This establishment was the last symbol to which the Immortals condescended; it marks a stage at which, judging that all undertakings are in vain, they determined to live in thought, in pure speculation. They erected their structure, forgot it and went to dwell in the caves. Absorbed in thought, they hardly perceived the physical world.

These things were told me by Homer, as one would speak to a child. He also related to me his old age and the last voyage he undertook, moved, as was Ulysses, by the purpose of reaching the men who do not know what the sea is nor eat meat seasoned with salt nor suspect what an oar is. He lived for a century in the City of the Immortals. When it was razed, he advised that the other be founded. This should not surprise us; it is famous that after singing of the war of Ilion, he sang of the war of the frogs and mice. He was like a god who might create the cosmos and then create a chaos.

To be immortal is commonplace; except for man, all creatures are immortal, for they are ignorant of death; what is divine, terrible, incomprehensible, is to know that one is immortal. I have noted that, in spite of religions, this conviction is very rare. Israelites, Christians and Moslems profess

60

immortality, but the veneration they render this world proves they believe only in it, since they destine all other worlds, in infinite number, to be its reward or punishment. The wheel of certain Hindustani religions seems more reasonable to me; on this wheel, which has neither beginning nor end, each life is the effect of the preceding and engenders the following, but none determines the totality. . . . Indoctrinated by a practice of centuries, the republic of immortal men had attained the perfection of tolerance and almost that of indifference. They knew that in an infinite period of time, all things happen to all men. Because of his past or future virtues, every man is worthy of all goodness, but also of all perversity, because of his infamy in the past or future. Thus, just as in games of chance the odd and even numbers tend toward equilibrium, so also wit and stolidity cancel out and correct each other and perhaps the rustic *Poem of the Cid* is the counterbalance demanded by one single epithet from the *Ecologues* or by an epigram of Heraclitus. The most fleeting thought obeys an invisible design and can crown, or inaugurate, a secret form. I know of those who had done evil so that in future centuries good would result, or would have resulted in those already past. . . . Seen in this manner, all our acts are just, but they are also indifferent. There are no moral or intellectual merits. Homer composed the *Odyssey;* if we postulate an infinite period of time, with infinite circumstances and changes, the impossible thing is not to compose the *Odyssey,* at least once. No one is anyone, one single immortal man is all men. Like Cornelius Agrippa, I am god, I am hero, I am philosopher, I am demon and I am world, which is a tedious way of saying that I do not exist.

The concept of the world as a system of precise compensations influenced the Immortals vastly. In the first place, it made them invulnerable to pity. I have mentioned the ancient quarries which broke the fields on the other bank; a man once fell headlong into the deepest of them; he could not hurt himself or die but he was burning with thirst; before they threw him a rope, seventy years went by. Neither were they interested in their own fate. The body, for them, was a submissive domestic animal and it sufficed to give it, every month, the pittance of a few hours of sleep, a bit of water and a scrap of meat. Let no one reduce us to the status of ascetics. There is no pleasure more complex than that of thought and we surrendered ourselves to it. At times, an extraordinary stimulus would restore us to the physical world. For example, that morning, the old elemental joy of the rain. Those lapses were quite rare; all the Immortals were capable of perfect quietude; I remember one whom I never saw stand up: a bird had nested on his breast.

Among the corollaries of the doctrine that there is nothing lacking compensation in something else, there is one whose theoretical importance is very small, but which induced us, toward the end or the beginning of the tenth century, to disperse ourselves over the face of the earth. It can be stated in these words: "There exists a river whose waters grant immortality; in some region there must be another river whose waters remove it." The number of rivers is not infinite; an immortal traveler who traverses the world will finally, some day, have drunk from all of them. We proposed to discover that river.

Death (or its allusion) makes men precious and pathetic. They are moving because of their phantom conditions; every act they execute may be their last; there is not a face that is not on the verge of dissolving like a face in a dream. Everything among the mortals has the value of the irretrievable and the perilous. Among the Immortals, on the other hand, every act (and every thought) is the echo of others that preceded it in the past, with no visible beginning, or the faithful presage of others that in the future will repeat it to a vertiginous degree. There is nothing that is not as if lost in a maze of indefatigable mirrors. Nothing can happen only once, nothing is preciously precarious. The elegiacal, the serious, the ceremonial, do not hold for Immortals. Homer and I separated at the gates of Tangier; I think we did not even say goodbye.

V

I traveled over new kingdoms, new empires. In the fall of 1066, I fought at Stamford Bridge, I do not recall whether in the forces of Harold, who was not long in finding his destiny, or in those of the hapless Harald Hardrada, who conquered six feet of English soil, or a bit more. In the seventh century of the Hegira, in the suburb of Bulaq, I transcribed with measured calligraphy, in a language I have forgotten, in an alphabet I do not know, the seven adventures of Sinbad and the history of the City of Bronze. In the courtyard of a jail in Samarkand I played a great deal of chess. In Bikaner I professed the science of astrology and also in Bohemia. In 1638 I was at Kolozsvár and later in Leipzig. in Aberdeen, in 1714, I subscribed to the six volumes of Pope's *Iliad;* I know that I frequented its pages with delight. About 1729 I discussed the origin of that poem with a professor of rhetoric named, I think, Giambattista; his arguments seemed to me irrefutable. On the fourth of October, 1921, the *Patna,* which was taking me to Bombay, had to cast anchor in a port on the Eritrean coast.* I went ashore; I recalled other very ancient mornings, also facing the Red Sea, when I was a tribune of Rome and fever and magic and idleness consumed the soldiers. On the outskirts of the city I saw a spring of clear water; I tasted it, prompted by habit. When I came up the bank, a spiny bush lacerated the back of my hand. The unusual pain seemed very acute to me. Incredulous, speechless and happy, I contemplated the precious formation of a slow drop of blood. Once again I am mortal, I repeated to myself, once again I am like all men. That night, I slept until dawn. . . .

After a year's time, I have inspected these pages. I am certain they reflect the truth, but in the first chapters, and even in certain paragraphs of the others, I seem to perceive something false. This perhaps produced by the abuse of circumstantial details, a procedure I learned from the poets and which contaminates everything with falsity, since those details can abound in the realities but not in their recollection. . . . I believe, however, that I have discovered a more intimate reason. I shall write it; no matter if I am judged fantastic.

The story I have narrated seems unreal because in it are mixed the events of two different men. In the first chapter, the horseman wants to know the name of the river bathing the walls of Thebes; Flaminius Rufus, who before has applied to the city the epithet of Hekatompylos, says that the river is the Egypt; none of these locutions is proper to him but rather to Homer, who makes express mention of the *Iliad* of Thebes Hekatompylos and who in the *Odyssey,* by way of Proteus and Ulysses, invariably says Egypt for Nile. In the second chapter, the Roman, upon drinking the immortal water, utters some words in Greek; these words are Homeric and may be sought at the end of the famous catalogue of the ships. Later, in the vertiginous palace, he speaks of "a reprobation which was almost remorse;" these words belong to Homer, who had projected that hor-

*There is an erasure in the manuscript; perhaps the name of the port has been removed.

63

ror. Such anomalies disquieted me; others, of an aesthetic order, permitted me to discover the truth. They are contained in the last chapter; there it is written that I fought at Stamford Bridge, that I transcribed in Bulaq the travels of Sinbad the Sailor and that I subscribed in Aberdeen to the English *Iliad* of Pope. One reads, *inter alia*: "In Bikaner I professed the science of astrology and also in Bohemia." None of these testimonies is false; what is significant is that they were stressed. The first of them seems proper to a warrior, but later one notes that the narrator does not linger over warlike deeds, but does over the fates of men. Those which follow are even more curious. A dark elemental reason obliged me to record them; I did it because I knew they were pathetic. Spoken by the Roman Flaminius Rufus, they are not. They are, spoken by Homer; it is strange that the latter should copy in the thirteenth century the adventures of Sinbad, another Ulysses, and should discover after many centuries, in a northern kingdom and a barbarous tongue, the forms of his *Iliad*. As for the sentence containing the name of Bikaner, one can see that it was fabricated by a man of letters, desirous (as was the author of the ship catalogue) of exhibiting splendid words.*

When the end draws near, there no longer remain any remembered images; only words remain. It is not strange that time should have confused the words that once represented me with those that were symbols of the fate of he who accompanied me for so many centuries. I have been Homer; shortly, I shall be No One, like Ulysses; shortly, I shall be all men; I shall be dead.

Postscript (1950).—Among the commentaries elicited by the preceding publication, the most curious, if not the most urbane, is biblically entitled *A Coat of Many Colors* (Manchester, 1948) and is the work of the most tenacious pen of Doctor Nahum Cordovero. It comprises some one hundred pages. The author speaks of the Greek centos, of the centos of late Latinity, of Ben Jonson, who defined his contemporaries with bits of Seneca, of the *Virgilius evangelizans* of Alexander Ross, of the artifices of George Moore and of Eliot and, finally, of "the narrative attributed to the

---

*Ernesto Sábato suggests that the "Giambattista" who discussed the formation of the *Iliad* with the antique dealer Cartaphilus is Giambattista Vico; this Italian defended the idea that Homer is a symbolic character, after the manner of Pluto or Achilles.

antique dealer Joseph Cartaphilus." He denounces, in the first chapter, brief interpolations from Pliny (*Historia naturalis*, V, 8); in the second, from Thomas de Quincey (*Writings*, III, 439); in the third, from an epistle of Descartes to the amabassador Pierre Chanut; in the fourth, from Bernard Shaw (*Back to Methuselah*, V). He infers from these intrusions or thefts that the whole document is apocryphal.

In my opinion, such a conclusion is inadmissible. "When the end draws near," wrote Cartaphilus, "there no longer remain any remembered images; only words remain." Words, displaced and mutilated words, words of others, were the poor pittance left him by the hours and the centuries.

Translated by James E. Irby.

Humor is a funny thing, as some anonymous wag once remarked: there's satire, slapstick, camp, situation-comedy, whimsy, and pure corn. R. A. Lafferty's story of modern homesteaders trying to take possession of a tract of land protected by an old Indian spell has a bit of all these elements—plus the disarming left-footed approach which makes every Lafferty story distinctively his own.

NARROW VALLEY R. A. Lafferty

In the year 1893, land allotments in severalty were made to the remaining eight hundred and twenty-one Pawnee Indians. Each would receive one hundred and sixty acres of land and no more, and thereafter the Pawnees would be expected to pay taxes on their land, the same as the White-Eyes did.

"Kitkehahke!" Clarence Big-Saddle cussed. "You can't kick a dog around proper on a hundred and sixty acres. And I sure am not hear before about this pay taxes on land."

Clarence Big-Saddle selected a nice green valley for his allotment. It was one of the half dozen plots he had always regarded as his own. He sodded around the summer lodge that he had there and made it an all-season home. But he sure didn't intend to pay taxes on it.

So he burned leaves and bark and made a speech:

"That my valley be always wide and flourish and green and such stuff as that!" he orated in Pawnee chant style, "but that it be narrow if an intruder come."

He didn't have any balsam bark to burn. He threw on a little cedar bark instead. He didn't have any elder leaves. He used a handful of jack-oak leaves. And he forgot the word. How you going to work it if you forget the word?

"Petahauerat!" he howled out with the confidence he hoped would fool the fates.

"That's the same long of a word," he said in a low aside to himself. But he was doubtful. "What am I, a White Man, a burr-tailed jack, a new kind of nut to think it will work?" he asked. "I have to laugh at me. Oh well, we see."

He threw the rest of the bark and the leaves on the fire, and he hollered the wrong word out again.

And he was answered by a dazzling sheet of summer lightning.

"Skidi!" Clarence Big-Saddle swore. "It worked. I didn't think it would."

Clarence Big-Saddle lived on his land for many years, and he paid no taxes. Intruders were unable to come down to his place. The land was sold for taxes three times, but nobody ever came down to claim it. Finally, it was carried as open land on the books. Homesteaders filed on it several times, but none of them fulfilled the qualification of living on the land.

Half a century went by. Clarence Big-Saddle called his son.

"I've had it, boy," he said. "I think I'll just go in the house and die."

"Okay, Dad," the son Clarence Little-Saddle said. "I'm going in to town to shoot a few games of pool with the boys. I'll bury you when I get back this evening."

So the son Clarence Little-Saddle inherited. He also lived on the land for many years without paying taxes.

There was a disturbance in the courthouse one day. The place seemed to be invaded in force, but actually there were but one man, one woman, and five children. "I'm Robert Rampart," said the man, "and we want the Land Office."

"I'm Robert Rampart Junior," said a nine year old gangler, "and we want it pretty blamed quick."

"I don't think we have anything like that," the girl at the

67

desk said. "Isn't that something they had a long time ago?"

"Ignorance is no excuse for inefficiency, my dear," said Mary Mabel Rampart, an eight year old who could easily pass for eight and a half. "After I make my report, I wonder who will be sitting at your desk tomorrow."

"You people are either in the wrong state or the wrong century," the girl said.

"The Homestead Act still obtains," Robert Rampart insisted. "There is one tract of land carried as open in this county. I want to file on it."

Cecilia Rampart answered the knowing wink of a beefy man at a distant desk. "Hi," she breathed as she slinked over. "I'm Cecilia Rampart, but my stage name is Cecilia San Juan. Do you think that seven is too young to play ingenue roles?"

"Not for you," the man said. "Tell your folks to come over here."

"Do you know where the Land Office is?" Cecilia asked.

"Sure. It's the fourth left-hand drawer of my desk. The smallest office we got in the whole courthouse. We don't use it much any more."

The Ramparts gathered around. The beefy man started to make out the papers.

"This is the land description," Robert Rampart began. "Why, you've got it down already. How did you know?"

"I've been around here a long time," the man answered.

They did the paper work, and Robert Rampart filed on the land.

"You won't be able to come onto the land itself, though," the man said.

"Why won't I?" Rampart demanded. "Isn't the land description accurate?"

"Oh, I suppose so. But nobody's ever been able to get to the land. It's become a sort of joke."

"Well, I intend to get to the bottom of that joke," Rampart insisted. "I will occupy the land, or I will find out why not."

"I'm not sure about that," the beefy man said. "The last man to file on the land, about a dozen years ago, wasn't able to occupy the land. And he wasn't able to say why he couldn't. It's kind of interesting, the look on their faces after they try it for a day or two, and then give it up."

The Ramparts left the courthouse, loaded into their camper, and drove out to find their land. They stopped at the house of a cattle and wheat farmer named Charley Dub-

68

lin. Dublin met them with a grin which indicated he had been tipped off.

"Come along if you want to, folks," Dublin said. "The easiest way is on foot across my short pasture here. Your land's directly west of mine."

They walked the short distance to the border.

"My name is Tom Rampart, Mr. Dublin." Six-year-old Tom made conversation as they walked. "But my name is really Ramires, and not Tom. I am the issue of an indiscretion of my mother in Mexico several years ago."

"The boy is a kidder, Mr. Dublin," said the mother Nina Rampart, defending herself. "I have never been in Mexico, but sometimes I have the urge to disappear there forever."

"Ah yes, Mrs. Rampart. And what is the name of the youngest boy here?" Charles Dublin asked.

"Fatty," said Fatty Rampart.

"But surely that is not your given name?"

"Audifax," said five-year-old Fatty.

"Ah well, Audifax, Fatty, are you a kidder too?"

"He's getting better at it, Mr. Dublin," Mary Mabel said. "He was a twin till last week. His twin was named Skinny. Mama left Skinny unguarded while she was out tippling, and there were wild dogs in the neighborhood. When mama got back, do you know what was left of Skinny? Two neck bones and an ankle bone. That was all."

"Poor Skinny," Dublin said. "Well, Rampart, this is the fence and the end of my land. Yours is just beyond."

"Is that ditch on my land?" Rampart asked.

"That ditch *is* your land."

"I'll have it filled in. It's a dangerous deep cut even if it is narrow. And the other fence looks like a good one, and I sure have a pretty plot of land beyond it."

"No, Rampart, the land beyond the second fence belongs to Holister Hyde," Charley Dublin said. "That second fence is the *end* of your land."

"Now, just wait a minute, Dublin! There's something wrong here. My land is one hundred and sixty acres, which would be a half mile on a side. Where's my half mile width?"

"Between the two fences."

"That's not eight feet."

"Doesn't look like it, does it, Rampart? Tell you what— there's plenty of throwing-sized rocks around. Try to throw one across it."

"I'm not interested in any such boys' games," Rampart exploded. "I want my land."

But the Rampart children *were* interested in such games.

69

They got with it with those throwing rocks. They winged them out over the little gully. The stones acted funny. They hung in the air, as it were, and diminished in size. And they were small as pebbles when they dropped down, down into the gully. None of them could throw a stone across that ditch, and they were throwing kids.

"You and your neighbor have conspired to fence open land for your own use," Rampart charged.

"No such thing, Rampart," Dublin said cheerfully. "My land checks perfectly. So does Hyde's. So does yours, if we knew how to check it. It's like one of those trick topological drawings. It really is a half mile from here to there, but the eye gets lost somewhere. It's your land. Crawl through the fence and figure it out."

Rampart crawled through the fence, and drew himself up to jump the gully. Then he hesitated. He got a glimpse of just how deep that gully was. Still, it wasn't five feet across.

There was a heavy fence post on the ground, designed for use as a corner post. Rampart up-ended it with some effort. Then he shoved it to fall and bridge the gully. But it fell short, and it shouldn't have. An eight foot post should bridge a five foot gully.

The post fell into the gully, and rolled and rolled and rolled. It spun as though it were rolling outward, but it made no progress except vertically. The post came to rest on a ledge of the gully, so close that Rampart could almost reach out and touch it, but it now appeared no bigger than a match stick.

"There is something wrong with that fence post, or with the world, or with my eyes," Robert Rampart said. "I wish I felt dizzy so I could blame it on that."

"There's a little game that I sometimes play with my neighbor Hyde when we're both out," Dublin said. "I've a heavy rifle and I train it on the middle of his forehead as he stands on the other side of the ditch apparently eight feet away. I fire it off then (I'm a good shot), and I hear it whine across. It'd kill him dead if things were as they seem. But Hyde's in no danger. The shot always bangs into that little scuff of rocks and boulders about thirty feet below him. I can see it kick up the rock dust there, and the sound of it rattling into those little boulders comes back to me in about two and a half seconds."

A bull-bat (poor people call it the night-hawk) raveled around in the air and zoomed out over the narrow ditch, but it did not reach the other side. The bird dropped below ground level and could be seen against the background of the other side of the ditch. It grew smaller and hazier as though at a distance of three or four hundred yards. The white bars on its wings could no longer be discerned; then the bird itself could hardly be discerned; but it was far short of the other side of the five foot ditch.

A man identified by Charley Dublin as the neighbor Hollister Hyde had appeared on the other side of the little ditch. Hyde grinned and waved. He shouted something, but could not be heard.

"Hyde and I both read mouth," Dublin said, "so we can talk across the ditch easy enough. Which kid wants to play chicken? Hyde will barrel a good-sized rock right at your head, and if you duck or flinch you're chicken."

"Me! Me!" Audifax Rampart challenged. And Hyde, a big man with big hands, did barrel a fearsome jagged rock right at the head of the boy. It would have killed him if things had been as they appeared. But the rock diminished to nothing and disappeared into the ditch. Here was a phenomenon—things seemed real-sized on either side of the ditch, but they diminished coming out over the ditch either way.

"Everybody game for it?" Robert Rampart Junior asked.

"We won't get down there by standing here," Mary Mabel said.

"Nothing wenchered, nothing gained," said Cecilia. "I got that from an ad for a sex comedy."

Then the five Rampart kids ran down into the gully. Ran *down* is right. It was almost as if they ran down the vertical face of a cliff. They couldn't do that. The gully was no wider than the stride of the biggest kids. But the gully diminished those children, it ate them alive. They were doll-sized. They were acorn-sized. They were running for minute after minute across a ditch that was only five feet across. They were going, deeper in it, and getting smaller. Robert Rampart was roaring his alarm, and his wife Nina was screaming. Then she stopped. "What am I carrying on so loud about?" she asked herself. "It looks like fun. I'll do it too."

She plunged into the gully, diminished in size as the children had done, and ran at a pace to carry her a hundred yards away across a gully only five feet wide.

That Robert Rampart stirred things up for a while then. He got the sheriff there, and the highway patrolmen. A ditch had stolen his wife and five children, he said, and maybe had killed them. And if anybody laughs, there may be another killing. He got the colonel of the State National

71

Guard there, and a command post set up. He got a couple of airplane pilots. Robert Rampart had one quality: when he hollered, people came.

He got the newsmen out from T-Town, and the eminent scientists, Dr. Velikof Vonk, Arpad Arkabaranan, and Willy McGilly. That bunch turns up every time you get on a good one. They just happen to be in that part of the country where something interesting is going on.

They attacked the thing from all four sides and the top, and by inner and outer theory. If a thing measures a half mile on each side, and the sides are straight, there just has to be something in the middle of it. They took pictures from the air, and they turned out perfect. They proved that Robert Rampart had the prettiest hundred and sixty acres in the country, the larger part of it being a lush green valley, and all of it being a half mile on a side, and situated just where it should be. They took ground-level photos then, and it showed a beautiful half mile stretch of land between the boundaries of Charley Dublin and Hollister Hyde. But a man isn't a camera. None of them could see that beautiful spread with the eyes in their heads. Where was it?

Down in the valley itself everything was normal. It really was a half mile wide and no more than eighty feet deep with a very gentle slope. It was warm and sweet, and beautiful with grass and grain.

Nina and the kids loved it, and they rushed to see what squatter had built that little house on their land. A house, or a shack. It had never known paint, but paint would have spoiled it. It was built of split timbers dressed near smooth with axe and draw knife, chinked with white clay, and sodded up to about half its height. And there was an interloper standing by the little lodge.

"Here, here what are you doing on our land?" Robert Rampart Junior demanded of the man. "Now you just shamble off again wherever you came from. I'll bet you're a thief too, and those cattle are stolen."

"Only the black-and-white calf," Clarence Little-Saddle said. "I couldn't resist him, but the rest are mine. I guess I'll just stay around and see that you folks get settled all right."

"Is there any wild Indians around here?" Fatty Rampart asked.

"No, not really. I go on a bender about every three months and get a little bit wild, and there's a couple Osage boys from Gray Horse that get noisy sometimes, but that's about all," Clarence Little-Saddle said.

"You certainly don't intend to palm yourself off on us as an Indian," Mary Mabel challenged. "You'll find us a little too knowledgeable for that."

"Little girl, you might as well tell this cow there's no room for her to be a cow since you're so knowledgeable. She thinks she's a short-horn cow named Sweet Virginia. I think I'm a Pawnee Indian named Clarence. Break it to us real gentle if we're not."

"If you're an Indian where's your war bonnet? There's not a feather on you anywhere."

"How you be sure? There's a story that we got feathers instead of hair on— Aw, I can't tell a joke like that to a little girl! How come you're not wearing the Iron Crown of Lombardy if you're a white girl? How you expect me to believe you're a little white girl and your folks came from Europe a couple hundred years ago if you don't wear it? There were six hundred tribes, and only one of them, the Oglala Sioux, had the war bonnet, and only the big leaders, never more than two or three of them alive at one time, wore it."

"Your analogy is a little strained," Mary Mabel said. "Those Indians we saw in Florida and the ones at Atlantic City had war bonnets, and they couldn't very well have been the kind of Sioux you said. And just last night on the TV in the motel, those Massachusetts Indians put a war bonnet on the President and called him the Great White Father. You mean to tell me that they were all phonies? Hey, who's laughing at who here?"

"If you're an Indian where's your bow and arrow?" Tom Rampart interrupted. "I bet you can't even shoot one."

"You're sure right there," Clarence admitted. "I never shot one of those things but once in my life. They used to have an archery range in Boulder Park over in T-Town, and you could rent the things and shoot at targets tied to hay bales. Hey, I barked my whole forearm and nearly broke my thumb when the bow-string thwacked home. I couldn't shoot that thing at all. I don't see how anybody ever could shoot one of them."

"Okay, kids," Nina Rampart called to her brood. "Let's start pitching this junk out of the shack so we can move in. Is there any way we can drive our camper down here, Clarence?"

"Sure, there's a pretty good dirt road, and it's a lot wider than it looks from the top. I got a bunch of green bills in an old night charley in the shack. Let me get them, and then

73

I'll clear out for a while. The shack hasn't been cleaned out for seven years, since the last time this happened. I'll show you the road to the top, and you can bring your car down it."

"Hey, you old Indian, you lied!" Cecilia Rampart shrilled from the doorway of the shack. "You *do* have a war bonnet. Can I have it?"

"I didn't mean to lie, I forgot about that thing," Clarence Little-Saddle said. "My son Clarence Bare-Back sent that to me from Japan for a joke a long time ago. Sure, you can have it."

All the children were assigned tasks carrying the junk out of the shack and setting fire to it. Nina Rampart and Clarence Little-Saddle ambled up to the rim of the valley by the vehicle road that was wider than it looked from the top.

"Nina, you're back! I thought you were gone forever," Robert Rampart jittered at seeing her again. "What—where are the children?"

"Why, I left them down in the valley, Robert. That is, ah, down in that little ditch right there. Now you've got me worried again. I'm going to drive the camper down there and unload it. You'd better go on down and lend a hand too, Robert, and quit talking to all these funny-looking men here."

And Nina went back to Dublin's place for the camper.

"It would be easier for a camel to go through the eye of a needle than for that intrepid woman to drive a car down into that narrow ditch," the eminent scientist Dr. Velikof Vonk said.

"You know how that camel does it?" Clarence Little-Saddle offered, appearing of a sudden from nowhere. "He just closes one of his own eyes and flops back his ears and plunges right through. A camel is mighty narrow when he closes one eye and flops back his ears. Besides, they use a big-eyed needle in the act."

"Where'd this crazy man come from?" Robert Rampart demanded, jumping three feet in the air. "Things are coming out of the ground now. I want my land! I want my children! I want my wife! Whoops, here she comes driving it. Nina, you can't drive a loaded camper into a little ditch like that! You'll be killed or collapsed!"

Nina Rampart drove the loaded camper into the little ditch at a pretty good rate of speed. The best of belief is that she just closed one eye and plunged right through. The car diminished and dropped, and it was smaller than a toy car. But it raised a pretty good cloud of dust as it bumped for several hundred yards across a ditch that was only five feet wide.

"Rampart, it's akin to the phenomenon known as looming, only in reverse," the eminent scientist Arpad Arkabaranan explained as he attempted to throw a rock across the narrow ditch. The rock rose very high in the air, seemed to hang at its apex while it diminished to the size of a grain of sand, and then fell into the ditch not six inches of the way across. There isn't anybody going to throw across a half mile valley even if it looks five feet. "Look at a rising moon sometime, Rampart. It appears very large, as though covering a great sector of the horizon, but it only covers one half of a degree. It is hard to believe that you could set seven hundred and twenty of such large moons side by side around the horizon, or that it would take one hundred and eighty of the big things to reach from the horizon to a point overhead. It is also hard to believe that your valley is five hundred times as wide as it appears, but it has been surveyed, and it is."

"I want my land. I want my children. I want my wife," Robert chanted dully. "Damn, I let her get away again."

"I tell you, Rampy," Clarence Little-Saddle squared on him, "a man that lets his wife get away twice doesn't deserve to keep her. I give you till nightfall; then you forfeit. I've taken a liking to the brood. One of us is going to be down there tonight."

After a while a bunch of them were off in that little tavern on the road between Cleveland and Osage. It was only a half mile away. If the valley had run in the other direction, it would have been only six feet away.

"It is a psychic nexus in the form of an elongated dome," said the eminent scientist Dr. Velikof Vonk. "It is maintained subconsciously by the concatenation of at least two minds, the stronger of them belonging to a man dead for many years. It has apparently existed for a little less than a hundred years, and in another hundred years it will be considerably weakened. We know from our checking out of folk tales of Europe as well as Cambodia that these ensorceled areas seldom survive for more than two hundred and fifty years. The person who first set such a thing in being will usually lose interest in it, and in all worldly things, within a hundred years of his own death. This is a simple thanato-psychic limitation. As a short-term device, the thing has been used several times as a military tactic.

"This psychic nexus, as long as it maintains itself, causes group illusion, but it is really a simple thing. It doesn't fool birds or rabbits or cattle or cameras, only humans. There is nothing meteorological about it. It is strictly psychological. I'm glad I was able to give a scientific explanation to it or it would have worried me."

"It is continental fault coinciding with a noospheric fault," said the eminent scientist Arpal Arkabaranan. "The valley really is a half mile wide, and at the same time it really is only five feet wide. If we measured correctly, we would get these dual measurements. Of course it is meteorological! Everything including dreams is meteorological. It is the animals and cameras which are fooled, as lacking a true dimension; it is only humans who see the true duality. The phenomenon should be common along the whole continental fault where the earth gains or loses a half mile that has to go somewhere. Likely it extends through the whole sweep of the Cross Timbers. Many of those trees appear twice, and many do not appear at all. A man in the proper state of mind could farm that land or raise cattle on it, but it doesn't really exist. There is a clear parallel in the Luftspiegelungthal sector in the Black Forest of Germany which exists, or does not exist, according to the circumstances and to the attitude of the beholder. Then we have the case of Mad Mountain in Morgan County, Tennessee, which isn't there all the time, and also the Little Lobo Mirage south of Presidio, Texas, from which twenty thousand barrels of water were pumped in one two-and-a-half year period before the mirage reverted to mirage status. I'm glad I was able to give a scientific explanation to this or it would have worried me."

"I just don't understand how he worked it," said the eminent scientist Willy McGilly. "Cedar bark, jack-oak leaves. and the word 'Petahauerat.' The thing's impossible! When I was a boy and we wanted to make a hideout, we used bark from the skunk-spruce tree, the leaves of a box-elder, and the word was 'Boadicea.' All three elements are wrong here. I cannot find a scientific explanation for it, and it does worry me."

They went back to Narrow Valley. Robert Rampart was still chanting dully: "I want my land. I want my children. I want my wife."

Nina Rampart came chugging up out of the narrow ditch in the camper and emerged through that little gate a few yards down the fence row.

"Supper's ready and we're tired of waiting for you, Robert," she said. "A fine homesteader you are! Afraid to come onto your own land! Come along now; I'm tired of waiting for you."

"I want my land! I want my children! I want my wife!" Robert Rampart still chanted. "Oh, there you are, Nina. You stay here this time. I want my land! I want my children! I want an answer to this terrible thing."

"It is time we decided who wears the pants in this family," Nina said stoutly. She picked up her husband, slung him over her shoulder, carried him to the camper and dumped him in, slammed (as it seemed) a dozen doors at once, and drove furiously down into Narrow Valley, which already seemed wider.

Why, that place was getting normaler and normaler by the minute! Pretty soon it looked almost as wide as it was supposed to be. The psychic nexus in the form of an elongated dome had collapsed. The continental fault that coincided with the noospheric fault had faced facts and decided to conform. The Ramparts were in effective possession of their homestead, and Narrow Valley was as normal as any place anywhere.

"I have lost my land," Clarence Little-Saddle moaned. "It was the land of my father Clarence Big-Saddle, and I meant it to be the land of my son Clarence Bare-Back. It looked so narrow that people did not notice how wide it was, and people did not try to enter it. Now I have lost it."

Clarence Little-Saddle and the eminent scientist Willy McGilly were standing on the edge of Narrow Valley, which now appeared its true half-mile extent. The moon was just rising, so big that it filled a third of the sky. Who would have imagined that it would take a hundred and eighty of such monstrous things to reach from the horizon to a point overhead, and yet you could sight it with sighters and figure it so.

"I had the little bear-cat by the tail and I let go," Clarence groaned. "I had a fine valley for free, and I have lost it. I am like that hard-luck guy in the funny-paper or Job in the Bible. Destitution is my lot."

Willy McGilly looked around furtively. They were alone on the edge of the half mile wide valley."

"Let's give it a booster shot," Willy McGilly said.

Hey, those two got with it! They started a snapping fire and began to throw the stuff onto it. Bark from the dog-elm tree—how do you know it won't work?

It *was* working! Already the other side of the valley seemed a hundred yards closer, and there were alarmed noises coming up from the people in the valley.

Leaves from a black locust tree—and the valley narrowed

77

still more! There was, moreover, terrified screaming of both children and big people from the depths of Narrow Valley, and the happy voice of Mary Mabel Rampart chanting "Earthquake! Earthquake!"

"That my valley be always wide and flourish and such stuff, and green with money and grass!" Clarence Little-Saddle orated in Pawnee chant style, "but that it be narrow if intruders come, smash them like bugs!"

People, that valley wasn't over a hundred feet wide now, and the screaming of the people in the bottom of the valley had been joined by the hysterical coughing of the camper car starting up.

Willy and Clarence threw everything that was left on the fire. But the word? The word? Who remembers the word?

"Corsicanatexas!" Clarence Little-Saddle howled out with confidence he hoped would fool the fates.

He was answered not only by a dazzling sheet of summer lightning, but also by thunder and raindrops.

"Chahiksi!" Clarence Little-Saddle swore. "It worked. I didn't think it would. It will be all right now. I can use the rain."

The valley was again a ditch only five feet wide.

The camper car struggled out of Narrow Valley through the little gate. It was smashed flat as a sheet of paper, and the screaming kids and people in it had only one dimension.

"It's closing in! It's closing in!" Robert Rampart roared, and he was no thicker than if he had been made out of cardboard.

"We're smashed like bugs," the Rampart boys intoned. "We're thin like paper."

"*Mort, ruine, ecrasement!*" spoke-acted Cecilia Rampart like the great tragedienne she was.

"Help! Help!" Nina Rampart croaked, but she winked at Willy and Clarence as they rolled by. "This homesteading jag always did leave me a little flat."

"Don't throw those paper dolls away. They might be the Ramparts," Mary Mabel called.

The camper car coughed again and bumped along on level ground. This couldn't last forever. The car was widening out as it bumped along.

"Did we overdo it, Clarence?" Willy McGilly asked. "What did one flat-lander say to the other?"

"Dimension of us never got around," Clarence said. "No, I don't think we overdid it, Willy. That car must be eighteen inches wide already, and they all ought to be normal by
78

the time they reach the main road. The next time I do it, I think I'll throw wood-grain plastic on the fire to see who's kidding who."

Ray Russell has written one novel, THE CASE AGAINST
SATAN, and a good number of shorter fantasies—most
of them, like the following, appearing originally in
Playboy, of which he is a distinguished former editor.
Here he turns his talents to a very old and rich fantasy
theme, and adds to it the more scientific idea of conservation of energy . . . or, in this case, conservation of
genius. A peculiarly effective juxtaposition, which you
may find bouncing around inside your head for some
while, like dissonant harmonies.

COMET WINE
Ray Russell

I'm a bloodhound. Ask anyone who knows me and they'll
tell you I'm a meticulous researcher, an untiring zealot, a
ruthless bloodhound when pursuing facts. I'm not a professional musician, granted; not even a gifted amateur; but my
fondness for music can't be disputed and my personal fund
of musical and musicological knowledge happens to be huge.
All the more remarkable (wouldn't you say?) that no catalog,
no concert program, no newspaper file, no encyclopedia, no
dictionary, no memoir, no interview, no history of music,
no grave marker has rewarded my efforts by surrendering
the name V. I. Cholodenko.

Such a person, it would seem, never existed. Or, if he did exist, became an Orwellian unperson who was whisked from this world as completely as were Ambrose Bierce, Judge Crater, or the passengers and crew of the *Marie Celeste*. I'm well aware of the transliteration problems regarding Russian names, and I've doggedly searched under the spellings Kholodenko, Tcholodenko, Tscholodenko, Shcholodenko and even Zholodenko, but to no avail. True, I haven't had access to archives within the Soviet Union (my letters to Shostakovich and Khachaturian appear to have gone astray), but I've queried Russian musicians on tour in the United States, and to none of them is it a familiar name.

Its exclusive appearance is in a ribbon-tied bunch of old letters, crisp and desiccated, purchased last year by me, along with items of furniture and art, at a private auction of the effects of the late Beverly Hills attorney Francis Cargrave. They had belonged to his grandfather, Sir Robert Cargrave, an eminent London physician, to whom they are addressed, and all were written, in elegant if somewhat epicene prose, by Lord Henry Stanton, a fashionable beau and minor poet of the period.

The curiosity, the enigma, lies in the fact that all the people mentioned in the three pertinent letters are real people, who lived, whose names and achievements are well-known—all, that is, but the name and achievements of Cholodenko. Even the briefly mentioned Colonel Spalding existed, as will be noted later. Down to the most insignificant details—such as the color of his famous host's eyeglasses—Lord Stanton's letters can be substantiated (the only exceptions, again, being the references to the elusive Cholodenko).

Is the man a fabrication? Was Stanton the perpetrator of an elaborate hoax? If so, I can't in all honesty understand why. The letters were written to his closest friend, a presumably sober pillar of the medical profession. Both men were no longer youngsters, and undergraduate pranks strike me as uncharacteristic of them.

But if it was not a prank, how can we explain the way Cholodenko has been ripped from history, his music not even a fading echo but a silence, a vacuum, completely forgotten, as totally unknown as the song the Sirens sang?

I don't presume to solve the mystery. I merely present the three letters "for what they're worth," and invite other bloodhounds to make what they will of them. Such bloodhounds will sniff out, as I did, a glaring discrepancy, for the very survival of these letters seems to discredit Lord Henry's colorful insinuations—but he would probably counter our incredulity, if he were here, by urbanely pointing out that if God proverbially moves in mysterious ways His wonders to perform, might not His Adversary do the same? For reasons of scholarship and accuracy, I haven't condensed or edited the letters in any way (except to eliminate the redundant addresses in all but the first), preferring to let even irrelevant or trivial observations stand, in the hope that they may contain clues that eluded me. I've also kept Stanton's not always standard, though phonetically accurate, transliterations. In a few places, I've inserted short bracketed notes of my own, in italics. The letters bear month and dates, but no year. Stanton being English, I assume these dates conform to the Gregorian calendar familiar to us, rather than to the old Julian calendar, which was still in use in Russia at the time. On the basis of internal evidence, such as the first performance of *Eugene Onegin,* I believe the letters to have been written in 1879.

5 April

Sir Robert Cargrave
Harley Street
London, England

My dear Bobbie,

No, do not scold me! I know full well that I have been a renegade and most delinquent comrade. If I seem to have avoided your home these many months; if I have neglected you, your dear Maude and your brood of cherubim—one of whom, young Jamey, must be quite ripe for Oxford by now! —then ascribe it, I pray you, not to a cooling of our friendship's fires nor to a bachelor's disdain for the familial hearthstone, but, rather, to my persistent vice, travel.

I have set foot on divers shores since last I sipped your sherry, old friend, and I write to you from St. Petersburg. Yes, I am cosily hugged by "the rugged Russian bear," a cryptic creature, I assure you, warm and greathearted, quick to laugh, and just as quick to plunge into pits of black *toská* —a word that haughtily defies translation, hovering mystically, as it does, somewhere between melancholy and despair. Neither melancholy nor despair, however, have dogged my steps here in this strange land. I have been most cheerful. There are wondrous sights to bend one's gaze upon; exotic food and drink to quicken and quench the appetite; fascinating people with whom to talk. To your sly and silent question, my reply is Yes!—there are indeed ladies here, lovely ones, with flared bright eyes and sable voices; lambent ladies, recondite and rare. There are amusing soirees, as well (I will tell you of one in a moment), and there are evenings of brilliance at the ballet and the opera.

The opera here would particularly captivate both you and your Maude. I am certain, for I know of your deep love of the form. How enviously, then, will you receive the news that just last month, in Moscow, I attended the premiere of a dazzling new *opus theatricum* by the composer Pyotr Chaikovsky. It was a work of lapidary excellence, entitled *Yevgeny Onyégin* (I transliterate as best I can from the spiky Cyrillic original), derived from a poem of that name by a certain Pushkin, a prosodist now dead for decades, who —my friend, Colonel Spalding tells me—enjoys a classical reputation here, but of whom I had not hitherto heard, since his works have not been translated into English, an error the colonel is now busy putting right. [*Lieutenant Colonel Henry Spalding's English translation, transliterated as "Eugene Onéguine," was published in London in 1881.*] The opera is a shimmering tapestry of sound, brocaded with waltzes and polonaises.

But St. Petersburg, I find, is richer in cultural life than even Moscow: I have been awed by the art treasures of The Hermitage, humbled by the baroque majesty of the Aleksandr Nevsky Cathedral, chastened by the mighty gloom of the Peter Paul fortress and properly impressed by the Smolny monastery and the Winter Palace. Apropos of winter, I have also been chilled to the marrow by the fiercest cold I have ever known. "Winter in April?" I can hear you say. Yes, the severe season stretches from November to April in this place, and the River Neva, which I can see, moonlit, from my window as I write, is frozen over, and has been thus, I am told, for the past six months! It is a great gleaming broadsword of ice, cleaving the city in two.

As for music: Just last night, thanks to a letter of introduction from Spalding, I was received at a famous apartment in the Zagoredny Prospekt—nothing ostentatious, a small drawing room, a few chairs, a grand piano, a table in the dining room loaded with the simplest food and drink . . . but what exceptional people were crowded, shoulder to shoulder in that place. It was the apartment of Rimsky-Korsakov, who, I was pleased to discover, is not only a gifted and amiable gentleman but speaks excellent English—an accomplishment not shared by many of his compatriots, whose social conversations are customarily couched in (or, at least, liberally laced with) French. The guests, myself excluded, were, to a man, composers and performers, some

(I later learned) being members of a *koochka*, or clan, of musicians of which Rimsky-Korsakov is the nucleus.

You will laugh when I tell you that, not five minutes after being welcomed into the *salon*, I committed a *faux pas*. Wishing to take part in the musical discussions, I minutely described and lavishly praised the Chaikovsky opera I had enjoyed so recently at the Moscow Conservatorium. My tall host's gentle eyes grew cold behind his blue-tinted spectacles (which he wears because of ailing sight) and I felt a distinct frost. The awkward moment soon passed, however, and a dark young man took me aside to dryly inform me that "Our esteemed Nikolai Andreyvich considers Chaikovsky's music to be in abominable taste."

"Do you share that opinion?" I asked.

"Not precisely, but I do feel Chaikovsky is not a truly Russian composer. He has let himself be influenced by bad French models—Massenet, Bizet, Gounod, and so on."

We were joined by a bloated, wild-haired, red-nosed, bleary-eyed but very courteous fellow who, after addressing me most deferentially, asked eagerly about the Chaikovsky work: "It is good, then, you think? Ah! Splendid! An excellent subject, *Onyégin*. I once thought of setting it myself, but it's not my sort of thing—Pyotr Ilyich is the man for it, there's no doubt. Don't you agree, Vassily Ivanovich?" he added, turning to my companion.

That intense young man shrugged. "I suppose so—but to tell the truth, I am growing weary of these operatic obeisances to Pushkin. One cannot blame a composer of the old school, such as Glinka, for setting *Ruslan and Lyudmila*, but what are we to think when Dargomizhsky sets not one but three Pushkin subjects—*Russalka*, *The Triumph of Bacchus* and *The Stone Guest;* when you joined the cortege five years ago with your own opera; and when Chaikovsky now follows the pattern with *Onyégin?*" He threw up his hands. "May that be the last!" he sighed.

"There is still *The Queen of Spades*," said the unkempt man, mischievously. "Perhaps you will undertake that one yourself?"

"Thank you, no," snapped the other (rather irritably, I thought). "I leave that to you."

"I may just do it," was the smiling reply, "unless Chaikovsky is too quick for me!" [*He was: Tchaikovsky's setting of "The Queen of Spades," or "Pique-Dame" was presented in 1890.*] *And, later, Rimsky-Korsakov drew upon Pushkin for his operas "Le Coq d'Or" and "Mozart and Salieri"; and Rachmaninoff also turned to Pushkin for his "Aleka."*] Elaborately excusing himself, the wild-haired man left us and began chatting with another group.

"Talented," my young friend said in appraisal of him after he left, "but he lacks technique. His scores are crude, grotesque, his instrumentation a disgrace. Of course, he isn't well. An epileptic. And, as you may have noted, he drinks heavily. Still, somehow, he goes on writing music. There is a tavern in Morskaia Street, called Maly Yaroslavets—any night you will see him there, drinking vodka, scribbling music on napkins, menus, the margins of newspapers, feverishly, almost as if—" He broke off.

"As if possessed?" I said.

"A somewhat lurid allusion, don't you think? No, I was about to say, 'almost as if his life depended on it'—as I suppose it does, for his interest in music is probably the only thing keeping him alive. To look at him now, Lord Henry, would you ever guess he was once an impeccably groomed Guards officer, of refined breeding, a wit, a ladies' man?" He shook his head dolorously. "Poor Mussorgsky," he sighed.

Looking slowly about the *salon,* he then said, "The *koochka* is not what it was, sir. Do you see that pathetic creature sitting in the corner?" The gentleman indicated indeed pathetic, a wraith who looked with glazed eye upon all who passed before him, responding feebly and mechanically to greetings, like an old man (although he was not old), then sinking back into motionless apathy. "That is, or was, the *koochka's* vital force, its spine, its heart, its tingling blood. It was in *his* apartment we were wont to meet, he who held the group together, his hands that firmly gripped the reins, his whip that goaded us to frenzied effort. No man was more steeped in the classical scores, no memory was so vast as his. Now look at him. A coffin. His mind blighted by a mysterious malady. There he sits. His *Tamara* languishes unfinished. Music has ceased to interest him, he who breathed exotic harmonies every minute of the day."

We had been walking toward this pitiful wreckage, and now my guide leaned close and spoke to him: "Mily Alekseyevich! How is it with you?" The man looked up and blinked vapidly; it was quite obvious he did not recognize the speaker. "It is I, Vassily Ivanovich," he was forced to add.

"Vas . . . sily . . . 'Van . . . ovich . . ." A small, crooked smile of recognition twisted the poor man's face for a moment, although the eyes did not kindle.

"Allow me to present an honored guest from England, Lord Henry Stanton. Lord Henry, Mily Balakirev."

The wretched fellow offered me a limp, dead hand, which I briefly shook; and then we left him, staring vacantly into empty air again. "Tragic," my Virgil murmured: "and the final offense is that poor Mily, who once was the most vociferous of scoffers, now mumbles prayers and bends his knee to icons."

"I hope you are not an unbeliever," I said lightly.

"I believe," he said—a reply that would have satisfied me, had it not been for its dark color, which seemed to imply meanings beyond the simple words.

"Surely," I asked him, "such ruination of body or mind is not typical of your group?"

"Mussorgsky and Balakirev are possibly extreme examples," he agreed. "But there, at the table, stuffing himself with *zakuski*," he said, indicating a man in the uniform of a lieutenant general of engineers, "is Cui, who suffers from the worst disease of all: poverty of talent. And Rimsky, whose soul is corroded by his envy of Chaikovsky."

The music of Chaikovsky's *Yevgeny Onyégin* still rang in my memory and I was therefore reminded of the poet on whose work the opera was founded. "You spoke of Pushkin some moments ago," I said. "I have been told he was an extraordinary poet. Why do you hold him in low esteem?"

"I do not," he replied. "Pushkin was a genius. But suppose your English musicians persisted in setting only the plays and verses of Shakespeare, ignoring today's English writers? This preoccupation with the past is stagnating most of Russian culture, and the music itself is as dated as its subject matter. Even Mussorgsky, whose crudeness is sometimes redeemed by flashes of daring, is being obtunded and made 'inoffensive' by Rimsky—a pedant who gets sick to the stomach at the sound of a consecutive fifth!"

Does it strike you, Bobbie, that this chap was annoyingly critical of his illustrious colleagues? It so struck me, and a little later in the evening I had an opportunity to challenge him—but at this precise moment in our conversation, we were joined by our host.

My initial "offense" regarding the music of Chaikovsky was now, happily, forgotten, and Rimsky's eyes were warm behind the blue lenses. "Ah, Lord Henry," he said, "I see you have met our young firebrand. Has he been telling you what old fogies we are, the slaves of tradition, and so on? Dear boy, for shame: Our English visitor will carry away a bad impression of us."

"No, no," I said, "his views are refreshing."

"He is our gadfly," Rimsky said, with a diplomatic smile.

"But we must all suspend our conversations—refreshing though they may be—and turn our attention to some music a few of our friends have consented to play for us."

We all found chairs, and a feast of sound was served. Mussorgsky provided accompaniment for a song sung by a basso they called Fyodr [*Not Chaliapin, of course, who was only six years old at the time; but possibly Fyodr Stravinsky, the singer-father of Igor*]; after which a chemist named Borodin played pungent excerpts from an uncompleted opera ("He's been at it for fifteen years," whispered my young companion. "Keeps interrupting it to work on symphonies. A chaotic man, disorganized. Bastard son of a prince.") Next, Rimsky-Korsakov himself played a lyrical piece I found charming, but which my self-appointed commentator deprecated as "conventional, unadventurous."

I had, by this time, had a surfeit of his vicious carping. Taking advantage of a lull in the musical offerings, I now turned to him and, with as much courtesy as I could summon and in a voice distinct enough to be heard by all, said, "Surely a man of such austere judgment will condescend to provide an example of his ideal? Will *you* not take your place at the keyboard, sir, so that others may play at critic?"

He proffered me a strange look and an ambiguous smile. A profound hush fell upon the room. Our host cleared his throat nervously. My heart sank as I realized that somehow, in a way quite unknown to me, I had committed another and possibly more enormous *faux pas!*

But I see the dawn has begun to tint the sky, and I have not yet been to bed. I will dispatch these pages to you at once, Bobbie, and resume my little chronicle at the very next opportunity.

Your peripatetic friend,
Harry

8 April

My dear Bobbie,

I left off, if I remember right, at that moment in Rimsky-Korsakov's apartment when I committed some manner of gauche blunder merely by suggesting that a rather unpleasant young man, who had been so superciliously critical of his colleagues, play something of his own composition for the assembled guests. The embarrassed silence that fell upon the room thoroughly discomfited me. What had I said? In what way was my suggestion awkward or indelicate? Was the young man bitterly hated by our famous host? Unlikely, for he was a guest. Did the poor fellow have no hands? Not so;

for, even now, he held wineglass and biscuit in long, slender fingers. I was bemused; I may have blushed. Only a moment passed, but it seemed an hour. Finally, the young man, still wearing the smirk with which he had greeted my challenge, replied, "Thank you, Lord Henry. I *shall* play something of my own, if our host gives me leave?" He cocked an eyebrow toward Rimsky.

Recovering his aplomb, Rimsky said hurriedly, "My dear fellow, of course. The keyboard is yours." And so, raking the room's occupants with an arrogant look, the young man swaggered to the piano and was seated.

He studied the keyboard for a moment, then looked up at us. "I am in the midst of composing an opera," he said. "It's source, you may be surprised to learn, is not a poem by the indispensable Pushkin or an old Slavonic tale. It is a modern novel, a book still in the writing, a work of revolutionary brilliance. It rips the mask of pretense and hypocrisy from our decadent society, and will cause an uproar when it is published. I was privileged to see it in manuscript—the author resides here in St. Petersburg. It is called *The Brothers Karamazov.* And this," he concluded, flexing his spidery fingers, "is the prelude to the first act of my operatic setting."

His hands fell upon the keys and a dissonant chord impaled our ears. Rimsky-Korsakov winced. Mussorgsky's bleared eyes went suddenly wide. Borodin's jaws, with a caviar savory half masticated, stopped chewing. The chord hung in the air, its life prolonged by the pedal, then, as the long fingers moved among the keys, the dissonance was resolved, an arresting modulation took place, a theme of great power was stated in octaves, and then that theme was developed, with a wealth of architectural ingenuity. The theme took wing, climbed, soared, was burnished with rich harmony, took on a glittering texture, yet not effete but with an underlying firmness and strength. The *koochka* and the other guests were transfixed, myself among them; Balakirev alone seemed unthrilled. Cascades of bracing sound poured from the piano. When the prelude reached its magnificent conclusion and the last breathtaking chord thundered into eternity, there was an instant of profound silence—followed by a din of applause and congratulatory cries.

The composer was immediately engulfed by his colleagues, who shook his hand, slapped his shoulders, plied him with questions about the opera. If I were pressed to find one word to best describe the general feeling exuded by these men, the word would be *surprise.* It was plain to me that they were stunned not only by the vigor and beauty of the music but by its source, the young gadfly. I wondered why.

My unvoiced question must have been written on my face, for at that moment Rimsky-Korsakov drew me aside and said, "You appear to be puzzled, Lord Henry. Permit me to enlighten you—although, I confess, I am extremely puzzled myself. The fact is, you see, that this is the very first time young Cholodenko has shown even the dimmest glimmer of musical talent!"

"What? But that prelude—"

"Astonishing, I agree. Daring, original, moving, soundly constructed. A little too dissonant for my taste, perhaps, but I have no hesitation in calling it a work of genius."

"Then how . . ." Incredulous, more baffled than ever, I stammered out my disbelief: "That is to say, a man does not become a genius overnight! His gifts must ripen and grow, his masterworks must be foreshadowed by smaller but promising efforts . . ."

Rimsky nodded. "Exactly. That is why we are all so surprised. That is why I am so puzzled. And that, you see, is why we were so uncomfortable when you asked Cholodenko to play. Hitherto, his attempts have been painfully inept, devoid of any creative spark, colorless, derivative, drab. And his piano playing! The awkward thumpings of an ape!"

"You exaggerate, surely."

"Only a little. The poor boy himself was aware of his shortcomings—shamefully aware. We tried to be polite, we tried to encourage him, we searched for compliments to pay him, but he saw through us and declined to play at these soirees."

"Yet he attends them."

"Yes, although his very presence has been a discomfort to himself and the rest of us. Music has a kind of insidious attraction for him; he is goaded by it as by a demon; he behaves almost as if . . ." He searched for words.

"As if possessed?" I said, for the second time that evening.

"As if it were food and drink to him. And yet, for some time now, he has been merely an observer."

"And a critic!"

"A caustic critic. He has been an embarrassment, an annoyance, but we tolerated him, we pitied him . . ."

"And now, suddenly . . ."

"Yes," said Rimsky. "Suddenly." The eyes narrowed behind their cool blue panes as he gazed across the room at the triumphant Cholodenko. "Suddenly he is a keyboard virtuoso and the creator of a masterpiece. There is a mystery here, Lord Henry."

And, at that, I burst out laughing!

Rimsky said, "You are amused?"

"Amused and appreciative," I replied. "It is a very good joke—you have my admiration, sir."

"Joke?"

"You had me completely gulled. An absolutely inspired hoax!"

Rimsky's brow now creased in an Olympian frown. "I do not waste time with hoaxes," he said with dignity, and walked stiffly away.

Determined not to be daunted by this, I pushed my way through to Cholodenko and shook his hand. "I am only a profane listener," I said, "and have no real knowledge of music, but my congratulations are sincere."

"Thank you, Lord Henry. You are most kind." His demeanor had undergone a subtle change: Victory and praise had softened the prickly edges of his character. How wrong, Bobbie, is the axiom of our mutual friend. Acton [Obviously, John Emerich Edward Dalberg-Acton, Eighth Baronet and First Baron, 1834-1902]. "Power corrupts," he says; "absolute power corrupts absolutely." This is bosh, and I've often told him so: It would be much truer to say, "Lack of power corrupts; absolute lack of power corrupts absolutely."

The soiree was nearing its end. As the guests began to leave, my curiosity impelled me to seek out Cholodenko and accompany him into the street.

The cold hit me like a cannon ball. Nevertheless, I strolled at Cholodenko's side, along the banks of the frozen Neva (the embankments, of Finnish gray and pink marble, were irridescent under the moon). Both of us were buried in enormous greatcoats of fur, but I was still cold.

"Be patient but a few more days," said my companion, "and you will see spring split open the land. Our Russian spring is sudden, like a beautiful explosion."

"I shall try to live that long," I said, shivering.

"You need a fire and some wine," he laughed. "Come—my apartment is only a few more steps . . ."

I was eager to learn more about this man, although custom urged me to make a token demur: "No, no, it is late—I should be returning to my quarters."

"Please," he said. "I am wide awake from this evening's triumph—I should not like to celebrate it alone."

"But I am a stranger. Surely your friends—"

Cholodenko snarled bitterly, "Those vultures? They condescended to me when they felt me their inferior; soon they will hate me for being their superior. Here is my door—I entreat you—"

My face felt brittle as glass from the cold. With chattering teeth, I replied, "Very well, for a little while." We went inside.

His apartment was small. Dominating it was a grand piano of concert size. Scores and manuscript paper were piled everywhere. Cholodenko built a fire. "And now," he said, producing a dust-filmed bottle, "we will warm ourselves with comet wine."

His strong thumbs deftly pushed out the cork and the frothing elixir spewed out into the goblets in a curving scintillant jet, a white arc that brought to mind, indeed, a comet's tail.

"Comet wine?" I repeated.

He nodded. "A famed and heady vintage from the year of the comet, 1811. This is a very rare bottle, one of the last in the world. Your health, Lord Henry."

We drank. The wine was unlike any I have ever tasted—akin to champagne. but somehow spicy, richer; dry, yet with a honeyed aftertaste. I drained the goblet and he poured again.

"A potent potation," I said with a smile.

"It makes the mind luminous," he averred.

I said, "That heavenly wanderer, for which it is named, imbued it with astral powers, perhaps?"

"Perhaps. Drink, sir. And then I will tell you a little story, a flight of fancy of which I would value your opinion. If you find it strange, so much the better! For, surely, one must not tell mundane stories between draughts of comet wine?"

Of that story, and of its effect on me, I will write soon.

Your friend,
Harry

12 April

My dear Bobbie,

Forgive the palsied look of my handwriting—I scribble this missive on the train that carries me from St. Petersburg, and the jiggling motion of the conveyance is to blame. Yes, I take my leave of this vast country, will spend some time in Budapest, and will return to London in time to celebrate your birthday. Meanwhile, I have a narrative to conclude—if this confounded train will let me!

The scene, you may recall, was the St. Petersburg apartment of Vassily Ivanovich Cholodenko. The characters, that enigmatic young man and your faithful correspondent. My head was light and bright with comet wine, my perceptions sharpened, as my host lifted a thick mass of music manuscript from the piano and weighed it in his hands. "The score of *The Brothers Karamazov*," he said. "It needs but the final ensemble. When it is finished, Lord Henry, all the impresarios in the country, in the world, will beg me for the privilege of presenting it on their stages!"

"I can well believe it," I rejoined.

"After that, other operas, symphonies, concerti . . ." His voice glowed with enthusiasm. "There is a book that created a scandal when it was published three years ago—*Anna Karenyina*—what an opera I will make of it!"

"My dear Vassily," I said, only half in jest, "I see a receptacle for discarded paper there in the corner. May I not take away with me one of those abandoned scraps? In a few short years, an authentic Cholodenko holograph may be priceless!"

He laughed. "I can do better than wastepaper," he said, handing me a double sheet of music manuscript from a stack on the piano. It was sprinkled with black showers of notes in his bold calligraphy. "This is Alyosha's aria from the second act of *Karamazov*. I have since transposed it to a more singable key—this is the old copy—I have no further use of it."

I thanked him, then said, "This story you wish to tell . . . what is it?"

"No more than a notion, really. Something I may one day fashion into a libretto—it would lend itself to music, I think. I would like your thoughts, as a man of letters, a poet."

"A very minor poet, I fear, but I will gladly listen."

He poured more wine, saying, "I have in mind a Faustian theme. The Faust, in this case, would possibly be a painter. But it would be patently clear to the audience from the opening moments of the first act—for his canvases would be visibly deployed about his studio—that he is a painter without gift, a maker of wretched daubs. In a poignant aria—baritone, I think—he pours out his misery and his yearnings. He aspires to greatness, but a cruel Deity has let him be born bereft of greatness. He rails, curses God, the aria ends in a crashing blasphemy. Effective, yes?"

"Please go on," I said, my curiosity quickened.

"Enter Lucifer. And here I would smash tradition and make him not the usual booming basso but a lyric tenor with a seductive voice of refined gold—the Fallen Angel, you see, a tragic figure. A bargain is reached. The Adversary will

92

grant the painter the gift of genius—for seven years, let us say, or five, or ten—and then will claim both his body and his immortal soul. The painter agrees, the curtain falls, and when it rises on the next scene, we are immediately aware of a startling transformation—the canvases in the painter's studio are stunning, masterful! A theatrical stroke, don't you agree?"

I nodded, and drank avidly from my goblet, for my throat was unaccountably dry. I felt somewhat dizzy—was it only the heady wine?—and my heart was beating faster. "Most theatrical," I replied. "What follows?"

Cholodenko sighed. "That is my dilemma. I do not know what follows. I had hoped you could offer something. . . ."

My brain was crowded with questions, fears, wild conjectures. I told myself that a composer was merely seeking my aid in devising an opera libretto—nothing more. I said, "It is a fascinating premise, but of course it cannot end there. It needs complications, development, reversal. Possibly, a young lady? . . . No, that's banal. . . ."

Suddenly, a face was in my mind. The remembrance of it, and the new implications it now carried, I found disturbing. The eyes in this face were dead, as blank as the brain behind them; the smile was vacuous and vapid: It was the face of that living corpse, Balakirev. My thoughts were racing, my head swam. I set down my goblet with a hand that, I now saw, was trembling.

Cholodenko's solicitous voice reached me as if through a mist: "Are you well, Lord Henry?"

"What? . . ."

"You are so very pale! As if you had seen—"

I looked up at him. I peered deep into the eyes of this man. *They* were not dead, those eyes! They were dark, yes, the darkest eyes I have ever seen, and deep-set in the gaunt face, but they were alive, they burned with fanatic fire. At length, I found my voice. "I am quite all right. A drop too much, I fear. . . ."

"Comet wine is unpredictable. Are you sure—"

"Yes, yes. Don't concern yourself." I inhaled deeply. "Now then, this opera story of yours . . ."

"You must not feel obligated to—"

"Suppose," I said guardedly, "that you invent another character. A fellow painter—but a man immensely gifted and acclaimed. You introduce him in Act One, prior to the appearance of Lucifer . . ."

"Yes?" said Cholodenko quickly.

"As the opera progresses, we watch an uncanny trans-

93

feral . . . we see the gifts of this great painter dim, in direct proportion to the rate with which your Faustian painter is infused with talent, until the great artist is an empty shell and his opposite number is a man of refulgent genius."

Cholodenko smiled sardonically. "The Devil robs Peter to pay Paul, is that it?"

"That is precisely it. What do you think of the idea?"

"It is arousing," he said, his dark eyes watching my face intently. "It is very clever." Then, waxing casual again, he asked, "But is it enough?"

"No, of course not," I said, rising and pacing. His eyes followed me, flickering from left to right and back again. "There must be the obligatory finale, wherein Lucifer returns after the stipulated time, and drags the condemned painter to fiery perdition. Quite a scene, that! Think what you could make of it."

"It's trite," he snapped. "The weary bourgeois idea of retribution. I detest it."

I stared at him, mouth agape. "My dear boy, you needn't bite my head off. It's merely an opera . . . isn't it?"

He mumbled. "I apologize. But that scene has been done before—Mozart, Gounod, Dragomizhsky . . ."

I shrugged. "Then we will change it."

"Yes, yes," he said, almost desperately. "We *must* . . . change it."

"What would you suggest? That your Faust be spared?"

"Why may he not be spared? Must he be punished because he wished to bring the world great art? . . ."

"No," I said slowly, "not for that."

"Then for what? Why must he be damned for all eternity? *Why*, Lord Henry?"

We were facing each other across the piano. He was leaning forward, his hands gripping the instrument's lid, his nails digging into the very wood. When I answered him, my voice was even and low:

"Because," I said, "of the man who was drained of his Godgiven genius to satisfy the cravings of your Faust. The man who was sucked dry and thrown aside. For that, someone must pay. For that, your Faust must burn in Hell."

"*No!*"

The syllable was torn from his depths. It rang in the room. "Why must he burn for that? He had no way of knowing whence that talent came! Even if, later, he began to suspect the truth, if he saw the great master wane as his own star ascended, there was nothing he could do, no way he could stop it, the pact had been sealed! The Fiend had tricked

94

him! Comprehend, if you can, the horror he would feel, the guilt, the shame, as he watched that blazing talent become cold ashes, sacrificed on the altar of his own ambition! He would hate and disgust himself, he would loathe himself far more than one would loathe a vampire—for a vampire drains only the blood of his victim, whereas *he . . .*"

Cholodenko's voice stopped, throttled by emotion. His face was a mask of anguish. Then he took a shuddering breath, straightened, and summoned the shadow of a laugh. "But what a very good story this must be, indeed, to sting us to such passion. I fear we are taking it too seriously."

"Are we?"

"Of course we are! Come, hand me your glass. . . ."

"I have had enough, thank you. Perhaps we both have."

"You may be right. It has made us irritable. I'm sorry I burdened you with my problems."

"Not at all. It is stimulating to collaborate with a fellow artist. But it is really very late, and I must go."

I reached for my greatcoat, but he gripped my arm. "No, please, Lord Henry. Stay. I beseech you. Do not leave me here . . . alone."

I smiled courteously, and gently extricated my arm from his grasp. I put on my coat. At the door, I turned and spoke. "That final scene," I said. "You wish something different from the usual plunge to Hell. Here is something that might prove piquant, and is certainly theatrical. . . ."

Although he did not respond, I continued:

"Lucifer drags your Faust down to The Pit, but the opera does not end, not quite. There is a little epilog. In it, those lustrous paintings fade before the audience's eyes and become empty canvases—I suppose that might be done chemically, or by a trick of lighting? And the poor chap whose gifts were stolen is restored to his former glory. As for your Faust—it is as if he never lived; even the memory of him is swallowed in Hell. How does that strike you?"

I do not know if he heard me. He was staring into the fire. I waited for a reply, but he said nothing and did not look at me. After a moment, I left.

Please pass on to Maude the enclosure you will find herein. It is the piece of music Cholodenko gave me—Alyosha's aria from *Karamazov*. Bid her play it (I am sure it is beautiful) and you will be the envy of London: the first of your circle to be granted a foretaste of a bold new opera that is certain to be greeted as a masterpiece.

Your friend,
Harry

Lord Henry Stanton's account of his Russian sojourn ends there. The other letters of his in the packet purchased at the Beverly Hills auction are interesting enough to possibly justify future publication, but all the material bearing upon what I may call The Great Cholodenko Mystery is contained in the three letters you have just read. To them, I can add nothing about Cholodenko, although I can supply some peripheral data available to any researcher willing to spend a little time digging into the history of Russian music:

In the years following Lord Henry's visit to Russia, Mily Balakirev enjoyed a miraculous recovery. He returned to his abandoned *Tamara,* completed it. and in 1882 saw it produced to acclaim so tremendous that it secured for him, in the following year, a coveted appointment as Director of the Court Chapel. He again became an active host, filling his home with musicians and others eager for his friendship and guidance. He composed his second symphony and worked on a piano concerto. He conducted. He organized festivals in homage to Chopin and Glinka. He personally prepared a new edition of Glinka's works. He energetically composed and edited music even into his retirement years, and outlived the other members of the *koochka* (with the single exception of Cui), dying in 1910 at the age of 73.

A final curiosity: A yellowing sheet of music paper, presumably the one Lord Henry mentioned, the page he said contained Alyosha's aria from *The Brothers Karamazov* in Cholodenko's own hand, actually is folded into his April 12th letter—but, except for the printer's mark and the orderly rows of staves, it is blank.

Katherine MacLean is a major name in the field of science fiction and fantasy even though she's published surprisingly few stories. This very short tale of a not-at-all alien being living within the human mind shows impressively why she's built such a reputation with so few words.

THE OTHER
Katherine MacLean

Tree shadows moved on the gray linoleum of the hospital floor, swaying like real leaves and twigs. Joey blurred his eyes to make the leaf shadows green.

The floor quivered slightly to foam-padded footsteps, and a man-shaped shadow appeared across the sunlight. That was Dr. Armstrong. He was kind. He always walked softly and then stood and shuffled when he hoped you would notice him.

The feet shuffled hopefully. When Joey concentrated on the doctor's shadow he could turn the head part pink, like a face.

Dr. Armstrong's voice said something. It was a pleasant light tenor voice, a little anxious.

"What did he say?" Joey asked the other, the one in his head who listened and calculated and explained.

"He asked *How are you?*"

"What did he mean?"

"He wants you to get up and be busy, like him," said the cool advice of his Other, his guardian and advisor. "That's what they all want."

"Not right now. I am watching the leaves. What shall we tell him?"

"Tell him, *Just about the same.*"

Joey made the effort, and spoke, hearing his own voice very close to his ears. He was ready to turn and look out the window now, but the doctor's feet were beside him, anxiously demanding his attention, afraid he would turn away.

"What did he say?" Joey asked the Other.

There was a pause, a barrier, a reluctance to speak, then the cool voice answered. "He asked about me."

"Was he—" Joey was alarmed. People meddled, people said things which got inside and hurt. And yet Dr. Armstrong had always been nice; he never critized, so far. "No —I don't want to know. Well—tell me a little."

The voice was indistinct. "Asked who you talk to—when you . . . before talking outside to him."

"Tell him it's you," Joey said, confident and warm. The voice was his friend, and Dr. Armstrong was his friend. They should know each other. The voice helped Dr. Armstrong. "Tell him it's you."

"What name? Authority people need names for existing things. They don't understand without names."

"What are you?"

"I am a construct. You made me."

"We can't tell him that. People punish me for making up people." Joey felt pain in his middle, near stomach and heart. It was hard to breath. "Mommee shouted and cried."

"We won't tell him that," the voice agreed.

Joey felt calmer. The voice was good; there had to be a good name for it, one that the outside others would approve. "We can find a name for you. There are so many words. What else are you?"

"I am part your mother and your father and little parts and feelings of anyone who ever worried about you and wanted you to stop doing things so that you would be all right and strangers would not be angry at you. And you made me into a grownup to talk to you. Many years. I've grown wise, Joey. I worry about you and want you to stop . . ."

"Don't bother me about that now," Joey said, withdrawing

himself in his head so that the voice was far away where he would not have to listen. "You explain to Dr. Armstrong that you are on his side, that you are grownup like him, and tell me what to do. I wouldn't know when to get up, or what people want. . . . They would be angry."

"Doctors don't want to talk to me. They want to talk to you, Joey. They don't ask how to do something: they ask what do you feel."

"I can't talk. They'd see me. I'd cry, and want to touch arms and rub cheeks. Talk for me. Tell them you're a doctor. Use their words."

Joey heard his voice close but too quiet and mumbly. He forced it louder. ". . . *father image, Dr. Armstrong. He tells me what is right to say. He is strict, so it is all right.*"

That sounded good. That sounded safe to say. Joey heard the musical tenor of Dr. Armstrong's anxious, well-intentioned voice. It would be praise.

Don't listen to it, Joey. It's not—

Pain and grief struck him in the middle, curling him over. Got to get away quickly or die. Make it not happen. Into the past, in the dark, in the comforting dark, before people could take away their love. He was lying on the floor, curled up, and the warm dark was wrapping around like a blanket.

But the feet still stood by, shuffling nervously. That past event must be finished before it could be forgotten. Joey took a deep breath, made a shouting effort, heard his distant scream and left it behind, screaming forever like a soundless sign on the wall of a deserted train station, at a distant place in time.

"*He said the wrong thing. Tell him to go away.*"

Outside-people do not know the roads and paths inside the world of image, memory, and dream: they stumble, blunder and destroy among the fragile things. He decided that he should not have listened and replied. When time came around to return from darkness to the world of light, he would be silent.

Doctor Armstrong, twenty-four years old, successful and considered brilliant, walked into his small office in the hospital. He carefully shut the door behind him and made sure his latch had caught before sitting at his desk.

He put his face down into his hands. (*He said the wrong thing. Tell him to go away.*) The article about Rosen's techniques had said that Rosen talked freely with his patients, discussing their fantasy worlds with them as if they were real, and explaining the meaning of the symbols to them.

99

Perhaps he should see it demonstrated before trying it again.

God! Joey had fallen from the chair and hit the floor already curled up, knees to chin, eyes shut, as if stunned and dead. Maybe he would be all right. Tomorrow, casual inquiry to the nurses . . . The nurses might blame him for Joey. How many other mistakes did they blame him for already?

Why was he sitting like this with his face in his hands? *I'm tired,* he thought. *Just tired.*

Doctor Armstrong leaned his face more heavily into his hands, his elbows braced on the desk as though he were tired. Tears trickled down between his spread fingers and splashed on the psychiatric journal on his desk.

It is not I who is weeping, he thought. *I am the cool and logical student, the observer of human actions. I can observe myself also, which proves that my body weeps. This wastes time I could use to study and to think.*

Tears trickled down between his spread fingers and splashed on the psychiatric journal.

It is not I who is weeping, he thought. *It is that other, the childish feeling in me, who can be wounded by love and hope, and pity and confusion, and being alone. I am an adult, a scientist. It is the other who weeps, the ungrown-up one we must conceal from the world.*

"*No one sees you,*" he said to the Other. "*You can weep for five minutes. This spasm will pass.*"

One of fantasy's greatest strengths is its ability to deal with emotional symbols far more directly than does most other fiction. Many of the monsters we meet in the best fantasy are horrific not for any scaly, fanged appearance, but for the chords they strike within us as we recognize archetypes of our deepest fears. Here Mildred Clingerman presents a very unsettling monster who becomes more fearful the smaller he gets. . . .

Mildred Clingerman

A RED HEART AND BLUE ROSES

I'm awake, I argued with the Spectator who watched all my dreams and commented on them with amusement or distaste. If I were asleep how should I know what time it was? And I did know, clearly. It was that reasonably quiet hour in the hospital after the visitors have all straggled out, when one's dinner is still only a rattling promise far away down the corridor. I was awake. But the Spectator only pointed silently into a deep chasm where a large Hospital still hunted Lewis Carroll's *Snark.*

"They sought it with thimbles," the Spectator urged, "They sought it with care . . ."

I obediently took up the refrain, "They pursued it with forks and hope; they threatened its life with a railway share—"

"My dear, are you very sick?" The warm, motherly Voice called across the dark blue void I was peering into.

"Oh no," I was cheerful about it. "They charmed it with smiles and soap." I opened my eyes, and after a moment or two I woke up. In the next bed a large pink woman had raised herself up to stare at me.

"You were asleep again," she accused me in a playful tone. "Off and on you've said some queer things today, but I haven't minded a bit. It's taken my mind off my troubles. Did you know your husband was here, and you slept right through the whole visiting hour?"

I considered this fact, turning it around and around to look at it. "He wore the wrong tie with that striped shirt." I was triumphant and positively awake.

"You were quite brutal about it," she agreed, "but he seemed awfully pleased."

I lay quietly for a while, as if I were resting smugly after immense effort.

"When did you come in?" I struggled to stay awake long enough to hear the answer, but her first words eluded me.

"—days ago," the woman was saying, "but they only moved me in here with you this morning. You were asleep. They had me in a private room, but they finally decided what I needed *least* was to be alone. I keep having nightmares, you see, about a tattooed—"

"—tapioca pudding, or you could have Jello, if you'd rather." The nurse was being firm about something. Her arms were faintly yellow and stringy with muscle. I sat up and ate the tapioca pudding.

The woman in the other bed was eating heartily from a loaded tray. She kept dipping her fork into something dark brown and succulent looking, and I suddenly felt quite pitiably betrayed and hungry. I drank a cup of tea, well sugared. "I'll have the Jello, too," I said, but the nurse and the tray were both gone.

". . . son in the Navy." It was morning, and the woman was shrugging into a pink bedjacket.

"Why, my son's in the Navy, too!" I hauled myself up to lean woozily against the pillow, and stared at her as if the hairbrush she was flourishing were a fairy wand.

"I know, dear, that's just what I was saying. Your husband told me. *My* son isn't in the Navy. He's in the
102

Army. They think that may be the source of half my trouble. The nightmares, you know. You see, my father and all my uncles were Navy. I married outside the Service, but I'd always supposed our son would choose to be Navy when the time came. Well, he didn't, at all." She sighed and picked stray hairs out of the brush. "He's been rather a disappointment in some ways. His Math wasn't good enough for Annapolis or West Point. Next year when he finishes his tour of duty he wants to apprentice to a mortician. Now, really, what kind of ambition would you call that?"

"An eminently respectable one?" I hazarded.

She shook the hairbrush at me admonishingly. "My, we *are* feeling better, aren't we?"

We were. After I'd wolfed a meager breakfast I was buoyed up enough to tell my roommate all (and more) than she wanted to know about my son in the Navy. "He's on one of the new Polaris submarines," I bragged. "Born and brought up on the desert, as he was, that boy lived and breathed Navy from babyhood, almost. And as for being underwater, we could never make him swim on the surface, and then in high school he joined a skindiving club, and they all sat around for hours on the bottom of a swimming pool."

"Does he get home very often?" She was frowning down at her fingernails.

"Not often," I said mournfully. "And he's dreadful about writing letters. But far too handy with the long distance telephone. Collect, of course."

"Of course. Clay's exactly the same." We nodded at each other solemnly, two middle-aged mothers with equally enormous phone bills.

"But tell me, does your boy ever bring any of his service buddies home? To stay, I mean, in your house."

"He hasn't so far," I said. "But I wouldn't mind if he did."

"That's what you think", she said darkly. "You'll need to be *very* careful. I daresay there's more than one orphan in the Navy. If that's what he was. . . ."

"Who?"

"Surely I mentioned him yesday? That boy—that man— that *thing* Clay brought home with him Christmas before last."

"I can remember Christmas before last," I said, "but yesday . . ."

She looked at me in astonishment. "But you had your eyes open, and you even made one or two rather pungent

103

comments. Do you mean to tell me you were asleep all day?"

"Oh, hardly asleep. What I was doing, I think, was concentrating on holding now, without allowing the last now and the next now to get away. It was very difficult. It took two hands to hold one now, and the other two kept falling away. I'm really very sorry. And the funny thing is I can actually juggle three oranges . . ." I hesitated and decided to be honest. "Sometimes."

She snorted, but I knew I was forgiven. "My dear, think nothing of it. It's entirely appropriate that only a six-handed woman could hear and understand the truth about Damon Lucas. I think he was some kind of fiend. My husband thinks he was a natural-born sponger. Rhoda—that's my daughter, she's nineteen and extremely pretty—thinks he's one of those weirdies who preys on older women. Clay says simply—and I quote—'the guy's a kook.' You see? Even the people he happened to can't agree on what he was. Maybe, in different ways, we're all biased." She paused to rub out the frown between her eyes. "I wouldn't care a bit if that could just be the end of it—a family mystery—with all of us sitting about now and then idly speculating about him. Why, he might even, in time, have turned into a family joke."

"Why hasn't he?" I was bitterly regretting all those hours yesterday devoted to that silly juggling game, when I might have been fitting together highly-colored bits of a jigsaw puzzle.

"How could we possibly turn him into a joke when he keeps turning up again? And each time getting younger and younger?"

I was getting desperate. "Will you be very kind," I said, "and start all over again at the very beginning and go along slowly, because I'm beginning to need six hands again."

"Of course I will. You poor darling, how thoughtless I've been." Her face smoothed out and she smiled at me as if I were three years old with all my buttons buttoned into the wrong holes. She looked so much like everybody's secret ideal of motherhood I suddenly wanted to lay my head on her full bosom and cry away a heartful of tears. Moreover, I was starving in this horrible hospital and nobody cared. I blew my nose and blinked my eyes clear and spoke coldly to the ceiling.

"You realize, I hope, that they have forgotten to give us any lunch."

"Well, dear, it's only nine o'clock." She got out of bed and fished in the drawer of her nightstand, then padded barefoot across the space between the beds. "Do have some of these chocolates. In fact, it would be a great favor to me if you'd eat all of them. I'm getting much too fat. But hide them from the nurse, won't you?" She leapt hurriedly back into bed, keeping a sharp watch on the door.

"I don't even know your name." I had eaten three chocolates before she'd stopped sighing and settling herself in bed.

"It's Pemberton. Katie Pemberton, age over forty and hips to match. You'd think, wouldn't you, that with a figure like mine I'd be perfectly safe from strange young men for the rest of my days? Well, I thought so, too, till Damon Lucas started following me around like a lap dog. At first sight we all thought he was handsome, in a blond and bland kind of way. Rhoda was prepared to be quite taken with him, I know, but after he'd been staying with us a few hours it became painfully clear that he wasn't taken with her. In fact, I don't believe he ever actually looked at her. Now, you can't call that normal, not for an unattached young man of twenty-six, and certainly not when the girl is as pretty as Rhoda. Philip thought—he's my husband—well, Philip got to worrying that maybe he was one of those you-know-whats, but after questioning Clay very closely and watching Damon when Clay was around, he soon saw that Damon was, if possible, even less taken with Clay than he was with Rhoda. It began to look as if he positively disliked Clay, and with every day that passed he seemed to dislike Clay more and more. By that time we were all uneasy about Damon, for one reason or another. Sometimes for no discernible reason at all."

Mrs. Pemberton sighed, and stared at the only picture in the room, a doe-eyed Christ blessing little children. "It was a queer kind of Christmas, I assure you."

"Why did Clay ever invite him? Were they good friends?"

"Oh, no. Clay had never seen him before they met in the waiting room at the bus station. You see, it was this way: Clay hadn't seriously expected to get a Christmas furlough, but at the last minute it came through, just too late for him to get any plane reservations. Two airlines were tied up by strikes, and the others had waiting lists miles long, so Clay phoned home—collect, of course—to tell me he'd take a bus. He told me later the bus station was mobbed by servicemen of all branches, all trying to get home for Christmas. Here and there in the crowd were soldiers and sailors who owned cars and who were wandering about looking for riders going in their direction to help pay driving expenses.

"Clay thought he might get home faster that way and began to look around for a ride going west. Finally, a fellow in civilian clothes came up to Clay and said he was driving to Phoenix, which of course was perfect for Clay, who jumped at the offer. But for once Clay used enough common sense to look over the car—an almost new racing Corvette—to take down the license plate number, get the fellow's name, and phone home again to tell me his plans and relay the details. Even if I'd openly disapproved, I doubt if Clay *could* have turned down that ride. On the phone he was lyrical about his chance to drive such a car—they were to spell each other at the wheel. I didn't like it. But it was Christmas time, and Clay's still such a child, in some ways. I just told him to be careful and then started praying the minute he hung up."

"Was there an accident?" I sincerely hoped not, but the fact remained that I was full of chocolates and contentment. It was blissful to lie in bed while a large pink mother told me stories.

"Not a serious accident. In New Mexico it was snowing, and Clay, who was driving and has had no experience of icy roads, skidded them into a ditch. They were stuck there seven hours till the Highway Patrol came along and lent them a shovel to dig themselves out. Even with that delay they made the trip—over two thousand miles—in an incredibly short time. I gather they barely paused for food and gasoline, and the only sleep they had was what one could snatch while the other drove. When they arrived on Saturday afternoon they were both red-eyed, muddy, and exhausted. It would have been inhuman of us not to offer Damon, along with Clay, a hot bath, food, and some sleep.

"Philip hurried to set up a camp cot in Clay's room and got out Clay's old sleeping bag to make an extra bed in a hurry. Clay's room is small, you see, and is built like a sea captain's cabin, very compact and shipshape—when he isn't in it—but with just the one bed. We'd remodeled the room that way when Clay was only ten, and I still hoped he'd be Navy. Well, never mind that. . . . After they'd showered and shaved and demolished ham sandwiches and several quarts of milk they both went to bed, and we didn't see them any more till late that evening. I had given up hovering around their closed door when finally Clay emerged, blinking and grinning and starved to death. Damon was still asleep in Clay's bed. When I broiled Clay a steak he told me a bit about Damon—all Clay had learned about him during the long hours of driving.

"Damon, he told me, was just out of the Navy, twenty-six years old, single, and planning to settle in Arizona, preferably up in Phoenix, where he had a distant relative, a second cousin, I think it was, whom he'd never met. The only relative he had left since his parents had been killed in a highway accident a few months back—a Labor Day accident, in fact. Clay, I could see, was quite haunted, as I was, by Damon's lonely future and particularly by the bleakness of this first Christmas since his parents' death. Their estate had been settled quickly and their home sold almost immediately after the double funeral. Damon had purchased the car with part of the insurance money and had enough left to spend a few months looking around for the right job and the place where he wanted to live.

"While he was telling me all this Clay ate the steak, a large green salad, and half a pecan pie. Long before he got to the pie and coffee I knew I was going to ask Damon to spend Christmas with us. I also knew that Clay would have been horrified at any other conclusion, in spite of the fact that he admitted he was not in any way drawn to Damon personally. Damon had been in another service, was several years older, and in Clay's own words was 'kinda funny-peculiar.' Clay's unspoken attitude was simplicity itself: Homeless cats, dogs and humans had to be fed, warmed and comforted at any season of the year. At Christmas they were to be especially cherished, 'just because.' It is this 'just because' quality in Clay that keeps me wavering between parental despair and delight. . . . I wouldn't have let him down for worlds."

Mrs. Pemberton found a tissue and blew her nose. She glanced sharply at me to make sure, I think, that I was still awake. I nodded at her urgently and after a moment she continued.

"Most house guests are disturbing, in my opinion. Even when they're the considerate kind. There's a different feeling about the rooms. There's a . . . well . . . a different smell in the air, almost. One's possessions begin either to look dreadfully shabby or too shinily new. And all at once family habits and customs begin to seem slovenly or just plain silly. I'll admit that there are two or possibly three people I know who can stay in my house and not affect my life in any way except to increase my pleasure and excitement. But even that can be wearing. You know the old saying about fish and guests beginning to smell after the third day. In Damon's case I should say he began to smell three seconds after he finally woke up and joined us all in the living room.

"To begin with, after brief nods to Philip and Rhoda—he ignored Clay—he addressed himself solely to me. 'That's a pretty good bed,' he said. 'The room's okay, too, but that cot sorta crowds it up. I took it down. Junior, here, can sleep in that other bedroom I found at the end of the hall. The bed in there's loaded with Christmas junk, but I guess he's big enough to unload it.' Then he rubbed his hands together briskly and gestured with his chin towards the kitchen. I suppose I was just sitting there staring at him with my mouth dropped open, because he walked over and chucked me under the chin. 'Well, *c'mon*, Mom,' says he. 'Feed me, your new boy's hungry!'"

"I hope you told him off *good*," I said. "I think I'd have stamped on his toes and ordered him out of the house."

"I wanted to," Mrs. Pemberton said grimly. "There was a long silence while each of us waited for somebody else to do or say something, but we were so appalled that finally all we did was giggle a little, and then pretend we hadn't. Then, hardly knowing what I meant to do, I got up and left the room, with Damon following close behind me. Philip got up and followed Damon. I went straight back to Clay's room, gathered up the folded camp cot, carried it into the spare bedroom, set it up—with Philip's help—and then unloaded all the wrapped Christmas gifts off the spare room bed onto the cot. Then with Philip and Damon still watching every move I made I carried Damon's suitcase into the spare room and plopped it down hard. 'You'll sleep here,' I said. That's the kind of stupid mistake people make when they're angry and off-balance."

"Why do you say that? I think it was a very natural thing to do."

"Don't you see? I gave Damon a foothold . . . implied he was staying. I suppose ever since I'd talked to Clay about asking him for Christmas I'd been idly thinking how I'd put Damon into the spare bedroom, and under the stress of the moment I just did the next thing I'd planned to do. It was automatic, like picking a stray thread off the living room rug when the house is on fire. I saw at once by the look on Philip's face that I'd done the wrong thing.

" 'Tonight,' Philip told Damon. 'You can stay here tonight. In the morning no doubt you'll want to continue your trip.' There was no mistaking Philip's meaning. Damon straightened up and stopped grinning. He turned rather

108

pale, and his eyes looked hurt and bewildered. 'I hope I haven't stepped out of line, sir,' he said. 'It was a joke—a funny—I planned it in the room when I woke up. My folks and I used to kid a lot that way. I guess it was being in a real home again that got me going like that.' He started to say something about 'Mom' and choked up and stopped talking.

"I could see Philip was softening. Philip comes of a very gentle breed with a tradition of hospitality that's all-embracing. It must have cost him a great deal of effort to speak out to Damon in the way he had. 'Very well, Damon,' he said. 'Come along now and we'll find you something to eat.' Philip left the room, and for just a second or two Damon and I were alone. We stared at each other and Damon shuffled his feet in a queer kind of little dance step, and started grinning again. 'Pop's a real nice little man,' he said softly. 'Real nice.' Then he winked at me and walked out. Later, when Philip and I were getting ready for bed, I tried to tell him about that wink and something of my dislike and distrust of the man, but none of it sounded very menacing to Philip. 'He's been badly brought up,' Philip said, 'but it's Christmas, and he's lonely and lost. You can see that. He isn't exactly our kind, as you say, though that does sound very snobbish, Katie. I think we ought to let him stay, so long as he behaves respectfully to you.' It was Damon's lack of respect for Philip that was bothering me, but I didn't say that. It isn't the kind of thing you like to point out to your husband.

"All this took place just five days before Christmas. Nobody ever actually asked Damon to stay. It just seemed to be taken for granted by all of us, including Damon. I was very busy cooking and cleaning. The children were out a great deal . . . Clay, tearing around in my car seeing his friends, and Rhoda, doing research in the University library for a paper she had to hand in after vacation, or else shopping for me. Philip, of course, was at work all day. Damon scarcely left the house at all, though the children asked him along, often. He treated their invitations with such obvious contempt, I marveled at their good manners towards him. But, then, all of us were strangely patient with him. I should certainly call it patience, in the beginning. Later, I thought it looked more like fear. . . . He slouched around after me most of the day, wearing a tight, skimpy T-shirt and an old pair of Clay's Levis. His own clothes were at the drycleaners, and he seemed to have just the one set of civilian clothes. We never saw any sign that he still had his Navy uniforms. He never talked about the Navy, either. The only way you could tell which service he'd been in was by the repulsive tattoo on his left arm. It was a big, dripping red heart, enclosing a blue anchor, and underneath it the word MOM, in red letters entwined with blue roses. He seemed very proud of it."

Mrs. Pemberton lay quietly for a while, as if stricken by the memory of the bleeding heart. Before she could rally herself to continue, our doctors arrived together, hearty and jocular, and both in a tearing hurry. With some prodding from the nurse who accompanied him, I managed to give my doctor a halting report of my behavior for the past twenty-four hours. He seemed to be as bored with it as I was, but as he left he gave me a paternal pat on the head, by way of forgiveness.

"Tomorrow we'll get *up*," he caroled, and left.

I scrupulously tried not to hear the conversation going on five feet away from me, but I couldn't help overhearing the parting remarks which Mrs. Pemberton's doctor was delivering in louder tones, as if reassurance for his patient lay mainly in drowning out her own faintly protesting voice.

"Fine, *fine*," he was roaring. "And if all goes well again tonight you can go home tomorrow. There's not a thing on earth wrong with you that time won't take care of, Haw, Haw. Time and a leetle self-discipline, Katie. Now, buck up and take your medicine like the big girl you are, and put that silly notion of yours right out of your mind. F'gawd's sake, girl, you're saner than I am and healthy as a horse. Control! That's all you need. . . . Well, then, *stop* thinking!" He plunged out of the room, flashing a fine set of teeth in my direction.

For some minutes I refrained from looking at Mrs. Pemberton. From the sounds of tissues being pulled from the box and various little sniffings, I felt sure she was crying. After a while, though, she poured herself a glass of water with so much banging of the vacuum pitcher, and then plumped her pillow so viciously I knew she'd recovered from her tears and was in the process of passing through anger to resignation. It didn't take her very long.

"Oh, well. . . ." she sighed. "Jim always was a tactless idiot, but he is a good doctor. And it's true—I'm feeling better. Last night is the first night in weeks I haven't screamed my lungs out, waking from that nightmare. You're lucky not to have heard me. They say I wail like a banshee, enough to lift the hair right off your head."

I was suddenly enlightened. "Has the nightmare anything to do with Damon?"

"It has everything to do with Damon," Mrs. Pemberton said. "When I finally told him to go I hoped and prayed that would be the last of him, but it hasn't been."

"You kicked him out?"

"On Christmas Eve," she nodded. "We had a ghastly scene . . . just Damon and I. The children were out, and Philip was in bed asleep. Of course, that scene had been building up in me for days. It takes a lot to make me explode that way, and a lot is what I'd been taking. . . .

"Mealtime, for instance. While I was preparing the meals, Damon would hang over me and watch every move I made. He was always sampling and meddling. If I wanted a certain butcher knife, Damon was sure to be fiddling with it, testing its sharpness or poking it into my chopping block. Sometimes he sang bloody ballads in a high voice—all about drowning somebody in a river after choking her to death, and most troubling of all, there were times when he'd giggle steadily for long, long minutes about nothing at all. At the table he talked very little, which was a blessing, but he ate so greedily and with so much noise that it was difficult to carry on a conversation. He *grabbed*, you see, and he took food right off Clay's plate, while Clay was talking. And suddenly, out of the silence, he'd laugh in that queer way, and always he kept his feet moving, as if he were dancing, even as he sat. Then, if somebody commented on the food . . . like, 'This pie is delicious,' Damon would swell visibly and say, 'My Mom made it. She likes to cook for her sailor boy.' What kind of answer do you make to a remark like that? One, I mean, that doesn't sound surly and ungracious. I'm not really old enough to be Damon's mother, and the way he kept calling me 'Mom' grated on me. More than anything else, it kept suspicion stirring in me. If your mother had been dead only four months, do you think you could call any other woman 'Mom' so easily?"

"Probably not," I said.

"Then there was the incident of the Christmas tree. The children have always decorated it so carefully. They take a great deal of pride in some of the old ornaments we have. Some are lovely. Some are rather awful. . . . There's a celluloid doll, for one thing, that has to have a prominent place on the tree, simply because we've always had it. Damon stepped on it and smashed it flat. Not quite an accident. . . . When Rhoda hung it, anyway, Damon got very loud and scornful. He kept sneering at their work and finally announced that next year we were going to have an aluminum tree with no ornaments at all, just lights. Before

I could remind him that next year he wouldn't be with us, he slammed out of the room.

"There were dozens of little incidents of that kind. Little things, maybe, but all together, very disturbing. When Clay and I tried to talk he was always butting in, always there, trying to draw my attention away from Clay, growing louder and louder and more excited. Clay only had a ten-day furlough, and I began to despair of ever having a moment alone with him. Often Clay would give up trying to talk to me and go to his room to nap behind a locked door. Somehow, in that house of always-open doors, we'd all begun to shut ourselves in. In Clay's case I could see reason in it. Damon had begun to raid Clay's wardrobe of all his civilian clothes, even after Damon's own clothes had been cleaned. Clay would be trying to dress for a party and would discover his best white shirt stuffed away, soiled, in Damon's room. Knowing Damon would be there for Christmas, I did extra shopping, of course, so he'd have some gifts under the tree. I bought clothes for him, since he seemed to need them. One afternoon I locked myself in my bedroom so I could wrap them nicely. I also wrapped a lovely, bulky gold-colored sweater for Clay as an extra surprise—one he'd especially admired in a store window, one day when he was with Rhoda in town. When I finished I put all those gifts with the others under the tree.

"I had baking to do that day, and for once Damon was somewhere else in the house, and I was thankful. Just before dinner he came swaggering in, wearing all the clothes I'd wrapped for his Christmas gifts, plus the gold sweater I'd bought for Clay. 'I don't like waiting, Mom,' he said. 'I saw my name on the packages.' I was so rattled I began to doubt myself. Maybe I *had* put Damon's name on Clay's sweater. Anyway, I wasn't sure, so I let it go. But the next morning I sent Rhoda to town to buy an identical sweater for Clay.

"By Christmas Eve I was strung up as tight as the strings on a fiddle. The children left with a crowd of young people to go caroling and to a party later. Philip and I turned out all the lights but the tree lights, drew up our chairs to the fireplace, and listened to Christmas music on the hi-fi. Damon, to our surprise, had roared away in his Corvette almost immediately after dinner. The house was beautifully peaceful without him. My doubts and fears began to melt away. About ten o'clock Philip went on to bed, but I decided to sit up awhile to savor more of the Christmas peace. Around eleven o'clock Damon walked in. I admit what

I was doing may have looked silly by some standards. . . .
The children have these old, beat-up, felt Christmas stockings
they still hang up at the fireplace every year. I had already stuffed Rhoda's with cosmetics and hair-rollers and
things like that. For Clay's I had shaving things, combs, pen-
cils, and other odds and ends. I was standing there smiling at
Clay's sock, which was stuck together inside the toe, where
years ago he'd deposited some half-chewed candy he didn't
like.

"Damon sidled over, wrenched the sock out of my hand
and dropped it on the fire. Before I had time to feel shock
or anger, I rescued the sock and saw that it wasn't scorched
much, then I whirled on Damon as if I were a buzz saw.
What did he mean by acting like that, I wanted to know.
And what in *hell* gave him the idea he could move into
my house and ruin my Christmas? I wasn't very ladylike
about it. I may have used even stronger language. . . .
When I reached the point at last where I could hear again
and see, Damon was trembling and mumbling, as pale as a
ghost. He was trying, I think, to say something about Clay's
being too old to hang up a stocking. That was enough to
set me off again, and I can't remember all the things I
said. When I ran down a little, Damon was still mumbling
and had shucked out of the gold sweater and was rolling
up his shirt sleeve to show me his left arm. It took a while
for me to focus my eyes and see what he was trying to
show me. He'd spent the evening in some nasty little tattoo
parlor, having an addition made to that horror on his
arm. It now read: MOM, I LOVE YOU.

"He was saying over and over, 'I did it for you, see?
Your Christmas present. . . . I did it for you.' Well, I simply
broke down and howled. I still don't know if I was laughing or crying. Damon danced around me sort of tentatively,
talking so fast I could scarcely make out what he was
saying. After my hysteria subsided a little I began to listen
very carefully, and this is the kind of thing I heard: He
had it all planned out; my children were almost grown up,
ready to leave home for good. He would take their place.
He would get a job and take care of me, always. Even
if the 'old man' died I wouldn't have to be alone, ever.
Nothing could make him leave me, ever, ever, ever. I was
his Mom. He had chosen me. Out of the whole world, he
had chosen me. I was his, and he was mine, for the rest
of our lives.

"It was like a chant. He kept repeating himself, and
the horror kept growing in me till I thought I'd scream.

113

When I couldn't stand it any longer I ran out of the room, wildly, just to get away from his voice. I was terrified that he would follow, but he didn't. I could hear him in the living room, still chanting. I washed my face in cold water at the kitchen sink and dried it with a paper towel. Then I went to the spare room and packed his things. I let myself out the back door and piled all his stuff into the Corvette. Then—quietly—I came back into the house and woke Philip. Eventually the two of us were able to persuade Damon to leave, but there were some hideous minutes when I thought we'd have to call the police . . . or an ambulance complete with straitjacket. I couldn't sleep that night. I was so afraid he'd come back."

"Did he?"

"No. He never came back to the house. I don't know where he went that night. He must have left town. For weeks we kept watching in traffic for his red Corvette, but we never saw it again. And for weeks I kept remembering his words—like a threat—just before he drove away. 'You'll see me again, Mom. You ain't ever gonna be rid of me, one way or another.' "

"Have you seen him again?"

Mrs. Pemberton bit her lower lip and looked at me with troubled eyes. "Not exactly," she said at last. "I may as well tell you the rest and if you decide I'm crazy, well—"

"I heard your doctor say you were saner than he is. I'll take the chance," I said.

"Very well then, dear. Six months later, when we'd just begun to forget Damon, or to get over him, at any rate, Philip got a long-distance phone call one night from the San Diego police. Our twelve-year-old runaway son, they said, had been picked up hanging around outside a tattoo parlor, and would we please come and get him or send the fares for him and an accompanying social worker. The boy had told them his name was Damon Pemberton, and that he was our son . . . our name and our address, everything. It took time to convince them we had no such son. We even had our local police department phone them to verify our statements. In the meantime, we learned, the boy had escaped from the detention home they'd put him in. We don't know to this day who or what the child was . . . or who put him up to it.

"The San Diego episode happened in June. In August Philip and I spent a weekend at the Grand Canyon. We were staying at that lodge right on the rim of the canyon. It was after dinner, and Philip was reading his paper in the lobby. I went out to watch the sunset, and I was strolling down the path along the rim. Behind me I heard somebody running in my direction. Then I could tell it was a child, gasping and crying, being chased by someone. I turned around just in time to brace myself as the little boy in front threw his arms around me, hiding his face in my skirt. He grabbed me with such force I almost lost my balance. A bigger boy had slowed down when he saw me and was hanging back. The little boy peered around at the big one who'd been chasing him. 'My Mom will fix you,' he said. 'You big old dumb nut.' The big boy turned and ran off, out of sight. The child gave me a big squeeze, then, and said, 'Mom, I love you.' While I was taking that in, he just sort of melted away into the dusk, but I could hear his running feet, and could hear him laughing. He was wearing a sailor cap, and just as he twisted away I saw he had an enormous tattoo on his left arm."

"Oh, surely not!" I said. "Or it was probably one of those transfers little boys delight in plastering themselves with. They do look like tattoos."

"Maybe," Mrs. Pemberton said. "Then last September Philip and I went fishing in the White Mountains. Now that we're older we don't bother about camping out. We rent a motel room in Show Low and Philip drives out very early to the trout streams and lakes. On this day I stayed behind, because I wanted to write some letters and wash my hair. It was still very early in the morning, not many people about. I'd had coffee with Philip at an all-night place on the highway and walked back to our motel alone. I hadn't been back in our room long before I heard a kind of scrabbling noise outside the door. I thought it was a maid, perhaps, though it was far too early for them to be coming around, or a yardman, raking the car park. I was sitting at the little desk, watching the door, when I saw a piece of paper come sliding under. Some kind of advertising, I thought. But when I picked it up I saw it was lined paper torn from a child's school tablet. On it was drawn, in red crayon, a dripping heart, and in staggering block letters, like those of a child in the second grade, it read *Mom I love you*. I don't know how long I stood there staring at it. I remember how the paper shook in my hands. I opened the door and looked out. There wasn't a soul stirring in the courtyard of the motel. I left my door open and ran out to look up and down the main street. Almost a block away a very small boy in a sailor suit was just turning the corner, crying as if his heart would

115

break. By the time I got to the corner, he was no longer in sight."

Mrs. Pemberton was sitting up in bed, half turned towards me, her eyes pleading with me for some answering word.

"Oh," I said reluctantly, and then hunted for something to add to it. "Coincidence?" I offered.

"I don't believe it," Mrs. Pemberton said sadly. "Oh, I *want* to. You don't know how much I'd like to think that I'm reading dark significance into unimportant little happenings. A few weeks ago I started having nightmares . . . brought on, I know, by far too many of these so-called coincidences, far too frequently occurring, and far too shattering in their impact on me. I haven't dared to tell anybody, even Philip, all the things I've half-seen and half-heard."

"Do you feel . . . well . . . persecuted?" I asked.

"I did for a long time. I felt hunted, and I was angry, And at last I was afraid. Afraid to walk down a street, afraid to answer the telephone, even afraid to sleep after the nightmares began."

"What is it in the nightmare that frightens you so much you scream?"

Mrs. Pemberton glanced at me in surprise. "Why, it's the baby, of course. I find it, you see, on my doorstep, and it's so sweet, so warm and talcum-powdery, and I'm so delighted with it. Then, as I hold it and rearrange its clothing—such delicate, lovely clothing—the blanket falls away and reveals that hideous tattoo on the baby's arm. . . ."

We didn't talk much more that day. Luncheon trays arrived and were carried away—mine, at least, very much lightened. Flowers were delivered and exclaimed over. Visitors sidled through our doorway, rested uneasily on the two chairs, or stood first on one foot and then the other, and finally, in great relief, hurried away. When the long day brought us once again to that fairly quiet hour before dinner, I asked Mrs. Pemberton the question that had been troubling me.

"If you no longer feel resentful or persecuted, how *do* you feel?"

"I've been puzzling about that," she said. "You know, the nightmare has changed. That's why you've never heard me scream. It isn't a real nightmare anymore. It's just a dream about a gift. Something fragile and of great value, which somebody has brought to me after great exertions and dangers. I accept it, but with immense reservations. My fingers refuse to close around it. I drop it, and it breaks. But it doesn't shatter like glass. It just lies there and bleeds.

116

. . . All that's left with me when the dream ends—the residue, you might say, for the daylight hours—is just sadness. Weary sadness, that's all."

After breakfast the next morning a pretty nurse's aide brought in the wheelchair for Mrs. Pemberton's departure. While the girl waited and watched, smiling at us, Mrs. Pemberton told me goodbye.

"I don't really need this." Mrs. Pemberton gestured to the wheelchair. "But this hospital is sinisterly determined that no discharged patient walk out of here on his own two feet."

"More Snark hunting," I said. She patted my hand warmly and was wheeled away.

"I'll be back in a moment," the nurse's aide called to me from the doorway. "To get you up in a chair. And I hear you're to go home tomorrow, too."

When she returned I asked anxiously, "So you think Mrs. Pemberton will be all right?"

"Right as rain," the girl said. "She was only in here for some tests and observation. After all, she *is* a little old to be starting another baby."

"Oh . . . yes," I said.

"She's a little scared, I think. But, you'll see, she'll perk up more and more; by the time that baby arrives, she'll be convinced there's not another baby like hers anywhere in the world."

"Oh, dear Lord," I said. "I hope not."

Editors presenting their own stories should do so dif-
fidently, so I'll say only that STANLEY TOOTHBRUSH
is the story I most enjoyed writing, which convinces me
that there must be a fair amount of good fun in its
rather wacky depiction of some problems resulting
from a peculiar psi power.

STANLEY TOOTHBRUSH
Terry Carr

The trouble was, Herbert decided as he stared baggily
into the mirror, that Joanie just didn't understand about
mornings. It was very important in this workaday world to
understand mornings: each day of the week had a different
character, and you had to bear that in mind. Monday, of
course, was just awful—it was hopeless morning, when you
had five days of work stretching like parallel lines out to
eternity or infinity or Friday when they would at last meet.
Tuesday was a foggy morning, when the lines were blurred
and you didn't want to think about it. By Wednesday you
were caught up in the office environment and it seemed
somehow, unthinkingly, reasonable that you should spend
most of your life doing something you didn't want to do, but
Thursday was anxious morning, when it began to dawn on

118

you anew that salvation Friday was coming. And Friday morning was the worst; that was the day when you could no longer resist measuring your sentence in hours.

Today was Friday, and to make it worse Joanie had kept him up till two that morning. A movie, a few drinks afterward at her apartment, and then she'd insisted on just walking around for over an hour, talking. Herbert lathered up his face and painfully began to scratch off the night's accumulation of beard.

He was in a quandary. If he put his foot down and told Joanie right out that he had to get more sleep on weeknights she'd just get mad and refuse to see him at all, most likely. But if he continued to take her out every night, missing sleep and stumbling around the office the next day like a badly-engineered windup toy, it wouldn't be long before he was dismissed. Either way, he'd soon be on the shelf . . . shelved by Joanie, or shelved by Mr. Blackburn.

His brain seemed fuzzy, and he found himself thinking irrationally about how silly that expression was. "On the shelf" . . . a ridiculous metaphor. In the first place, the word "shelf" was ridiculous all by itself. He ran the word through his brainclouds, several times—*shelf, shelf, shelf*. It didn't make sense; it was just a random collection of sounds. Did human animals really go around all the time trying to communicate with such pointless sounds? *Shelf, shelf.*

There was a terrible crashing and banging all through his apartment, and Herbert nearly took off his left nostril with the razor.

He ran out of the bathroom to find out what had happened, heedless of the soapsuds dripping on his livingroom rug. The noise had come mostly from the kitchen, and he went there first. He found his dishes (the ones that had been washed and put away) all over the floor in pieces; cans of soup and chili and jars of instant coffee and salad dressing were scattered at his feet. The cupboard doors stood open, one of them still swinging on its hinges.

There was obviously no one else in the apartment, so it must have been an earthquake or something, he decided. He hadn't felt it, but then in his condition this morning that wasn't surprising. He stood staring at the mess and decided that he had a headache too.

Well, there was nothing to do but clear it up. He stooped and began loading cans in his arms, thinking about how much it would cost him to replace the broken dishes, and when he went to put the cans back in the cupboard he found that there were no shelves left.

119

They weren't anywhere on the floor either; they had disappeared. No shelves? But that was silly. He opened the refrigerator and a head of lettuce rolled out onto the floor and a can of beer fell on his foot. The shelves in the refrigerator had vanished too.

Herbert didn't like this at all. He put the cans of soup down, kicked some dishes into a corner, and checked the closets. The shelves were gone there too. The bookcase by the door had collapsed, emptying onto the floor two dozen mysteries, short story collections by Damon Runyon and Ring Lardner, and numerous books on sex in history, secret societies and the like. When he went back into the bathroom he found that the shelves in the medicine cabinet had gone too, and half his supply of hair tonic was dripping into the sink.

He stood and pondered for a minute. Now let's see . . . he had been shaving, and thinking about Joanie, and then he had decided that the word "shelf" was . . . unbelievable. And all the shelves had disappeared, just like that. It was a perfectly clear chain of circumstances.

He decided this was a hell of a way to start a Friday morning.

There wasn't much he could do right now; he was already late at the office. He hurriedly finished shaving, left his razor in the sink, put on a tie, and went to work.

When he entered the office Marcia frowned at him from behind the switchboard, so he knew Mr. Blackburn was mad. He hung up his coat (noticing that the shelves hadn't disappeared from the closets here) and hurried to his desk.

In a moment the phone rang. "Mr. Blackburn would like you to step into his office," Marcia said.

Herbert went in, carrying with him the list of Los Angeles newspapers he had contacted for the Paperap ads. He didn't suppose he could change the subject, but he might as well try.

"Here's the list you wanted," he said briskly. "I'm not sure about the advisability of this Pasadena thing, but—"

"I wanted that list yesterday," Mr. Blackburn said calmly. "Put it down there. Why were you late this morning?"

"I'm sorry, sir; I had a little trouble at home."

"What kind of trouble?"

All my shelves blinked out of existence, Herbert said in his mind, trying it on for size. No, that wouldn't do at all."

"I cut myself shaving. Couldn't stop the bleeding for almost an hour—must have hit a vein or something. A wonder
120

I didn't bleed to death, sir, ha ha, then I would have been *really* late getting in."

Mr. Blackburn stared coldly at him. "See that it doesn't happen again," he said. "We don't want our employees cutting their throats every morning. Now go away."

Herbert went away. He sat at his desk for ten minutes thinking that he would really have to be sure to come in on time for the next several days. No more nonsense like this morning. And then he sat back in his chair and wondered how one went about seeing that his shelves didn't disappear.

Well, it had happened because he'd decided that "shelf" was a nonsensical word. Presumably it could happen again, if he got to thinking about some other words. That newspaper list he'd given to Mr. Blackburn, for instance—what if that had disappeared? After all—*noos-pay-per-lisst*—was pretty silly too. But he'd better not think about that.

His phone rang. "Mr. Blackburn would like you to step into his office," Marcia said.

"Yes, I know," said Herbert, knowing. He went in.

"Where's that list you just gave me?" said Mr. Blackburn.

"I'll look for it again," he said, and walked slowly back to his desk. He sorted through various sheets of paper on his desktop and in his drawers and within half an hour was able to make up a duplicate, which he gave to Mr. Blackburn.

Then he sat at his desk and frowned. He didn't like this one bit. He'd read a little about wild talents, of course—people who could tell what cards were before they were turned over, people who could control the roll of dice, who could read minds or see into the future. They were usually erratic, undependable, and often useless—like the lady in Pennsylvania who could tell where every frog within ten miles was at any given time, or the man out in Idaho who could hear the radiation from stars. It was undoubtedly something to do with the unused 4/5 of the brain—at least, that was as close as Herbert could come to a rational explanation of it. Something probably caused it.

And now he could make things disappear, snuffed out of existence, just because he didn't believe in certain words. That seemed to him even more unscientific, even more silly—a random wild talent for performing nonsensicalities. He couldn't suppress the feeling that a person with a talent should be able to use it for something useful.

He stared at the blank wall across from him and repeated over and over again in his mind, *Mr. Blackburn, Mr. Blackburn, Mr. Blackburn, Mr. Blackburn . . .*

121

Then he picked up the phone. "Marcia, is Mr. Blackburn still in his office?"

"Yes; he's on another line," she said.

"Oh." Herbert put the phone back down. Maybe it wouldn't work with just last names. Knowing a person's True Name had been quite important in magic circles for centuries—if you knew someone's True Name, it had been believed, you had immense power over him.

Perhaps because you could, at will, make him disappear?

He picked up the phone again. "Marcia, what's Mr. Blackburn's full name? His first and middle names, I mean."

"His first name is Chester. Wait a minute, I have his middle name here somewhere. . . ." There was a rustling. "Yes, his middle name is Hartwick, H-a-r-t-w-i-c-k."

"Thank you," Herbert said, and hung up. Now that was all very fine—Chester Hartwick Blackburn would be an easy name not to believe in. In fact, Herbert wondered for a moment how Mr. Blackburn had got this far through life without having been snuffed out that way. But perhaps no one else had Herbert's talent.

Chester Hartwick Blackburn, Chester Hartwick Blackburn, Chester Hartwick Blackburn, said Herbert in his mind. What a silly combination of syllables. Of course they were thoroughly meaningless.

He picked up the phone. "Is Mr. Blackburn still on that other line, Marcia?"

"Yes, he is."

"Are you sure? Can you just plug in for a second and see if he's still talking?"

"Just a minute. . . ." There were a few clicks. "Yes, he's still talking. Do you want me to connect you with him when he's off again?"

"God, no," Herbert muttered, and hung up.

Well, all right then—he couldn't will people out of existence simply by disbelieving in their names. All that business about True Names had been about some mythical abstraction, anyway, not just the name someone's parents might give them. Who could know what Mr. Blackburn's True Name was?

He stared at the clutter of papers on his desk, focusing about two inches beyond them and seeing them only as a white blur, while he continued to toy with the whole idea. A lot of the formulas devised by medieval magicians for conjuring the devil and various demons had involved using their True Names. And those strange chants they used in their preparations could have simply been the names of

122

various things, maybe forces, which prevented the other-world beings from getting in—sort of like deciding that doors didn't exist instead of getting up to open one when there was a knock. Maybe those old magicians had sat there muttering "Abracadabra" over and over because an abracadabra was some sort of closed door between this world and another, and if they disbelieved in the word the door would cease to bar the way.

Herbert sat up at his desk and frowned. But of course all this speculation was not only silly, but useless as well. Just the sort of thing a person could get to thinking about on a Friday morning. He hunched over his desk and got busy at his day's work.

That evening when he got home he carefully cleared up the kitchen and the medicine cabinet and closets and book-cases, stacking cans and bottles and galoshes on the floor or on ledges. ("Ledges" was a good, sensible word, Herbert decided, and carefully refrained from thinking about it any more.) Then he called Joanie.

"I was thinking of going dancing tonight," he said. "Shall I pick you up around eight?"

There was a short silence on her end. "Oh, Herbie honey, I think you'd better rest tonight—you were up awfully late last night, and you know how you complain. I've invited someone over to watch TV."

Herbert frowned. "But it's Friday night—I don't have to go to work tomorrow."

"Well, just the same, I think you should get some sleep," she said. "You've been looking so tired."

"Joanie, what's come over you?"

She laughed, a soft laugh that he always found delightful. "Well, actually, I've got a new beau, Herbie, and he's taking me out tonight. His name is Stanley."

"Stanley what?" Herbert said in a low voice.

She giggled. "Oh, Herbie! Stanley Toothbrush, then, because he always carries a toothbrush with him in case he ever wants to go somewhere suddenly. He used to live in Chicago, but one time he went to the store to buy some Kleenex and decided to come to New York instead, and he did. He's like that, so I call him Stanley Toothbrush. It fits him so much better than his real name."

"Yes, it seems to," Herbert growled. "Well, I hope the two of you will be very happy."

"What?" she said. "Herbie? You didn't believe me, did you? I was only joking, honey, you know that."

123

"Were you," he said.

"Well *of course*. Oh, Herbie, don't be silly. Edna is coming over tonight and we're going to watch television and do our nails. Honestly!"

"But I wanted to go dancing," he said.

"Well, not tonight, because Edna's on her way here already. Anyway, you ought to be proud of me, because you've been saying for a long time that you need more rest nights, and now I've finally—"

"I guess so," he said, and they said goodbye.

He set about fixing dinner for himself, heating beans and franks. He turned on the burner and slammed the pan down on it and then stood with his hands on his hips, irritably waiting for the water to boil. He usually wasn't so impatient about cooking, but tonight he was in a bad mood. Not enough sleep recently, for one thing.

But Joanie's imaginary boyfriend was worrying him too. Maybe he wasn't so imaginary at that. And come to think of it, who was Edna? Joanie had never mentioned her before. This was all very suspicious.

Of course, he really needn't worry too much, he thought, as he dropped the cold franks into the water. This Stanley Toothbrush didn't sound like much competition—a fellow with so little stability that he'd take off and move a thousand miles to another city overnight couldn't have much to offer a girl. No security, no future . . . He probably didn't shave either.

But still, his bipartisan mind told him, Stanley Toothbrush might be a fascinating person . . . just the sort of wild funloving, carefree Casanova that a girl could ruin herself over. And, since he was so lax about responsibilities, he probably didn't have a regular job and was therefore free to take Joanie out every night. He could probably sweep her off her feet while Herbert was struggling to keep his job.

It was all very unfair. Herbert certainly hoped that Stanley Toothbrush really didn't exist, as Joanie had assured him. And in fact, maybe it would be a good idea to do something about that himself. If ever he'd heard a person's True Name, it was Stanley Toothbrush.

Stanley Toothbrush must go. It was a quite senseless name in the first place, easy to disbelieve. *Stanley Toothbrush, Stanley Toothbrush, Stanley Toothbrush* . . .

At the end of an hour Herbert had to stop repeating Stanley's name in his head. He had said it so often that it had almost begun to sound real.

124

The next afternoon Herbert went to Joanie's apartment in person. He rang the bell and the little peephole opened, and he saw Joanie's blue left eye, trimmed with long dark lashes, looking at him.

"It's me," he said.

"Oh! Herbie!" Joanie sounded upset. "Herbie, you'll have to go away . . . I mean, come back later. I'm not decent."

"At three o'clock in the afternoon?"

"Well, I was going to . . . take a shower. I'm completely *nude*, without a *stitch*."

"That's fine," he said.

"Herbert!"

"All right; I'll come back in half an hour." He went out and killed time looking at the magazines in a drug store. He saw an ad for some toothpaste, and that reminded him of Stanley Toothbrush, whom he didn't want to think about because he didn't exist anyway, if he had ever existed. If he had, Herbert had done away with him, he hoped.

When he went back to Joanie's apartment and rang she opened the peephole at him again. "Oh, Herbie, can you—"

"Let me in, Joanie," he said decisively.

"But I'm still not—"

"Your eye is quite thoroughly made up," he said, "and I know that you never do your eyes until you're dressed. Now open the door."

Joanie made a small sound and her left eyebrow came down to show part of what must have been a much bigger frown. "Well, all right."

She opened the door and Herbert walked in. Standing by the door to the kitchen was a young man who could have been no one but Stanley Toothbrush.

"I didn't want you to—I was trying to get rid of him," Joanie whispered quickly to him, and then said aloud, "Herbert, this is Stanley . . . Stanley Toothbrush; I don't know his real last name."

"How do you do," said Herbert evenly.

Stanley Toothbrush waved casually at him, leaning against the wall and displaying even white teeth in a full, friendly smile. He had dark sandy hair and rugged features, and he stood at least six feet tall, much more impressive than Herbert's own five feet nine. His face had a day's stubble.

"We were just going off for a boat ride around Manhattan," said Stanley. "You can come too; we wouldn't mind."

"No!" said Joanie, and then when Herbert turned to look at her she said, "I mean yes of course you can come, but I was trying to—"

"Fine! Let's all go!" said Stanley, and picked up his weathered brown jacket from where it had been lying over the back of a chair.

Joanie was standing in the middle of the room, looking from one to the other of them helplessly. "I wasn't going to go in the first place," she said.

"But it's all settled," Stanley said reasonably, and led the two of them out the door. Herbert followed seethingly, not saying a word.

They caught a cab and arrived at the dock where the excursion boat was tied up just in time for the next trip. Several times Joanie tried to say something to Herbert, but he sat in such stony silence and Stanley continued to chatter so unconcernedly that each time she gave up with a shrug and a little frustrated sound.

"Now don't do anything unnecessary like paying," said Stanley when they approached the ramp. "Leave it to me; I have connections."

"I thought you would," Herbert muttered.

Stanley walked up to the ticket-taker and slapped him on the shoulder. Herbert couldn't hear what he was saying, but Stanley was smiling and laughing and occasionally nodding over at him and Joanie. The ticket man grinned back at him and waved them all on.

As they took their seats by the boat's railing Stanley leaned over and said confidentially to Herbert, "Took a little finagling, but don't worry about it. Had to tell him that Joanie was with you and I was showing the two of you the sights. I gave him a lot of stuff about young lovebirds—it probably would've made you sick to hear it, but he liked it." Then Stanley turned back to Joanie, who had been maneuvered into sitting on his other side, and started telling her about how he had worked for a few days on the building of the very boat they were on.

Herbert didn't listen. He stared blackly into the water which lapped against the boatside, repeating in his head, *Stanley Toothbrush, Stanley Toothbrush.* The name was frighteningly believable.

He looked up when a woman in her fifties sat down next to him, fussing with her bag and struggling to get out of her heavy coat. Herbert helped her with that and she laid the coat across her ample lap, and then he began to stare into the water again. But she wouldn't let him.

She tapped him on the shoulder. "Do you see the terribly handsome man standing on the quay?" she said softly. "The one with the dog? Well, that's my husband."

126

"Who, the dog?" said Herbert, coming up out of the water. "Oh, no, I'm sorry. Yes, he's very handsome."

"We were just married last week," she said, "and we've come to the big city for our honeymoon. But he has to stay and wait for me because O'Shaughnessy has heart trouble. He's almost twenty years old."

"Good heavens!" said Herbert, staring at her husband.

"He's an Irish wolfhound, and he won't drink his water," she said.

"Oh, yes, of course," Herbert said, and just then the boat started backing out from the pier.

He turned back to Stanley and Joanie. Stanley was pointing up the Hudson saying, "There's a fine little park up there, looks out on the river and is all terraced in the center and wild around the edges. Squirrels and all. We ought to go up there tomorrow."

"Well, I don't—" said Joanie helplessly.

"It's just a quick ride on the subway," Stanley said. "You've still got all those tokens you bought last night, haven't you?"

"Well, yes."

"Then fine, and it won't cost a thing," said Stanley.

"I think I have to powder my nose," she said, and got up and went off to the concessions area of the boat. She looked at Herbert as she passed, and made a pleading face. Herbert got up and followed her.

She stopped just inside the door to the concessions-room. "Herbie honey, I've been trying to get a word in edgeways. Honestly, he just showed up last night, and I'd never seen him before. I can't get rid of him."

"You had a date with me last night," Herbert said. "You could have told him that."

"But I *didn't.* I mean, I'd already told you I was going to stay home, and then Edna said she couldn't come—"

"Well, why was he hanging around anyway, if you didn't encourage him? And what do you mean, he came after you'd told me you were staying home? You'd already made a date with him when I called."

"But I *hadn't,* that's what I'm trying to tell you! I'd never seen him before, and I just made him up to tease you, Herbie. And then there he was, at my door, and what could I do?"

Herbert stared at her. "You really made him up when you were talking to me?"

"Yes, honestly, Herbie."

127

"And then he showed up, and his name is Stanley Tooth-brush?"

"Yes, and he has a toothbrush in his right pants pocket." She waved her hands. "I couldn't get rid of him all night—he insisted and he insisted, and I didn't want to hurt him. He's very sensitive, Herbie, you'd be surprised."

"*All night?*" said Herbert.

"Well, he slept right outside my apartment, right there in the hall, and I couldn't just send him away."

Herbert shook his head. "This has ceased to be ridiculous," he muttered.

"What?"

"Joanie, this is crazy, but you remember what I told you about the powers of the mind? That book I was reading? Well, *I've got it now!*"

Two passengers who had been standing next to him edged away.

"I mean I've got some crazy kind of wild talent," Herbert said more softly. "Listen, yesterday morning I was shaving, and I started thinking, I don't know why, about what a ridiculous word 'shelf' is. You know, if you say a word over and over often enough it loses all its meaning. So I did that with 'shelf,' and all of a sudden all the shelves in my apartment disappeared!"

"Herbert!"

"No, Joanie, I'm serious. I can show you the apartment—they're all gone, and things are all over the floor. So anyway, last night when you told me about Stanley, I tried to make him disappear too—but I said his name over and over so much that it began to make *sense*. And that must have been what happened, that's where he came from."

Joanie frowned and pursed her lips. "Herbie, if you're joking—"

"Now why would I joke about Stanley Toothbrush?" Herbert said. "He's no laughing matter!"

"Then show me," she said.

"What? Show you?"

"Make something disappear." She tapped her foot.

"Well . . . I mean, it's a wild talent, and it may not work just like turning it on and off."

"Herbert."

"All right, I'll try." He looked around the concession area, and spotted a man with a red moustache and a derby. He looked ridiculous, but Herbert couldn't decide whether it was the fault of the hat or the moustache. Well, either one would do.

128

"What do you think of that man over there?" he said to Joanie, and in his mind he said Moustache, *moustache.*

"That man?" she said.

"Yes." *Mus-tash*, he thought. *Muss-tash.*

"Oh!" Joanie put her fingers to her mouth in surprise.

The man muttered to his wife, "Demmed dreft in here." She stared at him and shuddered, and pointed, and he wrinkled his mouth and frowned and gasped and ran to the men's room.

Herbert smiled. "You see? And that's where Stanley Toothbrush came from."

"But what are we going to do?" she said.

"I don't know." Herbert's grin vanished. "Every time I try to make him disappear he just gets more real."

"Well, we've got to do something," Joanie said.

Stanley Toothbrush walked up behind them just then and said heartily, "How about something to eat? They have hotdogs here, and hamburgers, anything you want."

"I'm not hungry," Herbert said shortly, and went back to his seat by the rail. Stanley steered Joanie to the concessions stand and she bought two hotdogs.

The woman whose Irish wolfhound had heart trouble said to Herbert, "Have you noticed how wonderfully wet the river is today? The water just goes down and down, fathom after fathom or whatever they are."

"I'm afraid so," Herbert said abstractedly. "I hope your dog gets well soon."

"Oh, he won't," the woman said lightly. "He'll die in a week or so—married life is so hard on him. I'm afraid Arnold and I shock him with our behavior."

"Well, it's terrible when a dog's nerves start acting up," said Herbert, and then he grimaced and wondered why he let himself be drawn into such conversations. He leaned over the rail and stared into the water again.

"It's very wet, very wet," said the woman, "and I suppose there are fish in it."

"It's conceivable," said Herbert, and had a vision of a huge beast of a shark arcing out of the water and snapping Stanley Toothbrush from the boat, glom just like that.

"Oh dear!" said the woman suddenly, and Herbert looked up to see her pointing frantically down at the river. "I dropped my bag! Oh, my heavens! It's in the water! Back there!"

"Back where?" said Herbert. "It's probably sunk already."

He heard running footsteps, and suddenly Stanley was beside them, taking off his shoes. "You lost your purse, lady?"

"Yes, it's back there!"

129

"Hold my hotdog," Stanley said, and thrust it into the woman's hand and dived overboard. It wasn't a very good dive; he went end-over-end and hit the water feet-first, but he came up sputtering and swam strongly back to the area where the purse had been dropped. A crowd was gathering around Herbert and the woman.

"It's probably sunk to the bottom," Herbert said.

"Well, it was one of those new materials, plastic or something," said the woman, beaming happily at all the attention. "I think it was watertight. It may float."

"Did Stanley go in the water?" Joanie asked, coming up behind them.

"Yes—he's a good swimmer," Herbert said. "I always knew he would be."

The boat blew a whistle and swung around to pick up Stanley, while the loudspeaker told everyone to remain calm and stay in their seats. Stanley had almost reached the purse.

"How gallant of him!" said Joanie. "Herbie, you must admit that was a sweet thing for him to do."

Herbert looked slightly disgusted and shrugged. "It's a Stanley Toothbrush thing to do," he said. "If you're so impressed with him, just remember that I made him up."

"Well, you needn't be short with me," Joanie said. "And anyway, I'll bet Stanley is just some sort of wish-fulfillment of yours—he acts the way you secretly wish you could." She wrinkled her nose at him. "There, you see I read a book or two every now and then myself."

"I don't want to talk about it," said Herbert.

By the time the boat had returned to where Stanley was, he had come up with the purse dripping in his hand. The ship's crew lowered a ladder over the side and gave him a hand up, and Stanley immediately squished in wet stocking feet over to the Irish wolfhound woman and delivered her purse with a sloshy bow. Then he took his hotdog back from her.

"It was just wonderful of you to swim after it," the woman said to him. "You went over the side like a real-life Sir Walter Raleigh!"

Stanley gave a crooked grin and shrugged. "It wasn't much of a dive," he said around the hotdog.

"Wasn't he wonderful, my dear?" said the woman, to Joanie.

"Yes, I thought it was very gallant, that's the only word I can think of," she said.

"If only Arnold could have seen you!" said the woman.

"Arnold is her husband," Herbert explained, and added

130

under his breath, "Fortunately, he doesn't have heart trouble, like some dogs I know."

The woman was still beaming delightedly at Stanley, holding her dripping purse. Joanie was fluttering around him, trying to get his shirt off so it would dry, and Herbert felt quite disgusted. He shook his head and walked off around to the other side of the boat.

The rest of the excursion was thoroughly ruined for him. He sat apart from Stanley and Joanie, and when at one point she came over to him he was irritable and they had words. By the time the boat docked back at its point of departure over an hour later he was in a vile mood.

Stanley's clothes had dried a bit by then, and he had squeezed back into his shoes. "Well, what shall we do now?" he said lightly as they stepped off the boat.

"I think we should go to Herbert's apartment," said Joanie. "You could hang your clothes over the radiator, and we could all have a few drinks."

"While he sits there without any clothes on?" cried Herbert.

"Oh don't be silly; you can lend him some dry clothes to wear," she said, and took his arm to lead him off toward a waiting cab.

They did go to Herbert's apartment, and when they came in the door Herbert remembered that he had meant to buy some new shelves today. Books and cans were still tumbled on the floor, and it looked pretty bad.

Stanley looked around the place and said lightly, "Well, bachelor's apartment, eh? You should get a woman to take care of you, Herbie." Herbert glared at him.

Joanie glanced around briefly and then went to the kitchen, where Herbert always kept a bottle on the drainboard. "I'll mix some drinks," she said, "while you go in the bedroom and get out of those clothes, Stanley."

Stanley grinned and followed Herbert while he found some clean underwear, pants and shirt for him. He picked the oldest and most faded clothes he had. "Hang the clothes in the shower," he said, and went into the kitchen.

Joanie was cross. "You needn't be a bad sport about it," she said. "He does have some good qualities, as you can see."

"His ribs stick out." Herbert said.

"Oh, honestly, Herbie! Your whole attitude toward him is incredible. First you try to tell me that you . . . made him up, or *created* him or something, then you—"

"But I did!" said Herbert. "Or at least you did, and then

131

I brought him into existence by accident. He doesn't even belong here."

"Well, if you brought him into existence or whatever, then it's your own fault and it serves you right," she said. "Anyway, I don't believe that story about you and your whatever-it-is."

"It's a wild talent," said Herbert. "I told you."

"Well, you and your wild talons can just—"

"Wild talent, wild talent!" he said.

"What?"

"*Wild talent!* Good God, can't you—"

"Wild talent, wild talent," she said. "That's a silly name for it, don't you think? Herbie, why don't you go in the bedroom and see if Stanley is still there?"

"Of course he's still there, unless he suddenly went to Chicago," said Herbert.

"I doubt it," Joanie said, grinning. "For one thing, your shelves are back." She waved a hand at the cupboard.

"Well I'll be damned," Herbert said.

"Not necessarily. But do go see if Stanley is gone, please."

Herbert went. The bedroom was empty, the clothes he had given Stanley were lying on the floor, and though the showerstall showed where his wet clothes had dripped, Stanley Toothbrush wasn't there either.

Herbert went into the kitchen and kissed the back of Joanie's neck. "You're a genius," he said.

"Yes, and what's more I only mixed two drinks," she said. "Now tell me what we're going to do tonight."

Monday morning Herbert stared blearily into the mirror and decided that "morning" was the most ridiculous and idiotic word he had ever heard. But of course it did him no good.

Tom Disch is one of the most literarily ambitious writers in the sf field; he is constantly experimenting with form, style and content in his stories, often with fascinating results. The following Kafkaesque narrative, for instance: It might be the story of the last man on Earth, sitting alone in a room. Or it might be about what goes on *inside* one man, every man. Or, of course, both.

Thomas M. Disch
THE SQUIRREL CAGE

The terrifying thing—if that's what I mean—I'm not sure that "terrifying" is the right word—is that I'm free to write down anything I like but that no matter what I *do* write down it will make no difference—to me, to you, to whomever differences are made. But then what is meant by "a difference?" Is there ever really such a thing as change?

I ask more questions these days than formerly; I am less programmatic altogether. I wonder—is that a good thing?

This is what it is like where I am: a chair with no back to it (so I suppose you would call it a stool); a floor, walls, and a ceiling, which form, as nearly as I can judge, a cube; white, white light, no shadows—not even on the underside of the lid of the stool; me, of course; the typewriter. I have described the typewriter at length elsewhere. Perhaps I shall describe it again. Yes, almost certainly I shall. But not now. Later. Though why not now? Why not the typewriter as well as anything else?

Of the many kinds of questions at my disposal, "why" seems to be the most recurrent. Why is that?

What I do is this: I stand up and walk around the room from wall to wall. It is not a large room, but it's large enough for present purposes. Sometimes I even jump, but there is little incentive to do that, since there is nothing to jump *for*. The ceiling is quite too high to touch, and the stool is so low that it provides no challenge at all. If I thought anyone were *entertained* by my jumping . . . but I have no reason to suppose that. Sometimes I exercise: push-ups, somersaults, head-stands, isometrics, etc. But never as much as I should. I am getting fat. Disgustingly fat and full of pimples besides. I like to squeeze the pimples on my face. Every so often I will keep one sore and open with overmuch pinching, in the hope that I will develop an abscess and blood-poisoning. But apparently the place is germ-proof. The thing never infects.

It's well nigh impossible to kill oneself here. The walls and floor are padded, and one only gets a headache beating one's head against them. The stool and typewriter both have hard edges, but whenever I have tried to use *them,* they're withdrawn into the floor. That is how I know there is someone watching.

Once I was convinced it was God. I assumed that this was either Heaven or Hell, and I imagined that it would go on for all eternity just the same way. But if I were living in eternity already, I couldn't get fatter all the time. Nothing changes in eternity. So I console myself that I will someday die. Man is mortal. I eat all I can to make that day come faster. *The Times* says that that will give me heart disease.

Eating is fun, and that's the real reason I do a lot of eating. What else is there to do, after all? There is this little . . . nozzle, I suppose you'd call it, that sticks out of one wall, and all I have to do is put my mouth to it. Not the most elegant way to feed, but it tastes damn good. Sometimes I just stand there hours at a time and let it trickle in. Until *I have* to trickle. That's what the stool is for. It has a lid on it, the stool does, which moves on a hinge. It's quite clever, in a mechanical way.

134

If I sleep, I don't seem to be aware of it. Sometimes I do catch myself dreaming, but I can never remember what they were about. I'm not able to make myself dream at will. I would like that exceedingly. That covers all the vital functions but one—and there is an accommodation for sex too. Everything has been thought of.

I have no memory of any time before this, and I cannot say how long *this* has been going on. According to today's *New York Times* it is the Second of May, 1961. I don't know what conclusion one is to draw from that.

From what I've been able to gather, reading *The Times*, my position here in this room is not typical. Prisons, for instance, seem to be run along more liberal lines, usually. But perhaps *The Times* is lying, covering up. Perhaps even the date has been falsified. Perhaps the entire paper, every day, is an elaborate forgery and this is actually 1950, not 1961. Or maybe they are antiques and I am living whole centuries after they were printed, a fossil. Anything seems possible. I have no way to judge.

Sometimes I make up little stories while I sit here on my stool in front of the typewriter. Sometimes they are stories about the people in *The New York Times*, and those are the best stories. Sometimes they are just about people I make up, but those aren't so good because . . .

They're not so good because I think everybody is dead. I think I may be the only one left, sole survivor of the breed. And they just keep me here, the last one, alive, in this room, this cage, to look at, to observe, to make their observations of, to— I don't *know* why they keep me alive. And if everyone is dead, as I've supposed, then who are they, these supposed observers? Aliens? *Are* there aliens? I don't know. Why are they studying me? What do they hope to learn? Is it an experiment? What am I supposed to do? Are they waiting for me to say something, to write something on this typewriter? Do my responses or lack of responses confirm or destroy a theory of behavior? Are the testers happy with their results? They give no indications. They efface themselves, veiling themselves behind these walls this ceiling, this floor. Perhaps no human could stand the sight of them. But maybe they are only scientists, and not aliens at all. Psychologists at M.I.T. perhaps, such as frequently are shown in *The Times*: blurred, dotty faces, bald heads, occasionally a moustache, certificate of originality. Or, instead, young, crew-cut Army doctors studying various brainwashing techniques. Reluctantly, of course. History and a concern for freedom has forced them to violate their own

135

(privately-held), moral codes. Maybe I *volunteered* for this experiment! Is that the case? O God, I hope not! Are you reading this, Professor? Are you reading this, Major? Will you let me out now? I want to leave this experiment *right now*.

Yeah.

Well, we've been through that little song and dance before, me and my typewriter. We've tried just about every password there is. Haven't we, typewriter? And as you can see (can you see?)—here we are still.

They are aliens, obviously.

Sometimes I write poems. Do you like poetry? Here's one of the poems I wrote. It's called *Grand Central Terminal*. ("Grand Central Terminal" is the right name for what most people, wrongly, call "Grand Central Station." This —and other priceless information—comes from *The New York Times*.)

> *Grand Central Terminal*
> How can you be unhappy
> when you see how high
> the ceiling is?
>
>   My!
> the ceiling is high!
> High as the sky!
> So who are *we*
> to be gloomy here?
>
>   Why,
> there isn't even room
> to die, my dear.
>
> This is the tomb
> of some giant so great
> that if he ate
> us there would be
> simply no taste.
>
>   Gee,
> what a waste
> that would be
> of you and me.

And sometimes, as you can also see, I just sit here copying old poems over again, or maybe copying the poem that *The Times* prints each day. *The Times* is my only source of poetry. Alas the day! I wrote *Grand Central Terminal* rather a long time ago. Years. I can't say exactly how many years, though.

I have no measures of time here. No day, no night, no waking and sleeping, no chronometer but *The Times,* ticking off its dates. I can remember dates as far back as 1957. I wish I had a little diary that I could keep here in the room with me. Some record of my progress. If I could just save up my old copies of *The Times.* Imagine how, over the years, they would pile up. Towers and stairways and cosy burrows of newsprint. It would be a more humane architecture, would it not? This cube that I occupy does have drawbacks from the strictly human point of view. But I am not allowed to keep yesterday's edition. It is always taken away, whisked off, before today's edition is delivered. I should be thankful, I suppose, for what I have.

What if *The Times* went bankrupt? What if, as is often threatened, there were a newspaper strike! Boredom is not, as you might suppose, the great problem. Eventually—very soon, in fact—boredom becomes a great challenge. A stimulus.

My body. Would you be interested in my body? I used to be. I used to regret that there were no mirrors in here. Now, on the contrary, I am grateful. How gracefully, in those early days, the flesh would wrap itself about the skeleton; now, how it droops and languishes! I used to dance by myself hours on end, humming my own accompaniment—leaping, rolling about, hurling myself spread-eagled against the padded walls. I became a connoisseur of kinesthesia. There is great joy in movement—free, unconstrained speed.

Life is so much tamer now. Age dulls the edge of pleasure, hanging its wreaths of fat on the supple Christmas tree of youth.

I have various theories about the meaning of life. Of life *here.* If I were somewhere else—in the world I know of from *The New York Times,* for instance, where so many exciting things happen every *day* that it takes half a million words to tell about them—there would be no problem at all. One would be so busy running around—from 53rd St. to 42nd St., from 42nd St. to the Fulton Street Fish Market, not to mention all the journeys one might make *crosstown*—that one wouldn't have to worry whether life had a meaning.

In the daytime one could shop for a multitude of goods,

then in the evening, after a dinner at a fine restaurant, to the theatre or a cinema. Oh, life would be so full if I were living in New York! If I were free! I spend a lot of time, like this, imagining what New York must be like, imagining what other people are like, what I would be like with other people, and in a sense my life here is full from imagining such things.

One of my theories is that they (*you* know, ungentle reader, who they are, I'm sure) are waiting for me to make a confession. This poses problems. Since I remember nothing of my previous existence, I don't know what I should confess. I've tried confessing to everything: political crimes, sex crimes (I especially like to confess to sex crimes), traffic offenses, spiritual pride. My God, what *haven't* I confessed to? Nothing seems to work. Perhaps I just haven't confessed to the crimes I really did commit, whatever they were. Or perhaps (which seems more and more likely), the theory is at fault.

I have another theory th

A brief hiatus.

The Times came, so I read the day's news, then nourished myself at the fount of life, and now I am back at my stool.

I have been wondering whether, if I were living in that world, the world of *The Times*, I would be a pacifist or not. It is certainly the central issue of modern morality, and one would have to take a stand. I have been thinking about the problem for some years, and I am inclined to believe that I am in favor of disarmament. On the other hand, in a practical sense I wouldn't object to the bomb if I could be sure it would be dropped on me. There is definitely a schism in my being between the private sphere and the public sphere.

On one of the inner pages, behind the political and international news, was a wonderful story headlined: BIOLOGISTS HAIL MAJOR DISCOVERY. Let me copy it for your benefit:

Washington D.C.—Deep-sea creatures with brains but no mouths are being hailed as a major biological discovery of the twentieth century.

The weird animals, known as pogonophores, resemble slender worms. Unlike ordinary worms, however, they have no digestive system, no excretory organs, and no means of breathing, the National Geographic Society says. Baffled scientists who first examined pogonophores believed that only parts of the specimens had reached them.

Biologists are now confident that they have seen the whole animal, but still do not understand how it manages to live. Yet they know it does exist, propagate, and even think, after a fashion, on the floors of deep waters around the globe. The female pogonophore lays up to thirty eggs at a time. A tiny brain permits rudimentary mental processes.

All told, the pogonophore is so unusual that biologists have set up a special phylum for it alone. This is significant because a phylum is such a broad biological classification that creatures as diverse as fish, reptiles, birds, and men are all included in the phylum Chordata.

Settling on the sea bottom, a pogonophore secretes a tube around itself and builds it up, year by year, to a height of perhaps five feet. The tube resembles a leaf of white grass, which may account for the fact that the animal went so long undiscovered.

The pogonophore apparently never leaves its self-built prison, but crawls up and down inside at will. The wormlike animal may reach a length of fourteen inches, with a diameter of less than a twenty-fifth of an inch. Long tentacles wave from its top end.

Zoologists once theorized that the pogonophore, in an early stage, might store enough food in its body to allow it to fast later on. But young pogonophores also lack a digestive system.

It's amazing the amount of things a person can learn just by reading *The Times* every day. I always feel so much more *alert* after a good read at the paper. And creative. Herewith, a story about pogonophores:

STRIVING
The Memoirs of a Pogonophore

Introduction

In May of 1961 I had been considering the purchase of a pet. One of my friends had recently acquired a pair of tarsiers, another had adopted a boa constrictor, and my nocturnal roommate kept an owl caged above his desk.

A nest (or school?) of pogs was certainly one-up on their eccentricities. Moreover, since pogonophores do not eat, excrete, sleep, or make noise, they would be ideal pets. In

139

June I had three dozen shipped to me from Japan at considerable expense.

A brief interruption in the story: Do you feel that it's credible? Does it possess the *texture* of reality? I thought that by beginning the story by mentioning those other pets, I would clothe my invention in greater verisimilitude. Were you taken in?

Being but an indifferent biologist, I had not considered the problem of maintaining adequate pressure in my aquarium. The pogonophore is used to the weight of an entire ocean. I was not equipped to meet such demands. For a few exciting days I watched the surviving pogs rise and descend in their translucent white shells. Soon, even these died. Now, resigned to the commonplace, I stock my aquarium with Maine lobsters for the amusement and dinners of occasional out-of-town visitors.

I have never regretted the money I spent on them: man is rarely given to know the sublime spectacle of the rising pogonophore—and then but briefly. Although I had at that time only the narrowest conception of the thoughts that passed through the rudimentary brain of the sea-worm ("Up up up Down down down"), I could not help admiring its persistence. The pogonophore does not sleep. He climbs to the top of the inside passage of his shell, and, when he reaches the top, he retraces his steps to the bottom of his shell. The pogonophore never tires of his self-imposed regimen. He performs his duty scrupulously and with honest joy. He is *not* a fatalist.

The memoirs that follow this introduction are not allegory. I have not tried to "interpret" the inner thoughts of the pogonophore. There is no need for that, since the pogonophore himself has given us the most eloquent record of his spiritual life. It is transcribed on the core of translucent white shell in which he spends his entire life.

Since the invention of the alphabet it has been a common conceit that the markings on shells or the sand-etched calligraphy of the journeying snail are possessed of true linguistic meaning. Cranks and eccentrics down the ages have tried to decipher these codes, just as other men have sought to understand the language of the birds. Unavailingly, I do not claim that the scrawls and shells of *common* shellfish can be translated; the core of the pogonophore's shell, however, can be—for I have broken the code!

With the aid of a United States Army manual on cryptography (obtained by what devious means I am not at liberty to reveal), I have learned the grammar and syntax of the pogonophore's secret language. Zoologists and others who would like to verify my solution of the crypt may reach me through the editor of this publication.

In all thirty-six cases I have been able to examine, the indented traceries on the insides of these shells have been the same. It is my theory that the sole purpose of the pogonophore's tentacles is to follow the course of this "message" up and down the core of his shell and thus, as it were, to think. The shell is a sort of externalized stream-of-consciousness.

It would be possible (and in fact it is an almost irresistible temptation), to comment on the meaning that these memoirs possess for mankind. Surely, there is a philosophy compressed into these precious shells by Nature hcrelf. But before I begin my commentary, let us examine the text itself.

The Text

I

Up. Uppity, up, up. The Top.

II

Down. Downy, down, down. Thump. The Bottom.

III

A description of my typewriter. The keyboard is about one foot wide. Each key is flush to the next and marked with a single letter of the alphabet, or with two punctuation signs, or with one number and one punctuation sign. The letters are not ordered as they are in the alphabet, alphabetically, but seemingly at random. It is possible that they are in code. Then there is a space bar. There is not, however either a margin control or a carriage return. The platen is not visible, and I can never see the words I'm writing. What does it all look like? Perhaps it is made immediately into a book by automatic linotypists. Wouldn't that be nice? Or perhaps my words just go on and on in one endless line of writing. Or perhaps this typewriter is just a fraud and leaves no record at all.

Some thoughts on the subject of futility:

I might just as well be lifting weights as pounding at these keys. Or rolling stones up to the top of a hill from which they immediately roll back down. Yes, and I might as well tell lies as the truth. It makes no difference what I say.

That is what is so terrifying. Is "terrifying" the right word?

I seem to be feeling rather poorly today, but I've felt poorly before! In a few more days I'll be feeling all right again. I need only be patient, and then . . .

What do they want of me here? If only I could be sure that I were serving some good *purpose*. I cannot help worrying about such things. Time is running out. I'm hungry again. I suspect I am going crazy. That is the end of my story about the pogonophores.

A hiatus.

Don't *you* worry that I'm going crazy? What if I got catatonia? Then *you'd* have nothing to read. Unless they gave *you* my copies of *The New York Times*. It would serve *you* right.

You: the mirror that is denied to me, the shadow that I do not cast, my faithful observer, who reads each freshly-minted *pensée*; Reader.

You: Horrorshow monster, Bug-Eyes, Mad Scientist. Army Major, who prepares the wedding bed of my death and tempts me to it.

You: Other!

Speak to me!

YOU: What shall I say, Earthling?

I: Anything so long as it is another voice than my own, flesh that is not my own flesh, lies that I do not need to invent for myself. I'm not particular, I'm not proud. But I doubt sometimes—you won't think this is too melodramatic of me?—that I'm real.

YOU: I know the feeling. (Extending a tentacle) May I?

I: (Backing off) Later. Just now I thought we'd talk. (You begin to fade.)

There is so much about you that I don't understand. Your identity is not distinct. You change from one being to another as easily as I might switch channels on a television set, if I had one. You are too secretive as well. You should get about in the world more. Go places, show yourself, enjoy life. If you're shy, I'll go out with you. You let yourself be undermined by fear, however.

YOU: Interesting. Yes, definitely most interesting. The

142

subject evidences acute paranoid tendencies, fantasizes with almost delusional intensity. Observe his tongue, his pulse, his urine. His stools are irregular. His teeth are bad. He is losing hair.

I: I'm losing my mind.

YOU: He's losing his mind.

I: I'm dying.

YOU: He's dead.
(Fades until there is nothing but the golden glow of the eagle on his cap, a glint from the oak leaves on his shoulders.) But he has not died in vain. His country will always remember him, for by his death he has made this nation free.
(Curtain. Anthem.)

Hi. It's me again. Surely you haven't forgotten *me?* Your old friend, me? Listen carefully now—this is my plan. I'm going to escape from this damned prison, by God, and *you're* going to help me. 20 people may read what I write on this typewriter, and of those 20, 19 could see me rot here forever without batting an eyelash. But not number 20. Oh no! He—*you*—still has a conscience. He/you will send me a Sign. And when I've seen the Sign, I'll know that someone out there is trying to help. Oh, I won't expect miracles overnight. It may take months, years even, to work out a foolproof escape, but just the knowledge that there is someone out there trying to help will give me the strength to go on from day to day, from issue to issue of *The Times*.

You know what I sometimes wonder? I sometimes wonder why *The Times* doesn't have an editorial about me. They state their opinion on everything else—Castro's Cuba, the shame of our Southern States, the Sales Tax, the first days of Spring.

What about me!

I mean, isn't it an injustice the way *I'm* being treated? Doesn't anybody care, and if not, why not? Don't tell me they don't know I'm here. I've been years now writing, writing. Surely they have some idea. Surely *someone* does!

These are serious questions. They demand serious appraisal. I insist that they be *answered*.

I don't really expect an answer, you know. I have no false hopes left, none. I know there's no Sign that will be shown me, that even if there is, it will be a lie, a lure to go on hoping. I know that I am alone in my fight against this injustice. I know all that—and *I don't care!* My will is still unbroken, and my spirit free. From my isolation, out of the stillness, from the depths of this white, white light, I say this to you—I DEFY YOU! Do you hear that? I said: I DEFY YOU!

Dinner again. Where does the time all go to?

While I was eating dinner I had an idea for something I was going to say here, but I seem to have forgotten what it was. If I remember, I'll jot it down. Meanwhile, I'll tell you about my other theory.

My *other* theory is that this is a squirrel-cage. You know? Like the kind you find in a small town park. You might even have one of your own, since they don't have to be very big. A squirrel-cage is like most any other kind of cage except it has an exercise wheel. The squirrel gets *into* the wheel and starts running. His running makes the wheel turn, and the turning of the wheel makes it necessary for him to keep running inside it. The exercise is supposed to keep the squirrel healthy. What I don't understand is why they put the squirrel in the cage in the first place. Don't they know what it's going to be like for the poor little squirrel? Or don't they care?

They don't care.

I remember now what it was I'd forgotten. I thought of a new story. I call it "An Afternoon at the Zoo." I made it up myself. It's very short, and it has a moral. This is my story:

AN AFTERNOON AT THE ZOO

This is the story about Alexandra. Alexandra was the wife of a famous journalist, who specialized in science reporting. His work took him to all parts of the country, and since they had not been blessed with children, Alexandra often accompanied him. However, this often became very boring, so she had to find something to do to pass the time. If she had seen all the movies playing in the town they were in, she might go to a museum, or perhaps to a ball game, if she was interested in seeing a ball game that day. One day she went to a zoo.

Of course it was a small zoo, because this was a small town. Tasteful but not spectacular. There was a brook that meandered all about the grounds. Ducks and a lone black swan glided among the willow branches and waddled out

144

onto the lake to snap up bread crumbs from the visitors. Alexandra thought the swan was beautiful.

Then she went to a wooden building called the "Rodentiary." The cages advertised rabbits, otters, raccoons, etc. Inside the cages was a litter of nibbled vegetables and droppings of various shapes and colors. The animals must have been behind the wooden partitions, sleeping. Alexandra found this disappointing, but she told herself that rodents were hardly the most important thing to see at any zoo.

Nearby the Rodentiary, a black bear was sunning himself on a rock ledge. Alexandra walked all about the demi-lune of bars without seeing other members of the bear's family. He was an enormous bear.

She watched the seals splash about in their concrete pool, and then she moved on to find the Monkey House. She asked a friendly peanut vendor where it was, and he told her it was closed for repairs.

"How sad!" Alexandra exclaimed.

"Why don't you try *Snakes and Lizards?*" the peanut vendor asked.

Alexandra wrinkled her nose in disgust. She'd hated reptiles ever since she was a little girl. Even though the Monkey House was closed she bought a bag of peanuts and ate them herself. The peanuts made her thirsty, so she bought a soft drink and sipped it through a straw, worrying about her weight all the while.

She watched peacocks and a nervous antelope, then turned off onto a path that took her into a glade of trees. Poplar trees, perhaps. She was alone there, so she took off her shoes and wiggled her toes, or performed some equivalent action. She liked to be alone like this, sometimes.

A file of heavy iron bars beyond the glade of trees drew Alexandra's attention. Inside the bars there was a man, dressed in a loose-fitting cotton suit—pajamas, most likely—held up about the waist with a short rope. He sat on the floor of his cage without looking at anything in particular. The sign at the base of the fence read:

Chordate.

"How lovely!" Alexandra exclaimed.

Actually, that's a very old story. I tell it a different way every time. Sometimes it goes on from the point where I left off. Sometimes Alexandra talks to the man behind the bars. Sometimes they fall in love, and she tries to help him escape. Sometimes they're both killed in the attempt, and that is *very* touching. Sometimes they get caught and are

145

put behind the bars *together*. But because they love each other so much, imprisonment is easy to endure. That is also touching, in its way. Sometimes they make it to freedom. After that, though, after they're free, I never know what to do with the story. However, I'm sure that if I were free myself, free of this cage, it would not be a problem.

One part of the story doesn't make much sense. Who would put a person in a zoo? Me, for instance. Who would do such a thing? Aliens? Are we back to aliens again? Who can say about aliens? I mean, *I* don't know anything about them.

My theory, my best theory, is that I'm being kept here by people. Just ordinary people. It's an ordinary zoo, and ordinary people come by to look at me through the walls. They read the things I type on this typewriter as it appears on a great illuminated billboard, like the one that spells out the news headlines around the sides of The Times Tower on 42nd Street. When I write something funny, they may laugh, and when I write something serious, such as an appeal for help, they probably get bored and stop reading. Or vice versa perhaps. In any case, they don't take what I say very seriously. None of them care that I'm inside here. To them I'm just another animal in a cage. You might object that a human being is not the same thing as an animal, but isn't he, after all? They, the spectators, seem to think so. In any case, none of them is going to help me get out. None of them thinks it's at all strange or unusual that I'm in here. None of them think it's wrong. That's the terrifying thing.

"Terrifying?"

It's not terrifying. How can it be? It's only a story, after all. Maybe *you* don't think it's a story, because you're out there reading it on the billboard, but I know it's a story because I have to sit here on this stool making it up. Oh it might have been terrifying once upon a time, when I first got the idea, but I've been here now for years. Years. The story has gone on far too long. Nothing can be terrifying for years on end. I only *say* it's terrifying because, you know, I have to say something. Something or other. The only thing that could terrify me now is if someone were to come in. If they came in and said, "All right, Disch, you can go now." That, truly, would be terrifying.

Like Jorge Luis Borges, Peter S. Beagle is an excellent fantasy writer who is largely unknown among readers of the genre. His first novel, A FINE AND PRIVATE PLACE, was pure fantasy, as is his second, an as-yet-untitled book to appear next year. He is also known as a prominent Tolkien enthusiast; and far from least among his fantasy credits is the following fable of death, beauty, love, bravery . . . and other qualities, good and bad.

Peter S. Beagle
COME LADY DEATH

This all happened in England a long time ago, when that George who spoke English with a heavy German accent and hated his sons was King. At that time there lived in London a lady who had nothing to do but give parties. Her name was Flora, Lady Neville, and she was a widow and very old. She lived in a great house not far from Buckingham Palace, and she had so many servants that she could not possibly remember all their names; indeed, there were some she had never even seen. She had more food that she could eat, more gowns than she could ever wear; she had wine in her cellars that no one would drink in her lifetime, and her private vaults were filled with great works of art that she did not know she owned. She spent the last years of her life giving parties and balls to which the greatest lords of England—and sometimes the King himself—came, and she was known as the wisest and wittiest woman in all London.

But in time her own parties began to bore her, and though she invited the most famous people in the land and hired the greatest jugglers and acrobats and dancers and magicians to entertain them, still she found her parties duller and duller. Listening to court gossip, which she had always loved, made her yawn. The most marvelous music, the most exciting feats of magic put her to sleep. Watching a beautiful young couple dance by her made her feel sad, and she hated to feel sad.

And so, one summer afternoon she called her closest friends around her and said to them, "More and more I find that my parties entertain everyone but me. The secret of my long life is that nothing has ever been dull for me. For all my life, I have been interested in everything I saw and been anxious to see more. But I cannot stand to be bored, and I will not go to parties at which I expect to be bored, especially if they are my own. Therefore, to my next ball I shall invite the one guest I am sure no one, not even myself, could possibly find boring. My friends, the guest of honor at my next party shall be Death himself!"

A young poet thought that this was a wonderful idea, but the rest of her friends were terrified and drew back from her. They did not want to die, they pleaded with her. Death would come for them when he was ready; why should she invite him before the appointed hour, which would arrive soon enough? But Lady Neville said, "Precisely. If Death has planned to take any of us on the night of my party, he will come whether he is invited or not. But if none of us are to die, then I think it would be charming to have Death among us—perhaps even to perform some little trick if he is in a good humor. And think of being able to say that we had been to a party with Death! All of London will envy us, all of England!"

The idea began to please her friends, but a young lord, very new to London, suggested timidly, "Death is so busy. Suppose he has work to do and cannot accept your invitation?"

"No one has ever refused an invitation of mine," said Lady Neville, "not even the King." And the young lord was not invited to her party.

She sat down then and there and wrote out the invitation. There was some dispute among her friends as to how they should address Death. "His Lordship Death" seemed to place him only on the level of a viscount or a baron. "His Grace Death" met with more acceptance, but Lady Neville said it sounded hypocritical. And to refer to Death as "His Majesty" was to make him the equal of the King of England, which even Lady Neville would not dare to do. It was finally decided that all should speak of him as "His Eminence Death," which pleased nearly everyone.

Captain Compson, known both as England's most dashing cavalry officer and most elegant rake, remarked next, "That's all very well, but how is the invitation to reach Death? Does anyone here know where he lives?"

"Death undoubtedly lives in London," said Lady Neville, "like everyone else of any importance, though he probably goes to Deauville for the summer. Actually, Death must live fairly near my own house. This is much the best section of London, and you could hardly expect a person of Death's importance to live anywhere else. When I stop to think of it, it's really rather strange that we haven't met before now, on the street."

Most of her friends agreed with her, but the poet, whose name was David Lorimond, cried out, "No, my lady, you are wrong! Death lives among the poor. Death lives in the foulest, darkest alleys of this city, in some vile, rat-ridden hovel that smells of—" He stopped here partly because Lady Neville had indicated her displeasure, and partly because he had never been inside such a hut or thought of wondering what it smelled like. "Death lives among the poor," he went on, "and comes to visit them every day, for he is their only friend."

Lady Neville answered him as coldly as she had spoken to the young lord. "He may be forced to deal with them, David, but I hardly think that he seeks them out as companions. I am certain that it is as difficult for him to think of the poor as individuals as it is for me. Death is, after all, a nobleman."

There was no real argument among the lords and ladies that Death lived in a neighborhood at least as good as their own, but none of them seemed to know the name of Death's street, and no one had ever seen Death's house.

"If there were a war," Captain Compson said, "Death would be easy to find. I have seen him, you know, even spoken to him, but he has never answered me."

"Quite proper," said Lady Neville. "Death must always

speak first. You are not a very correct person, Captain."
But she smiled at him, as all women did.

Then an idea came to her. "My hairdresser has a sick child, I understand," she said. "He was telling me about it yesterday, sounding most dull and hopeless. I will send for him and give him the invitation, and he in his turn can give it to Death when he comes to take the brat. A bit unconventional, I admit, but I see no other way."

"If he refuses?" asked a lord who had just been married.

"Why should he?" asked Lady Neville.

Again it was the poet who exclaimed amidst the general approval that this was a cruel and wicked thing to do. But he fell silent when Lady Neville innocently asked him, "Why, David?"

So the hairdresser was sent for, and when he stood before them, smiling nervously and twisting his hands to be in the same room with so many great lords, Lady Neville told him the errand that was required of him. And she was right, as she usually was, for he made no refusal. He merely took the invitation in his hand and asked to be excused.

He did not return for two days, but when he did he presented himself to Lady Neville without being sent for and handed her a small white envelope. Saying, "How very nice of you, thank you very much," she opened it and found therein a plain calling card with nothing on it except these words: *Death will be pleased to attend Lady Neville's ball.*

"Death gave you this?" she asked the hairdresser eagerly. "What was he like?" But the hairdresser stood still, looking past her, and said nothing, and she, not really waiting for an answer, called a dozen servants to her and told them to run and summon her friends. As she paced up and down the room waiting for them, she asked again, "What is Death like?" The hairdresser did not reply.

When her friends came they passed the little card excitedly from hand to hand, until it had gotten quite smudged and bent from their fingers. But they all admitted that, beyond its message, there was nothing particularly unusual about it. It was neither hot nor cold to the touch, and what little odor clung to it was rather pleasant. Everyone said that it was a very familiar smell, but no one could give it a name. The poet said that it reminded him of lilacs but not exactly.

It was Captain Compson, however, who pointed out the one thing that no one else had noticed. "Look at the handwriting itself," he said. "Have you ever seen anything more graceful? The letters seem as light as birds. I think we have wasted our time speaking of Death as His This and His That. A woman wrote this note."

Then there was an uproar and a great babble, and the card had to be handed around again so that everyone could exclaim, "Yes, by God!" over it. The voice of the poet rose out of the hubbub saying, "It is very natural, when you come to think of it. After all, the French say *la mort*. Lady Death. I should much prefer Death to be a woman."

"Death rides a great black horse," said Captain Compson firmly, "and wears armor of the same color. Death is very tall, taller than anyone. It was no woman I saw on the battlefield, striking right and left like any soldier. Perhaps the hairdresser wrote it himself, or the hairdresser's wife."

But the hairdresser refused to speak, though they gathered around him and begged him to say who had given him the note. At first they promised him all sorts of rewards, and later they threatened to do terrible things to him. "Did you write this card?" he was asked, and "Who wrote it, then? Was it a living woman? Was it really Death? Did Death say anything to you? How did you know it was Death? Is Death a woman? Are you trying to make fools of us all?"

Not a word from the hairdresser, not one word, and finally Lady Neville called her servants to have him whipped and thrown into the street. He did not look at her as they took him away, or utter a sound.

Silencing her friends with a wave of her hand, Lady Neville said, "The ball will take place two weeks from tonight. Let Death come as Death pleases, whether as man or woman or strange, sexless creature." She smiled calmly. "Death may well be a woman," she said. "I am less certain of Death's form than I was, but I am also less frightened of Death. I am too old to be afraid of anything that can use a quill pen to write me a letter. Go home now, and as you make your preparations for the ball see that you speak of it to your servants, that they may spread the news all over London. Let it be known that on this one night no one in the world will die, for Death will be dancing at Lady Neville's ball."

For the next two weeks Lady Neville's great house shook and groaned and creaked like an old tree in a gale as the servants hammered and scrubbed, polished and painted, making ready for the ball. Lady Neville had always been very proud of her house, but as the ball drew near she be-

151

gan to be afraid that it would not be nearly grand enough for Death, who was surely accustomed to visiting in the homes of richer, mightier people than herself. Fearing the scorn of Death, she worked night and day supervising her servants' preparations. Curtains and carpets had to be cleaned, goldwork and silverware polished until they gleamed by themselves in the dark. The grand staircase that rushed down into the ballroom like a waterfall was washed and rubbed so often that it was almost impossible to walk on it without slipping. As for the ballroom itself, it took thirty-two servants working at once to clean it properly, not counting those who were polishing the glass chandelier that was taller than a man and the fourteen smaller lamps. And when they were done she made them do it all over, not because she saw any dust or dirt anywhere, but because she was sure that Death would.

As for herself, she chose her finest gown and saw to its laundering personally. She called in another hairdresser and had him put up her hair in the style of an earlier time, wanting to show Death that she was a woman who enjoyed her age and did not find it necessary to ape the young and beautiful. All the day of the ball she sat before her mirror, not making herself up much beyond the normal touches of rouge and eye shadow and fine rice powder, but staring at the lean old face she had been born with, wondering how it would appear to Death. Her steward asked her to approve his wine selection, but she sent him away and stayed at her mirror until it was time to dress and go downstairs to meet her guests.

Everyone arrived early. When she looked out of a window, Lady Neville saw that the driveway of her home was choked with carriages and fine horses. "It all looks like a great funeral procession," she said. The footman cried the names of her guests to the echoing ballroom. "Captain Henry Compson, His Majesty's Household Cavalry! Mr. David Lorimond! Lord and Lady Torrance!" (They were the youngest couple there, having been married only three months before.) "Sir Roger Harbison! The Contessa della Candini!" Lady Neville permitted them all to kiss her hand and made them welcome.

She had engaged the finest musicians she could find to play for the dancing, but though they began to play at her signal not one couple stepped out on the floor, nor did one young lord approach her to request the honor of the first dance, as was proper. They milled together, shining and murmuring, their eyes fixed on the ballroom door. Every time they heard a carriage clatter up the driveway they seemed to flinch a little and draw closer together; every time the footman announced the arrival of another guest, they all sighed softly and swayed a little on their feet with relief.

"Why did they come to my party if they were afraid?" Lady Nevile muttered scornfully to herself. "I am not afraid of meeting Death. I ask only that Death may be impressed by the magnificence of my house and the flavor of my wines. I will die sooner than anyone here, but I am not afraid."

Certain that Death would not arrive until midnight, she moved among her guests, attempting to calm them, not with her words, which she knew they would not hear, but with the tone of her voice, as if they were so many frightened horses. But little by little, she herself was infected by their nervousness: whenever she sat down she stood up again immediately, she tasted a dozen glasses of wine without finishing any of them, and she glanced constantly at her jeweled watch, at first wanting to hurry the midnight along and end the waiting, later scratching at the watch face with her forefinger, as if she would push away the night and drag the sun backward into the sky. When midnight came, she was standing with the rest of them, breathing through her mouth, shifting from foot to foot, listening for the sound of carriage wheels turning in gravel.

When the clock began to strike midnight, everyone, even Lady Neville and the brave Captain Compson, gave one startled little cry and then was silent again, listening to the tolling of the clock. The smaller clocks upstairs began to chime. Lady Neville's ears hurt. She caught sight of herself in the ballroom mirror, one gray face turned up toward the ceiling as if she were gasping for air, and she thought, "Death will be a woman, a hideous, filthy old crone as tall and strong as a man. And the most terrible thing of all will be that she will have my face." All the clocks stopped striking, and Lady Neville closed her eyes.

She opened them again only when she heard the whispering around her take on a different tone, one in which fear was fused with relief and a certain chagrin. For no new carriage stood in the driveway. Death had not come.

The noise grew slowly louder; here and there people were beginning to laugh. Near her, Lady Neville heard young Lord Torrance say to his wife, "There, my darling, I told

153

you there was nothing to be afraid of. It was all a joke."

"I am ruined," Lady Neville thought. The laughter was increasing; it pounded against her ears in strokes, like the chiming of the clocks. "I wanted to give a ball so grand that those who were not invited would be shamed in front of the whole city, and this is my reward. I am ruined, and I deserve it."

Turning to the poet Lorimond, she said, "Dance with me, David." She signaled to the musicians, who at once began to play. When Lorimond hesitated, she said, "Dance with me now. You will not have another chance. I shall never give a party again."

Lorimond bowed and led her out onto the dance floor. The guests parted for them, and the laughter died down for a moment, but Lady Neville knew that it would soon begin again. "Well, let them laugh," she thought. "I did not fear Death when they were all trembling. Why should I fear their laughter?" But she could feel a stinging at the thin lids of her eyes, and she closed them once more as she began to dance with Lorimond.

And then, quite suddenly, all the carriage horses outside the house whinnied loudly, just once, as the guests had cried out at midnight. There were a great many horses, and their one salute was so loud that everyone in the room became instantly silent. They heard the heavy steps of the footman as he went to open the door, and they shivered as if they felt the cold breeze that drifted into the house. Then they heard a light voice saying, "Am I late? Oh, I am so sorry. The horses were tired," and before the footman could reenter to announce her, a lovely young girl in a white dress stepped gracefully into the ballroom doorway and stood there smiling.

She could not have been more than nineteen. Her hair was yellow, and she wore it long. It fell thickly upon her bare shoulders that gleamed warmly through it, two limestone islands rising out of a dark golden sea. Her face was wide at the forehead and cheekbones, and narrow at the chin, and her skin was so clear that many of the ladies there —Lady Neville among them—touched their own faces wonderingly, and instantly drew their hands away as though their own skin had rasped their fingers. Her mouth was pale, where the mouths of the other women were red and orange and even purple. Her eyebrows, thicker and straighter than was fashionable, met over dark, calm eyes that were set so deep in her young face and were so black, so uncompromisingly black, that the middleaged wife of a middle-aged lord murmured, "Touch of the gypsy there, I think!"

"Or something worse," suggested her husband's mistress.

"Be silent!" Lady Neville spoke louder than she had intended, and the girl turned to look at her. She smiled, and Lady Neville tried to smile back, but her mouth seemed very stiff. "Welcome," she said. "Welcome, my lady Death."

A sigh rustled among the lords and ladies as the girl took the old woman's hand and curtsied to her, sinking and rising in one motion, like a wave. "You are Lady Neville," she said. "Thank you so much for inviting me." Her accent was as faint and as almost familiar as her perfume.

"Please excuse me for being late," she said earnestly. "I had to come from a long way off, and my horses are so tired."

"The groom will rub them down," Lady Neville said, "and feed them if you wish."

"Oh, no," the girl answered quickly. "Tell him not to go near the horses, please. They are not really horses, and they are very fierce."

She accepted a glass of wine from a servant and drank it slowly, sighing softly and contentedly. "What good wine," she said. "And what a beautiful house you have."

"Thank you," said Lady Neville. Without turning, she could feel every woman in the room envying her, sensing it as she could always sense the approach of rain.

"I wish I lived here," Death said in her low, sweet voice. "I will, one day."

Then, seeing Lady Neville become as still as if she had turned to ice, she put her hand on the old woman's arm and said, "Oh, I'm sorry, I'm so sorry. I am so cruel, but I never mean to be. Please forgive me, Lady Neville. I am not used to company, and I do such stupid things. Please forgive me."

Her hand felt as light and warm on Lady Neville's arm as the hand of any other young girl, and her eyes were so appealing that Lady Neville replied, "You have said nothing wrong. While you are my guest, my house is yours."

"Thank you," said Death, and she smiled so radiantly that the musicians began to play quite by themselves, with no sign from Lady Neville. She would have stopped them, but Death said, "Oh, what lovely music! Let them play, please."

So the musicians played a gavotte, and Death, unabashed by eyes that stared at her in greedy terror, sang softly to herself without words, lifted her white gown slightly with
155

both hands, and made hesitant little patting steps with her small feet. "I have not danced in so long," she said wistfully. "I'm quite sure I've forgotten how."

She was shy; she would not look up to embarrass the young lords, not one of whom stepped forward to dance with her. Lady Neville felt a flood of shame and sympathy, emotions she thought had withered in her years ago. "Is she to be humiliated at my own ball?" she thought angrily. "It is because she is Death; if she were the ugliest, foulest hag in all the world they would clamor to dance with her, because they are gentlemen and they know what is expected of them. But no gentleman will dance with Death, no matter how beautiful she is." She glanced sideways at David Lorimond. His face was flushed, and his hands were clasped so tightly as he stared at Death that his fingers were like glass, but when Lady Neville touched his arm he did not turn, and when she hissed, "David!" he pretended not to hear her.

Then Captain Compson, gray-haired and handsome in his uniform, stepped out of the crowd and bowed gracefully before Death. "If I may have the honor," he said.

"Captain Compson," said Death, smiling. She put her arm in his. "I was hoping you would ask me."

This brought a frown from the older women, who did not consider it a proper thing to say, but for that Death cared not a rap. Captain Compson led her to the center of the floor, and there they danced. Death was curiously graceless at first—she was too anxious to please her partner, and she seemed to have no notion of rhythm. The Captain himself moved with the mixture of dignity and humor that Lady Neville had never seen in another man, but when he looked at her over Death's shoulder, she saw something that no one else appeared to notice: that his face and eyes were immobile with fear, and that, though he offered Death his hand with easy gallantry, he flinched slightly when she took it. And yet he danced as well as Lady Neville had ever seen him.

"Ah, that's what comes of having a reputation to maintain," she thought. "Captain Compson too must do what is expected of him. I hope someone else will dance with her soon."

But no one did. Little by little, other couples overcame their fear and slipped hurriedly out on the floor when Death was looking the other way, but nobody sought to relieve Captain Compson of his beautiful partner. They danced every dance together. In time, some of the men present began to look at her with more appreciation than terror, but when she returned their glances and smiled at them, they clung to their partners as if a cold wind were threatening to blow them away.

One of the few who stared at her frankly and with pleasure was young Lord Torrance, who usually danced only with his wife. Another was the poet Lorimond. Dancing with Lady Neville, he remarked to her, "If she is Death, what do these frightened fools think they are? If she is ugliness, what must they be? I hate their fear. It is obscene."

Death and the Captain danced past them at that moment, and they heard him say to her, "But if that was truly you that I saw in the battle, how can you have changed so? How can you have become so lovely?"

Death's laughter was gay and soft. "I thought that among so many beautiful people it might be better to be beautiful. I was afraid of frightening everyone and spoiling the party."

"They all thought she would be ugly," said Lorimond to Lady Neville. "I—*I* knew she would be beautiful."

"Then why have you not danced with her?" Lady Neville asked him. "Are you also afraid?"

"No, oh, no," the poet answered quickly and passionately. "I will ask her to dance very soon. I only want to look at her a little longer."

The musicians played on and on. The dancing wore away the night as slowly as falling water wears down a cliff. It seemed to Lady Neville that no night had ever endured longer, and yet she was neither tired nor bored. She danced with every man there, except with Lord Torrance, who was dancing with his wife as if they had just met that night, and, of course, with Captain Compson. Once he lifted his hand and touched Death's golden hair very lightly. He was a striking man still, a fit partner for so beautiful a girl, but Lady Neville looked at his face each time she passed him and realized that he was older than anyone knew.

Death herself seemed younger than the youngest there. No woman at the ball danced better than she now, though it was hard for Lady Neville to remember at what point her awkwardness had given way to the liquid sweetness of her movements. She smiled and called to everyone who caught her eye—and she knew them all by name; she sang constantly, making up words to the dance tunes, nonsense words, sounds without meaning, and yet everyone strained
157

to hear her soft voice without knowing why. And when, during a waltz, she caught up the trailing end of her gown to give her more freedom as she danced, she seemed to Lady Neville to move like a little sailing boat over a still evening sea.

Lady Neville heard Lady Torrance arguing angrily with the Contessa della Candini. "I don't care if she is Death, she's no older than I am, she can't be!"

"Nonsense," said the Contessa, who could not afford to be generous to any other woman. "She is twenty-eight, thirty, if she is an hour. And that dress, that bridal gown she wears—really!"

"Vile," said the woman who had come to the ball as Captain Compson's freely acknowledged mistress. "Tasteless. But one should know better than to expect taste from Death, I suppose." Lady Torrance looked as if she were going to cry.

"They are jealous of Death," Lady Neville said to herself. "How strange. I am not jealous of her, not in the least. And I do not fear her at all." She was very proud of herself.

Then, as unbiddenly as they had begun to play, the musicians stopped. They began to put away their instruments. In the sudden shrill silence, Death pulled away from Captain Compson and ran to look out of one of the tall windows, pushing the curtains apart with both both hands. "Look!" she said, with her back turned to them. "Come and look. The night is almost gone."

The summer sky was still dark, and the eastern horizon was only a shade lighter than the rest of the sky, but the stars had vanished and the trees near the house were gradually becoming distinct. Death pressed her face against the window and said, so softly that the other guests could barely hear her, "I must go now."

"No," Lady Neville said, and was not immediately aware that she had spoken. "You must stay a while longer. The ball was in your honor. Please stay."

Death held out both hands to her, and Lady Neville came and took them in her own. "I've had a wonderful time," she said gently. "You cannot possibly imagine how it feels to be actually invited to such a ball as this, because you have given them and gone to them all your life. One is like another to you, but for me it is different. Do you understand me?" Lady Neville nodded silently. "I will remember this night forever," Death said.

"Stay," Captain Compson said. "Stay just a little longer." He put his hand on Death's shoulder, and she smiled and leaned her cheek against it. "Dear Captain Compson," she said. "My first real gallant. Aren't you tired of me yet?"

"Never," he said. "Please stay."

"Stay," said Lorimond, and he too seemed about to touch her. "Stay. I want to talk to you. I want to look at you. I will dance with you if you stay."

"How many followers I have," Death said in wonder. She stretched one hand toward Lorimond, but he drew back from her and then flushed in shame. "A soldier and a poet. How wonderful it is to be a woman. But why did you not speak to me earlier, both of you? Now it is too late. I must go."

"Please stay," Lady Torrance whispered. She held on to her husband's hand for courage. "We think you are so beautiful, both of us do."

"Gracious Lady Torrance," the girl said kindly. She turned back to the window, touched it lightly, and it flew open. The cool dawn air rushed into the ballroom, fresh with rain but already smelling faintly of the London streets over which it had passed. They heard birdsong and the strange, harsh nickering of Death's horses.

"Do you want me to stay?" she asked. The question was put, not to Lady Neville, nor to Captain Compson, nor to any of her admirers, but to the Contessa della Candini, who stood well back from them all, hugging her flowers to herself and humming a little song of irritation. She did not in the least want Death to stay, but she was afraid that all the other women would think her envious of Death's beauty, and so she said, "Yes. Of course I do."

"Ah," said Death. She was almost whispering. "And you," she said to another woman, "do you want me to stay? Do you want me to be one of your friends?"

"Yes," said the woman, "because you are beautiful and a true lady."

"And you," said Death to a man, "and you," to a woman, "and you," to another man, "do you want me to stay?" And they all answered, "Yes, Lady Death, we do."

"Do you want me, then?" she cried at last to all of them. "Do you want me to live among you and to be one of you, and not to be Death anymore? Do you want me to visit your houses and come to all your parties? Do you want me to ride horses like yours instead of mine, do you want me to wear the kind of dresses you wear, and say the things you would say? Would one of you marry me, and would the rest of you dance at my wedding and bring gifts to my children? Is that what you want?"

"Yes," said Lady Neville. "Stay here, stay with me, stay with us."

Death's voice, without becoming louder, had become clearer and older; too old a voice, thought Lady Neville, for such a young girl. "Be sure," said Death. "Be sure of what you want, be very sure. So all of you want me to stay? For if one of you says to me, no, go away, then I must leave at once and never return. Be sure. Do you all want me?"

And everyone there cried with one voice, "Yes! Yes, you must stay with us. You are so beautiful that we cannot let you go."

"We are tired," said Captain Compson.

"We are blind," said Lorimond, adding, "especially to poetry."

"We are afraid," said Lord Torrance quietly, and his wife took his arm and said, "Both of us."

"We are dull and stupid," said Lady Neville, "and growing old uselessly. Stay with us, Lady Death."

And then Death smiled sweetly and radiantly and took a step forward, and it was as though she had come down among them from a great height. "Very well," she said. "I will stay with you. I will be Death no more. I will be a woman."

The room was full of a deep sigh, although no one was seen to open his mouth. No one moved, for the golden-haired girl was Death still, and her horses still whinnied for her outside. No one could look at her for long, although she was the most beautiful girl anyone there had ever seen.

"There is a price to pay," she said. "There is always a price. Some one of you must become Death in my place, for there must forever be Death in the world. Will anyone choose? Will anyone here become Death of his own free will? For only thus can I become a human girl."

No one spoke, no one spoke at all. But they backed slowly away from her, like waves slipping back down a beach to the sea when you try to catch them. The Contessa della Candini and her friends would have crept quietly out of the door, but Death smiled at them and they stood where they were. Captain Compson opened his mouth as though he were going to declare himself, but he said nothing. Lady Neville did not move.

"No one," said Death. She touched a flower with her
160

finger, and it seemed to crouch and flex itself like a pleased cat. "No one at all," she said. "Then I must choose, and that is just, for that is the way that I became Death. I never wanted to be Death, and it makes me so happy that you want me to become one of yourselves. I have searched a long time for people who would want me. Now I have only to choose someone to replace me and it is done. I will choose very carefully."

"Oh, we were so foolish," Lady Neville said to herself. "We were so foolish." But she said nothing aloud; she merely clasped her hands and stared at the young girl, thinking vaguely that if she had had a daughter she would have been greatly pleased if she resembled the lady Death.

"The Contessa della Candini," said Death thoughtfully, and that woman gave a little squeak of terror because she could not draw her breath for a scream. But Death laughed and said, "No, that would be silly." She said nothing more, but for a long time after that the Contessa burned with humiliation at not having been chosen to be Death.

"Not Captain Compson," murmured Death, "because he is too kind to become Death, and because it would be too cruel to him. He wants to die so badly." The expression on the Captain's face did not change, but his hands began to tremble.

"Not Lorimond," the girl continued, "because he knows so little about life, and because I like him." The poet flushed, and turned white, and then turned pink again. He made as if to kneel clumsily on one knee, but instead he pulled himself erect and stood as much like Captain Compson as he could.

"Not the Torrances," said Death, "never Lord and Lady Torrance, for both of them care too much about another person to take any pride in being Death." But she hesitated over Lady Torrance for a while, staring at her out of her dark and curious eyes. "I was your age when I became Death," she said at last. "I wonder what it will be like to be your age again. I have been Death for so long." Lady Torrance shivered and did not speak.

And at last Death said quietly, "Lady Neville."

"I am here," Lady Neville answered.

"I think you are the only one," said Death. "I choose you, Lady Neville."

Again Lady Neville heard every guest sigh softly, and although her back was to them all she knew that they were sighing in relief that neither themselves nor anyone dear to themselves had been chosen. Lady Torrance gave a little

161

cry of protest, but Lady Neville knew that she would have cried out at whatever choice Death made. She heard herself say calmly, "I am honored. But was there no one more worthy than I?"

"Not one," said Death. "There is no one quite so weary of being human, no one who knows better how meaningless it is to be alive. And there is no one else here with the power to treat life"—and she smiled sweetly and cruelly—"the life of your hairdresser's child, for instance, as the meaningless thing it is. Death has a heart, but it is forever an empty heart, and I think, Lady Neville, that your heart is like a dry riverbed, like a seashell. You will be very content as Death, more so than I, for I was very young when I became Death."

She came toward Lady Neville, light and swaying, her deep eyes wide and full of the light of the red morning sun that was beginning to rise. The guests at the ball moved back from her, although she did not look at them, but Lady Neville clenched her hands tightly and watched Death come toward her with her little dancing steps. "We must kiss each other," Death said. "That is the way I became Death." She shook her head delightedly, so that her soft hair swirled about her shoulders. "Quickly, quickly," she said. "Oh, I cannot wait to be human again."

"You may not like it," Lady Neville said. She felt very calm, though she could hear her old heart pounding in her chest and feel it in the tops of her fingers. "You may not like it after a while," she said.

"Perhaps not." Death's smile was very close to her now. "I will not be as beautiful as I am, and perhaps people will not love me as much as they do now. But I will be human for a while, and at last I will die. I have done my penance."

"What penance?" the old woman asked the beautiful girl. "What was it you did? Why did you become Death?"

"I don't remember," said the lady Death. "And you too will forget in time." She was smaller than Lady Neville, and so much younger. In her white dress she might have been the daughter that Lady Neville had never had, who would have been with her always and held her mother's head lightly in the crook of her arm when she felt old and sad. Now she lifted her head to kiss Lady Neville's cheek, and as she did so she whispered in her ear, "You will still be beautiful when I am ugly. Be kind to me then."

Behind Lady Neville the handsome gentlemen and ladies

162

murmured and sighed, fluttering like moths in their evening dress, in their elegant gowns. "I promise," she said, and then she pursed her dry lips to kiss the soft, sweet-smelling cheek of the young lady Death.

Every now and then you come across a story with an idea that makes so much sense you wonder why no one ever thought of it before. It may even be a thoroughly ridiculous idea, such as the one presented here by Curt Clark, but if all the facts fit . . .

NACKLES
Curt Clark

Did God create men, or does Man create gods? I don't know, and if it hadn't been for my rotten brother-in-law the question would never have come up. My *late* brother-in-law? Nackles knows.

It all depends, you see, like the chicken and the egg, on which came first. Did God exist before Man first thought of Him, or didn't He? If not, if Man creates his gods, then it follows that Man must create the devils, too.

Nearly every god, you know, has his corresponding devil. Good *and* Evil. The polytheistic ancients, prolific in the creation (?) of gods and goddesses, always worked up nearly enough Evil ones to cancel out the Good, but not quite. The Greeks, those incredible supermen, combined Good and Evil in *each* of their gods. In Zoroaster, Ahura Mazda, being Good, is ranged forever against the Evil one, Ahriman. And we ourselves know God and Satan.

But of course it's entirely possible I have nothing to worry about. It all depends on whether Santa Claus is or is not a god. He certainly *seems* like a god. Consider: He is omniscient: he knows every action of every child, for good or evil. At least on Christmas Eve he is omnipresent, everywhere at once. He administers justice tempered with mercy. He is superhuman, or at least non-human, though conceived of as having a human shape. He is aided by a corps of assistants who do *not* have completely human shapes. He rewards Good and punishes Evil. And, most important, he is believed in utterly by several million people, most of them under the age of ten. Is there any qualification for godhood that Santa Claus does not possess?

And even the non-believers give him lip-service. He has surely taken over Christmas; his effigy is everywhere, but where are the manger and the Christ child? Retired rather forlornly to the nave. (Santa's power is growing, too. Slowly but surely he is usurping Chanukah as well.)

Santa Claus *is* a god. He's no less a god than Ahura Mazda, or Odin, or Zeus. Think of the white beard, the chariot pulled through the air by a breed of animal which doesn't ordinarily fly, the prayers (requests for gifts) which are annually mailed to him and which so baffle the Post Office, the specially-garbed priests in all the department stores. And don't gods reflect their creators' (?) society? The Greeks had a huntress goddess, and gods of agriculture and war and love. What else would we have but a god of giving, of merchandising, and of consumption? Secondary gods of earlier times have been stout, but surely Santa Claus is the first fat primary god.

And wherever there is a god, mustn't there sooner or later be a devil?

Which brings me back to my brother-in-law, who's to blame for whatever happens now. My brother-in-law Frank is—or was—a very mean and nasty man. Why I ever let him marry my sister I'll never know. Why Susie *wanted* to marry him is an even greater mystery. I could just shrug and say Love Is Blind, I suppose, but that wouldn't explain how she fell in love with him in the first place.

Frank is—Frank was—I just don't know what tense to use. The present, hopefully. Frank is a very handsome man in his way, big and brawny, full of vitality. A football player; hero in college and defensive linebacker for three years in pro ball, till he did some sort of irreparable damage to his left knee, which gave him a limp and forced him to find some other way to make a living.

165

Ex-football players tend to become insurance salesmen; I don't know why. Frank followed the form, and became an insurance salesman. Because Susie was then a secretary for the same company, they soon became acquainted.

Was Susie dazzled by the ex-hero, so big and handsome? She's never been the type to dazzle easily, but we can never fully know what goes on inside the mind of another human being. For whatever reason, she decided she was in love with him.

So they were married, and five weeks later he gave her her first black eye. And the last, though it mightn't have been, since Susie tried to keep me from finding out. I was to go over for dinner that night, but at eleven in the morning she called the auto showroom where I work, to tell me she had a headache and we'd have to postpone the dinner. But she sounded so upset that I knew immediately something was wrong, so I took a demonstration car and drove over, and when she opened the front door there was the shiner.

I got the story out of her slowly, in fits and starts. Frank, it seemed, had a terrible temper. She wanted to excuse him because he was forced to be an insurance salesman when he really wanted to be out there on the gridiron again, but I want to be President and I'm an automobile salesman and *I* don't go around giving women black eyes. So I decided it was up to me to let Frank know he wasn't to vent his pique on my sister any more.

Unfortunately, I am five feet seven inches tall and weigh one hundred thirty-four pounds, with the Sunday *Times* under my arm. Were I just to give Frank a piece of my mind, he'd surely give me a black eye to go with my sister's. Therefore, that afternoon I bought a regulation baseball bat, and carried it with me when I went to see Frank that night.

He opened the door himself and snarled, "What do *you* want?"

In answer, I poked him with the end of the bat, just above the belt, to knock the wind out of him. Then, having unethically gained the upper hand, I clouted him five or six times more, and then stood over him to say, "The next time you hit my sister I won't let you off so easy." After which I took Susie home to *my* place for dinner.

And after which I was Frank's best friend.

People like that are so impossible to understand. Until the baseball bat episode, Frank had nothing for me but undisguised contempt. But once I'd knocked the stuffings out of him, he was my comrade for life. And I'm sure it was sincere; he would have given me the shirt off his back, had I wanted it, which I didn't.

(Also, by the way, he never hit Susie again. He still had the bad temper, but he took it out in throwing furniture out windows or punching dents in walls or going downtown to start a brawl in some bar. I offered to train him out of maltreating the house and furniture as I had trained him out of maltreating his wife, but Susie said no, that Frank had to let off steam and it would be worse if he was forced to bottle it all up inside him, so the baseball bat remained in retirement.)

Then came the children, three of them in as many years. Frank Junior came first, and then Linda Joyce, and finally Stewart. Susie had held the forlorn hope that fatherhood would settle Frank to some extent, but quite the reverse was true. Shrieking babies, smelly diapers, disrupted sleep and distracted wives are trials and tribulations to any man, but to Frank they were—like everything else in his life—the last straw.

He became, in a word, worse. Susie restrained him I don't know how often from doing some severe damage to a squalling infant, and as the children grew toward the age of reason Frank's expressed attitude toward them was that their best move would be to find a way to become invisible. The children, of course, didn't like him very much, but then who did?

Last Christmas was when *it* started. Junior was six then, and Linda Joyce five, and Stewart four, so all were old enough to have heard of Santa Claus and still young enough to believe in him. Along around October, when the Christmas season was beginning, Frank began to use Santa Claus's displeasure as a weapon to keep the children "in line"—his phrase for keeping them mute and immobile and terrified. Many parents, of course, try to enforce obedience the same way: "If you're bad, Santa Claus won't bring you any presents." Which, all things considered, is a negative and passive sort of punishment, wishy-washy in comparison with fire and brimstone and such. In the old days, Santa Claus would treat bad children a bit more scornfully, leaving a lump of coal in their stockings in lieu of presents, but I suppose the Depression helped to change that. There are times and situations when a lump of coal is nothing to sneer at.

In any case, an absence of presents was too weak a punishment for Frank's purposes, so last Christmastime he invented Nackles.

Who is Nackles? Nackles is to Santa Claus what Satan is to God, what Ahriman is to Ahura Mazda, what the North Wind is to the South Wind. Nackles is the new Evil.

I think Frank really *enjoyed* creating Nackles; he gave so much thought to the details of him. According to Frank, and as I remember it, this is Nackles: Very very tall and very very thin. Dressed all in black, with a gaunt gray face and deep black eyes. He travels through an intricate series of tunnels under the earth, in a black chariot on rails, pulled by an octet of dead-white goats.

And what does Nackles do? Nackles lives on the flesh of little boys and girls. (This is what Frank was telling his children; can you believe it?) Nackles roams back and forth under the earth, in his dark tunnels darker than subway tunnels, pulled by the eight dead-white goats, and he searches for little boys and girls to stuff into his big black sack and carry away and eat. But Santa Claus won't let him have *good* boys and girls. Santa Claus is stronger than Nackles, and keeps a protective shield around little children, so Nackles can't get at them.

But when little children are bad, it hurts Santa Claus, and weakens the shield Santa Claus has placed around them, and if they keep on being bad pretty soon there's no shield left at all, and on Christmas Eve instead of Santa Claus coming down out of the sky with his bag of presents Nackles comes up out of the ground with his bag of emptiness, and stuffs the bad children in, and whisks them away to his dark tunnels and the eight dead-white goats.

Frank was proud of his invention, actually proud of it. He not only used Nackles to threaten his children every time they had the temerity to come within range of his vision, he also spread the story around to others. He told me, and his neighbors, and people in bars, and people he went to see in his job as insurance salesman. I don't know how many people he told about Nackles, though I would guess it was well over a hundred. And there's more than one Frank in this world; he told me from time to time of a client or neighbor or bar-crony who had heard the story of Nackles and then said, "By God, that's great. That's what *I've* been needing, to keep *my* brats in line."

Thus Nackles was created, and thus Nackles was promulgated. And would any of the unfortunate children thus introduced to Nackles believe in this Evil Being any less than they believed in Santa Claus? Of course not.

This all happened, as I say, last Christmastime. Frank invented Nackles, used him to further intimidate his already-
168

intimidated children, and spread the story of him to everyone he met. On Christmas Day last year I'm sure there was more than one child in this town who was relieved and somewhat surprised to awaken the same as usual, in his own trundle bed, and to find the presents downstairs beneath the tree, proving that Nackles had been kept away yet another year.

Nackles lay dormant, so far as Frank was concerned, from December 25th of last year until this October. Then, with the sights and sounds of Christmas again in the land, back came Nackles, as fresh and vicious as ever. "Don't expect *me* to stop him!" Frank would shout. "When he comes up out of the ground the night before Christmas to carry you away in his bag, don't expect any help from *me!*"

It was worse this year than last. Frank wasn't doing as well financially as he'd expected, and then early in November Susie discovered she was pregnant again, and what with one thing and another Frank was headed for a real peak of ill-temper. He screamed at the children constantly, and the name of Nackles was never far from his tongue.

Susie did what she could to counteract Frank's bad influence, but he wouldn't let her do much. All through November and December he was home more and more of the time, because the Christmas season is the wrong time to sell insurance anyway and also because he was hating the job more every day and thus giving it less of his time. The more he hated the job, the worse his temper became, and the more he drank, and the worse his limp got, and the louder were his shouts, and the more violent his references to Nackles. It just built and built and built, and reached its crescendo on Christmas Eve, when some small or imagined infraction of one of the children—Stewart, I think—resulted in Frank's pulling all the Christmas presents from all the closets and stowing them all in the car to be taken back to the stores, because this Christmas for sure it wouldn't be Santa Claus who would be visiting this house, it would be Nackles.

By the time Susie got the children to bed, everyone in the house was a nervous wreck. The children were too frightened to sleep, and Susie was too unnerved herself to be of much help in soothing them. Frank, who had taken to drinking at home lately, had locked himself in the bedroom with a bottle.

It was nearly eleven o'clock before Susie got the children all quieted down, and then she went out to the car and brought all the presents back in and ranged them under the tree. Then, not wanting to see or hear her husband any more that night—he was like a big spoiled child throwing a tantrum—she herself went to sleep on the living-room sofa.

Frank Junior awoke her in the morning, crying, "Look, Mama! Nackles *didn't* come, he *didn't* come!" And pointed to the presents she'd placed under the tree.

The other two children came down shortly after, and Susie and the youngsters sat on the floor and opened the presents, enjoying themselves as much as possible, but still with restraint. There were none of the usual squeals of childish pleasure; no one wanted Daddy to come storming downstairs in one of his rages. So the children contented themselves with ear-to-ear smiles and whispered exclamations, and after a while Susie made breakfast, and the day carried along as pleasantly as could be expected under the circumstances.

It was a little after twelve that Susie began to worry about Frank's non-appearance. She braved herself to go up and knock on the locked door and call his name, but she got no answer, not even the expected snarl, so just around one o'clock she called me and I hurried on over. I rapped smartly on the bedroom door, got no answer, and finally I threatened to break the door in if Frank didn't open up. When I still got no answer, break the door in I did.

And Frank, of course, was gone.

The police say he ran away, deserted his family, primarily because of Susie's fourth pregnancy. They say he went out the window and dropped to the back yard, so Susie wouldn't see him and try to stop him. And they say he didn't take the car because he was afraid Susie would hear him start the engine.

That all sounds reasonable, doesn't it? Yet I just can't believe Frank would walk out on Susie without a lot of shouting about it first. Nor that he would leave his car, which he was fonder of than his wife and children.

But what's the alternative? There's only one I can think of: Nackles.

I would rather not believe that. I would rather not believe that Frank, in inventing Nackles and spreading word of him, made him real. I would rather not believe that Nackles actually did visit my sister's house on Christmas Eve.

But did he? If so, he couldn't have carried off any of the children, for a more subdued and better-behaved trio of youngsters you won't find anywhere. But Nackles, being brand-new and never having had a meal before, would need *somebody*. Somebody to whom he was real, somebody not

170

protected by the shield of Santa Claus. And, as I say, Frank was drinking that night. Alcohol makes the brain believe in the existence of all sorts of things. Also, Frank was a spoiled child if there ever was one.

There's no question but that Frank Junior and Linda Joyce and Stewart believe in Nackles. And Frank spread the gospel of Nackles to others, some of whom spread it to their own children. And some of whom will spread the new Evil to other parents. And ours is a mobile society, with families constantly being transferred by Daddy's company from one end of the country to another, so how long can it be before Nackles is a power not only in this one city, but all across the nation?

I don't know if Nackles exists, or will exist. All I know for sure is that there's suddenly a new level of meaning in the lyric of that popular Christmas song. You know the one I mean:

You'd better watch out.

J. G. Ballard's fascination with myth-figures has given his fiction a dreamlike intensity unmatched by the work of any other modern fantasist. Here he turns his talents to a curiously muted story of guilt spanning many centuries . . . a story as haunting as its central figure.

THE LOST LEONARDO
J. G. Ballard

The disappearance—or, to put it less euphemistically—the theft of the *Crucifixion* by Leonardo da Vinci from the Museum of the Louvre in Paris, discovered on the morning of April 19, 1968, caused a scandal of unprecedented proportions. A decade of major art thefts, such as those of Goya's *Duke of Wellington* from the National Gallery, London, and collections of impressionists from the homes of millionaires in the South of France and California, as well as the obviously inflated prices paid in the auction rooms of Bond Street and the Rue de Rivoli, might have been expected to accustom the general public to the loss of yet another over-publicized masterpiece, but in fact the news of its disappearance was received by the world with genuine consternation and outrage. From all over the globe thousands of telegrams poured in daily at the Quai d'Orsay and the Louvre, the French consulates at Bogata and Guatemala City were stoned, and the panache and finesse of press attachés at every embassy from Buenos Aires to Bangkok were strained to their not inconsiderable limits.

I myself reached Paris over twenty-four hours after what was being called "the great Leonardo scandal" had taken place, and the atmosphere of bewilderment and indignation was palpable. All the way from Orly Airport the newspaper headlines on the kiosks blazoned the same story.

As the Continental Daily Mail put it succinctly:

LEONARDO'S CRUCIFIXION STOLEN
£5 Million Masterpiece Vanishes from Louvre

Official Paris, by all accounts, was in uproar. The hapless director of the Louvre had been recalled from a UNESCO conference in Brasilia and was now on the carpet at the Elysée Palace, reporting personally to the President, the Deuxième Bureau had been alerted, and at least three ministers without portfolio had been appointed, their political futures staked to the recovery of the painting. As the President himself had remarked at his press conference the previous afternoon, the theft of a Leonardo was an affair not only for France, but for the entire world, and in a passionate plea he enjoined everyone to help effect its speedy return. (Despite the emotionally charged atmosphere, cynical observers noticed that this was the first crisis of his career when the Great Man did not conclude his peroration with "Vive La France.")

My own feelings, despite my professional involvement with the fine arts—I was, and am, a director of Northeby's, the world-famous Bond Street auctioneers—by and large coincided with those of the general public. As the taxi passed the Tuileries Gardens I looked out at the crude half-tone illustrations of da Vinci's effulgent masterpiece reproduced in the newspapers, recalling the immense splendor of the painting, with its unparalleled composition and handling of chiaroscura, its unsurpassed technique, which together had launched the High Renaissance and provided a beacon for the sculptors, painters and architects of the Baroque.

Despite the two million reproductions of the painting sold each year, not to mention the countless pastiches and inferior imitations, the subject matter of the painting still retained its majestic power. Completed two years after da

Vinci's *Virgin and St. Anne,* also in the Louvre, it was not only one of the few Leonardos to have survived intact the thousand eager hands of the retouchers of four centuries, but was the only painting by the master, apart from the dissolving and barely visible *Last Supper,* in which he had handled a composition with a large landscape and a huge gallery of supporting figures.

It was this latter factor, perhaps, which gave the painting its terrifying, hallucinatory power. The enigmatic, almost ambivalent expression on the face of the dying Christ, the hooded serpentine eyes of the Madonna and Magdalene, these characteristic signatures of Leonardo became more than mere mannerisms when set against the huge spiral concourse of attendant figures that seemed to swirl up into the distant sky across the Place of Bones, transforming the whole image of the crucifixion into an apocalyptic vision of the resurrection and judgment of mankind. From this single canvas had come the great frescoes of Michelangelo and Raphael in the Sistine Chapel, the entire schools of Tintoretto and Veronese. That someone should have the audacity to steal it was a tragic comment on mankind's respect for its greatest monuments.

And yet, I wondered as we arrived at the offices of Galleries Normande et Cie in the Madeleine, had the painting really been stolen at all? Its size, some 15 feet by 18 feet, and weight—it had been transferred from the original canvas to an oak panel—precluded a single fanatic or psychopath, and no gang of professional art thieves would waste their time stealing a painting for which there would be no market. Could it be, perhaps, that the French government was hoping to distract attention from some other impending event?— though nothing less than the re-introduction of the monarchy and the coronation of the Bourbon Pretender in Notre Dame would have required such an elaborate smoke-screen.

At the first opportunity I raised my doubts with Georg de Stael, the director of Galleries Normande with whom I was staying during my visit. Ostensibly I had come to Paris to attend a conference that afternoon of art dealers and gallery directors who had also suffered from thefts of major works of art, but to any outsider our mood of elation and high spirits would have suggested some other motive. This, of course, would have been correct. Whenever a large stone is cast into the turbid waters of international art, people such as myself and Georg de Stael immediately take up our positions on the bank, watching for any unusual ripple or malodorous bubble. Without doubt the theft of the Leonardo would reveal a good deal more than the identity of some crackpot cat burglar. All the darker fish would now be swimming frantically for cover, and a salutary blow had been struck at our official establishment.

Such feelings of revenge obviously animated Georg de Stael as he moved with dapper, light-footed ease around his desk to greet me. His blue silk summer suit, well in advance of the season, glittered like his smooth brilliantined hair, his svelte rapacious features breaking into a smile of roguish charm.

"My dear Charles, I assure you, categorically, the confounded picture has actually gone"—Georg shot out three inches of elegant chalk-blue cuff and snapped his hands together—"puff! For once everyone is speaking the truth. What is even more remarkable, the painting was genuine."

"I don't know whether I'm glad to hear that or not," I admitted. "But it's certainly more than you can say for most of the Louvre—and the National Gallery."

"Agreed." Georg straddled his desk, his patent leather shoes twinkling in the light. "I had hoped that this catastrophe might induce the authorities to make a clean breast of some of their so-called treasures, in an attempt, as it were, to dispel some of the magic surrounding the Leonardo. But they are in a complete fuddle."

For a moment we both contemplated what such a sequence of admissions would do to the art markets of the world— the price of anything even remotely genuine would soar— as well as to the popular image of Renaissance painting as something sacrosanct and unparalleled. However, this was not to gainsay the genius of the stolen Leonardo.

"Tell me, Georg," I asked, "who stole it?" I assumed he knew.

For the first time in many years Georg seemed at a loss for an answer. He shrugged helplessly. "My dear Charles, I just do not know. It's a complete mystery. Everyone is as baffled as you are."

"In that case it must be an inside job."

"Definitely not. The present crowd at the Louvre are beyond reproach." He tapped the telephone. "This morning I was speaking to some of our more dubious contacts— Antweiler in Messina and Kokoschka in Beirut—and they are both mystified. In fact, they're convinced that either the whole thing is a put-up affair by the present regime, or else the Kremlin itself is involved."

"The Kremlin?" I echoed incredulously. At the invocation

of this name the atmosphere heightened, and for the next half an hour we spoke in whispers.

The conference that afternoon, at the Palais de Chaillot, offered no further clues. Chief Detective-Inspector Carnot, a massive gloomy man in a faded blue suit, took the chair, flanked by other agents of the Deuxieme Bureau. All of them looked tired and dispirited; by now they were having to check up on some dozen false alarms each hour. Behind them, like a hostile jury, sat a sober-faced group of investigators from Lloyds of London and Morgan Guaranty Trust of New York. By contrast, the two hundred dealers and agents sitting on the gilt chairs below the platform presented an animated scene, chattering away in a dozen languages and flying a score of speculative kites.

After a brief résumé, delivered in a voice of sepulchral resignation, Inspector Carnot introduced a burly Dutchman next to him, Superintendent Jurgens of the Interpol bureau at The Hague, and then called on M. Auguste Pecard. This merely confirmed that the security arrangements at the Louvre were first-class and that it was absolutely impossible for the painting to have been stolen. I could see that Pecard was still not entirely convinced that it had gone.

". . . the pressure panels in the floor surrounding the painting have not been disturbed, nor have the two infrared beams across its face been broken. Gentlemen, I assure you it is impossible to remove the painting without first dismantling the bronze frame. This alone weighs eight hundred pounds and is bolted into the wall behind it. But the electric alarm circuit which flows through the bolts was not interrupted . . ."

I was looking up at the two life-size photographs of the front and reverse faces of the painting fastened to the screens behind the dais. The latter showed the back of the oak panel with its six aluminum ribs, contact points for the circuit and a mass of chalked graffiti enscribed over the years by the museum laboratories. The photographs had been taken the last time the picture was removed for cleaning, and after a brief bout of questioning it transpired that this had been completed only two days before the theft.

At this news the atmosphere of the conference changed. The hundred private conversations ceased, colored silk handkerchiefs were returned to their breast pockets.

I nudged Georg de Stael. "So that explains it." Obviously the painting had disappeared during its period in the labora-

176

tory, where the security arrangements would be less than foolproof. "It was not stolen from the *gallery* at all."

The hubbub around us had restarted. Two hundred noses once again were lifted to scent the trail. So the painting had been stolen, was somewhere at large in the world. The rewards to the discoverer, if not the Legion of Honor or a Knighthood, then at least complete freedom from all income tax and foreign exchange investigations, hovered like a specter before us.

On the way back, however, Georg stared somberly through the window of the taxi.

"The painting *was* stolen from the gallery," he said to me pensively. "I saw it there myself just twelve hours before it vanished." He took my arm and held it tightly. "We'll find it, Charles, for the glory of Northeby's and the Galleries Normande. But, my God, my God, the man who stole it was a thief out of this world!"

So began the quest for the missing Leonardo. I returned to London the next morning, but Georg and I were in regular contact by telephone. Initially, like all the others on its trail, we merely listened, ears to the ground for an unfamiliar footfall. In the crowded auction rooms and galleries we waited for the indiscrete word, for the giveaway clue. Business, of course, was buoyant; every museum and private owner with a third-rate Rubens or Raphael had now moved up a rung. With luck the renewed market activity would uncover some distant accomplice of the thief, or a previous substitute for the Leonardo—perhaps a pastiche *Mona Lisa* by one of Verocchio's pupils—would be jettisoned by the thief and appear on one of the shadier markets. If the hunt for the vanished painting was conducted as loudly as ever in the outside world, within the trade all was quiet and watchful.

In fact, too quiet. By rights something should have materialized, some faint clue should have appeared on the fine filters of the galleries and auction rooms. But nothing was heard. As the wave of activity launched by the displaced Leonardo rolled past and business resumed its former tempo, the painting became just another on the list of lost masterpieces.

Only Georg de Stael seemed able to maintain his interest in the search. Now and then he would put through a call to London, requesting some obscure piece of information about an anonymous buyer of a Titian or Rembrandt in the late 18th Century, or the history of some damaged copy by a pupil of Rubens or Raphael. He seemed particularly interested in works known to have been damaged and subsequently restored, information with which many private owners are naturally jealous of parting.

Consequently, when he called to see me in London some four months after the disappearance of the Leonardo, it was not in a purely jocular sense that I asked: "Well, Georg, do you know who stole it yet?"

Unclipping a large briefcase, Georg smiled at me darkly. "Would it surprise you if I said 'yes'? As a matter of fact, I don't know, but I have an idea, a hypothesis, shall we say. I thought you might be interested to hear it."

"Of course, Georg. So this is what you've been up to."

He raised a thin forefinger to silence me. Below the veneer of easy charm I noticed a new mood of seriousness, a cutting of conversational corners. "First, Charles, before you laugh me out of your office, let me say that I consider my theory completely fantastic and implausible, and yet"—he shrugged deprecatingly—"it seems to be the only one possible. To prove it I need your help."

"Given before asked. But what is this theory? I can't wait to hear."

He hesitated, apparently uncertain whether to expose his idea, and then began to empty the briefcase, taking out a series of looseleaf files which he placed in a row facing him along the desk. These contained what appeared to be photographic reproductions of a number of paintings, areas within them marked with white ink. Several of the photographs were enlargements of details, all of a high-faced, goatee-bearded man in medieval costume.

Georg inverted six of the larger plates so that I could see them. "You recognize these, of course?"

I nodded. With the exception of one, Rubens' *Pieta* in the Hermitage Museum at Leningrad, I had seen the originals of them all within the previous five years. The others were the missing Leonardo *Crucifixion*, the *Crucifixions* by Veronese, Goya and Holbein, and that by Poussin, entitled *The Place of Golgotha*. All were in public museums—the Louvre, San Stefano in Venice, the Prado and the Ryksmuseum, Amsterdam—and all were familiar, well-authenticated master-works, center-pieces, apart from the Poussin, of major national collections. "It's reassuring to see them. I trust they're all in good hands. Or are they next on the mysterious thief's shopping list?"

Georg shook his head. "No, I don't think he's very interested in these. Though he keeps a watching brief over them." Again I observed the marked change in Georg's manner, the reflective private humor. "Do you notice anything else?"

I compared the photographs again. "They're all crucifixions. Authentic, except perhaps in minor details. They were all easel paintings." I shrugged. "What else?"

"They all, at some time, have been stolen." Georg moved quickly from right to left. "The Poussin from the Chateau Loire collection in 1822, the Goya in 1806 from the Monte Cassino monastery, by Napoleon, the Veronese from the Prado in 1891, the Leonardo four months ago as we know, and the Holbein in 1943, looted for the Herman Goering collection."

"Interesting," I commented. "But few master-works haven't been stolen at some time. I hope this isn't a key point in your theory."

"No, but in conjunction with another factor it gains in significance. Now." He handed the Leonardo reproduction to me. "Anything unusual there?" When I shook my head at the familiar image he picked another photograph of the missing painting. "What about that one?"

The photographs had been taken from slightly different perspectives, but otherwise seemed identical. "They are both of the original *Crucifixion*," George explained, "taken in the Louvre within a month of its disappearance."

"I give up," I admitted. "They seem the same. No— wait a minute!" I pulled the table light nearer and bent over the plates, as Georg nodded. "They're slightly different. What is going on?"

Quickly, figure by figure, I compared the photographs, within a few moments seized on the minute disparity. In almost every particular the pictures were identical, but one figure out of the score or more on the crowded field had been altered. On the left, where the procession wound its way up the hillside toward the three crosses, the face of one of the bystanders had been completely repainted. Although, in the center of the painting, the Christ hung from the cross some hours after the crucifixion, by a sort of spatio-temporal perspective—a common device in all Renaissance painting for overcoming the static nature of the single canvas—the receding procession carried the action backward through time, so that one followed the invisible presence of the Christ on his painful last ascent of Golgotha.

The figure whose face had been repainted formed part of the crowd on the lower slopes. A tall powerfully built man in a black robe, he had obviously been the subject of special care by Leonardo, who had invested him with the magnificent physique and serpentine grace usually reserved for his depiction of angels. Looking at the photograph in my left hand, the original unretouched version, I realized that Leonardo had indeed intended the figure to represent an angel of death, or rather, one of those agents of the unconscious, terrifying in their enigmatic calm, in their brooding ambivalence, who seem to preside in his paintings over all man's deepest fears and longings, like the gray-faced statues that stare down from the midnight cornices and pediments of the necropolis at Pompeii.

All this, so typical of Leonardo and his curious vision, seemed to be summed up by the face of this tall angelic figure. Turned almost in profile over the left shoulder, the face looked up toward the cross, a faint flicker of pity investing the gray saturnine features. A high forehead, slightly flared at the temples, rose above the handsome semitic nose and mouth. A trace of a smile, of compassionate resignation and understanding, hung about the lips, providing a solitary source of light which illuminated the remainder of the face partly obscured by the shadows of the thundering sky.

In the photograph on my right, however, all this had been altered completely. The whole character of this angelic figure had been replaced by a new conception. The superficial likeness remained, but the face had lost its expression of tragic compassion. The later artist had reversed its posture altogether, and the head was turned away from the cross and over the right shoulder toward the early city of Jerusalem whose spectral towers rose like a city of Miltonic hell in the blue dusk. While the other bystanders followed the ascending Christ as if helpless to assist him, the expression on the face of the black-robed figure was arrogant and critical, the tension of the averted neck muscles indicating that he had swung his head away almost in disgust from the spectacle before him.

"What is this?" I asked, pointing to the latter photograph. "Some lost pupil's copy? I can't see why—"

Georg leaned forward and tapped the print. "*That* is the original Leonardo. Don't you understand, Charles? The version on your left which you were admiring for so many minutes was superimposed by some unknown retoucher, only a few years after da Vinci's death." He smiled at my scepticism. "Believe me, it's true. The figure concerned is only a minor part of the composition; no one had seriously examined it before, as the rest of the painting is without doubt
180

original. These additions were discovered five months ago shortly after the painting was removed for cleaning. The infrared examination revealed the completely intact profile below."

He passed two more photographs to me, both large-scale details of the head, in which the contrasts of characterization were even more obvious. "As you can see from the brush-work in the shading, the retouching was done by a right-handed artist, whereas we know, of course, that da Vinci was left-handed."

"Well . . ." I shrugged. "It seems strange. But if what you say is correct, why on earth was such a small detail altered? The whole conception of the character is different."

"An interesting question," Georg said ambiguously. "Incidentally, the figure is that of Ahasuerus, the Wandering Jew." He pointed to the man's feet. "He's always conventionally represented by the crossed sandal-straps of the Essene Sect, to which Jesus himself may have belonged."

I picked up the photographs again. "The Wandering Jew," I repeated softly. "How curious. The man who taunted Christ to move faster and was condemned to rove the surface of the earth until the Second Coming. It's almost as if the retoucher were an apologist for him, superimposing this expression of tragic pity over Leonardo's representation. There's an idea for you, Georg. You know how courtiers and wealthy merchants who gathered at painters' studios were informally incorporated into their paintings—perhaps Ahasuerus would move around, posing as himself, driven by a sort of guilt compulsion, then later steal the paintings and revise them. Now there *is* a theory."

I looked across at Georg, waiting for him to reply. He was nodding slowly, eyes watching mine in unspoken agreement, all trace of humor absent. "Georg!" I exclaimed. "Are you serious? Do you mean—"

He interrupted me gently but forcefully. "Charles, just give me a few more minutes to explain. I warned you that my theory was fantastic." Before I could protest he passed me another photograph. "The Veronese *Crucifixion*. See anyone you recognize? On the bottom left."

I raised the photograph to the light. "You're right. The late Venetian treatment is different, far more pagan, but it's quite obvious. You know, Georg, it's a remarkable likeness."

"Agreed. But it's not only the likeness. Look at the pose and characterization."

Identified again by his black robes and crossed sandal straps, the figure of Ahasuerus stood among the throng on the crowded canvas. The unusual feature was not so much that the pose was again that of the retouched Leonardo, with Ahasuerus now looking with an expression of deep compassion at the dying Christ—an altogether meaningless interpretation—but the remarkable likeness between the two faces, almost as if they had been painted from the same model. The beard was perhaps a little fuller, in the Venetian manner, but the planes of the face, the flaring of the temples, the handsome coarseness of the mouth and jaw, the wise resignation in the eyes, that of some well-traveled physican witnessing an act of barbaric beauty and power, all these were exactly echoed from the Leonardo.

I gestured helplessly. "It's an amazing coincidence."

Georg nodded. "Another is that this painting, like the Leonardo, was stolen shortly after being extensively cleaned. When it was recovered in Florence two years later it was slightly damaged, and no further attempts were made to restore the painting." Georg paused. "Do you see my point, Charles?"

"More or less. I take it you suspect that if the Veronese were now cleaned a rather different version of Ahasuerus would be found. Veronese's original depiction."

"Exactly. After all, the present treatment makes no sense. If you're still skeptical, look at these others."

Standing up, we began to go through the remainder of the photographs. In each of the others, the Poussin, Holbein, Goya and Rubens, the same figure was to be found, the same dark saturnine face regarding the cross with an expression of compassionate understanding. In view of the very different styles of the artists, the degree of similarity was remarkable. In each, as well, the pose was meaningless, the characterization completely at odds with the legendary role of Ahasuerus.

By now the intensity of Georg's conviction was communicating itself to me physically. He drummed the desk with the palm of one hand. "In each case, Charles, all six paintings were stolen shortly after they had been cleaned —even the Holbein was looted from the Herman Goering collection by some renegade S.S. after being repaired by concentration camp inmates. As you yourself said, it's almost as if the thief was unwilling for the world to see the true image of Ahasuerus' character exposed, and deliberately painted in these apologias."

"But Georg, you're making a large assumption there. Can you prove that in each case, apart from the Leonardo, there is an original version below the present one?"

"Not yet. Naturally galleries are reluctant to give anyone the opportunity to show that their works are not entirely genuine. I know all this is still hypothesis, but what other explanation can you find?"

Shaking my head, I went over to the window, letting the noise and movement of Bond Street cut through Georg's heady speculations. "Are you seriously suggesting, Georg, that the black-robed figure of Ahasuerus is promenading somewhere on those pavements below us now, and that all through the centuries he's been stealing and retouching paintings that represent him spurning Jesus? The idea's ludicrous!"

"No more ludicrous than the theft of the painting. Everyone agrees it could not have been stolen by anyone bounded by the laws of the physical universe."

For a moment we stared at each other across the desk. "All right," I temporized, not wishing to offend him. The intensity of his *idée fixe* had alarmed me. "But isn't our best plan simply to sit back and wait for the Leonardo to turn up again?"

"Not necessairily. Most of the stolen paintings remained lost for ten or twenty years. Perhaps the effort of stepping outside the bounds of space and time exhausts him, or perhaps the sight of the original paintings terrifies him so—" He broke off as I began to come forward to him. "Look, Charles, it *is* fantastic, but there's a slim chance it may be true. This is where I need your help. It's obvious this man must be a great patron of the arts, drawn by an irresistible compulsion, by unassuageable feelings of guilt, toward those artists painting crucifixions. We must begin to watch the sale rooms and galleries. That face, those black eyes and that haunted profile—sooner or later we'll see him, searching for another *Crucifixion* or *Pieta*. Cast your mind back—do you recognize that face?"

I looked down at the carpet, the image of the dark-eyed wanderer before me. *Go quicker,* he had taunted Jesus as he passed bearing the cross toward Golgotha, and Jesus had replied: *I go, but thou shalt wait until I return.* I was about to say "no," but something restrained me, some reflex pause of recognition stirred through my mind. That handsome Levantine profile, in a different costume, of course, a smart dark-striped lounge suit, gold-topped cane and spats, bidding through an agent . . .

"You *have* seen him?" Georg came over to me. "Charles, I think I have too."

I gestured him away. "I'm not sure, Georg, but . . . I almost
183

wonder." Curiously it was the retouched portrait of Ahasuer-us, rather than Leonardo's original, which seemed more real, closer to the face I felt sure I had actually seen. Suddenly I pivoted on my heel. "Confound it, Georg, do you realize that if this incredible idea of yours is true this man must have spoken to Leonardo? To Michelangelo, and Titian and Rembrandt?"

Georg nodded. "And someone else too," he added pensively.

For the next month, after Georg's return to Paris I spent less time in my office and more in the sale rooms, watching for that familiar profile which something convinced me I had seen before. But for this undeniable conviction I would have dismissed Georg's hypothesis as obsessive fantasy. I made a few tactful inquiries of my assistants, and to my annoyance two of them also vaguely remembered such a person. After this I found myself unable to drive Georg de Stael's fancies from my mind. No further news was heard of the missing Leonardo—the complete absence of any clues mystified the police and the art world alike.

Consequently, it was with an immense feeling of relief, as much as of excitement, that I received five weeks later the following telegram:

CHARLES. COME IMMEDIATELY. I HAVE SEEN HIM. GEORG DE STAEL.

This time, as my taxi carried me from Orly Airport to the Madeleine, it was no idle amusement that made me watch the Tuileries Gardens for any sight of a tall man in a black slouch hat sneaking through the trees with a rolled-up canvas under his arm. Was Georg de Stael finally and irretrievably out of his mind, or had he in fact seen the phantom Ahasuerus?

When he greeted me at the doorway of Normande et Cie his handshake was as firm as ever, his face composed and relaxed. In his office he sat back and regarded me quizzically over the tips of his fingers, evidently so sure of himself that he could let his news bide its time.

"He's here, Charles," he said at last. "In Paris, staying at the Ritz. He's been attending the sales of 19th and 20th Century masters. With luck you'll see him this afternoon."

For once my incredulity returned, but before I could stutter my objections Georg silenced me.

"He's just as we expected, Charles. Tall and powerfully built, with a kind of statuesque grace, the sort of man who moves easily among the rich and nobility. Leonardo and

Holbein caught him exactly, that strange haunted intensity about the eyes, the wind of deserts and great ravines."

"When did you first see him?"

"Yesterday afternoon. We had almost completed the 19th Century sales when a small Van Gogh—an inferior copy by the painter of *The Good Samaritan*—came up. One of those painted during his last madness, full of turbulent spirals, the figures like tormented beasts. For some reason the Samaritan's face reminded me of Ahasuerus. Just then I looked up across the crowded auction room." Georg sat forward. "To my amazement there he was, sitting not three feet away in the front row of seats, staring me straight in the face. I could hardly take my eyes off him. As soon as the bidding started he came in hard, going up in two thousands of francs."

"He took the painting?"

"No. Luckily I still had my wits about me. Obviously I had to be sure he was the right man. Previously his appearances have been solely as Ahasuerus, but few painters today are doing crucifixions in the *bel canto* style, and he may have tried to redress the balance of guilt by appearing in other roles, the Samaritan for example. He was left alone at 15,000—actually the reserve was only ten—so I leaned over and had the painting withdrawn. I was sure he would come back today if he was Ahasuerus, and I needed 24 hours to get hold of you and the police. Two of Carnot's men will be here this afternoon. I told them some vague story and they'll be unobtrusive. Anyway, naturally there was the devil's own row when this little Van Gogh was withdrawn. Everyone here thought I'd gone mad. Our dark-faced friend leaped up and demanded the reason, so I had to say that I suspected the authenticity of the painting and was protecting the reputation of the gallery, but if satisfied would put it up the next day."

"Clever of you," I commented.

Georg inclined his head. "I thought so too. It was a neat trap. Immediately he launched into a passionate defense of the painting—normally a man with his obvious experience of sale rooms would have damned it out of hand—bringing up all sorts of details about Vincent's third-rate pigments, the back of the canvas and so on. The *back* of the canvas, note, what the sitter would most remember about a painting. I said I was more or less convinced, and he promised to be back today. He left his address in case any difficulty came up." Georg took a silver-embossed card from his pocket and read out: " '*Count Enrique Danilewicz, Villa d'Est,*
185

Cadaques, Costa Brava.' " Across the card was inscribed: *Ritz Hotel, Paris.*

"Cadaques," I repeated. "Dali is nearby there, at Port Lligat. Another coincidence."

"Perhaps more than a coincidence. Guess what the Catalan master is at present executing for the new Cathedral of St. Joseph at San Diego . . . ? One of his greatest commissions to date. Exactly! A crucifixion. Our friend Ahasuerus is once more doing his rounds."

Georg pulled a leather-bound pad from his center drawer. "Now listen to this. I've been doing some research on the identity of the models for Ahasuerus—usually some petty princeling or merchant-king. The Leonardo is untraceable. He kept open house, beggars and goats wandered through his studio at will, anyone could have got in and posed. But the others were more select. The Ahasuerus in the Holbein was posed by a Sir Henry Daniels, a leading banker and friend of Henry VIII. In the Veronese by a member of the Council of Ten, none other than the Doge-to-be, Enri Danieli —we've both stayed in the hotel of that name in Venice. In the Rubens by Baron Henrik Nielson, Danish Ambassador to Amsterdam, and in the Goya by a certain Enrico Da Nella, financier and great patron of the Prado. While in the Poussin by the famous dilenttante, Henri, Duc de Nile."

Georg closed the notebook with a flourish. I said: "It's certainly remarkable."

"You don't exaggerate. Danilewicz, Daniels, Danieli, Da Nella, de Nile and Nielson. Alias Ahasuerus. You know, Charles, I'm a little frightened, but I think we have the missing Leonardo within our grasp."

Nothing was more disappointing, therefore, than the failure of our quarry to appear that afternoon.

The transfer of the Van Gogh from the previous day's sale had fortunately given it a high lot number, after some three dozen 20th Century paintings. As the bids for the Kandinsky's and Leger's came in, I sat on the podium behind Georg, surveying the elegant assembly below. In such an international gathering, of American connoisseurs, English press lords, French and Italian aristocracy, colored by a generous sprinkling of ladies of the demi-monde, the presence of even the remarkable figure Georg had described would not have been overconspicuous. However, as we moved steadily down the catalogue, and the flashing of the photographers' bulbs became more and more wearisome, I began to wonder whether he would appear at all. His seat in the front row remained reserved for him, and I waited impatiently for this fugitive through time and space to materialize and make his magnificent entry promptly as the Van Gogh was announced.

As it transpired, both the seat and the painting remained untaken. Put off by Georg's doubts as to its authenticity, the painting failed to reach its reserve, and as the last sales closed we were left alone on the podium, our bait untaken.

"He must have smelled a rat," Georg whispered, after the attendants had confirmed that Count Danilewicz was not present in any of the other sale-rooms. A moment later a telephone call to the Ritz established that he had vacated his suite and left Paris for the south.

"No doubt he's expert at sidestepping such traps. What now?" I asked.

"Cadaques."

"Georg! Are you insane?"

"Not at all. There's only a chance, but we must take it! Inspector Carnot will find a plane. I'll invent some fantasy to please him. Come on, Charles, I'm convinced we'll find the Leonardo in his villa."

We arrived at Barcelona, Carnot in tow, with Superintendent Jurgens of Interpol to smooth our way through customs, and three hours later set off in a posse of police cars for Cadaques. The fast ride along that fantastic coastline, with its monstrous rocks like giant sleeping reptiles and the glazed light over the embalmed sea, reminiscent of all Dali's timeless beaches, was a fitting prelude to the final chapter. The air bled diamonds around us, sparkling off the immense spires of rock, the huge lunar ramparts suddenly giving way to placid bays of luminous water.

. The Villa d'Est stood on a promontory a thousand feet above the town, its high walls and shuttered moorish windows glistening in the sunlight like white quartz. The great black doors, like the vaults of a cathedral, were sealed, and a continuous ringing of the bell brought no reply. At this a prolonged wrangle ensued between Jurgens and the local police, who were torn between their reluctance to offend an important local dignitary—Count Danilewicz had evidently founded a dozen scholarships for promising regional artists—and their eagerness to partake in the discovery of the missing Leonardo.

Impatient of all this, Georg and I borrowed a car and chauffeur and set off for Port Lligat, promising the Inspector that we would return in time for the commercial airliner which was due to land at Barcelona from Paris some two hours later, presumably carrying Count Danilewicz. "No doubt, however," Georg remarked softly as we moved off, "he travels by other transport."

What excuse we would make to penetrate the private menage of Spain's most distinguished painter I had not decided, though the possibility of simultaneous one-man shows at Northeby's and Galleries Normande might have appeased him. As we drove down the final approach to the familiar tiered white villa by the water's edge, a large limousine came toward us, bearing away a recent guest.

Our two cars passed at a point where the effective width of the road was narrowed by a nexus of pot-holes and for a moment the heavy saloons wallowed side by side in the dust like two groaning mastodons.

Suddenly, Georg clenched my elbow and pointed through the window.

"Charles! There he is!"

Lowering my window as the drivers cursed each other, I looked out into the dim cabin of the adjacent car. Sitting in the back seat, his head raised to the noise, was a huge Rasputin-like figure in a black pin-stripe suit, his white cuffs and gold tie-pin glinting in the shadows, gloved hands crossed in front of him over an ivory-handled cane. As we edged past I caught a glimpse of his great saturnine head, whose living features matched and corroborated exactly those by so many hands upon so many canvases. The dark eyes glowed with an intense luster, the black eyebrows rearing from his high forehead like wings, the sharp curve of the beard carrying the sweep of his strong jaw forward into the air like a spear.

Elegantly suited though he was, his whole presence radiated a tremendous restless energy, a powerful charisma that seemed to extend beyond the confines of the car. For a moment we exchanged glances, separated from each other by only two or three feet. He was staring beyond me, however, at some distant landmark, some invisible hillcrest forever silhouetted against the horizon, and I saw in his eyes that expression of irredeemable remorse, of almost hallucinatory despair, untouched by self-pity or any conceivable extenuation, that one imagines on the faces of the damned.

"Stop him!" Georg shouted into the noise. "Charles, warn him!"

Our car edged upward out of the final rut, and I shouted through the engine fumes:

"Ahasuerus! Ahasuerus!"

His wild eyes swung back, and he rose forward in his seat, a black arm on the window ledge, like some immense half-crippled angel about to take flight. Then the two cars surged apart, and we were separated from the limousine by a tornado of dust. Enchanted from the placid air, for ten minutes the squall seethed about us.

By the time it subsided and we had managed to reverse, the great limousine had vanished.

They found the Leonardo in the Villa d'Est, propped against the wall in its great gilt frame in the dining room. To everyone's surprise the house was found to be completely empty, though two manservants who had been given the day off testified that when they left it that morning it had been lavishly furnished as usual. However, as Georg de Stael remarked, no doubt the vanished tenant had his own means of transport.

The painting had suffered no damage, though the first cursory glance confirmed that a skilled hand had been at work on a small portion. The face of the black-robed figure once again looked upward to the cross, a hint of hope, perhaps even of redemption, in its wistful gaze. The brush-work had dried, but George reported to me that the thin layer of varnish was still tacky.

On our feted and triumphant return to Paris, Georg and I recommended that in view of the hazards already suffered by the painting no further attempts should be made to clean or restore it, and with a grateful sigh the director and staff of the Louvre sealed it back into its wall. The painting may not be entirely by the hand of Leonardo da Vinci, but we feel that the few additions have earned their place.

No further news was heard of Count Danilewicz, but Georg recently told me that a Professor Henrico Daniella was reported to have been appointed director of the Museum of Pan-Christian Art at Santiago. His attempts to communicate with Professor Daniella had failed, but he gathered that the Museum was extremely anxious to build up a large collection of paintings of the Cross.

In the past few years there's been some commotion in England following the discovery that witchcraft is still (or again) practiced in certain secret enclaves, both in cities and countryside. Keith Roberts, probably the most talented new story-teller England has given us in the last decade, has taken some of this background, mixed it with humor and a faultless ear for dialect, and created a delightful teenaged witch named Anita who has a simple predilection for Trouble. But trouble is not always a simple matter, as Anita discovers in this not-so-lighthearted story.

TIMOTHY
Keith Roberts

Anita was bored; and when she was bored odd things were liable to happen. Granny Thompson, who studied her granddaughter far more closely than she would have cared to admit, had been noticing a brooding look in her eyes for some days. She cast about for chores that would keep her mind off more exotic mischief for a time. "There's the 'en run" intoned the old lady. "That wants a good gooin'-uvver fer a start. 'Arf the posts orl of a tip, 'oles everywheer. . . .

An' the path up ter the you-know-wot. Nearly *went* on that, yisdey. Place gooin' orl of 'eap, an' yer sits there *moanin'*. . . ."

Anita sneered. "Chicken runs. Paths up to you-know-whats. I want to do something *interesting*, Gran. Like working a brand new spell. Can't we—"

"No we *kent!*" snapped the old lady irritably. "Spells, spells, kent think o' nothink but *spells*. You wants ter look a bit lively, my gel. Goo on out an' earn yer kep, sit there chopsin'. . . . Goo on, git summat *done*. Git some o' that fat orf yer. . . ."

Anita hissed furiously. She was very proud of her figure.

"Mackle up that there chair-back in the wosh'ouse," snarled Granny, warming to her theme. "Tek the truck down to ole Goody's place an' git them line props wot's bin cut an' waitin' arf a month. Git rid of orl that muck an' jollop yer chucked down by the copper 'ole a week larst *Toosdey*. Git the three o'clock inter Ket'rin', save my legs fere a change. 'Ole 'eap o' stuff we're run out on. . . ."

"Oh *please* Gran, not today. . . ."

Granny Thompson softened a little. She didn't like goin to Kettering either. "Well goo on uvver to Aggie Everett's then an' git a couple of 'andfuls o' flour . . . an' watch she dunt put no chiblins o' nuthink in *with* it. Aggie's sense o' wot's funny ent the same as anybody normal. . . . An' when yer gits back yer kin goo up an' git orl that birdsnest muck out o' the *thack*. I ent avin' that game agin, wadn't the same fer a month larst time I went up that there ladder. . . ."

Anita fled, partly to escape her Granny's inventiveness, partly because there was some truth in the crack about her weight. In the winter she seemed to store fat like a dormouse, there was no answer to it; she'd tried a summer dress on only a day before and there had been too much Anita nearly everywhere. She decided to make a start on the chicken run. Levitation and spellraising were all very well in their way but there was something peculiarly satisfying once in a while in taking ordinary wood and nails and a perfectly normal hammer and lashing about as vigorously as possible. She rapidly tired of the job though. The rolls of wire netting were recalcitrant, possessed of a seemingly infinite number of hooks and snags that all but defied unravelment; once undone, they buried themselves gleefully in her palms. And the ground was soaked and nasty so that worms spurted out whenever she tried to drive a post. Anita leaned on the somewhat disheveled end frame of the run and yawned. She probed the mind of the nearest of its occupant and got back the usual moronic burbling about the next feeding-time. Hens are easily the most boring of companions.

Anita snorted, pushed back her hair, wiped her hot face and decided to go to Aggie's for the flour. She knew her Granny still had a good stock of practically everything in the larder and that the errand was only an excuse to get her out from underfoot for a while, but that didn't matter. She could take the long path round the far side of Foxhanger; perhaps the wood creatures were waking up by now.

She walked between the trees, well muffled in jeans, boots and donkey jacket. As she moved she scuffed irritably at twigs and leaves. She hated this time of the year with a peculiar loathing. February is a pointless sort of month: neither hot nor cold, neither winter nor spring. No animals, no birds, the sky a dull, uniform gray. . . . Anita hung her head and frowned. If only things would get a move on. . . . There were creatures in old tree stumps and deep in the ground but the few she was able to contact were dozy and grumpy and made it quite clear they wanted to be left alone for another six weeks, longer if possible. Anita decided she would like to hibernate, curled paws over nose in some brown crackling lair of leaves. Another year she really must try it; at least she might wake up feeling like doing something.

If she had expected any comfort from Aggie Everett she was disappointed. The old lady was morose; she had recently developed a head cold, and treated herself with a variety of ancient remedies and felt as she put it "wuss in consiquence." She was wearing a muffler knotted several times round her thin neck; her face was pale and even more scrinched-looking than usual while her nose, always a delicate member, glowed like a stoplight. She confided to Anita that things "orl wanted a good shove, like"; her nephews would be coming down for the spring equinox and there were great plans for festivities but until then the Witches' Calendar was empty. The boys were away making cardboard boxes in far-off Northampton and there was nothing to do, nothing to do at all. . . .

On the way back Anita took a shortcut across part of the Johnsons' land and saw Timothy on the horizon. Lacking anything better to do, she detoured so as to pass close by where he stood. She couldn't help noticing that Timothy looked as depressed as she felt. He had been made the previous spring to keep the birds off the new crops, so he was nearly a year old; and for nine months now he had had nothing to do but stand and be rained on and blown

192

about by the wind and stare at the crown of Foxhanger wood away across the fields. Anita nodded mechanically as she trudged past. "Afternoon, Timothy. . . ." But it seemed he was too tired even to flap a ragged sleeve at her. She walked on.

Twenty yards away she stopped, struck by a thought. She stood still for a moment, weighing possibilities and feeling excited for the first time in weeks. Then she went back, stepping awkwardly on the chunky soil. She set the flour down, put her hands on her hips and looked at Timothy with her head on one side and her eyes narrowed appraisingly.

His face was badly weathered, of course, but that was unimportant; if anything, it tended to give him character. She walked up to him, brushed the laps of his coat and tilted his old floppy hat to a more rakish angle. She made motions as if parting his wild straw hair. Timothy watched her enigmatically from his almond-shaped slits of eyes. He was a very well built scarecrow; the Johnson boys had put him together one weekend when they were home from College and Anita, who loved dolls and effigies, had watched the process with delight. She prodded and patted him, making sure his baling-wire tendons had not rotted from exposure. Timothy was still in good order; and although he was actually held up by a thick stake driven into the ground he had legs of his own, which was a great advantage. Anita walked round him, examining him with the air of a connoisseur. There were great possibilities in Timothy.

She moved back a few paces. Her boredom was forgotten now; she saw the chance of a brand new and very interesting spell. She squatted on her heels, folded her arms and rocked slightly to aid concentration. Around her, winter-brown fields and empty sky waited silently; there was no breath of wind. Anita opened her eyes, and ran through the incantation quickly to make sure she had it firmly set in her mind. Then she waved a hand and began to mutter rapidly.

A strange thing happened. Although the day remained still something like a breeze moved across the ground to Timothy. Had there been grass it might have waved; but there was no grass, and the soil twinkled and shifted and was still again. The wind touched the scarecrow and it seemed his shoulders stiffened, his head came up a trifle. One of his outstretched arms waved; a wisp of straw dropped from his cuff and floated to the ground. The stake creaked faintly to itself.

193

Anita was vastly pleased. She stood and did a little jig; then she looked around carefully. For a moment she was tempted to finish the job on the spot and activate Timothy; but the Johnson farmhouse was in sight and scarecrows that talk and walk and sing maybe and dance, are best not seen by ordinary folk. Anita scurried off with her head full of plans. Twenty yards away she remembered the flour and went back for it. Timothy stirred impatiently on his post and a wind that was not a wind riffled the ragged tails of his coat. "Sorry," called Anita. "I'll come back tonight; we can talk then. Besides, I'd better look up the rest of the trick, just to be sure." She skipped away, not turning back again, and Timothy might or might not have waved. . . .

The sky was deep gray when she returned, and the swell of land on which the scarecrow stood looked dark and rough as a dog's back. Timothy was silhouetted against the last of the light, a black drunken shape looking bigger than he really was. Anita breathed words over him, made passes; then she undid the wire and cord that held him to his stake and Timothy slid down and stood a little uncertainly on his curious feet. Anita held his arm in case he tumbled and broke himself apart. "How do you feel?" she asked.

"Stiff," said Timothy. His voice had a musty, earthy sort of quality and when he opened his mouth there was an old smell of dry soil and libraries. Anita walked slowly with him across the furrows; for a time he tottered and reeled like an old man or a sick one, then he began to get more assurance and strode out rapidly. At first his noseless round face looked odd in the twilight but Anita soon got used to it. After all, Timothy was a personality, and personalities do not need to be conventionally handsome. She crossed the field with the scarecrow jolting beside her, headed for the cover of the nearest trees.

She found Timothy's mind was as empty as a thing could be; but that was part of his charm, because Anita could stock it with whatever she wanted him to know. At first the learning process was difficult because one question had a knack of leading to a dozen others and often the simplest things are hardest to explain. Thus:

"What's night?"

"Night is now. When its dark."

"What's dark?"

"When there isn't any light."

"What's light?"

194

"Er. . . . Light is when you can see Foxhanger across the fields. Dark is when you can't."

"What's 'see' . . . ?"

Anita was on firmer ground when it came to the question of scarecrows.

"What's a scarecrow?"

"A thing they put in a field when there are crops. The birds don't come because they think it's a man."

"I was in a field. Am I a scarecrow?"

"No, you're not. Well, maybe once on a time, but not any more. I changed you."

"Am I a man?"

"You will be. . . ." And Anita leaned on the arm of the giant and felt the firmness of his wooden bones, and was very proud.

Timothy was back in his place by first light and Anita spent some time scuffing out tracks. When the scarecrow walked he had a way of plonking his feet down very hard so they sank deeply into the ground. If old Johnson saw the marks he might take it into his head to wait up and see what queer animal was on the prowl, and Anita hated the thought of Timothy being parted by a charge from a twelve bore. She was only just beginning to find out how interesting he could be.

During the following weeks Granny Thompson had little cause for complaint. She rarely saw her granddaughter; in the daytime Anita was usually mugging up fresh spellwork, or trying with the aid of a hugely battered Britannica to solve some of the more brilliant of Timothy's probings; and at night she was invariably and mysteriously absent. Her granny finally raised the question of these absences.

"*Gallivantin'!*" snorted the elder Thompson. "Yore got summat *on*, I knows that. The question is, *wot?*"

"But Gran, I don't know what you mean. . . ."

"Kep me up 'arf the night larst night," pronounced Granny. "I could 'ear yer, gooin' on. Chelp chelp chelp, ev'ry night alike, but I kent 'ear nothing *answer*. . . ." And then with a suddenly gimlet-like expression, "Yore got a *bloke* agin my gel, that's wot. . . ."

"Really, Gran," said Anita primly. "The very *idea*. . . ."

"Anita, what's a witch?"

"I've told you a dozen times, Timothy. A witch is somebody like me or Gran, or Aggie Everett I suppose. We can . . . talk to all sorts of people. Like yourself. Normal folk can't."

195

"Why can't other people talk to me?"

"Well, the . . . it's hard to explain. It doesn't matter anyway; you've got me. I talk to you. I made you."

"Yes, Anita. . . ."

"I've got a new dress," said Anita, pirouetting. Timothy stood stiffly by the gate and watched her. "An' new shoes . . . but I'm not wearing them tonight because I don't want the damp to spoil them. I've got all new things because it's spring." She held her hand out to Timothy and felt the brittle strength in him as he helped her over the gate. He had a sort of clumsy courtesy that was all his own.

"Anita, what's spring?"

Anita was exasperated. "It's when . . . ah, the birds come back from Africa, don't ask me where's Africa because I shan't tell you . . . and there's nice scents in the air at night and the leaves come on the trees and you get new clothes and you can go out and everything feels different. I like spring."

"What's 'like'?"

Anita stopped, puzzled. "Well, it's . . . I don't know. It's a feeling you have about people. I like you, for instance. Because you're gentle and you think about the things I think about." Overhead a bat circled and dipped and the evening light showed redly through his wings and for a moment he almost spoke to Anita; then he saw the gauntness walking with her along the path and spun back up into the sky. "I shall have to teach you about liking," said Anita. "There's still so many things you don't know." She pelted ultrasonics after the noctule but if he was still in range he didn't answer. "Come on, Timothy," she said. "I think we'll go to Deadman's Copse and see if the badgers are out yet."

"Spells," said Anita. "Marjoram and wormsblood and quicksilver and cinnabar. Mandrakes and tar and honey. Divination by sieve and shears. Can you remember all that?"

"Yes, Anita."

"You've got a very good brain, Timothy; you remember practically everything now. You've got most of the standard manual word for word, and I only read it through to you once. You really could be very useful. . . . I think you're developing what they call a Balanced Personality. Though there's so much to put in, I still keep remembering bits I haven't done. . . . Would you like to learn poetry?"

"What's poetry?"

Anita fumed momentarily, then started to laugh. "I'm tired of defining things; it gets harder all the time. We shall

just have to do some, that's all; I'll bring a book tomorrow."
And the day after she brought the book; it was one of
her treasures, heavy and old and bound with leather. She
opened Timothy's mind till he could read Shakespeare better
than a man, then they went to Drawback Hill to get a
dramatic setting and Anita found Timothy's withered lips
were just right for the ringing utterances of the old mad
Lear. Next night they did a piece of *Tempest,* choosing
for it the ghostly locale of Deadman's Copse. Anita read
Ariel, althought as she pointed out she was a little too well-
developed for the part. Timothy made a fine Prospero;
the cursing boomed out in great style although the bit
about pegging people in oaks was if anything rather too
realistic. When Timothy spoke the words Anita could see
quite clearly how bad it would be to get mixed up with the
knotty entrails of a tree as big as that.

The next day it rained, making the ground soggy and
heavy. Mud covered Anita's ankles before she was halfway across the field. Timothy looked a little sullen and
there was a pungent, rotting smell about his clothing that
she found alarming. "It's no good," she said, "we shall just
have to get you under cover. I hate the idea of you standing out all the time; I don't expect you mind, though."

"Anita, what's 'mind'?"

By mid-April Anita would normally have been busying
herself about a hundred and one things connected with the
field creatures and their affairs, but she was still mainly
preoccupied with Timothy. Somehow she had stopped thinking of him as a scarecrow; the thing she had woken up
was beginning to work by itself now and often when she
came to release him he would bubble with notions of his
own that had come to him in the gray time before the
sun drained away his power. He asked her how she knew
the bats called each other and why she was always sure
when the weasel was too close for comfort; so she gave
him a sixth sense, and portions of the seventh, eighth and
ninth for good measure. Then she could leave him standing on watch in his field and scurry off on her own business
and Timothy would tattle and wheeze out the night's news
when next he saw her. He found out where the fieldmice
were building, and how the hedgepigs were faring on their
rounds; then one of the hares under Drawback was taken
by a lurcher and Timothy heard the scream and told
Anita stiffly, making the death seem like a lab report; and
Anita angrily gave him emotions and after that the tears

197

would squeeze from somewhere and roll down his football face whenever he thought about killing.

A week later Anita came home with the dawn to find her Granny waiting for her. "This," said the old lady without preamble, " 'as gotta *stop*."

Anita flung herself down in one of the big armchairs and yawned. "Wha', Gran. . . ."

"Gallivantin' " said Granny Thompson sternly. "Muckin' about wi' that gret thing uvver at the Johnsonses. *Ugghhh*. . . . Giz me the creeps it does straight. . . . Gret mucky thing orl straw an' stuff, sets yer teeth on edge ter *think* on it. . . ." She crossed to one of the little windows and opened it. A breeze moved cold and sweet, ruffling Anita's hair. The room was shadowy but the sky outside was bright; somewhere a bird started to sing, all on his own. "*Gallivantin'!*" said Granny again, as if to clinch matters.

Anita was nearly asleep; she'd used a lot of power that night and she was very tired. She said dreamily, "He's not a thing, Gran. He's Timothy. He's very sweet. I invented him, he knows about everything. . . ." Then a little more sharply, "*Gran!* How did you know—"

Granny Thompson sniffed. "I knows wot I *knows*. . . . There's ways an' means, my gel. . . . Some as even you dunt know, artful though yer might be. . . ."

Anita had a vision of something skulking in hedgerows, pouring itself across open ground like spilled jam. A very particular vision this, it lashed its tail and spat. She said reproachfully "You didn't play fair. You used a Familiar. . . ."

Granny looked virtuous. "I ent sayin' I *did*, an' there agin I ent sayin' I *didn't*. . . ."

"It was Vortigern," said Anita, pouting. "It must have been. None of the others would peach on me. But *him*. . . ."

"Never mind 'ow I *knows*," said Granny Thompson sternly. "Or 'oo tole me. The thing is, yore gone fur *enough*. Any more an' I wunt be responsible, straight I wunt. . . ."

"But Gran, he's nice. And . . . well, I'm sorry for him. I don't like to think of him being left on his own now. It would be . . . well, like somebody dying almost. He's too clever now, can't just . . . *eeeooohhh* . . . jus' leave him li' that. . . ."

"Clever," muttered Granny, looking at the wall and not seeing it. "That ent no call fer pity. . . . You save yer pity fer the next world me gel, there ent no place fer it 'ere . . . . Brains, pah. Straw an' dirt an' muck orf the fields, that's brains. Same with 'im, same with 'em orl. You'll learn. . . ."

But the homily was lost on Anita; she had incontinently fallen asleep.

She dreamed of Timothy that morning, woke and slept again to see if he would come back. He did; he was standing far away in his field and waving his arms to her and calling but his voice was so thick and distant she couldn't hear the words. But he wanted something, that was plain; and Anita woke and blinked, thought she knew what it was, and forgot again. She rubbed her eyes, saw the sunlight, felt the warmth of the air. It was lunchtime, and the day was as hot as June.

The fields were dark and rough and a full moon was rising. Anita crossed the open ground behind Foxhanger. A hunting bird called, close and low; she stopped and saw distant woods humped on their hills, looking like palls of smoke in the moonhaze. Timothy was waiting for her, a tiny speck a long way off in the night. When she reached him he looked gaunter than ever; his fingers stuck out in bundles from his sleeve, and his hat was askew. The night wind stirred his coat, moonlight oozed through the tatters and rags. Anita felt a queer stirring inside her; but she released him as usual and Timothy wriggled from the stake and dropped awkwardly to the ground. He said, "It's a lovely night, Anita." He took an experimental step or two. "After you'd gone this morning my leg broke; but I mended it with wire and it's all right again now." Anita nodded, her mind on other things. "Good," she said. "Good, Timothy, that's fine. . . ."

In February the ground had been bare and red-brown; now the harshness was lost under a new green hair. That was the corn Timothy had been made to protect. She took his arm. "Timothy," she said. "Let's walk. I'm afraid I've got an awful lot to say."

They paced the field, on the path that was beaten hard where the tractor came each day; and Anita told Timothy about the world. Everything she knew, about people dying, and living, and hoping; and how all things, even good things, get old and dirty and worn-out, and the winds blow through them, and the rain washes them away. As it has always been, as it will be forever until the sun is cold. "Timothy," she said gently, "one day . . . even my great Prince will be dust. It will be as though He had never been. He, and all the people of His house. Nobody knows why; nobody ever will. It's just the way things are."

Timothy jolted gravely alongside; Anita held his thin

199

arm and although he had no real face she could tell by his expression that he understood what she was saying. "Timothy," she said. "I've got to go away. . . ."

"Yes, Anita. . . ."

She swallowed. "It's right what Gran says. You're old now and nearly finished and there are so many other things to do. I haven't been fair, Timothy. You've just been a . . . well, a sort of toy. You know . . . I wasn't ever really interested in you. You were just something I made when I was bored. You sort of grew on me."

"Yes, Anita. . . ."

They turned at the farthest end of their walk. The air was wine-warm on her face and arms and Timothy smelled faintly of old brass spoons and what he was thinking about it was impossible to say. "It's spring now," said Anita. "It's the time you put on a new dress and do your hair and find someone nice you can drive with or talk with or just walk along with and watch the night coming and the owls and the stars. They're the things that have to be done because they start right deep down inside you, in the blood. It's the same with animals nearly, they wake up and everything's fresh and green, and it's as if winter was the night and summer is one great long day. . . ."

They had reached Timothy's stake. In the west the sky was still turquoise; an owl dropped down against the light like a black flake of something burned. Anita propped Timothy against his post. He seemed stiffer already and more lifeless somehow. She put his hat right; it was always flopping down. As she reached up she saw something shine silver on his wizened-turnip face. She was startled, until she remembered she had given him feelings. Timothy was crying.

She hugged him then, not knowing what to do. She felt the hardness of him and the crackling dryness, the knobs and angles of his bits-and-pieces body. "Oh, Timothy," she said. "Timothy I'm sorry, but I just can't go with you any more. There won't be any spells for you after this, I've taken the power off. . . ." She stepped back, not looking at him. "I'll go now," she said. "This way's best, honestly. I won't tie you back onto your stick or anything, you can just stand here awhile and watch the bats and the owl. And in the morning you'll just sort of fade away; it won't hurt or anything. . . ." She started to walk off down the slope, feeling the blades of new corn touch her calves. "Goodbye, Timothy," she called.

Something iron-hard snagged at her. She fell, rolled over

horrified and tried to get up. Her ankles were caught; she wriggled and the night vanished, shut away by rough cloth that smelled of earth. "Love," croaked Timothy. "Please, Anita, love. . . ." And she felt his twiggy fingers move up and close over her breasts.

She looped like a caterpillar caught by the tail and her fists hit Timothy squarely, bang-bang. Dust flew, and the seeds of grass; then Anita was up and running down the hill, stumbling over the rough ground, and Timothy was close behind her, a flapping patch of darkness with his musty old head bobbing and his arms reaching out. His voice floated to her through the night. "Anita . . . *love*. . . ."

She reached the bottom of the field tousled and too shocked to defend herself at all, cut across the Johnsons' stackyard with Timothy still hard on her heels. A dog volleyed barks, subsided whimpering as he caught the strange scent on the air. Back up the hill, a doubling across Home Paddock; a horse bolted in terror as old cloth flapped at his eyes. Near the hedge Timothy gained once more, but he lost time climbing the gate. Anita spun round fifty yards away. "Timothy, *go back! Timothy, no!*"

He came on again; she took three deep breaths, lifted her arm and flung something at him that crackled and fizzed and knocked a great lump of wadding from his shoulder. One arm flopped down uselessly but the rest of him still thumped towards her. Anita was angry now; her face was white in moonlight and there was a little burning spot on each cheek and her mouth was compressed till her lips were hardly visible at all. "Scarecrow!" she shouted. "Old dirty thing made of straw! *Spiders' home!*" She'd had time to aim; her next shot took Timothy full in the chest and bowled him backwards. He got up and came on again although he was much slower.

Anita waited for him on the little bridge over the Fyne-brook. She stood panting and pushing the hair out of her eyes with each hand in turn and the rage was white-hot now and choking her. Around her, brightnesses fizzed and sparkled; as Timothy came within range she hit him again and again, arms and legs and head. Pieces flew from him and bounced across the grass. He reached the bridge but he was only a matchstick man now, his thin limbs glinting under tatters of cloth. Anita took a breath and held it, shut her eyes then opened them very wide, made a circle with her hands, thrust fire at Timothy. His wooden spine broke with a great sound; what was left of him folded in the middle, tumbled against the handrail of the bridge. He fell feet over head into the stream. The current seized him, whirling him off; he fetched up twenty yards away and lay quiet, humped in a reedbed like a heap of broken umbrellas.

Anita moved forward one foot at a time, ready to bolt again or throw more magic; but there was no need. Timothy was finished; he stayed still, the water rippling through his clothes. A little bright beetle shot from somewhere into his coatsleeve, came out at the elbow and sculled away down the stream. Timothy's face was pressed into mud so he could see nothing, but his voice still whispered in Anita's mind. *"Please . . . please. . . ."*

She ran again, faster than ever. Along beside the brook, across the meadow, through Foxhanger, up the garden path. She burst into the kitchen of the cottage, spinning Granny Thompson completely round. Took the stairs three at a time and banged her bedroom door shut behind her. She flung herself on the bed and sobbed and wrapped blankets around her ears; but all night long, until the last of the power ran down, she could hear Timothy thinking old moldy thoughts about rooks and winds, and worms in the thick red ground.

The adventures of brave young princes traveling through far lands on noble quests form a large and respectable part of the literature of fantasy. But surely not all princelings could be brave and thoroughly upright in character; surely some of them would fall short of heroic stature under the pressures and travails of a Quest, might even prove to be rascals or reprobates. Here Avram Davidson—in a story which appears here for the first time anywhere—tells of one such prince, Mallian sonHazelip, sent forth by his father to find a medicine for the ills of his native land, which has been struck most low by the effects of the Great Gene Shift. (Readers who may wish for more of Mallian's adventures will find an earlier encounter in the story BUMBERBOOM, in WORLD'S BEST SCIENCE FICTION: 1967 — Ace Book A-10.)

BASILISK
Avram Davidson

The shadow of a large bird fell athwart the path one morning as the earliest mists cleared away. Two men were approaching upon one horse, and Thrag of the watchtower by the South-East Way made present haste to scurry down

203

and confront them. He who held on to the reins was a young man of sturdy build, his brown beard attrimmed into two points, with a cunning cast to his broad mouth. Riding abaft was an older and thinner one with a boney brow and gray eyes of the sort which at first seem almost blind but soon enough disclose themselves as seeing more than common well.

"Greetings, blessings, salutations and welcome, Venturers," Thrag sang out, his splay feet slapping the familiar stones as he came hoppitting down and leapt in front of them. He held his arms wide, as though he would gladly embrace them, his gesture somever sufficing to halt the old horse. "Fortune favor you—"

"Sun shine upon you, Snagglebeard," the first rider said, commencing to guide the horse sideways roundabout him.

"—and grant you all your just desires," said the downcomer, skipping to the side. As the rider with a sigh and a grunt reined in his mount and raised his thick brows, he upon the ground said, "Much do we welcome those of a jesting and humorsome disposition, such as you, my young, to this Tawallis Land. As a mere point of referential accuracy, a hem hum hum, my style it is Thrag the father of Throg, and I farm the watchtower (such as you may see above yonder there, affollowing my finger) by this SouthEast Way from the True Lord of Tawallis. Again, welcome, and again."

He brushed his drooping browhairs out of his deepset eyes and he looked at them with a fever-bright stare, glance twitching from one to the other; and then with his long and filthy fingers he preened him a burr from his long and blacky beard, and smirked.

The second rider considered the rocks and trees of the narrow Way and pursed his pucker lips. "What crops does that aforesaid tower yield you, Thrag the father of Throg?— a curious custom of designature, but one not quite without merit, referring to the future rather than the past—what engender you upon your farm, farmer Thrag?"

Thrag hawked a humor from his throat and spat into the bushes. "In border entry fees and duties and duanes, such as the True Lord holds the advowsons of, my post engenders an approximate hundred measures of moneys per solar year," he said; "of which the yield to me is a fifth of some, a half of several, and a three quarters of another," he said, sighing and lifting his cluttered beard. "I am but the party of the third part, and the fuller fractions of the usufruct go into the treasuries of Trig the father of Treg, fat man and farmer-general; only my indomitable piety constrains me to hope that Fortune continue to favor him. Pray descend from your palfrey and allow us to proceed with the tiresome but requisite details of business, welcome Venturers."

He reached for the nag's bridle, but it tittuped away from his filthy finger-claws at its master's movement. The air, despite the early hour, was hot and close. "Alas, Thrag," the first rider said, "I sorrow for your ill-requited toils, exposed as you are alike to the clemencies and inclemencies of the weather—and moreover to the point: that you have nothing to reward you for downcoming to us from your aerie, inasmuch we have neither baggage nor ware, and moreover I bear letters of passage from a potent and friendly power such as to constitute a diplomatical immunity from all such customs and charges, for I am Mallian sonHazelip, lawfully begotten eldest malechild of the High Man to the Hereditor of Land Qanaras: allow me to read to you—"

But Thrag courteously assured him that there needed not such readings and that he neither questioned Mallian's own statement nor doubted that the True Lord would on presentation of the fee-tallies return everything which had been paid. "A mere formality, but one which Trig the tax-farmer will without uncertainty require at my hands. Descend, my highborn young and squire; descend, do; the fees will be nominal and slight as can be, as a gentility to one of your native land." He reached again his hand to the bridle and this time he caught hold of it.

Mallian banished the scowl which settled on his face and smiled and said, "Much do I appreciate the gentility, Thrag, but as a mere matter of form and principal I must decline. Unhand the bridle, I beg of yor, for, aged as this horse is, he is still of so mettlesome an humor that I fear he might quite without my desiring it bruise you upon the many sharp rocks and stones."

And the man behind him spoke up and declared, in a tone of fretful caution, "There is moreover nothing to be gained by assessments, sir duanier, for out of mere humility and a desire to give no countenance to sumptuary extravagances, we travel as you see without baggage and (as I can assure you) without funds."

Thrag raised his eyes and voice in praise of such exemplary conduct. "Nevertheless," he pointed out, "the horse has a value, that budget which you bear has something in it, and all is necessary to examine and adjudicate. I am empowered to make no exemptions and am indeed under contractual obligation to unloose the savage dogs which even now move restlessly and but await my signal." He turned his head and gestured with his free hand and there broke upon their ears an horrid yelping and a most fierce barking and baying and howling.

Mallian's squire shuddered. "As assuredly as my name is Zembac Pix," he exclaimed, "that dog is ahungry. Take my warm cloak for quittance, give us the talley, and return—good Thrag!—and toss the beast a faggot of beef or at least a piece of bread."

Thrag's browhairs squirled like serpents and his mouth beneath its clotted moustachioes moved into a leer. "*Dog,* faithful Zembac Pix? Your ears deceive you, there is a full pack of *dogs:* harken!" Again he threw out his hand and turned his head and again the chorus of horrid yelping and most fierce barking and baying and howling broke upon the thicky air. "Furthermore, the cloak is not alone sufficient, and—" But further word said he not, for whilst he was saying Zembac Pix had doffed and furled the cloak and struck him heavily upon the head with that corner of the garment into which leaden weights were sewn. Down went Thrag, groveling his snagglebeard into the dust, and rose not up.

Zembac Pix leaped off and chopped at the supine throat with the edge of his hand, stiffly. "Mount up, mount up!" cried Mallian, impatiently. "This nag which the knackers rejected can scarcely run faster than a shoat, let alone a pack of guard-dogs!"

But Zembac Pix smiled and swaggered and shook his head. "Ah no a hum, master-lord," he denied; "there are no guard-dogs, not even one. Saw you not how he sought to distract our eyes by throwing out his hand, or how to conceal his lips he turned his head? But I noted the nevertheless and telltale movements of his throat: twas a mere ventriloquy and trick, my master-lord, and I cannot forgive such a deceit. It is my opinion, though I am a potecary and not deeply learned in the medicine of law, tis my opinion that his false and treacherous dealings give us a substantial charge upon the estate of this Thrag the father of Throg—and such a one for precisions as he would not but approve our promptly moving to settle probate, a hem hum hum!"

Widely then Mallian's mouth moved up at each corner and he leapt from his horse and led it and tethered it hidden from sight in a cleft to one side of the gorge. "For my own part," he declared, as they scrambled up the slight but visible path, "I disdain all such sorts of booties and plunders. But the necessities of Land Qanaras, as well as the insult just offered it, do require support, and that of a substantial nature. Ah, woe! Qanaras!" he cried, weepingly, "Great was she among the Lands!—until came that accursed and maledicted Great Gene Shift, which according to oldwives' tales was caused by temporary instability of Orb Sun itself, thus—"

Zembac Pix, as Mallian, panting, paused for breath, waggled his head. "Aye, thus they say, the beldames: thus letting loose a flood of particles which deadly damage remains yet with us, a long after the said flood has ceased. But I believe it not, nor befits it me to so believe. Has any sober man yet seen Orb Sun casting off a particle? A hum hum no. But the evil and maleficent medicines of the crook Dwerfymen caused it."

So up they scrabbled and clumb the near flat face of the scarp, with threbble-spittings and curses upon the whole stunty race of Dwerfs and all their works: till they came at length to the tower itself.

This was a great rugged cairn of huge stones, such as must originally have been erected by the roistering race of the Gigants and none other: and by them with no great ease, either. Sturdy sticks sufficient to provide a sole if somewhat insecure pathway were thrust deeply into the crevices and interstices, and upon the top was built the doubtless vantage of the late Thrag the father of Throg out of similar sticks, and straws: inchoate and noisome and greatly resembling the nest of some insanitary eagle-bird: bones lay hither and there, some with flegs of rotting flesh still green upon them. And some not so green.

"Ough!" exclaimed Mallian. "What a vulture, if indeed no worse, was this reprobate duanier! Seemingly he fed upon the corses of any such as had the ill-fate to die nearabout him."

But Zembac Pix, his bony face gone a trifle grayer than usual, said that he feared it was indeed the "worse"—that the Thrag had never a faggot of beef nor crumb of bread save that which he devised himself from the persons of single and unarmed travelfolk. "—and the diseases they died of was the skulk Thrag himself, may Fortune forfend from us a like fate at any time in any place: and now let us see if there are discernables as to where he might have secreted those customs-dues and border-fees which I misdoubt he ever reported to or divided with Trig the father of Treg, the farmer-general . . . if indeed that fat and covetous magnate has any existence outside the conversations of the ogreous Thrag."

They prodded the stinking thatch of the nesty floor until

finding one place which seemed less firmly trodden down than the rest. Using one of the other sticks as digging tool, they delved and dugged and pried: presently they came upon a sort of small square door of worked wood, and this, when lifted up and out and away, disclosed an as it were chamber within the cairn. And all this space was filled with leathern sacks tied tightly at the mouths with leathern thongs. They had no more than slashed open one of them and peered inside at the tight-packed mass of rings and armills and ear-bobbles with which it was crammed, when a curious noise asmote their ears.

Coming down towards them through the air with slow and lazy flaps of its blacky wings was a huge and hideous vulture-eagle. For a moment the thought common to both of them was that this their standing-place was after all a nest of some great and grisly bird, videlicet *this* great and grisly bird, and they both bethought them of how far it was down and how bestrewn with sharp stones it was at the bottom. But even as they stooped where they were, hearts swollen and cold with fear, and before they could reflect that birds neither amass man-treasure nor pack the same into sacks of hide, the great bird espied them. The great bird blinked, and the great bird reacted for all the world like a woman come upon unclothed at a moment when she has neither expected nor desired to be so come upon. The great bird saw them and screamed and almost fell from its place in the air, betangled in its pinions and plummeting a ways before it got command of itself again.

Then it screamed a once more, but on a different note, one not of dismay but of quite rage, and it commenced to climb, its talons out a-claw. Instantly and very swift Mallian took in hand both sling and stones and sent first one and then another and another whuzzing through the air. The bird screamed thrice and mounted high and took its departure, gouts of blood streaming down upon the foul nest, and it croak in thick dismay.

"It limps—well-slung," admired Zembac Pix.

Mallian grunted. "True . . . but who knows whither or on what purpose that Hell-bird has gone, or when it may return and with what company? Hasten. Hasten."

They dropped one of the treasure-sacks over the side. It at once burst and scattered its contents. Mallian thereupon climbed down the perilous stick-way, eye cautiously scanning sky for a sign of any returning raptor-bird; once below he set to and soon had broken off enough branches from

208

the evergreens as to hazard further sacks being dropped upon the pile of springy limbs. And these did not burst.

It was not easy to rig a packing which enabled the scrannel nag to bear the burden they now proceeded to put upon it. And of course neither of them could now ride, let alone both. But they consoled them that they might soon enough purchase horses of sound limb and good wind, both saddle- and pack-. This they found a cheery thought and one which acted as balm to their feet.

"At last," said Mallian, in high delight, "I shall be able to purchase and outfit me as befits an High Man's son. Fortune alone knows what humility of soul and agony of mind I have suffered since my trappings were villainously stolen from me by the wicked Bandy folk (foul kith and spraddle-legged Dwerfs!) during my unsuccessful raid upon them and their riches. But enough; I am not one to dwell snuvvelingly upon the irremediable past. I shall, as I say, purchase princes' gear . . . for myself. For you, my loyal and learned Zembac Pix, will be boughten vestments of costly weave in the habit of the Order of Sages: eh? What say you?"

And Zembac Pix allowed a faint smile to widen his thin lips a trifle and he expressed his extreme gratitude and his assurance that he would most certainly have been admitted to the mysterie and medicine of that Order, had it not been for jealousy and ill-will and evil dealings on the parts of sundry petty sages: "Upon whom a bloody flux," he concluded. "I snap my fingers at them and defy them to say me aught as I don my rightful habits."

They had reached the crest of the hill which marked the border of that fell gorge, and without counseling together they stopped and looked back. Deep it was, and gloomy, and upon the edge of ridge and sky they saw the small prickle which was the gaunt cairn and tower of Thrag the father of Throg. Their eyes met and they exchanged sated and knowing smirks. And then there brake upon their ears the sound of an horrid yelping and a most fierce barking and baying and howling, as it was of a many dogs in the middling distance. Smiles they had no more for each other or at all. Zembac Pix seized a switch and smote the horse athwart the pinbones and Mallian pulled at the bridle with all his weight and might. And thus in haste and in affright and in terror they passed over the crown of the hill and out of sight of the gorge.

But the noise of the dogs still rang in their ears.

Down fell the land, a descent full of windings amid wastes and boulders and rain-slod slopes, with scrubby trees and never a smoke nor a roof nor a sight of man.

"Nor a woman," added Mallian, thinking aloud, and with much restrospective discontentment.

Zembac Pix quirked his lips. "Contain your natural impatience on this point, master-lord. Once it is known that a, in effect, princeling of wealth and manners is among them, women will not be wanting. I envy you both prospect and fulfilment, regretting only that the dignity and circumspection incumbent upon one clad in the habit of the Order of Sages will, alas and a hem hum hum, confine me utterly to covert and clandestine lecheries." And he sighed and smacked his lips.

By and by they saw before them the delineaments of settled soil: fields, and trees in rows and ranks, and houses large and small. It was as the road broadened that they heard a hail from the right hand side and saw riding toward them a stout man upon a stout mare, and riding behind *him* a slavey man holding a white umbrella to shield his master from the sun. The landowner had smoothly shaven chops and the lackey wore a straggle beard of reddish hue.

"Fortune favor you," the former said—adding, "Although, as you may adduce, I am the proprietor of all these fallows and fruit trees on either edge of the road, it is not by virtue of such that I will question you, but merely out of an wholesome and amiable curiosity. My style is Cape the father of Cope, and what is yours and from what Land do you come and for what purpose do you enter Tawallis Land and by the South-East Way?"

They devised and told him names and false provenances on the moment's spur, and a smooth tale to the effect that they were traveling merchants of jewels and baubletry and hoped to sell the same to the worthy and high-born subjects of the Land's True Lord. "At a good profit, my noble senior," said Zembac Pix, whose tongue was more accustomed to the glib talk of merchantry than Mallian's was. "At a good profit I will admit, for such is our necessity and custom, howsomever as you will be our first customer in all your land we will not scruple to offer you goodly bargains in hopes that your pleasure therein will provide equally goodly omens for our stay and traffic: so."

Landowner Cope chuckled and rubbed his plump palms. "We will see, we will see! But the truth is that I have a several wives and sundry freemates, and they all of them harry me for gifts and presents. Open your bales, gemsters,

210

then, and let us see and observe at least a sampling thereof."

He and his servitor dismounted and Mallian and Zembac Pix selected a sack at random and commenced to unloose the leathern thongs which bound its throat. But no sooner had they done so when an horrid yelping and a fierce barking and a baying and a howling sound from a middling far off, and they started and spilled a somewhat from the sack by inadvertancy.

"Fortune favor us, senior, but you have savage-seeming dogs," exclaimed Mal, finding once again his voice.

Cape stared at them from round and pop eyes. "Dogs? *I* have no dogs. Only Thrag the father of Throg has dogs . . . or, rather I should say, *had* dogs! for it is all too plain that you have between you asslain him and appropriated to yourself his many richnesses."

Zembac Pix with trembling fingers rebound the mouth of the sack, and the distressful howlings died away. "Hem hem, you mistake the situation, noble senior. The fact is that only one of these sacks pertains to the late Thrag—a most piteous case—he fell headlong when his footing gave way as he descended his tower with the bag he had besought us to bring as part-payment to one Farmer-General Trig the father of Treg—a favor we were glad to do and which has since his untimely demise become unto us as it were a semi-sacred trust. *One* sack, senior mine. . . .

"But the others are our own rightful property. Twas only by an inadvertency we opened this other. Hem a hum, partner, hand down that other one there: so; thus—"

Scowling intently, he loosed the leather knot and let slip the leather cord. And at once the quiet of the fields and trees was severed by an horrid yelping and a fierce barking and a baying and a howling, seemingly a somewhat nearer than before. Zembac Pix nighly bound a finger in his haste to close and tie shut the second sack, and he cast an eye in agony at Mal, who, wide mouth open and slack, stared only.

Cape shook his head and sighed. "No, no, this mime and play avails nothing. It is plain that you and you have slain Thrag the father of Throg and that his brute hounds pursue you both and your booty. For my own part I care not a twig for Thrag alive or dead, as he was neither my kin nor a shareholder in any contract of my own shareholding, and further he was a most foul fellow."

Mallian and Zembac Pix exchanged glances which were twin counsels of despair, and the former then said, "Landowner, it seems that you are too keen for us to further dissimulate. We will conceal nothing from you. The fact is that

211

Thrag, not content with collecting his lawful dues and duanes, did attempt to rob and to slay us: we merely acted in self-defense. Moreover, an examination of the fell Thrag's lair disclosed that he had both robbed and slain a muckle many, single and unarmed venturers, one must suppose. And that not content with secreting the thefts, he had feasted on their flesh. To slay such a one is not only not a crime, it is a meritorious act for the public health and weal."

Cape began to mount his mare, and said, grunting, foot in stirrup, "Doubtless . . . doubtless. . . . I neither make nor decide the public polity. But certain things are contractually clear: a share of whatever Thrag collected belongs to Trig, and likewise a share of what is Trig's is the True Lord's. What behooves me now is to secure your persons and plunders and hand over the both to the Patrol, to alert and alarm whom I must now depart. Flight would be futile, so I advise you to make yourselves a comfort, and remain right here. You may refresh you upon the smaller windfalls of the fruit-trees, but I will not tolerate your plucking of what still hangs on the boughs. Sun shine upon you; it will not be long."

He hoisted him into the saddle. Mallian cried, "Hold, sir Cape! A proposal—share and share alike, and no words spoken to any?"

"Naturally," said Cape, with a slight sigh, "the possibility of this was the first thing which occurred to me. But it will not do, no no, a hum hum hum; there are spies everywhere and the matter would be bound to become known. Anon, then—" He kicked his horse, but before she could more than start, Mal had slung him a shot-stone which thunked upon the head of Cape the father of Cope, and he fell heavily from his saddle and the horse trod upon his head.

The slavey man slid backwards over the beast's tail and, contenting himself that his master was indeed dead, flailed the corpse with his white umbrella, uttering umbrages and maledictions. "Pettoo upon the worst of masters," he concluded with a spet, then whirled around and bowed a flourishing bow. "My style it is Rud," he announced, mockingwise. "No one's son and no one's father, and my proposal it is that under your direction, bravoes, we rouse my fellow slaveys and possess ourselves of the deceased Cape's wives, freemates, and moveable chattles; after which we depart incontinently from this Tawallis Land and throw ourselves upon the known mercies of the Confoederate Kings of the Dwerfs: otherwise a sundry dreadful things are like to befall the three of us."

Mallian, with a small scowl, denounced the unsocial and

untoward suggestion. "Far be it from me," he said, "son of a High Man, to encourage a spirit of sedition among the proletary; indeed, were your straggle beard of but another color I would inflict a persecution upon you: but all men know that reddlebeards bring bad luck, as witness the termination of the late Cape.

"Since, however, you are of an addled mind to seek the mercies of the Bandy kings, I will not prevent your doing so. In fact, you may have our own horse to depart upon . . . as soon as you untie those sacks . . . and advise us an information or two. . . ."

The work was soon done of transference, the air was rich and sweet from the orchards—although Cape's offer of windfalls and warning against plucking were alike fictitious, it being far too early for either. Rud's informations did not take long, either. Of the (it now proved) famous dogs of Thrag the father of Throg, he knew little more than that they were a by-word: mothers frightened their children with the fear of them, and on dour nights when the winds whuffled round the houses it was said that one was actually hearing the hounds of Thrag. But he did not know that anyone had ever actually claimed to have ever seen them. And he gave them divers data about Cape and his households and about the True Lord and other signal features of Tawallis Land. And then they suffered him to depart.

It seemed somehow unfitting to the dignity of the deceased to be trundling him along attop the plunder-bags, and it was in addition not unlikely that the question might be asked: how had this big burden of bags been packed by a mere two men before they had the use of Cape's fat mare? And in order to spare the bereaved family any such distractions they sought about for a safe place to secure the treasures in. By good fortune they after a ways noticed a small stone building set abback behind the road, the key to which was a dangle on the ring of keys which had been in Cape's pouch and was now in Mal's. Fortunately also it contained but a few several pieces of items such as axes and adzes and barrow-wheels and was thus able to contain the plunder-bags with room to spare.

"Well-kept land and fields and groves," Zembac Pix observed approvingly as they next proceeded onward. "Fortunate one might think would be the owner of all, plus the as yet unseen by us houses and barns and mills and slavey folk and wives and freemates"—he sighed. "But what is all this to one of whom Fortune has mysteriously required that his horse should tread upon his head; what? Nothing. . . .
213

What think you of this most disturbing matter of the dogs, master-lord?"

A spasm passed upon Mallian's face. He growled. "You said there were no dogs! You assured me it was a mere ventriloquy!" He bared his teeth at the one-time potecary.

Zembac Pix skipped about to the off side of the horse. "Hem a hum, gracious lordling! Wrath is at all times to be avoided; it has been the known cause of many a fatal cachexy or affluxes of the nose or lungs. . . . I was quite certain that it *was* a mere ventriloquy. Saw you not how whenever he would have us hear them, how he flung out his hand to distract our eyes and turned aside his head so we might not see his lips move? Consider, consider: how is it that we never other heard them whilst he did live, except he performed thus?"

But Mallian, twixt his teeth, said that he would consider also the disturbing circumstances that each time they opened the plunder-bags they heard the baying and the barking and the horrid howling yelping of the hounds of Thrag—"and each time they seem to be nearer," he said, a-moan. Zembac Pix pointed out that, for a one, they had up in the vulture-room opened a plunder-bag without hearing the hounds; and, for a second, they had at the exit to the gorge heard the hounds although they had not opened a bag.

"It is most curious and does not for a certain seem to follow any known laws," Zembac Pix mused. "Moreover there is the matter of the great vulture-bird: clearly there is or was a deft connection betweenst it and the felon Thrag. And anent this a thought or two occur to me: Did perhaps that ugly bird espy out incomers for that dour duanier, being rewarded by the gift of the bones of some to pick? In such case we had slandered somewhat the memory of the dead by categorizing him as a cannibal when he was merely a murderer. Or—"

They turned a slight curve in the road and abruptly the orchard came to an end. "Yonder is the House of Cape," said Mal, a somewhat unnecessarily.

A rednose steward coming along stopped and lifted up his hands and voice as he saw them. "Woe and affliction!" he cried. "What has happened to Cape the father of Cope, the best of masters? —Help me to lift him down, and then I will summon his ladies to administer therapeutic attentions to him: woe!"

But Mal and Zembac Pix sighed deeply. "He is beyond the aid of such," they declared. "This very mare threw him and then trod upon his head—observe, observe, steward, the mark of her fatal hoof-shoe! All occurred in a trice as sir Cape was welcoming us, and he had but time to utter the single word *Teresilda* before he expired."

The steward arose from examining the corse. "He is surely extinct," he muttered, and spurned the body with his foot. "Pettoo upon the worst of masters," he declared. "His death terminates my contract, and with it my most unwilling respect. . . . However, I will tarry on a bit out of mere respect to Teresilda, the favorite freemate, an open-handed lady who always treated the loyal and diligent steward Snop with generosity and appreciation unlike a few several I could mention. As foreign strangers you will not have known that whomsoever is named in dying breath is legally assumed to be either guilty of the dead man's death, or his residuary legatee. The former will of course not apply, as Teresilda has been sitting all day in her hall with her maids, appricking at the broidered work upon her frame . . . but it has oft enough been a nice point at law: whether to load with riches or with chains the one named in a death's-word naming, hi a ho hem. Hither along with me, by favor, seniors. By the back ways, as not to disturb the delicate sensibilities of several."

Teresilda, whom they eventually reached by devious turnings, was a blackhaired woman of ripe charms, who, fatigued from broidering, lay upon a couch eating sugared fruits from a bowl. The steward Snop first made quick work of latching the doors of her hall, then said, "Cape's dead and named you. No one else knows."

Quickly she sat up and her color changed a few times. She quickly pressed Snop's hand, asked if the strangers were witness to the last word, assured them of her eternal favor, and inquired of the deceased's keys. Then she allowed herself to weep, then—with a sudden frown—demanded to know where the slaveyman Rud had been and was now. Zembac Pix told her that they had bid him follow with their own horse, but that he fell gradually behind and then galloped off with the stolen steed. "Whither?" she asked. "Thither," he said, with a gesture.

"To Tawallis Town. He thinks no doubt to steal his freedom whilst we are bemused with this tragic occurrence. But may I be sold a slavey to the Gollocks, who have no hair, if I do not alert upon him the Patrol to seize and punish him for his double defalcation," she declared; "to say nothing that his loss would diminish my rightful share in the estate." Her eyes gleamed. "To Erna, Arna, and Orna, his contracted wives, their dotal shares must be returned with interest—they

215

will be wild, the dullards, wild!—to be not one of them named as I was named!—for they and everyone else know that Cape married them for capital gain alone, whereas he chose me for looks and lust! So: to that thinblooded scholar, Cope, goes his assigned portion of the rest by right of primogeniture, and it is up to him to arbitrate with his lawful brothers and half-brothers as to the amount of their subshares; and no concern of mine." She rubbed her white and nice and plump hands, adorned with many a gem and jewel. "But all the rest and residue of the estate is mine!—save for the horses, which go by right of equity to the freemates' children, even though they no longer need them to flee from the sons of the wives as was once the practice; well; they may have them, though I shall buy a few back— But everything else is mine! The other freemates need have no fear I shan't make them customary presents, though be sure they have feathered well their own nests, as who of course can blame them?"

She directed Snop to draw up a testament of her name having been named in the dying breath of the no-more-breathing Cape for the strangers and witnesses to sign, also to alert the Patrol upon the scaped slavey man Rud, next to place double locks all round the estate, and lastly she directed, with some reluctance, "Announciation of the death had better be made. But first bribe such of the stout and astute servants and slaveys as are not utterly in the cause of any other, and promise them reasonable promises. But the testament first."

Here Zembac Pix cleared his throat and somewhat shook his head. "What, not?" she exclaimed, dismayed. "Why not?"

"Because, bereaved-lady," he explained, "it is against our own native pieties either to sign statements of pursue after reddlebeards the same day as a death. I solicit you to indulge us in this small matter or two. Tomorrow we may certainly sign, tomorrow by all means alert the Patrol. Only not today. Superstitious this may be, but suffer it to go unobjected."

Discontent upon her full features struggled a moment with other emotion, next she smiled. "Certainly," she said. "We must respect all religions and nonreligions, whatsoever forms they take. Tomorrow will do well enough, seniors—at which time you will delight me (no nay upon it; I insist) by selecting an horse, the pick of the stud, to replace that stolen by the thrall Rud. The estate shall bear the cost, which it can well afford. But for the meanwhile, you have clearly traveled far, and steward Snop before doing aught else shall guide

216

you to the guest house and provide you with all things necessary for your refreshment. It would be an ill hospitality to restrain you here in my hall, which—so soon as I finish my sugared fruits—must resound with grievous cries and bitter lamentation for my late lord and lovely."

They left her making a selection between an apricock and a quince.

Snop bowed and rubbed his rufous nose and signaled to a two of the maids to follow along with him and the twain guests; the maids were old and blear-eyed and Mallian frowned slightly at this, for such seemed to him a curious notion of hospitality. But he intercepted the shaveling of a glance between Snop and Teresilda in which, by illuminating sudden flash of thought, he saw the reason for it. And held his peace.

They passed along a mall lined with flowering trees and paved with wide smooth flags between which grew spicy herbs, and awaited on the broad doorstep of the guest house while Snop worked the key and leaned upon the door. He had gotten it open and stood a moment giving directions to the maids when a great black shadow passed across the area and—so it seemed to Mallian, who stared, aghast—part of it broke off and swelled and—

Zembac Pix, with a cry, hurled himself against Mallian, who fell against the steward, who knocked down the maids. And, as they all five lay astumbled on the floor, a boulder crashed down upon the threshold and cracked in two. A great cry and croak of rage rang out upon the air. One of the maids mumbled an enchantation and they saw the form of a great vulture-eagle go pinioning its way upwards and off.

The steward's face had gone the color of plaster. "Surely you have saved some of our lives," he said. "I have never heard of such a thing before as a bird's picking up a boulder and flying off with it, let alone of its dropping the same with intent of killing. I dread me that it is nothing else but some sort of drear omen, likely connected with our late master's death."

But Zembac Pix pshushed and poo'd the notion. "You attribute human conceipts to a mere brute bird," he said. "Yonder one without doubt mistook the boulder for a tortoise and dropped it with nothing else intended than the cracking of its shell for the meat. And it has no more to do with your late master's death than that this is the reason for us happening to be here at the moment the stone fell."

Steward and servantmaids seemed not totally convinced, but Mallian began to stride about the guest house and
217

so they were constrained to let the matter lie and to company him in his stridings. The steward in particular was profuse and active, urging the twain guests not to linger among the clutter upon the ground floor—for, he said, it was a rural practice in Tawallis Land to use that floor for storage—but to mount up to the more light and properly furnished upper floors. "The late lord's late father, landowner Cupe," he said, pressing them gently onward, "was given to the purchasing of many objects of art, the which you see abbundled and abbound here. But tastes change and fashions differ, and"— he unlocked the doors upon the upper landing—"in this chamber are rugs and couches, in this next one are vessels of old wine goblets for drinking, in this one and in this one are presses and cabinets containing a many changes of clean garments and among these are sure to be those fitting to your sizes. Here is also a library of brightly-inscribed books containing many pictures, and here is the steam-bath wherein the maids will at once kindle fires and draw water." He begged a permission to withdraw to go about his many pressing tasks, for he said that once the tragic news were known, the estate would cause an ant-hill to seem peaceable.

"This bath," said Mallian, tossing yet another kid of water upon the hot stones and observing with satisfaction the hissing outflux of vapors, "reminds me of such as we have in home. And, as whenever I think of home, tears rise into my eyes and fall addown my cheeks. It is fortunate that all is wet and steamy droplets on my face and hence no particular moisture may be discerned from another. . . . Home! Qanaras! —Can it be?" he inquired, beating his hairy body vigorous with a small besom of saponiferous herb: "—that I show insufficient concern for the problems besetting my dear native land?"

Zembac Pix flailed his own smooth limbs and shook his head.

"It cannot be," he said.

Mal sighed, but would not let the subject drop. "Of course it cannot be," he agreed. "Yet, this being so, why do all my such concerns turn out ill? It has long been clear to me that I ought to be my father's heir rather than either of my beloved brothers—lying Valendar and incurably immature Tassefont—and when our father sent us forth on envoyage intended both to find the proper medicine to solve our country's woes and to confirm (for such was certainly the meaning of his words) . . . to confirm his entirely proper opinion that I was the proper successor—"

"It cannot be," said Zembac Pix, who had perhaps lost the thread of this rather involved sentence. On observing Mallian's face, already red with heat, grow redder still, he hastily amended himself: "It cannot be other than as you have said, lordling!"

Mal grunted and mumbled, then went on. "When the High Man my father sent us out, I say, my intents were all for our country and none selfishly for myself. The raid upon the Dwerfymen, the attempt to invest Land Nor with the great gun Bumberboom, alike as with my stay among the Pseudomorphs, were intended only the better to finance my quest. Why then did they fail? Whence such malign reversals of what must be the designs of Fortune? Did I offer any initial offense to Thrag the father of Throg? Or to Cape the father of Cope? None. Nary a bittle. Twas their own personal perversities which brought about their deaths. And yet I ask myself: do I do arright to stay even so much as a single night at ease here? Ought I not to pass along and beg upon the ways?—saying, as it were, 'Seniors . . . Gentles . . . such and so is the misfortune of Land Qanaras, and can it be that you know where a medicine may be found to advise us how to recover therefrom?' Ought?"

Zembac Pix cast a kid of water over him, and crouched as the favor was returned. Then he said, "A hem hum, master-lord, I understand your concern as well as though I were a natal of Land Qanaras myself. I yearn, I burn, to follow whilst you do as suggested."

"You do?" said Mal, a trifle surprised.

He did (he said). But he begged that further consideration might be given the point. Was it not possible that the name and face of both Mallian sonHazelip and of Land Qanaras might be diminished if the quest was carried on afoot by two men, humbly clad? Would a serious and a proper attention be paid either to them or (which was more by far important) to their question? And—

"Enough," said Mallian. "I yield. You have persuaded me. My impulsive zeals must and shall be curbed. The cause of Qanaras requires that we be comely clad and lavishly outfitted. I see that now. It would be simply managed if we might merely purchase sumptuous items from this estate's store of such; alas that those hangman treasure bags somehow seem to convey to the mysterious dogs of Thrag a warning whenever they are opened. Therefore we must tarry here until it may somehow be managed to acquire fund or gear."

He stepped out into the next room and buried himself

from head to shin in an enormous towel-cloth. "Or perhaps both," he said. He heard a short squeak of astonishment from Zembac Pix, and peered his face out through the folds of the toweling. Sitting in a chair and facing him was a stout woman with shrewd small black eyes and a gray moustache, behind whom stood with lowering faces three tall and heavy men whom he identified as being of the race of Gollocks, who have no hair.

"We had not expected the honor of this visit, madame or lady," said Mallian. "And though I hastily add it is not less welcome for all of that, still, our natures are so excessively modest that we constrain to ask you that you await outside upon our dressing so as to—but you understand."

She gave a baritone guffaw. Faint, grim smiles fled across the mouths of her guardy-men, exposing thick yellow tushes. "You may be reassured," she said, "as to your commendable modesties. I am the mother of children and a married woman. That is, I *was* a married woman. . . . Strangers and venturers, you see before you the bereaved Matron Orna, seniormost widow of the late Cape the father of Cope; woe and affliction!"

Mal said, "Hem. . . ."

Zembac Pix said, "Hum. . . ." He said, "You are then the mother of Cape, elder son of the late deceased?"

Matron Orna scowled. "That puling fool never came forth from my womb! No . . . my children are daughters, as like to me, the dearlings, as heifers to the cow. Pity them, the orphans! For, while tis true that I will get me my dowery returned, still, that is but one dowery—and I have two daughters!"

It was with visible feeling that Mallian informed her that he himself was affianced to a daughter of his own land, whose laws required the most rigorous monogamy—and Zembac Pix, with equal emotion, regretted he was prevented from offering marriage by the rule of the Order of Sages demanding the most painstaking public celibacy.

"So be it, then," said the widow, with a sigh. "Did I indicate so much as the quiver of a doubt, my Gollock guardsmen here would hastily dislocate your limbs and snatch out your inward parts— But be at ease! I believe you. . . . Still, still, my daughters must be provided for: to this you agree? I am glad. A hum hum, handsome lads—is it perhaps possible that you mis-heard my convir's dying word? Did he not perhaps utter the syllables *Orna?* Or even those of *Nananda* and *Thasanda,* our daughters dear? You hesitate—you are not sure— A well, well. Search your memories tonight. I have it on excellent foundation that the cuckoldrix Teresilda, not content with having whilst you were in the bath stolen the key-ring of Cape which you were safely keeping—"

Mallian exclaimed, and groped a moment in his clothes . . . then let them fall . . . then smiled a trifle. . .

"Stolen via the person of her leman, the steward Snop, the keys, I say—Teresilda, not content with this, intends—I may assure you—once your signatures are obtained upon the testament, to denounce you to the True Lord as spies, unlicensed aliens, interlopers, and what-not else; so little sense of gratitude has she. Whereas *I*, rest assured, should a search of recollection convince you that it was *my* name or my daughter's—"

"A hem hum," Mallian said, looking at Zembac Pix.

"Hem a hum," Zembac Pix said looking at Mallian.

The widow arose and moved forward. Her Gollock guards moved one step behind, fingers twitching thickly. "Do not retreat from me, younglings," the Matron said, "firstly, because that would eventually bring you flat against the doubt-less still-hot stones of the steam-bath; and, secondly, because I desire nothing more, momently, than to examine that one key which I observe hanging upon your breast, son Mallian, peeping as it were slyly from the thicket thereupon. You have not heard the complaints and grumbles of the poxy Snop and Teresilda, as I have heard, that one key lacks from Cape's key-ring. By coincidence it happens that I know the missing one to be that of the stone shed wherein my convir Cape had at my request hidden moneys of my own which I had entrusted unto him for safekeeping. Allow me, allow me—"

Mallian assured her that it could not be the same key and that his key fitted no other lock than that of his mother's tomb, wherein he wonted to go for mournings and lamentations upon the anniversary of her demise: as fresh in his memory as though years had not passed. And he rearranged the towel and he stepped behind Zembac Pix, holding him firmly so that the potecary could not asquirm away.

Matron Orna brushed a tear out of her gray moustache. "How I honor such a sentiment!" she declared. "Yes, yes, I see that it is not the same key. Nevertheless and in hopes that my own issue will be as true to my memory as you to hers, allow me but to touch it a one moment only—" She swiftly reached out her right hand and, as Mallian parried it, thrust with her left hand into his bosom and grasped the key a moment. "Enough," she said. "I thank you. I feel the better for the touch. . . . Well a hum, my sons, and now I must and shall leave you. On the morrow you will sign the testaments, and I adjure and assure you, should you remember that the proper dying word of Cape was *Orna*, or *Nananda*, or *Thasanda*, rest satisfied that I and they will most generously endow you."

She paused at the door. She sighed. "Otherwise," she said—and sighed. Her Gollock guardy men looked at them and growled and scowled and flexed their hairless muscles.

The door closed upon all four.

After a moment Mal said, "At least now perhaps I may finish drying myself." He moved the key to rub his chest; he frowned. "I will swear," he said, taking off both key and cord, "that she did not hold it more than the merest moment . . . it is assuredly the same key . . . yet it feels a somehow different. . . "

The potecary took it from him, looked at it closely, held it to his nose, and hissed in upon his breath. "This is nothing else but wax of bees' nests!" he cried. "For shame, I say it plain, for shame my master-lord, to be cozened by so old a trick! For whilst she distracted you with her nasty right-hand, within her left concealed she had a bolus of bee-wax, into which she enprinted the key! Ah, there is a cunning-most granny for you," he exclaimed, admiringly. "Almost could I bring myself to wed a clever crone like that . . . almost."

And when Mal, distressed and agitated, commenced to form a plan that they two should forthwith steal a horse from the stud to lade the treasure-bags upon and thence flee without tallying further, Zembac Pix counseled nay. "Keys are not thus quickly copied," he said. "A mold must be made, a cast next contrived, and a several filings performed, and so on . . . not the work of less than hours. Still, a hum a hum, there can be no harm at all in taking a small walk about the grounds and, as I am sure the estate prides itself upon its stud, none in paying that a visit of a quiet nature and such as will give us some idea of its laying out. These things are always well to know—hum hey?"

Mallian's mouth widened more and he winked and he flicked the ends of his bifurcated beard. They finished drying and combing and dressing them, and then they descended to the lower floor, passing through the rows and ranks of long objects wrapped in sacking and cordage which constituted the out-moded collection of the long late Cupe the father of Cape, and slipped out onto the grounds. It was the dusky hour of the day, and no one was about, though in this and in that building they saw lamps begin to twinkle and they smelled the evenfires and the evenmeals and they heard now and then the sounds of voices from within.

Quietly and inconspicuously in the blue-gray garments they had selected from the wide collection upstairs they two made their way towards stables and stable-yards. Therein were all manner of fine horses, roans and grays and sable-blacks, cobs and stallions and fillies, colts and mares. Mallian's mouth almost watered, to see this fine wealth of horse-flesh, and he was embarrassed by his inability to choose. So suddenly did the voice sound out of the gloaming that he had barely a time to seize Zembac Pix by the throat and sink with him into a shadow, before he saw two men approach nearby.

"How goes the watch, half-brother?" asked the voice.

And a second voice replied, "Well enough, half-brother. As yet no signs of skulkers or of seizers."

The first made an angry growl, then, "A good thing," it said; "yet I trust none but our fellow bastard-brothers, sons of the freemates. Let me but smell any others roundabout here, plotting and planning to light upon our rightful share of our father's estate, and I will cut their throats a-twain."

"I will look upon their livers," said the second.

"I will have their heads off."

"I will flay their hides and peg them on the barns to dry."

They went on to further descriptions and delineations, but neither Mallian nor Zembac Pix had stayed to listen, crawling backwards upon hands and knees as they were. And thus they carried on until they found themselves upon the threshold of the guest house once again.

A woman's voice said, "A curious posture, guesty men—"

"A psychomaterial exercise incumbent upon those of our philosophy at this phase of the moon," said Mallian, rising up gracefully; "madame, matron, or lady, as the case itself may be. Fortune favor you, and I would invite you to join us for evenmeal but that I am uncertain of any such having been provided." He squinted into the darkness. Certain it was that this woman's figure was unlike that of Orna's, which had much resembled a very large sack of groats; but more he could not see because of the darkness.

The woman laughed softly and drew from beneath the folds of her costume a small lamp fitted with a translucent shade. "Snop, the favorite of Teresilda, was here a somewhat earlier," she said, smoothing her long tawny hair and smiling with her loose red mouth, "with announced intention of summoning you to dine with her, and went off in an alarm on not finding you."

Mallian clucked his tongue. "I must instantly pursue after him," he said, his stomach commencing to grumble, "lest he think me ill-disposed towards his lady's hospitality."

The woman put out her hand and took the stuff of his tunic allightly between two of her fingers. "It is all the rumor of this estate that Teresilda had provided you with her twain ugliest maids of a purpose, the which being that you should sate yourself on neither of them but that afterwards when all the night itself is asleep she herself intends to call and cosset you."

He smirked in the darkness. "Let her but try," he said, "that I might give an exemplar of my indomitable chastity."

She cast up her eyes in admiration, then her mouth down in woe. "For (as she said) it is little enough that I have ever seen of it, being but a bittle more than a child when my hag mother dulceted me away from my dollies, saying, 'Come, Lusilla, and we will go and visit folk.' —A malediction upon that day and its doings, which saw me sold as an alleged freemate unto Cape the father of Cope; may his belly swell as mine has never! For which reasons I have ever loathed and abhorred the touch of such as the aforesaid goat and randyman, and even misliked their conversation. But you assure me you are chaste?"

"I do assure you."

She sighed and smiled and said that in such case she might not mislike his conversation at all. And she agreed to take up her lamp and light their way abovestairs, but she insisted that it be without the conversation or company of Zembac Pix, who was (she said) far too old to be chaste. Nor would she accept his references as member of the Order of Sages. "They be such dirty devils in the dark," she declared. The potecary preened and pleaded guilty and agreed to mount guard upon the lower staircase lest the conversation be subject to an abrupt interruption which its free flow might not survive. He supplied him with a manuscripta from the library and found it a fascinating illustrated history of the splendid tortures inflicted by the long late Cupe the father of Cape upon his recalcitrant debtors. So the time passed and seemed but a moment before Lusilla came tripetting with her lamp in her hand and a faint half-smile upon her reddle mouth.

"Had you good conversation?" he enquired, returning in.

"Capital," said Mallian, smoothing his beard. "It is surprising how many recondite and intricate figures of speech she has at her fingertips. . . . And now let you and I go assearch of Snop and supper."

Zembac Pix said he hoped that his master-lord had not so exhausted his conversational resources as to have none left for dame Teresilda. Mal grinned. "Food will feed the fires," he said. "Teresilda. A hum hum. . . . If the Matron Orna was true-spoken and Teresilda and her steward Snop have indeed noted the absence of that one key, then she will be full of zeals to get it back. It might be best," he said, thoughtfully, groping under his shirt, "for you to retain it yourself, Zembac Pix, lest . . . lest . . ." He ripped off first tunic, then shirt, then trews, and groped and slapped and searched himself. Over and over again.

But of the key to the stone shed, there was no sign.

Mal sat on the edge of the couch holding his neck in his hands. "A several score thousand curses upon all Tawallis Land," he groaned; "and in particular upon all this particular estate. The longer we stay and tarry, the less we have. My only purpose in compounding the falsity about the dying word of Cape was to make usage of Teresilda and the residual heritage which I adjudged her (from the slavey man Rud's brief comments) the most competent to seize hold of. But Rud made no mention of Snop. A further curse upon Rud! I can only console myself a trifle with the thought that the trull Lusilla might meet whenat the keyhole of the stone shed the crone Orna and her brute guard of Gollocks!"

Zembac Pix said that he himself found it but less than a trifle consoling. And they brooded bitterly upon the ingrate and the treacherous whole house of Cape, until there came a rappeting upon the doors, and in came the two aged servant maids.

"A woe and an affliction, that such things be done!" cried the first.

"Hide! Flee!" shrilled the other.

And with many a wail and a headshake they explained that Matron Arna, second widow of Cape, and his other twain freemates by names Ulu and Iä, had made a compact one and all. "To wit, that they will menace you to sign a testament that Cape had named any one of them instead of Teresilda, and will divide the residuary amongst them all in equals. And should you fail or in anywise refuse," they went on, "the wicked women and their slavey men and servants purpose to slay the both of you and say that they saw you slaughter the late Cape!"

Mallian threw his hands out in horror. "Perjury!" he cried.

And Zembac Pix wept that the children of men should stoop to such disorder.

But the old women consoled them. "Even though our late

lord assented that we be assigned servant to Teresilda, still, we have a care for the honor of his name." They produced from beneath their apronskirts a pottle of liquor each. "You, young guest, are already stripped: good. You, senior, must haste to do the same. And both of you must instantly and thoroughly annoint yourselves with this liquor which has the essential property of making you, if not precisely invisible, then at least unnoticeable to the hostile eye."

Zembac Pix swore upon all his craft as a potecary that there was none such a substance. But then there came the sound of a number of people approaching loudly, and he made swift to cast off his every clout and clothes and to smear his limbs and head and trunk as Mallian was already doing.

"Am I begun to be unnoticeable?" he enquired. "Has it yet begun to work?"

"Indeed, there does seem to be a difference in your appearance," Mallian answered. "But I will not tarry to ascertain just what—"

The old women opened the doors and lighted them down the stairs with lamps, but scarcely had they reached the bottom floor when they stopped, the both of them, and moved no more of either lip or limb.

It was not until the next day that Cope the son of Cape arrived at the estate. His mother, Matron Erna, urged him to stay with her. But he replied that until all was probated and settled, he felt it more seemly to tarry at the guest house, whither he next proceeded. There he was met by the two old maid-servants whom he had most loved whenas a child, and they kissed him and becrooned him and made him welcome. "But woe and affliction! what dreadful things have here occurred and happened these late days!" they cried, a weeping-wise.

"A hem hum yes," he agreed. "Still: all men must die."

This they could not but assent to. "Nevertheless, we refer not to your father's death alone," they pointed out, "but to the unseemly and drear events concerning Teresilda and Snop and Orna and her Gollocks, as well as Lusilla: videlicet that they had all a somehow—and we will not ask *how*— came into possession, it would seem, of sundry baggages of treasure belonging to Thrag the father of Throg. And when they opened them to seek what was inside, woe and affliction! there came first an horrid yelping and then a most fierce barking and a baying and a howling and next from nowhere came the grue hounds or dogs of Thrag the father of Throg and attacked and slew the all of them. . . . Which next proceeded to come hither to this guest house and all but on the very threshold did the same work of destruction upon Arna and Ulu and Iä. Ah, and how they did scream! but we never liked them very much. After which the hounds snuffled and whuffled about the premises and then they got them gone, for a good thing, too!"

Cope agreed that the events were both inexplicable and horrorful. "But it behooves us," he said, "to look upon the bright and positive side of events: the abrupt deaths you mention have muchly simplified the probate and distribution of the estate, to which I am now the residuary as well as principal (by primogeniture) heir."

They agreed that this was so, and—doting upon him and delighting in his presence—they thanked him from their hearts for saving them an approach to doubting the beneficent decrees of Fortune. "But enough of lallying here below in the clutter and the rummage," they said. "Come up above and let us fix all things to your pleasure. Mind your steps, our dear."

He followed, looking about him with mild curiosity. "It beseems me," he observed, "that there is more of this stuff on hand each time I come here. What, precisely, are all these objects abbundled up in sacking and in cords?"

The old ones informed him that they represented the statuary collection begun and profusely added to by his long late grandfather, Cupe the father of Cape. "A wisely and a prudent man," they said; "and one which did teach us a sundry several useful tricks of sorts. Would you see a sampling, child?"

Cope shuddered his nose and shook his head. "He may have been all you say," he declared. "But it is well-known that he had a most execrable taste in art. No, no: I desire not to see a thing. For all I care," he concluded, mounting the steps to the upper floor, "they may stay here forever."

The combination of innocence and evil in a child can be one of the most chilling things in the world—especially if the child is your stepdaughter who has cold, calculated plans to murder you . . . and *most* especially if you have photographic proof from the future that she's going to succeed. . . .

THE EVIL EYE
Alfred Gillespie

The first sentence he typed was filled with mistakes: "El;zab eth is probsbly circlin g the biulding right now like a lonne Shoshone circling a burning wagoon."

"*Wagoon?*" Charlie said aloud, and snorted out a laugh that in turn led him to spill some gin on his bathrobe.

It was only ten-thirty at night, but Charlie had had half a dozen Martinis by six o'clock (such was his despair), and then another three or four by eight-thirty, when he'd tucked El;zab eth into her bed and repaired to the studio with a bottle of gin cradled in his arm. He'd stripped to his underwear, removed his aluminum leg, tossed it away from him, and fallen back onto the day bed in a deep and dreadful sleep.

He woke up, soaked with sweat, at half-past ten, his

228

head wracked with pain in at least four vital places, and he knew he would have to see the night through in a sitting position somewhere. As the leg was out of reach halfway across the room and Charlie was in no condition to crawl after it, he struggled to the edge of the bed, somehow got the robe around him, and hopped heavily to the table on which his electric typewriter crouched like a cannon. Surprisingly, he fell only once en route.

And now he sat, the cigarette pendant at his lip, letting out clouds of smoke, and pecked at the typewriter. Each character was whacked home electronically—*zzkak zzkak*. It gave him a certain feeling of permanence; it was all damn-the-torpedoes-full-speed-ahead, and no changing anything, not even with a string of obliterating z's. His right eye wept continually.

I have (he wrote) drunk a wagoonful of gin tonight so that I would have no trouble sleeping, and you see where it's got me. Exactly five jumps across the floor to the alphabet machine. I shall set down the story of me and that monster child out there in the night, and the camera, if it exists—and I think it does—and all the rest of it. I shall set it down neatly in the straight he-said-she-said manner of Homer, and you'll get no boozy philosophy out of me, no soul searchings, no dialectics—in a's and q's and other precise symbols like *¢@½?%$. I think *¢@½?%$ is a much better expression than the stuff you hear in barracks rooms and school buses.

Elizabeth.

Outside my window somewhere, I'm convinced, a small, nine-year-old bat girl named Elizabeth, my stepdaughter, is circling and circling and circling in for the kill. Why the *¢@½?%$ would she want to kill a sweet, middle-aged, forty-year-old bindle stiff like me?

I haven't the foggiest; that's the truth.

Last night, which is when I brought the camera home as a peace token after having been away for two days and one night—well, last night, under a purpling sky, I drove north out of New York City and skimmed like a bee with a sore rear end through Westchester County. The light was on in Elizabeth's room. That's her window just over the front door—the window from which she threw herself on one impressive occasion. My Volkswagen came scrunching up the driveway off the dirt lane to the house, and into the carport that connects the frame house to the studio, where

I make my living designing book jackets and things. The darkness by then had become a large black something of some kind kneeling over the two buildings. It was leaning on its forearms and breathing warmly on us. Through a front window, I could see Mrs. Cleary back in the kitchen preparing dinner. I beeped the horn and came grunting out of the car, pulling the camera and the portfolio after me.

Mrs. Cleary dried her long fingers on her apron as I came swinging into the kitchen, the prodigal returned, and gave me the full benefit of her thin face and her eyes, dead and dry as a cigarette ash. Then she ticked off her report, flatly and quickly. There was stew for dinner, Mr. Mc-Lenahan, she said, ready in about twenty minutes. The potatoes were ready now. The peas were in their pot. Elizabeth, she reported, seemed a bit pale tonight, though Mrs. Cleary had run her hand over the child's forehead and it seemed cool. (It's a wonder the child hadn't taken a bite at the hand.) Liz was in her room now, the dearie, doing her homework. There had been no trouble at school today, for a welcome change. Oh, but the light on the stairs was burned out, had Mr. McLenahan noticed? (Mrs. Cleary, as you've observed, has as much vivacity as the early Rosalind Russell.) The little James boy, Pete, had stopped by to see if Elizabeth had wanted to hunt frogs across the way, but, of course, she hadn't. Oh, yes, Mrs. C wouldn't be eating with Liz and me that night because her sister, Miss Kelly, was staying with her in town through the week. And she wouldn't be in tomorrow (meaning today) if that was OK with me, because she and her sister planned on journeying up to Mrs. Cleary's brother-in-law Henry's place in North Salem for the day. Well, sir, she would see me in a couple of days, then, and good night. Rosalind Russell, I hope, never had a first-act soliloquy like *that* one to get off.

Goodbye, ol' Pussycat Cleary! And good sailing!

I need a drink to salute her going. Wait while I make myself a bone-dry cocktail. That's a Martini without vermouth, ice cubes, or glass, and you take it directly from the bottle.

Cheers.

Charlie McLenahan shuddered at the sudden onslaught of gin but gulped it down manfully and then squinted off into the night. There was no moon, no stars to illuminate the small figure of Elizabeth (perhaps) standing quite still out there by the young elm, or stepping soundlessly across the gravel. He went back to his typing.

I heard the old woman's car leaving the driveway (he wrote) and turning down the road. As the silence closed in like a black, collapsing parachute in the dark, the time was at hand to summon the child to dinner. "Child!" I cried. "Dinner!" But there was no reply.

I clicked the light switch on the wall, but nothing happened. The bulb, as Mrs. Cleary had reported, was *kaput*. As I climbed the stairs to Elizabeth's room—the slow way some one-legged men do, two actions to a step—the swinging door to the kitchen quite suddenly swang, or swung, or maybe swinged a little shut, as it was in the habit of doing, cutting off all the light but that thin, bright strip under the bedroom door. I was breathing the way a bulldog will after a roughhousing. "Hello, puff puff!" I called aloud at about the halfway point. "Liz! Soup's on!" And in answer the thin line of light vanished silently. I said to myself, "The little &%$#?@¢." But I hobbled on, muttering, "Come on now, puff, puff, Liz," as I neared the top of the stairs.

I knew, at least, that she couldn't lock the door, because I'd done away with the key weeks ago after she'd succeeded in locking herself in for the day. My hand was on the doorknob and I paused a moment. The back of my neck had gone a bit cold. "Liz!" I called again, getting an edge of paternal authority into my voice. But after I'd given her a count of one-two-three-four-five, I said, "I'm comin' in," maybe a bit gruffly, and opened the door and stepped inside.

The blackness of the bedroom wasn't quite as *total* as what I'd walked out of, and I was able, without too much trouble, to get to the desk by the window. "Honey, that's no way to fire off a great welcome to the guy who keeps you in Nancy Drew books, and Jujyfruits, and all," I said. Or something equally as effective. The desk lamp, which was the only implement of electrification in the room, was gone. "Give me the lamp, huh?" I said. Then I struck a match and saw her standing in the corner with the frilly little-girl's lamp in her hands. I let the match burn out and lit a second one, but she was already returning the lamp to the desk and plugging it into the wall. The room seemed to burst into light. Liz stood and, giving her grand old stepfather a wide berth, made for the door. "Hold on," I said, and grabbed hold of her hand before she could get

231

it away. I pulled her after me to the bed. It hardly seemed the hand of a nine-year-old. More like five.

"Come on!" I said. "You're giving the fellow who's in love with you a damned rough time, do you know that?"

She said nothing. Her eyes, which are dark brown, are terribly large—too large for beauty, too round and wide and moist and lifeless. Usually her hair is parted in the middle and pulled back tightly into long, black pigtails. Her skin, you know, is white as a shell. I remember holding a buttercup under her chin once, not long ago, and her whole face seemed to turn gold in its reflection. I took the buttercup away, and she was chalk once more.

As I sat holding her on the edge of the bed, I touched her face with my finger just below her right eye and then just below her left. "What," I asked her as gravely as I could, "did one eye say to the other?"

I waited, but she said nothing, only looked away from me with a petulant shrug. "Do you know?" I asked.

"No," she whispered.

"No?" I inquired rather loudly.

"No!" she shouted.

" 'Something has come between us and it smells.' "

She looked quickly up at me and then away again, but no smile came within three city blocks of her lips.

"That's a pretty lousy joke," I said, "but I've known nine-year-olds to throw up laughing at it. Do you know about elbows?" I asked her.

She shook her head.

"Well, then, pinch your elbow."

She touched her left elbow with her right hand.

"Go ahead, *pinch* it. Pinch the skin behind it."

She pinched it lightly.

"No, hard!"

She gave it a good one.

"There, you see? You can pinch your elbow all you want, any time, and it'll never hurt. But that's a secret, and I don't want you blabbing it all over the place to Pete James or Mrs. Cuthbert or Mrs. Cleary or Sister Angela Marie."

"I don't tell secrets," she muttered.

"*What?*"

"*I don't* tell secrets!"

"Oh. Like what?"

"If I told you—"

"*What?*"

"*If I told you—*"

232

"Yes?"

"Then it would . . . be *told.*"

"It *what?*"

"*Would be told!*"

She struggled to get away.

"Hold on! Whoa!" I said. "Look. I'll let you go if you answer one question. OK?"

"Maybe," she whispered.

"Do you like me?"

"No."

And she dug her elbow hard in my ribs to give her leverage enough to get across the room. But I still held fast, idiot that I was.

"But that's only half the question," I said.

"No fair!" she complained.

"Shh. *Why* don't you like me?"

"*I don't know.*"

And she struggled again, her eyes going blurry in the angry tears.

"Why?"

"Because you're a cripple," she said.

"Ah, go on, I just walk a little funny. What's the reason, Liz?"

"You killed her, you killed her," she said in a whimper.

I let the girl go. At the door, before sliding out into the darkness, she turned and looked at me directly with a look so full of hate that the dimes and quarters melted in my pocket. But I noticed that she was, quite unthinkingly, pinching her left elbow between two fingers of her right hand. Earlier when, of course, I should have released her immediately, I'd held onto her; and now, when I should have been drawing the whole story out of her, I was letting her go. To go mulling off behind the house. To go brooding among the night trees. But I'm basically—and metabolically—an ignorant man.

When I had the dinner dished out. I called to her, "Liz!"

Nothing.

"Liz! Dinner! Come on, old woman!"

Nothing.

"I got you something, did you know?"

Nothing.

"A camera!"

She came slowly out of the shadowed carport and into the kitchen.

"Yes," I said, "a camera, Liz. Now sit down and eat your dinner, because you won't be getting the camera until

233

the morning, when the sun is out. People don't give cameras in the dark. That sort of thing has a curse attached to it."

Charlie stopped typing because a long ash had fallen from his cigarette into the typewriter and in blowing it away he had sent a cloud of ash up into his face. He rubbed his eyes with his knuckles and decided he wanted to walk around a bit. In a kind of diving motion, he bent sideways off the chair until the palms of his hands came flat against the floorboards. Then he allowed his rump to come crashing down, sending the chair flying. He crawled, lurching, to the aluminum leg, an elaborate contraption he would buckle onto his half-thigh and around his hips. It took him a full, exhausting three minutes on his back to get into the thing. Then he had a devil of a time climbing to a standing position. He hobbled quite eccentrically to a far corner where a cane stood, then circumnavigated the room almost with a swagger, peering out of the windows set in the southern and western walls; unlocking and opening the door leading (north) into the carport; and leaning out into the night. He was surprised that it was so chilly, and was about to close the door quickly behind him when, just beyond the hunched automobile, he thought he saw the vague silhouette of a small girl standing still as a snow sculpture in the night.

"Liz?" he said softly.

But suddenly he found himself back inside the studio, sagged against the closed door, and breathing deeply and rapidly. He thought he'd heard, very faintly but nearby, a giggle. And it frightened him.

Charlie righted the chair and slumped back into it, slept for half a minute with his fingers jammed into his eyes, awakened considerably refreshed, and recommenced his account of his life with Liz—yes, and Ann too, and Agnes the beagle, and the camera.

The camera (he tippy-tapped, *zzkak*, *zzkak*, ever so lightly on the infernal machine).

Actually, I bought the camera (I'm told) the day before yesterday. Norb Hutchinson was the fellow who told me, and he should know, because he was present at the ceremony. Norb is a hell of a fine guy, all ear and no lip, and I am as fond as I can be of that long, sallow, crumpled face of his. He has a high tolerance for other people's witticisms and sad confidences, a quality I am too twitchy to share. I guess I'd never told anybody about my malignant stepdaughter (that's the word I used—malignant)

234

until the day before yesterday at lunchtime with Norb Hutchinson at the bar of the *Plume Rouge* on East Forty-sixth Street.

The Plume's usual circle of art directors, copywriters, printer's representatives and magazine editorial people gave us a large hello when we entered. I get a reception in the Plume each time I enter that would be the envy of a king. (The fact that I am still only six or seven weeks widowed may add to the glamour, of course, but I doubt it.)

It's all a matter of style, y'see.

I come in with the end of a cigarette in my mouth, sending up enough smoke to blot out New Jersey. I go like a dump truck to the coat room to prop my portfolio against one wall and let the owner's wife pull the topcoat off me. Because ol' Charlie—or "the old man," as many of my friends, including my late wife, have referred to me—has never learned to remove a garment correctly, one sleeve comes off inside out, and the black arm band falls slackly about my left wrist in the entanglement. I run a hand swiftly through my pepper-and-salt hair, which has the consistency of kelp, and then pull the arm band up above my elbow. I'm a slightly-less-than-pretty fellow—a Dylan Thomas, I've been told, and without the poetry. I've put on weight in recent months, especially in the weeks since Anne was killed. My breathing is violent at times—"like the snorts that would escape through the blow-hole of an asthmatic whale," as one of my friends put it. My clothes are too tight in some places and too baggy in others. And my limp, which was never slight, now seems more pronounced than ever, as though some tinsmith were trimming the old metal leg by a quarter inch every Tuesday. Now I know—and it isn't immodesty, I swear—that the lunch crowd at the Plume, men with whom I've been working, drinking and jawing for years, love me almost extravagantly. They love me for my style, because in a stylish way I seem to be going to the dogs for *them*. They can smoke too much, drink too much, get into debt too deeply, risk their jobs by staying too long at lunch each day, and sink ever more quickly into the bad habits of middle age, and somehow not show a mark for it all. I'm their own picture of Dorian Gray, coughing away into my cupped hand (a final hurrah before something definitive strikes) or showing up in the art department of some swanky-danky magazine with eyes glowing red like exit signs, and then blowing my nose into a handkerchief that is already weighing down my hip pocket the way a revolver would. The unregenerate regulars at the Plume know that no matter how sickly they might feel, or how conscience stricken, I feel even worse, and I have more, each morning, to regret.

"You need a haircut, old man," one of the regulars said that day.

"Old man, when's your cookbook coming out?"

"Move over, Jack, and make room for the old man."

I thanked my companions and hoisted myself onto a stool.

"Old man, what'll you have today?" (This from François, the bartender—the upstart!)

Old man this, old man that; it's just a case of sweet, boozy camaraderie, that's all.

I remember the talk was about my being forty, which is no age to be, and then about putting on weight.

"Ah, I eat like a bird. A pelican."

I sank into a reverie and the conversations struck up once more around me. I glared into my Martini as an important thought struck into me like a javelin out of nowhere at all:

I wonder if Elizabeth thinks that I killed her mother! That it was none other than me—Charlie McLenahan!— over there in the park letting fly with the pistol! Eh? That the "old man" with the gun, who was described simply as "the old man" in the radio report—the only report Liz heard! —was really me!?!

Masculine intuition—that's what it was. And hardly more than twenty-four hours before the little gargoyle said it herself! "You killed her, you killed her."

By two o'clock, the Plume regulars were off at their tables putting away great heaps of *osso buco* and eggplant *parmigiana*, and only Norb and I sat hunched at the bar. Ann Carmody McLenahan, I was telling him in the slick tones of a newscaster, was shot to death one afternoon, a little short of two months ago, as she was about to cross Fifty-ninth Street to enter the swank Plaza Hotel on the arm of a former bit player in Tarzan movies ("See here, ape man, you show us the elephant graveyard or we kill the monkey, *comprenez?*"). Mention of the square-rigged young actor was news to Norb, as the chap had not been cited in the newspaper accounts except as a detached witness. The accident, of course, was an awful, terrible, monstrous freak. It was even bad melodrama. And old man, preparing to blow his brains out in Central Park across the way, had fired his lousy pistol prematurely and by accident, and the stray bullet tore into Anne's back, killing her instantly. The wild improbability of the event slapped it squarely on the

236

front pages of the evening papers and the next morning's one tabloid. "Blonde socialite" and "main-stem beauty" were the archaic descriptions of Ann used most frequently by the reporters. But because the story had no mystery to it—the old man turned himself in to a mounted policemen minutes after the shot—the papers dropped poor Ann, as they'd drop a poorly fought welterweight fight, within hours.

I told Norb I knew the actor pretty well, and he was a good-enough joker. Probably he'd already strolled casually into half a dozen affairs of this kind and would take that walk again because—well, he's who he is, and the world is full of good-looking, well-bred women who become jelly at the sound of a British accent. After her first husband died, Ann went a long time without men, and she was a girl who needed a baritone voice and a hairy leg around the house. Here I'd gone forty years without marriage. Thirty-eight, anyway. Didn't know what it was. Wasn't even sure I wanted it. Then there was Ann with her beagle dog, Agnes, on a leash, and her darlin' little daughter, Liz, skipping along behind. How could a hedgehog like me *not* want to have that creamy face of Ann's—that green-eyed, intelligent, alive, *pretty* face—looking at me all the time and kissing my ugly mug and cleaning up the crumbs I left behind?

I had a damn good marriage, I told Norb. It had a run of only two years—two years and a couple of months and a couple of days—but it was good while it lasted. And I was a gentle and constant lover, and I think Ann rather loved me too. Oh, I had my slouchy side. I was gone a good bit of the time. Holed up here at the Plume. Or at the Font. Or at Tim's. And I left my ties around the backs of chairs and my dental floss on the sink. So Ann met an actor with a chin like a hard, minuscule backside and an eye full of electric sparks short-circuiting away, and she had a short, sweet fling. I don't begrudge it to her. Not really.

Yes, I do. I begrudge the hell out of it.

I waved the bartender into making another round of drinks.

"Why do you still wear the arm band?" Norb wanted to know.

"For the kid, really. She's nine years old, and all I am to her is bad news. I think she connects me up with Ann's accident. Who knows? I even ran over her dog a couple of months ago, shortly before Ann's death. Didn't I tell you about it?"

"Yeah, I remember."

"Right in the dirt road that goes by our house. Not a moving thing within miles, except Agnes. That ¢@½°&%$#
237

dopey dog, Agnes. I think she thought the left front tire was vulcanized Ken-L-Ration. Liz was inconsolable. She's never really talked or listened to me since. But anyhow, the arm band. I want the thing to stay on as evidence that I *care*, despite the way she's been carrying on since the funeral, the malignant little wretch!"

I snickered. "Sorry, Norb, old fellow. I use words like that—malignant, gargoyle, monster child, bat girl—and I'd better wash my mouth out, because I don't really mean those words. Somewhere, in an interior organ of some sort, I love the kid. Or, if the word isn't love, then—well, at the very least, I'm *concerned* about her. I want her to be happy, because the truth is the little bloodsucker breaks my heart."

Norb and I left the Plume drunk, got drunker, and the next morning in Norb's studio, and Norb sitting at the drawing board, dragging deeply at a cigarette and staring morosely at the sunshine flooding the street below. "Hello, old man," Norb said. "God, you snore."

"Of course I do. And somebody's been at your face with the green paint."

He told me I'd been in no condition to drive home the night before, but that I'd phoned Mrs. Cleary and asked her to stay on for the night. And she'd given me one of her Irish lectures.

I shall not describe the pain I found myself in, from my lower regions to my cranium, except to say that no comparable sensation or group of sensations has been felt since the invention of ether. It was in this condition, then, that I was introduced to the camera. It stood on the file cabinet at the foot of the daybed on which I'd slept so violently all night. It was made completely of metal, with a black lacquer finish that was coming off. A leather strap ran across the top like the handle of a briefcase. The lens, which was facing away from me, was encased in a silver cone, giving the camera a faint resemblance to a lantern. Obviously, it was home-made. It was also terribly heavy and, upon close inspection, it proved to be geared for instant developing, in the Polaroid manner.

I'd bought the thing, Norb told me, for six dollars from a pawnbroker who had a shop on the east side of Third Avenue somewhere in the mid-Forties. The man had tried to sell me a battered old box camera, but I'd have none of it. "Don't you have one just as cheap, but different? Crazy?" I said.

"You mean nuts?" the man asked.

"Yah. For a nutty kid, a nutty camera," Norb said that I said.

And out had come this contraption that seemed half miner's lamp, half lunch box. It had been left with him, the pawnbroker told us (Norb said), by a thin little man with an indoor face—the face, perhaps, of a hen-pecked inventor who'd just lost a billion-dollar race with a large film company by only five minutes.

Oh, yes, to test the camera, I'd taken a picture of the spire of the Chrysler Building. Considering the shape I was in, the snapshot was just fine.

"Im! Possible!" were the words uttered by the pawnbroker when he saw the picture. And: "To tell you the truth, kid, I didn't think it'd work."

Charlie permitted his head to dip slowly forward in sleep, until his nose was snugly pressed against the margin-release button of the typewriter. Minutes later, he grunted "Huh" suddenly, excitedly, and lifted his head from the machine. He glanced quickly to his right in time to see—or perhaps, to sketch, in his despair-logged mind—a small darting movement. The door had been opened just a bit, six inches or so, and the small hand flew from the outside doorknob the instant Charlie turned. He lurched violently across small distance to the door, fell against it, opened it wide, and looked out. "What the hell!" he growled and, finding the cane in his hand, stalked out onto the gravel.

He was certain that he saw a pint-sized shadow far across the house. He turned and headed back to the carport, taking fast steps up the drive to the door. The wall switch inside still lit no lights, of course, and Charlie swore. From the drawer of the table that stood at the foot of the staircase he removed a flashlight and then hobbled, step by step, to the child's bedroom, the beam of the flashlight jerking to left and right ahead of him. There was no strip of illumination showing beneath the door. He walked directly across the room to the bed, keeping the flashlight beam diverted behind him and to one side so that it wouldn't awaken the girl if she was there and was asleep.

She was there. And dimly Charlie could see that she lay on her side facing him, with her lips parted slightly and her breathing coming slow and deep. Charlie placed a hand on her forehead and was surprised to find the child was quite cool. He turned off the flashlight and placed it on the desk.

"I'm an ash," he told himself. "a stupid, ignorant, selfish, frightened, unmitigated, total, and complete ash!"

And he went down the stairs again as quietly as he could. But then, once again, at the bottom of the stairs, the knowledge hit him that the child had followed him out of the room and was standing, this second, at the top of the staircase. He turned and then cursed himself for having left the flashlight behind. There was something, something the size of Elizabeth, at the bedroom door wasn't there?

"Liz," Charlie said, barely audibly, but no response came.

And as he made his way back to the studio, he knew she was with him all the way.

Only maybe she wasn't.

Maybe it was just Charlie McLenahan's grief following him around. But whatever it was—something mortal, something imagined, something loving, or something lethal—it frightened him cold.

After he'd closed the studio door behind him, he locked it. And he had a drink. He looked at his watch. Twenty to three. There was no telling how long he had slept—three minutes or a couple of hours—because he'd already written a respectable sheaf of unnumbered pages, some filled, some half empty, without once glancing at his watch, and with no idea of his speed. He seemed to be going like a Thompson submachine gun, *zzkak zzkak zzkakkakakakak*, but maybe that was only a gin-soaked impression too. Maybe he was tapping it out in the more uncertain rhythms of a cap pistol. Tap. Tap. Taptap. Tap.

Maybe: that was the word he was tapping a moment later.

Maybe (he wrote) is a word that somehow defines my entire experience with Elizabeth. We got off to a fuzzy, maybe, start the day I met her and lifted her onto my knee and tried to give her a kiss, only to have her turn her face away so that the kiss landed somewhere behind the left ear. "Pew, you smell," she said—her first words, and I shall hang onto them always.

Of course I *did* smell occasionally of Martinis, which can sometimes give one's neighbor the impression of being downwind of an onion field. I did smell of cigarettes, certainly. And of uncared-for bachelorhood.

By and large, though, she was civil enough to me, though we never became friends, even when Ann was alive. Liz was a quiet and rather remote child. She would open up from time to time—though never, I regret, when I was present. She and Ann would horse around somewhere and when I'd enter the room—run for your lives! Bad news! Poison gas!

Liz would stalk out of the room, the grand vizier stalking out of the peace conference.

She was a very religious child, as I was at her age and as, in many ways, I still am. She loved the atmosphere of church, as I did and do. She loved the nuns and the rosaries and the holy water and the confessional and the shiny linoleum everywhere. She even loved school (the creep!) and was good at her new mathematics and her ancient catechism answers. "Why did God make you?" "God made me to know Him to love Him, and to serve Him in this world and forever in the next."

After she had thrown herself out of that second-floor window—furious, I suppose, that her mother, in death, had abandoned her—and lay grunting a long while on the grass with the wind and the pride knocked out of her, but not the fury; after her almost week-long hunger strike—a week marked by thefts from the breadbox and the deep freeze; after she had set fire to (a) her wastebasket, (b) the gardener's shed behind the house, (c) *my* wastebasket, and (d), quite unsuccessfully, the studio; and after she had run away twice and been returned twice—well, after all these raucous events had transpired one upon the other following Ann's funeral, I took this small cuckoo and occasional arsonist to see Sister Angela Marie, her teacher, and thence to Mother Paul Jude, the principal, both of whom Liz admires inordinately.

"She's . . . *changeable*," Sister Angela Marie said. "She can be sullen one moment in class, and, five minutes later when the children are in church for stations, she seems almost radiant. What kind of food does Mrs. Cleary pack for Elizabeth's lunch? Perhaps her food is wrong."

Mother Paul Jude, who is not a dope, recommended psychiatry, which has been my own prescription from the beginning ("First psychiatry, then electrocution."), and told me about the nun's pet psychiatrist, a fellow in Pound Ridge, New York, who consents to listen to children for twenty-five dollars an hour. Elizabeth has only just started her visits, of course, so there have been no reports, no findings, no diagnoses yet. Give the good old doc time, I say. Shortly after my own autopsy in the Westchester County morgue, I suspect he will find a key to the child's problem.

But I haven't mentioned the snapshots yet. I must.

Yesterday morning, the morning of the great hangover, I worked straight through at Norb Hutchinson's place. I worked all the afternoon, too, on an illustration that wasn't due at the advertising agency until today. I figured I could

241

do the job a day in advance, deliver it, come home, and then stay at home the following day (the one I've just been through) working on a couple of book covers for a guy I know.

Anyhow, I went home, as I've recorded. Met Mrs. Cleary, said goodbye, tangled with Liz, put her to bed, as I've recorded. Then I had a few drinks because that seems to be the pattern of my life these last weeks, and slept like a grizzly bear. Leaped to the ceiling at the sound of the alarm this morning. Cooked breakfast. And . . .

"Hello, Liz."

She has this kittenish, hands-behind-the-back, let's-walk-close-to-the-walls-today kind of mood about her, though she is still no more talkative than a bay scallop. She is looking for something. She is good about straightening her long black stockings and washing her dirty neck. She is on the move. Silently.

Of course! "The camera!" I exclaim, snapping my fingers.

She darts a quick, thankful look at me, though if I were to measure the wattage of that gratitude flashing there in her eye I'd give it two and a half—about enough to kindle a fire-fly's abdomen.

Elizabeth liked the camera. She almost—not quite—smiled when I placed it on the breakfast table in the kitchen. She circled the table once and looked at the camera closely. "I love it," she said. She tried to lift it and found it so terribly heavy she had to use two hands. "I just love it."

I suggested that she take one picture before leaving for school. She agreed. She carried the thing before her with two hands holding the leather strap, much as she would carry a pail brimming with water, and went outside. I watched her from the front door as the explosion of morning sunlight—or maybe it was the cigarette I'd just lit—set a deep, needle-point pain going in the central area of my brainpan.

She was saying, "Ah, please, let me take a picture of you, Charlie."

"Nah, my face would burn a hole in the paper." But she was (for her) so happy and talkative that I couldn't risk a change in mood. "OK," I said, as her face began to harden, "where?"

"Back of the house, in the sun."

I stood against a section of white wall, bunching up my face like a closed fist in the early-morning sun. "I'm going to count," she said. "One."

"Don't I get a blindfold or a cigarette?"

"Two. *Three!*"

She pushed a button on the side of the machine, an action that set off a barely audible bzzzzzz-click somewhere in its middle that lasted more than a full second. The button popped back out to its normal position with the click. "There's nothing happening," she said.

I took a couple of steps toward her: "It's developing the picture. Don't worry. Whistle a song."

But her mood of delight was fast slipping away. "It's such a *stupid* thing!"

"Why don't you put it down on the old stump until it's ready, Liz?"

The smile was gone entirely when she looked up at me and said, carefully, "Elizabeth." She added, "I want to hold it."

It seemed half a lifetime before she tore the snapshot against the blade in the bottom of the camera and uttered her definitive comment: "But you're not *in* it!"

"Not in it?"

I stumped over to her and looked over her shoulder at the ridiculous thing. It contained nothing but a number of horizontal boards painted white—perhaps flaking just a bit—with the shadow of an eave slanting across the top left corner of the photograph. "I do seem to have a blank expression," I managed to say, despite the pang that shot through an inner pocket of my spleen. "Maybe it wasn't aimed just right, Liz," I said.

"But it was!"

She tossed the snapshot over her shoulder to the grass, as you might toss away a burned match, then placed the camera on the oak stump and walked off—or, rather, walked *out*. "It's an *ignorant* camera," she cried back at me, "and I hate it, and I hate you, and I don't want it."

"Well, that covers the situation nicely," I said, and then lifted my voice in my best quarter-deck manner: "Elizabeth! Here! Bring the camera into the house! And pick up th—"

The screen door slammed shut behind her.

We were sitting on the stump, the camera and I, when Liz drifted down the driveway on her way to the intersection where the school bus would pick her up. She never looked our way.

I shall not comment just now upon my philosophical musings or conjecturings regarding the snapshot beyond reporting that I examined it carefully and detected, beneath a clothesline hook that truly exists at this very moment in time, a rust stain on the outer wall of the house that does not. The general condition of the paint job in the picture (flaky) was a libel upon our homestead's current epidermis (smooth as nail-polish). In a kind of sedate panic, I left the camera and snap-shot on the stump, and, somehow got to the studio and even managed to do some work on a jacket for a book. The hours passed, and I confess that I had a nip or two to help them along. It must have been about four o'clock that I looked up from my work to see Elizabeth crossing the lawn toward the road.

It was the first I knew that she was home from school. The camera rode on her left arm while she held the snap-shot close to her face, inspecting it with an intensity you would find only in the face of a watchmaker looking into the workings of a pocket watch that has been run over by a bus. I tapped on the window with the end of the T square, and then went to the window and (This can't all be hap-pening just a few short hours ago, can it? It can.) opened the window all the way. I called out. "There's stuff in the kitchen. Crackers. Milk."

Without turning, she called back, "I *had* them."

"About to take another picture?"

"Yes."

"Of what?"

"Pete James."

Pete, a four-year-old with a head of tousled black hair that gives him an eternally startled look, lives down the road from us. He had appeared at the foot of the drive precisely on cue and hollered out, "Hey, Elizabeth! You wanna go froggin'?"

No, she didn't—not that minute, anyhow—but she had a better idea. *Uh*-uh, he said, he had to go catch a frog for his mother. Wait, she called to him, and then said that if he, Peter James, didn't come right on over to her in sixty sec-onds he'd be sorry.

Pete climbed the steep lawn to the girl. Stand against the house, she ordered. You're gonna do something bad, gonna hurt, he said. No, she promised. Picture! You're gonna take my picture! Sure, and you can see it right after, she prom-ised. *Right* after? Yup, and then she'd go frogging with him, honest. He smiled a huge, gleaming smile for the camera, his eyes tight shut. Bzzzzzz-click. OK, Elizabeth? Yes, Pete, you can relax. Let's see, huh? Pete, I *can't* go catching frogs this afternoon, I'm too busy, you go on now, get out of here, scram. I *won't* scram. Yes, you will, Peter James, you will if I have to run you off with a large rifle. I wanna see

244

my picture. Well, you can't, because I have to send the film away to be developed, to Rochester, to Kodiak, Alaska, to President Johnson. *Scram!*

She walked quickly around him and into the house, and Pete, after a moment's hesitation, came running behind her. But she was standing in the doorway holding the screen door open for him. She seized him by the face and pushed him backward onto the ground, hard.

That final gesture of Elizabeth's had me half out of the window. "Elizabeth!"

Pete picked himself up and came crying to me, but I couldn't make out a word the kid was saying among the sobs. "Be a good boy, Pete, and go catch yourself a frog somewhere," I told him.

My spit had turned to gunpowder. But I didn't go up to Liz's bedroom because I didn't want to risk a show-down on her battlefield. It would be here, on mine. I stalked the studio room, preparing a loud speech. The speeches I make up and then do not deliver, by the way, are among the finest pieces of rhetoric in all of Western literature.

On about my thirtieth circumnavigation of the room, I detected a slight movement to the right of the drawing board and once again peered from the window. There was Elizabeth, standing in the driveway, with her bicycle just behind her on its side. She was taking a picture of the house and studio.

I forced myself to walk slowly to the open window. I forced my face and voice into a measure of passivity. "Elizabeth, come on in a minute."

She did not reply. She lifted her bicycle, placed the camera in the basket on the handlebars, coasted to the road, and began pedaling toward town. I bellowed out her name, but it was no use.

I stalked over to the house and up the stairs to her room. A snapshot, in a dozen pieces, was in the wastebasket. I brought them back to the studio with me and glued them together on a piece of Bristol board. It was the picture of a tall young man with short black hair, his eyes squinting in the sun. He was standing, as Pete had stood, before the front wall of the house, wearing a well-cut suit and a dark tie. One side of his mouth was pulled into a grin—the same pull-of-the-mouth that will transform Pete's face even now, as he concentrates on a game of skill (like pouncing upon a frog), or a repair job (like realigning the bleached-white skeleton of a snake that's gotten out of whack in a rain-storm). The young man in the picture, I was happy to note, looked sensitive, warm-natured, and well-to-do. I'd placed his age at about twenty-four. And because Liz has a distant cousin of just that age, I was sure she was able to guess at Pete James's age in the picture, too, with a reasonable accuracy.

"Ah, come on, Pete!" I said aloud to the picture as I stomped about the room. "When you're twenty-four, I'll be sixty," I hollered. "Sixty! A spry, waltzing, wenching sixty!"

I don't know what time it was—maybe five—when the phone rang.

"Charlie? Mabel Cuthbert."

Through the tired voice I could see her tired, sweet face, with the pale freckles big as dimes on it, and her gray hair swept back into a bun, and something badly wrong with her. Some of her acquaintances think it's cancer, and I wouldn't be much surprised. She said she shouldn't be calling me telling me about anything so trivial, but—

Mabel had been cleaning a room upstairs in her house down the road when she saw Liz, acting like a bank robber, walk her bike in under the branches of a huge fir tree that's Mable's pride and joy. ("Why, anyone could hide a water buffalo in there and get away with it," she said.) Mrs. Cuthbert was unable to resist her curiosity, so she came out of the house and peered into the tree.

Elizabeth was studying a snapshot when Mabel had come snooping into the piny lair. The girl asked her: "Mrs. Cuthbert, can you tell how old a tree is just by looking at it?"

"I don't know. What kind of tree?"

"A maple."

"If it's young, perhaps, but not if it's old."

"It's young."

"Let's see, Elizabeth."

After wrestling with a should-she or shouldn't-she decision for a painful moment. Liz handed the old girl the snapshot. The McLenahan manse, according to the photograph, was only barely recognizable, Mabel told me. Ivy grew all over the north wall and the chimney. (The place has never seen ivy in its life!) Flamingos, leprechauns, and other garden cuties paraded across the lawn in the front of the place; ships' running lights ornamented both doors; and the studio—

"—wasn't there, was it?" I said, feeling sicker than ever.

Mabel snorted. "Exactly! But how did you know, Charlie?"

"Extrasensory perception, honey."

Where the studio had stood, a maple now grew—a tree that had been around, Mabel guessed, oh, a good fifteen to twenty years, more like twenty. The woods beyond, she said, were a little "ratty" in the picture.

"Ratty?"

"Yes, ratty," she said. "Some of the trees in the very first line are dead—long dead—and haven't been removed. And one or two of them show up black."

"Black?"

"Scorched."

And that, in essence, was her story.

Liz, "looking like the cat that ate the canary," had walked her bike onto the road and had pedaled off toward home.

As I hung up the phone, I saw Elizabeth returning—the attempt to make it all the way up the gravel drive, the slight skid, the dismounting, the abandonment of the bicycle at the door of the house. I caught her eye and waved her into the studio. She came slowly, something strangely *tight* about her, as though she were straining every fibre in her to refrain from bursting into laughter, or dancing a tarantella. I jiggled the keys in my pocket frantically in accompaniment.

"Elizabeth—" I began.

"Yes, Daddy?" she said, showering sparks of pure love everywhere in the room. I could have wrung her lollipop-stem neck.

"Elizabeth, I wish—"

"—that I weren't so mean to Pete?"

"Yes, well, *that* for a starter. I think it would be nice if you'd be nice to me too."

"I'm sorry, Daddy." With a *smile!*

"But I'm putting aside that particular speech for another occasion. Right now I want to make you an offer." She walked about the room as I talked, running an index finger over things. "I'm taking you to live somewhere else. New experiences. New friends. New—"

She scowled suddenly and wheeled on me. "Where?"

"Oh . . ." I wondered myself where to begin another life. "Manhattan."

"No."

"It's a different tempo. Theater. Noise. We'll go off somewhere for a while Europe, maybe. You've nev—"

"No," she said. "I'll never leave here. That's something I know." She said it flatly, with her back to me.

"Let me tell you something, small pussycat. Something important. We're leaving this house tomorrow, you and me.

the day after today. And we'll never return to it. I'll have somebody else pack up for us later. Huh? We'll drive in to the Algonquin Hotel in the morning. Eh? And from there on out, we'll improvise. What do you think about that?"

At the word "tomorrow" she had stiffened. Thoughts chased one another across her face like dark, medieval armies sweeping across a ruined plain. One could almost hear—cronk! crunk! clang! oof!—the clangor of the broad-axes upon cuirass and shield. But then there came a sudden terrible quiet. I think I can call it a "quiet," can't I? And, after quite a long pause, a filthy little smile caught the corners of her mouth. "All right, Daddy."

It was the small, hard smile that finished the sentence for me: All right, Daddy-o, then it will have to be tonight, won't it, old pal?

Forgive me while I groan. Ohh, my God, I'm tired. And I can't stay with this thing. I can't. Not with the last thing of all. The final snapshot. The one that cinched the whole thing. Tied it up. Turned the key. Threw the switch. Dropped the blade. Struck the spark. I need a drink. No, a cigarette. No, a drink *and* a cigarette. And then I'll tell you about death.

But Charlie hadn't even the energy to raise the bottle or light the cigarette. For a full two minutes the typewriter became his pillow again, and he would doubtless have drifted back into sleep, despite his determination to see the night through and his account completed, but a fit of coughing shook him up violently. His round, red, blue-black eyes slowly opened, and Charlie found himself staring at an image that was first colored a bright orange, then a blurred, dull gray-black coming into sharp focus. The door. In the door, a small square window. And the window itself cut into four narrow panes. The two at the left perfectly framed the face of a child with eyes hard and dark and lifeless as coal.

As Charlie sat up, the child's face grew smaller and then disappeared altogether.

Charlie snorted, "Hnf!" and muttered drunkenly a few indeterminate words as he tried to find the end of a bent cigarette with the flame in his match. The match burned his fingers, and he catapulted it into the air. It landed on a mound of pencil sketches done on tracing paper and started a small fire which Charlie beat out with a sketch pad. He hurled the cigarette into the wastebasket. He dug a fresh cigarette from the pack and got it going without too much difficulty. "Gotta finish the job," he told himself. "Gotta gotta gotta gotta gotta fininish the jobobob." Somewhere in himself he found the strength to resume his typewritten account of his conversation with Elizabeth in the studio.

"All right Daddy"—that's what she'd said with that small, hard smile of hers like the smile a nightclub comic throws to a heckler.

I said to her, "But you don't know how it will all turn out, do you?"

"How *what* will turn out?"

"The accident."

She raised her eyebrows, meaning the look to be disarmingly quizzical.

"We know, both of us," I went on, "that there has been an accident scheduled, don't we?"

"An accident." The look was a hmm-what-have-we-here? Wary.

"And we know what kind of accident it will be."

Another small needle of light ignited in the witch girl's eyes.

"Fire." She'd formed the word with her lips, but no sound was uttered.

"Fire," I said. "Correct! Right here in the studio."

"Here."

Her conversation, you note, was not voluble. but I understand brevity of speech is common among nine-year-old patricides. Or maybe the word should be step-patricides.

"But there's something vital that we still don't know, Elizabeth. And that's what will happen to . . ." I paused.

"Elizabeth," she whispered.

"Yes again. We can't let any accidents take place, eh?—unless we know just exactly how Elizabeth will make out. Shall I take your picture? It's hardly the dinner hour yet, not even five-thirty, and we've got plenty of sunlight."

(I hear the words, but they're deep and slow, like a seventy-eight-rpm record played at forty-five.)

Now the thoughts that fled across her face were of a different sort, ending in a suspended emotion very close, I think, to despair. She nodded gravely, and we walked together to the out-of-doors.

(I see us walking together, as a bystander would, but each step takes an eternity, like the graceful sweep of a slow-motion movie.)

On the lawn, across which the trees stretched their shadlows in long sloping lines to the house, I took her picture with the camera. "Say cheese," I said and got the tight little paper-clip smile. Bzzzzzz-click.

"What do you think you'll look like?" I asked as I handed her the camera. "A movie star? Or an oyster?"

"An oyster."

"Then what noise is it, Liz, that annoys an oyster, do you know?"

"*Please* shut up."

"Don't you know?"

"A noisy noise!"

"No, you're wrong. The noise that annoys an oyster is faint, ever so faint. It's the scraping sound—skkkkk!—of the oysterman's knife just beginning to go to work on her front door."

Elizabeth shivered.

"Do you hear it?" I asked her.

"Hear what?"

"The oysterman's knife. It's your last chance. I want to begin to make a real life for you. Let me do it?"

"You hate me."

"I don't anything of the kind. I love you, kitten. Here, let me throw that cam—"

She twisted away from me. "No! You hate me and you've killed everything. Everything! And I'll see the picture. I'm *going* to see the picture no matter what!"

Elizabeth stood very still with the camera held before her in both hands. The picture, when it finally appeared, was that of a young nun, just short of her thirtieth birthday or just beyond it, of the same order as that of Sister Angela Marie and Mother Paul Jude. I can't describe the young nun's face as happy, but there was a resignation in it that seemed frozen there, a calm mask over a tortured memory. The eyes were large, even larger than I imagined they could be, but darkly shadowed. A smile, a rather knowing smile, touched the lips. And it was the smile that did it. I knew at that first glance, that I'd lost the war, just as surely as though some dark enemy had turned a flamethrower on me. I looked at Liz to see how the picture affected her. Her mouth twitched with excitement. In my inner most mind, I thought I detected the sound, ever so faint, of the oysterman's knife.

Death is the end of everything we know and maybe of everything else too. It's the lid coming down. It's every regret we have for failure. It's a black, asphyxiating cloud. And waiting for it is worse than waiting for pain. It's waiting for the zero, the nothing, the stopping of the intelligence that lives, like a gray shimmering pearl, somewhere behind our eyes. Death, believe me, is a lonely business. I believe in God and in eternity, but I don't (just now at least) believe in my place with Him in it. There's just the *skkkkk!* of the knife. And then the dark. And there's only one way to wait for it that I know. You drink. And then you drink some more. And then you

Charlie McLenahan did get to finish his account of his life and hard times with Liz—as much as he could know, that is—but with not even seconds to spare. When he became aware that the room was filled with smoke, and that, in fact, there were intimations of real red fire to his right, Charlie rolled up the forty-odd pages he'd typed into a tight cylinder and jammed them into the pocket of his robe as one would thrust a sword into a scabbard. In fleeing the studio, he fell badly once, giving his right hip a terrible wrench, and then had a devil of a job making it to the door on his elbows. The door needed unlocking, which delayed things a bit. (He'd knocked the key out of the lock and had trouble finding it.) All in all, it took him a long, wearying four minutes before he was breathing the clear, cool, almost cold night air.

He coughed a good deal as he lay on the gravel halfway down the driveway, and emitted a few indescribable noises from deep inside him. Elizabeth flew out of the house, shouting, "Daddy! Daddy!" with a shrillness that was close to hysteria. She asked him, over and over, what the matter was, but his attempts to answer came out only as grotesque wheezes and grunts. The child sobbed in apparent fear and threw her arms around him. Charlie cried a bit himself. And by the time he could get a word out, the studio was most dramatically afire. Charlie sent the child to the house to put in an emergency phone call. When she returned to him, helpless on the gravel, her eyes were still wide with excitement. She helped him to the car, so that he could move it down to the road, free of the blaze and out of the way of the volunteer firemen. Through the dark hours, they sat side by side, propped against a tree by the road, watching the fire brigade hose down the blaze in the studio and in the trees beyond. The flames never reached to the house.

At one point in their vigil, Charlie somehow muttered into the child's ear the fact that he, Charlie, had not had anything to do with the death of her mother; and Elizabeth, genuinely surprised at his stupidity, said that of course she knew he had

251

nothing to do with the violent end of Ann Carmody McLenahan. A crazy old man in Central Park had done that. He'd shot her. And he hadn't even meant to.

But then—

Charlie stopped. Then why had the girl called him a murderer?

Agnes!

Of course!

Liz thought he'd killed that silly beagle bitch Agnes out of sheer wanton malice! Charlie began, very quietly, to laugh, and his shoulders shook against the tree trunk, and tears coursed down his cheeks. Liz looked at him quizzically, but he could say nothing through his exhausted giddiness. He'd tell her another time, in another place.

Then the giddiness was gone. Charlie turned to the child. Why had she been up all night, sneaking around like a ¢@#$%& leprechaun?

But she hadn't, she said, and her puzzled look was entirely convincing. She'd been in bed. Asleep. His gruntings in the driveway here had awakened her and, in fact, had given her a good scare.

Charlie shook again with laughter that was not too far removed from weeping. She'd been in her room all the time! The fire had not been started by Elizabeth—it must have been his own discarded cigarette! And probably even the snapshots were only sick little flashes from his own burning imagination! Martini dreams, knitted from pure dog hair —the hair of the hair of the hair of the dog that began biting him in earnest just a few days ago, or a few weeks, at the bar at the Plume!

"Show me the picture of the house," he said, almost in a whimper.

"Picture of the house?"

"Describe it to me, then," he said.

"How?"

"Was there ivy? A maple tree? Santa Clauses? Reindeer? Imps? Leprechauns?"

"*Leprechauns?*"

"What, then?"

"The house," she said, shrugging. "I don't know what you're talking about, Daddy."

Charlie sighed, like a man reaching home.

There is little to add to the story. The next day, Charlie looked everywhere for the camera, even in the ashes of the studio, but he found nothing. A couple of weeks later he put the house up for sale and took Liz off with him to New

York. They lived, as he'd suggested, at the Algonquin. They went to James Bond movies, ballets, slick new musicals, even ball games. Norb Hutchinson and Charlie's other close friends at the Plume decided that the old man and his small stepdaughter were hitting it off quite well together in the big city, and Norb was extremely pleased when he learned that Charlie and Liz were sailing to Europe for the summer. Norb, of course—and everyone at the Plume—was naturally shocked to the ends of his being when he heard that, on their fourth night out from New York, while Charlie and Liz were taking a turn together, alone on the deck, Charlie fell overboard and was lost.

The little girl, in a profound state of shock, was flown back to New York from Europe and was met at Kennedy Airport by some cousins of her mother's. She lived with them only a short time, though, because she was quite unhappy, always drifting about like a new moth in a breeze. She had, they noticed with sympathy, a strange habit of holding her right arm behind her and pinching her left elbow.

In the end, the cousins gave up. They bowed to the child's entreaties and gave her over to the Church.

Here's a quick checklist of recent releases of
ACE SCIENCE FICTION BOOKS

F-titles 40¢   M-titles 45¢   G-titles 50¢
H-titles 60¢   N-titles 95¢

If you are missing any of these, they can be obtained directly from the publisher by sending the indicated sum, plus 5¢ handling fee per copy, to Ace Books, Inc. (Dept. MM), 1120 Ave. of the Americas, New York, N. Y. 10036

CLASSICS OF GREAT SCIENCE-FICTION

from ACE BOOKS

If you want to keep up with the best science fiction stories of the year, you will want to get your copy of:

WORLD'S BEST SCIENCE FICTION

1967

Selected and Edited by

Donald A. Wollheim and Terry Carr

Outstanding stories and novelettes from the science fiction and fantasy magazines of the world, including great tales by Roger Zelazny, Brian W. Aldiss, Frederik Pohl, Philip K. Dick, Avram Davidson, Michael Moorcock, and others.

"Entertaining and imaginative"
    —*Publishers Weekly*

Ace Book A-10   75¢

Ace Books, Inc. (Dept. MM)
1120 Avenue of the Americas
New York, N.Y. 10036